A STRANGER'S TOUCH

Lila gasped aloud at the sound of Garrett's voice as his strong hands snapped out to clamp onto her upper arms and she was suddenly whirled around and thrust into the darkness of the corner. Pinned against the wall with the hard, male length of his body, Lila rasped, "Let me go, damn you! Wh-what are you doing in here, anyway? I thought you were in the bunkhouse."

"You were wrong."

Garrett crushed her tighter, effortlessly subduing her struggles as he whispered against her lips, "You're not foolin' me. I know what you've been doin' with Knox. You've been tryin' to use him to put me out of your mind, but it's not workin', is it, darlin' . . ." Garrett did not wait for her response as he continued hotly. "It's not workin' because every time you're in Knox's arms, you think of what it would be like if *I* was holdin' you instead. Every time he kisses you, you think of what it would be like if *I* was kissin' you instead, and every time he touches you . . ."

Garrett cursed low in his throat the moment before he closed the tantalizing distance between their lips. His kiss was angry and demanding, and unexpectedly soul-shattering as it surged relentlessly deeper. It seared Lila's mind and body with brilliant, blinding colors that left only the sensation of Garrett's warm breath against her skin and the male taste of him in her mouth as he laved the hollows there with increasing ardor. He was consuming her with his passion. The weight of his muscular strength moving against her womanly softness was silk against steel . . . an ecstasy just short of pain . . .

ZEBRA BOOKS
KENSINGTON PUBLISHING CORP.

ZEBRA BOOKS are published by

Kensington Publishing Corp.
475 Park Avenue South
New York, NY 10016

First Printing: October, 1993

Printed in the United States of America

Prologue

Lawrence, Kansas—Friday, August 21, 1863

The ignoble force gathered secretly, silently, on the wings of the night. Sweeping stealthily over the border toward the sleeping Kansas town, it paused, a vicious bird of prey clothed in noble grey. The first shaft of dawn the awaited signal, it swooped down on the defenseless people within with the thunder of four hundred horses, guns barking indiscriminate death and destruction.

Blood! Smoke! Fire! The screams of the anguished and dying!

He remembered it all! It was a blurred nightmare from which he could not seem to awaken as he was raised to his feet in a fevered daze at the first sounds of gunfire and delivered to safety in a cellar room.

The feral yells drew closer. The gunfire grew louder. The holocaust began. Through the muddied cellar window he saw the barn burst into flames. He watched his father run into the yard. He saw the old man's body jerk spasmodically when the bullets struck him. He heard his mother's cry as she rushed toward his father and fell to her knees at his side. He saw his young blond wife race to their aid, horror in her eyes as her running step came to an abrupt halt beside them. He felt her terror as she glanced back toward the cellar window, then looked at the burning barn. He knew what she was thinking. The wagon . . . the horses . . . their only escape . . .

He shouted a warning, a protest that went unheard as she started toward the flaming structure. He strained to stand, but his weakened limbs could not support him. Collapsing back against the cot, he watched in silent panic as his wife reached the barn and disappeared within.

No, Elizabeth! No!

Anguished cries were still ringing in his mind when his mother stood abruptly. Her rounded shoulders shuddered as she looked down at her lifeless husband, then up at the blazing barn. He called out aloud when, in an unexpected rush, his mother followed Elizabeth inside.

The gunfire grew louder, and within moments, his view of the burning structure was obscured by horsemen in military grey. His father's still form was trampled heedlessly under their horses' hooves as the barn fire burned brighter, higher.

He heard a loud crack, then gasped aloud as the barn exploded fully into flames. Mesmerized with the horror of it, he watched as the roof fluttered and swayed in a deadly dance, as the charred planking quivered and black smoke billowed out of the doorway through which the two women had disappeared minutes earlier.

A silent plea rose inside him. It turned into a desperate prayer that went unanswered as the barn gave a final shudder, then crashed to the ground in a blaze of flying sparks.

The tortured cry that rang from his lips went unheard

in the deadly din beyond the cellar walls. His pain of loss more grievous than his physical wounds, he cursed his impotence and the fate that had held him helpless witness to the deaths of those he loved.

Aware that his fevered consciousness was gradually fading, he uttered a final, tormented prayer—that this time he, too, would never awaken.

But . . . oh, God . . . he did.

One

Kansas—1879

The full skirt of her scarlet traveling dress brushing the seats as she passed, Lila Chesney walked swiftly down the narrow railway car aisle. The matching plume on her black straw hat bobbed as she glanced nervously over her shoulder. Relief flickered in her eyes when she saw no one had entered the car behind her.

The train jerked into motion with a piercing whistle as Lila scanned the crowded car for an unoccupied seat. There were only two. One was beside a grinning, nattily dressed drummer with an open sample case on his lap. The other was beside a demurely dressed young woman who was the sole female occupant of the car. Her decision swiftly made, Lila slipped her bag onto the overhead rack and sat beside the woman.

Tension a tight knot inside her, Lila waited. The appreciative silence and open speculation that had greeted her appearance gradually lapsed back into conversation sparked by unabashed profanity and loud guffaws so common to the spontaneity of the frontier as she assessed her fellow passengers furtively. They were a varied lot, not unlike those she had left behind in the

Golden Steer Saloon a short time earlier. Men with shaggy mustaches and beards, wearing buckskins, gun-belts, and slouched broad-brimmed hats abounded, as did the odors she knew were destined to grow stronger as the journey progressed. Fancy-booted ranchers and soberly dressed farmers completed the picture, with the lone, leering drummer seeming to have been tossed in for good measure.

Above it all hung the inevitable cloud of blue tobacco smoke, growing ever larger.

Yes, everything appeared normal . . .

Switching her attention to the landscape outside the window, Lila studied it intently as the train whistle blasted once more. She leaned forward to peruse the railroad track to the rear. Satisfied they were not being pursued, she released a relieved breath.

The woman beside her moved, calling Lila's attention for the first time to the startling differences between the two female images reflected side by side in the window glass. Although both were of the same approximate age and coloring, the upward sweep of Lila's own light hair, her brightly painted features and eye-catching attire were carefully calculated to make the most of her natural assets. In direct contrast, the other woman's efforts seemed calculated to make the least of them. Her brown traveling costume was unadorned and drab. The close-fitting bonnet, under which she wore her hair pulled back from a center part into a severe bun, did little to promote her appeal. Her ordinary features, untouched by artificial color of any kind, were all but obscured by awkward, wire-rimmed spectacles resting low on the bridge of her nose. In all, Lila's seatmate was a pathetic little wren of a woman, an image that was further perpetuated as she turned jerkily to face her, blinked her small eyes, and whispered in a thin, quaking voice, "I . . . I think I'm going to be sick."

Lila jumped back spontaneously. "Not on me, you're not!"

The sharpness of her response set the young woman aback. Seizing the advantage, Lila instructed tightly, "Take a deep breath . . . that's it. Now close your eyes and sit still. Don't move until your stomach is feeling settled again."

"But—"

"Do what I told you!"

The woman snapped her eyes obediently closed.

Silence reigned for long minutes before Lila's seatmate slowly opened her eyes. Her tone apologetic, she whispered, "I . . . I'm feeling better now, thank you. But I feel I must warn you that it won't last." At Lila's responsive frown, the young woman continued with a feeble attempt at reassurance, "Oh, you needn't fear that you'll catch an illness from me. I'm not sick." Appearing to seek understanding with her intense gaze, the young woman rasped, "It's my inner agitation that's the problem. I made an error in judgment, you see . . . a big mistake . . . and it's about to catch up with me."

Lila stiffened. The story of her life . . . Of all the luck! Three passenger cars on the train and she had to sit next to a woman who was running away, just as she was!

Not realizing her expression had adequately conveyed her thoughts, Lila was startled as the young woman spoke again in dead earnest.

"I'm not running away from anything, if that's what you're thinking. It's not what's behind me that's frightening me. It's what's ahead of me . . ." The woman gulped. "I . . . I just don't know what to do!"

The young woman's small, nearsighted eyes brimmed as she squinted at Lila in silent appeal.

A colorful string of curse words galloped across Lila's mind as she squinted back. She had problems of her own! She didn't have the time or the inclination to listen to a stranger's dilemma, no matter how pathetic she was. Her sympathy had been used up long ago, in any case, and when it came right down to the line, she wasn't qualified to give advice to this timid young woman, or anyone else.

Lila kept her silence as her seatmate's eyes continued their forlorn appeal.

Damn!

Those eyes didn't blink.

Double damn!

They didn't blink even once.

Damn, damn, damn . . .

Not even *one, goddamned time* . . .

"All right!" Lila gritted her teeth. "Tell me about it."

The young woman nodded gratefully.

And the torrent of words began.

The sun had long before slipped below the horizon as the train roared along the tracks. Darkness had brought a silence upon the passenger car that was broken only by the rhythmic clacking of the rails, an occasional blast of the train whistle, and snores of passengers sprawled in various positions of uncomfortable sleep.

Modesty Parkins, as the plain young woman had identified herself, had allowed her rambling recitation to trail to a halt a half hour earlier. Visibly shaken, she had then carefully removed her sober bonnet and placed it on the overhead rack, smoothed her hair, and waited for Lila to comment.

She was still waiting.

Lila looked up at the rack where her brilliantly plumed hat rested beside Modesty's sober bonnet much like a magnificent peacock beside a solemn pea hen. It was strange how the young woman's story paralleled her own. Like her, Modesty had been orphaned at an early age and been left to fend for herself in a hard world. Like her, she had done the best she could to make a life for herself—but that was where their stories diverged onto different paths.

A spark of warmth flickered briefly to life inside Lila. She'd been more fortunate than Modesty. She had had Billy. Dear Billy . . . troubled and troublesome Billy. Her brother had been two years younger than her ten years when they had been sent to the orphanage. He had been rebellious against the hand fate had dealt them. He was rebellious still.

Lila glanced again at Modesty. Plain Modesty, sober Modesty, had behaved well in the orphanage and had been repaid by being hired out into domestic service until she had grown old enough to be sent out on her own into a life of frugal servitude. Timid Modesty had taken only one aggressive step in her entire life—which she now regretted with all her heart.

The generous curve of Lila's lips tightened. Such had not been the case for her. The heartless punishments meted out to her rebellious brother at the orphanage had lit a fire in her heart that had not yet been contained. Seizing the first opportunity, she had run away with her brother in tow, and at the age of fourteen she had begun supporting them both by using her natural singing voice as well as other natural assets to make their way.

Like Modesty . . . and *unlike* Modesty, Lila had done what she needed to do to survive. She had made mistakes. Some more painful than others had left deep scars, but if she had some regrets . . . well, she did not indulge them. Dear Billy, with his bright, engaging smile and the wounded look that remained hidden behind his eyes for only her to see, had always been first with her. That would never change.

The rhythm of the rails changed subtly, interrupting Lila's thoughts, and her stomach tightened. Another stop and another tense few moments was approaching when she would survey the platform for any new passengers who might pose a threat. That process had been repeated over and again as the stops had trailed past one by one, as she had followed Modesty's story with half an ear while her heart pounded like a captive bird in her breast.

Glancing beside her, Lila saw the silent Modesty still awaited her advice. She almost laughed. The lame leading the blind . . .

The scarlet feather on Lila's hat bobbed with the rhythm of the train. It waved at her, mocking her with its brilliant display. It teased her, taunted her . . . until—

Slowly drawing herself up straight, Lila turned to look into the patient brown eyes of the young woman seated beside her. Was there any courage hidden behind all the self-censure and apprehension she read there?

The dark velvet of her eyes direct and compelling, Lila was determined to find out.

The first shaft of daylight peeked through the soot-stained train window, awakening Lila with a snap. Disoriented, she glanced around her, then closed her eyes as the events of the previous day flooded back into her mind.

Pinkerton . . . Even now the name sent shivers down her spine. She had not seen the Pinkerton detective who had come to town, but just the word that he was asking questions about her had been enough to send her running.

Her heart again pounding, her dark eyes growing frantic, Lila looked around the crowded car once more. The buckskin-clad fellow snoring noisily a few feet away . . . the drummer sleeping with his head against the windowpane—both had showed particular interest in her during the previous day, but the interest men showed in her was nothing new. Surely neither of them could be the Pinkerton.

"Lila . . ."

Jumping with a start, Lila turned toward her seatmate with a frown.

"I'm sorry. I didn't mean to startle you."

"No, it's all right." Lila attempted a smile. "Your stop is coming up within the hour, isn't it?"

The young woman swallowed nervously and nodded, peering at her with her intense, nearsighted eyes.

"Don't worry. It's going to be all right."

Nodding again without response, Modesty drew herself slowly to her feet. Adjusting her glasses, she took her toilette case and bonnet off the rack above her and turned toward the tightly curtained ladies' dressing room at the rear of the car.

Silent as Modesty disappeared behind the curtain, Lila glanced around the car again. Her fellow passengers were beginning to stir. A fellow in a dark suitcoat glanced her way, as did a cowboy with a droopy mustache. Could either of them be the Pinkerton?

Impelled by a sudden sense of urgency, Lila stood

up and reached for her hat and case. She was uncomfortable and anxious, but she consoled herself that when she was freshly washed and groomed, she would be a new woman.

That thought giving her temporary respite from agitation, Lila walked to the rear of the car. Raising the curtain, she slipped out of sight.

DEER TRAIL! NEXT STOP DEER TRAIL IN FIVE MINUTES!

The curtains at the rear of the swaying rail car moved in response to the conductor's call. Stepping back into sight, Lila raised a hand to the clean line of her upswept hair. She lowered her freshly kohled lashes, curved her brightly rouged lips in a semismile, then adjusted her hat to a low, jaunty angle on her forehead before starting back down the aisle. She stumbled unexpectedly, regained her balance, and proceeded carefully to her seat. Sitting, she turned to stare out the window in silent contemplation.

The curtain of the ladies' dressing room moved again as Modesty exited in a nervous step. Her face dutifully scrubbed, her hair tightly bound and covered with the sober bonnet, her dowdy traveling outfit freshly brushed, she tripped awkwardly as she started down the aisle. Adjusting her glasses, she continued forward, her chin lowered with embarrassment.

The abrasive screech of the train's brakes signified the next station was fast approaching as Modesty reached her seat. Her knuckles white as she gripped the backrest, she met Lila's eyes in silence before reaching up for her carpetbag. Pausing for a brief, sober goodbye when the train jerked to a final halt, she then turned and walked unsteadily toward the door of the car.

Tripping again as she started down the steps, Modesty clutched the railing for support and stepped down onto the station platform. A departing whistle sounded as she peered over the wire rims of her glasses to check the immediate area. Satisfied no other passengers had disembarked, she widened her circle of vision.

So this was Deer Trail. She gave a low grunt of disgust. It was nothing more than a whistle-stop, but it would have to do.

Pushing her spectacles back up the bridge of her nose, Modesty stepped forward only to stumble again. A muttered curse escaped her lips as she attempted to adjust to the distortion of her vision. Gripping her bags tighter, she mumbled through gritted teeth, "Damn! *She* can't see without her glasses, and *I* can't see with them!"

Realizing her spontaneous cursing would betray her where her appearance would not, *Lila* reassumed the modest posture of her new identity. She was no longer the bold, vivacious Lila Chesney. The backward and uncertain Modesty had become she and she—an involuntary shiver shook Lila—she had become Modesty.

"Modesty . . . ?"

The sound of a deep male voice behind her turned Lila slowly. Pushing her glasses down on her nose so she might see more clearly, she felt a tug in the pit of her stomach that bore no relation to her former anxiety as she viewed the man standing there.

Tall, well built, brown hair, and eyes as blue as the sky overhead—she recognized him from the blurred photo the *old* Modesty had showed her. He was the man the virginal Modesty had met only by mail, the stranger she had agreed to marry before trepidation had overwhelmed her and escape had become imperative.

He was Luther Knox.

Her husband-to-be.

Smiling shyly, her eyes demurely lowered, Lila took a short step toward him.

Two

He heard them again, the sounds of terror that came on the wings of the night. Gunshots, screaming, the sound of pounding hooves.

He smelled the smoke. He felt the fear. He relived the pain.

He saw *her* . . .

She was running from the burning barn, but the glow of her hair was no longer golden. It was red . . . ablaze with fire! He called out in horror as she came closer. He struggled to escape the mire in which he was bound, to reach her, to save her, but he sank deeper. She called out to him, stretching out her hand. The wedding band he had placed on her finger caught the light of the flames, momentarily blinding him, but he regained his sight to see . . . to see . . .

She was being consumed . . . his Elizabeth, his wife, the woman he loved more than life. Eyes that had been as clear and serene as a mountain pool were dark, empty sockets of fire. Lips that had given him comfort without words, breathed hot, greedy flames. Hands that had been gentle, tender, loving, were blackened stalks, reaching for him.

He struggled to touch her hand, to reach her, to join

her, but the mire held him fast. It held him safe. It held him from the oblivion he prayed would overwhelm him.

And then she was gone.

Shaken, Garrett Harrison awoke from the smoke-shrouded shadows of his dream with a start. He raised a hand to his perspired brow to shield his eyes from the grey light of morning seeping through the slit in the window shade. Another dawn had come to dispel his nightmares, but he wasn't ready . . . not yet.

His throat thick, his heart still pounding, Garrett took a steadying breath. Dropping his hand back to the bed, he pulled himself abruptly to a seated position and looked around the small hotel room. He saw walls that bore the marks of countless careless guests before him, a night table with a single, smoke-blackened lamp, a washstand with a chipped pitcher, and a solitary grey towel.

His strong features drawing into a frown, Garrett threw back the coverlet and drew himself up to his full, towering height. The wooden planking was cool under his feet, but he was oblivious to the chill as he walked toward the washstand and splashed water into the bowl. Picking up the soap, he worked up a brisk lather and rubbed it against his face, chest, and arms, knowing that the ritual cleansed his mind as well as his body and allowed time for the shadows of the night to fade.

Relieved and refreshed minutes later, Garrett looked into the stained washstand mirror. The peculiarly light eyes staring back at him from beneath dark brows were cold, and the face reflected there was hard. His unruly black hair was longer than style demanded, but that was all right. His neglect of shaving for the past few days had already produced an impressive growth of beard that lent a touch of menace to the sharp planes of his face, but that was all right, too. The changes on the outside were reflective of the changes the years had wrought on the inside, and he cared little who saw them.

Turning abruptly, Garrett reached for his shirt. He sniffed it, frowned, and tossed it aside, then reached into his saddlebag for another. He remembered when he had been a young man of twenty and his shirts had smelled of fresh air and sun. He remembered that Elizabeth had worked to keep them that way, just for the love of him.

His frown darkening, Garrett shrugged his shirt over the broad expanse of his shoulders. An old wound cried out in response, but he ignored its nagging whine as he drew up his pants and stepped into his boots. Turning, he withdrew his gun from his belt and checked it briefly before slipping it back into the holster and strapping it around his hips. He settled it comfortably there, then reached for his coat and hat.

Giving the room a last glance, Garrett adjusted the brim of his hat low onto his forehead and, stepping out into the hallway, closed the door behind him. His step rapid, he was at the staircase to the ground floor within moments—a hard man, a cold man, a man with a purpose.

The wooden staircase to the second floor of the two-story frame structure in Denver's busiest section echoed with the heavy, rapid sound of Garrett's footsteps. Pausing briefly to listen outside the hallway door marked with a distinctive drawing of "the eye that never sleeps," he pushed it open. He was closing the door behind him as a man emerged from the inner office. The fellow was much smaller than he, of an unimpressive build. He was wearing wire-rimmed spectacles and was neatly dressed, his closely trimmed, reddish-brown hair combed back from a round face dominated by a large handlebar mustache. The impression the man gave was of a quiet, well-mannered clerk, but that impression was negated by the authority in his voice the moment he spoke.

"So ye're here at last." Walking toward him, James McParland extended his hand. The disarming smile so much a part of his engaging personality was not in evidence. The reason became obvious as he snapped, "It's too bad ye're too late."

Accepting his hand, Garrett remained as sober as McParland.

"I didn't get your message until two days ago. I came here immediately. I'm too late for what?"

McParland's smooth cheek twitched, revealing the personal intensity that had raised him to the position of superintendent of the Pinkerton Detective Agency's Denver office as he spoke again. "We were as close as we've ever been to catchin' Bart Forbes and his gang of thievin' murderers."

"Forbes!" Memory flashed. Gunshots . . . smoke . . . fire . . . Garrett felt a familiar inner rage. "What happened?"

"I can't tell ye what happened. We had one of our best operatives followin' a woman who's connected with the gang, but he—"

"Followin' a woman?" Garrett's interruption was accompanied by a sneer. "That was a waste of time! You know damned well Forbes and his gang change women the way they change their shirts."

"Ye're wrong there, me bucko. This woman's been appearin' in our investigations for the past year, and we were finally able to track her down. She would've led us to the gang sooner or later."

Garrett felt a familiar prickling along his spine. "So? Spit it out, McParland! I don't have any patience for this cat-and-mouse game. I had a hard night."

"Every night's a hard night for ye, isn't it, Harrison?"

McParland's unexpected comment stopped Garrett cold. He didn't care to look back and count the years he had been working for the Pinkerton Agency. He didn't want to recall the long, lost days and nights, the parts he had played, the deceits he had practiced, the times he had used his gun, and the lives that had come to an early end as a result. All had been necessary steps toward the goal that had given his life purpose. He had shared his silent dedication with no one during that time, much less this fellow whose bespectacled eyes seemed suddenly to see deep inside him.

Resenting McParland's steady stare almost as much as he resented his words, Garrett responded with a deepening of his drawl that was just short of a growl. "What's it to you how I spend my nights, McParland?"

McParland paused again, silently measuring Garrett's hostility. "I'd think a better question would be how I come to know what I do about ye, Harrison. But since ye didn't ask, I'll tell ye anyway, and I'll tell ye this way." The smaller man's jaw tightened. "Ye know about the years I spent undercover with the Molly Maguires . . ." Garrett did not respond, but McParland nodded. "Aye, ye know, all right. Ye know I was responsible for bringin' an end to that bloodthirsty organization in the Pennsylvania coal fields when even the government of this country had given up on bringin' them in. But did ye know that I'd not be able to count the times that I was spit upon and called an *informer* for the work I did there, that I was asked more times than I care to remember how I could've made meself live with the men of the old sod during those years, shared their lives and their confidences, and then betrayed them to the law? And did ye know that as many condemned the work I did as applauded it?"

Pausing to search Garrett's face, McParland nodded again. "Aye, I can see ye did not. So I'll tell ye now what I've not bothered to explain to others, just so ye might understand how I know what I do about ye. I did what I did because them men I helped bring to the bar of justice were murderers—a disgrace to their Irish blood. I did what I did for the Church, for my race, and for my country, and once I had set me mind to the task, I did not deter. But did ye know that the thing that drove me to continue was the *faces in me dreams*—the dead faces of them the Mollies had killed with their growin' madness? Aye, them faces haunted me, and I know . . . I saw it in yer eyes from the first . . . that similar dreams haunt ye."

Garrett did not respond, preferring instead to let the smaller man continue.

"Ye're a wise man, Harrison. Aye, allowin' me to make me point before respondin', so I'll make this short and sweet. I see in ye the same dedication that drove me to carry through to the end in that unpleasant affair. That's what's needed to bring in this gang of thievin' murderers when all else has failed, and I'm about to set ye to the task."

Garrett's eyes narrowed. "You said you already have one of your best men on that job."

"I do."

"So?"

Smiling for the first time, McParland was transformed into the smooth-tongued Irishman he was known to be. "I'm thinkin' *two* of my best men will be better than one for this job."

Garrett glowered in lieu of a smile, the reasoning behind McParland's unexpected personal revelations suddenly clear.

"So, that's it. Sorry to disappoint you, but you've got the wrong man, McParland. I work alone."

"Ye want Forbes, don't ye?"

Garrett maintained his silence.

"Forbes was part of Quantrill's raiders . . ."

Garrett's broad shoulder twitched as familiar echoes rang in his mind.

"Forbes wasn't just a member of the band. He was one of Quantrill's lieutenants . . ."

Garrett's shoulder twitched again.

"I won't be sendin' one man out on this investigation, Harrison. We've already lost three investigators tryin' to get Forbes. Ye did yer part in puttin' the Reno brothers behind bars, and I'd not have called ye in off the James case if I didn't think I could better use ye here." McParland paused. "But ye'll be workin' with a partner on this or ye won't be workin' on it at all."

Garrett's expression did not change. "I work alone."

"Not this time. I'll not lose any more good men because of stubbornness." McParland's voice dropped a notch lower. "Ye know as well as I that Forbes is one of the worst to come out of Quantrill's band. He's grown more vicious with every bank and train robbery he and his gang's committed in the years since. We need yer help on this now before we lose the bastard again."

The lilting rhythm of McParland's brogue rang with sincerity as he added quietly, "We never needed ye more."

The silence between the two men lengthened before Garrett heard himself say, "I work my own way."

"It won't be as difficult as ye think to work with this fella—just a matter of watchin' each other's back."

"Who's the other operative?"

"Jake Hobbs."

"Hobbs . . ." Garrett paused again. "I don't know him, but I've heard of him."

Quick to pick up the acceptance growing in Garrett's tone, McParland smiled more broadly. "He's a good man, but he's at a true loss right now. He's waitin' to meet with ye. He thought it best not to be seen with ye here."

"What about the woman?"

McParland's smile faded. "Hobbs will fill ye in on her. With the two of ye workin' together, we'll get Forbes's whole gang. I have no doubt of that." Garrett did not dissent, and McParland's satisfaction was obvious. "Aye, we're goin' to get them this time. I feel the certainty of it in me bones."

Garrett was walking back down the staircase to the street, the heels of his hand-tooled boots echoing hollowly in the empty hallway behind him when he realized for the first time that the small Irishman and he did indeed have something in common. Somehow he, too, had a feeling in his bones . . .

The heat of the day had already begun to fade as Garrett made his way along the crowded street. Denver had grown in the years since he had first seen it, but the aura of the frontier remained. The streets still teemed with the traffic of freight trains, farm wagons, and the slow amble of itinerant cowboys out for a time on the town. The business establishments lining the walks reflected the trade they served, with prospector's equipment and gunsmiths sharing equal space with haberdashery and furniture stores. A distance away, children raced along the street with a dog barking at their heels, adding to a growing din that was overwhelmed by music resounding from the gaudy false fronts of numerous saloons sprinkled among the more sober establishments.

Most garish of all the saloons was the Palace, located in a prime spot on the corner, toward which Garrett walked with a deceptively casual step.

Garrett's eyes narrowed with cautious scrutiny of the area as he reviewed in his mind the conversation he had had with McParland earlier that day.

Bart Forbes . . .

Garrett's stomach clenched spasmodically. He had known the moment he had received McParland's summons that it was important because only the greatcst urgency would have induced McParland to take him away from his investigation in progress. And somehow, he had known it concerned Bart Forbes.

The bright sunlight faded as the gloom of the cellar room years earlier returned to Garrett's mind. It had been weeks before he had awakened in a military hospital lucid enough to face the events of that horrendous day, and lucid enough to realize that although he had been brought home from that same military hospital weeks earlier to spend what was expected to be the last few days of his life with his family, only he had ultimately survived.

The deadening ache inside Garrett returned with memories he could not evade. He remembered the day he was released from the hospital. A bitter, angry man, he had returned to serve until the end of the war, and he recalled the day two years later when he heard the news that William Clarke Quantrill had died from wounds received in an encounter with Union forces. His rage had been boundless because it had not been *he* who had killed him.

The war had ended a short time before Quantrill's death, but the seeds Quantrill had sown had since borne malevolent fruit. One after another of his vicious raiders began scourging the land with tactics he had taught them. The list of the infamous was endless—the Reno brothers, the James boys, the Youngers, the Farringtons . . . and the Bart Forbes gang.

Garrett's lips tightened. Through a quirk of fate only a few years earlier, he had learned that Bart Forbes had led the actual raid on his family's farm. He had sworn never to forget it.

The sound of bawdy music grew louder, interrupting Garrett's dark thoughts and exorcising ghosts of the past as he neared the Palace Saloon. His eyes narrowed in assessment as he pushed his way through the swinging doors. He was far removed from the idealistic, twenty-year-old youth he had been when he was carried down to that cellar room—and he was glad. He had learned the hard way that there was no place in the world for foolish idealism, for weakness, indecision, or any of the qualities that stood between him and the things he had sworn to do.

Crossing the floor of the crowded saloon, Garrett leaned his powerful frame against the bar and assessed the lively scene. Painted women, bearded men, the smell of beer and cheap perfume pervaded as conversation rose to the level of a shout in competition with ribald laughter and relentless music from a piano in the corner. It was no better or worse than the scores of similar saloons that had served his purposes in a variety of ways through the years.

Garrett caught the bartender's eye. He was holding a drink moments later when he felt a slender hand slide up his sleeve. A buxom brunette leaned casually against his side, challenging his unsmiling gaze as he turned to look down at her.

"Lonesome, big fella?"

The saloon girl's narrow brows rose speculatively as he maintained his silence.

"What does it take to make you smile, handsome?" Her eyelashes fluttering over experienced eyes, she whispered huskily, "Because whatever it is, I'm ready for it." She inched closer. "Just about anything . . ."

Feeling a familiar stirring, Garrett trailed his slitted gaze over the dancehall girl's upswept hair, across her small, painted features and parted lips. His attention lingered on the full white swells rising above the deeply cut neckline of her dress, and the stirring grew stronger.

Garrett slid his arm around the saloon girl's waist. Her soft female flesh was warm under his hand as he cupped her breast and whispered huskily, "What's your name, sweetheart?"

"My name's Lulu, but if you don't like that name, you can call me anything you want . . . just as long as you call me."

"Lulu's fine." Garrett lowered his head to cover the girl's lips with a seeking kiss. She protested as he drew back to add, "I'll call you, all right. You can depend on it. But right now I'd appreciate it if you'd take yourself off. I'm goin' to be busy for a little while."

Lulu hesitated, her disappointment obvious. "Is that a promise?"

"It is."

Lulu smiled. "I'll be waiting . . ." Sweeping her hand across the bulge below his belt, she whispered, "I sure as hell will . . ."

Waiting only until the flushed bar girl slipped back into the crowd, Garrett emptied his glass and caught the bartender's eye once more.

"Do you have a room available upstairs?"

The fellow nodded. "Number four's empty."

"That'll do just fine." Reaching into his pocket, Garrett slapped down a small roll of bills. "Give me a bottle and two glasses."

Moments later, he was ascending the staircase to the second floor.

Grateful to be out of sight of the room below as he turned into the narrow upstairs hallway, Garrett pushed open the door of the room marked with the numeral 4 and walked inside. He scanned it briefly. A rumpled bed, a nightstand with a dirty lamp, and a small table and chairs. Kicking one of the chairs out from under the table, Garrett sat down and poured himself a drink.

He did not have to wait long.

Sliding his hand to his holster at the sound of a step in the hallway, Garrett remained motionless as the door slowly opened.

Sample case in hand, *the drummer* met his gaze briefly before slipping inside and closing the door behind him.

The big man rose as Jake Hobbs entered the room, and Hobbs studied him silently. He had heard about Garrett Harrison. Harrison's reputation within the agency was almost legendary. He had been at the job since the cessation of the war and he was damned good at it. He was intense . . . obsessed. He made few mistakes and had little patience for them.

Momentarily discomfited, Hobbs continued his silent assessment. He was vaguely surprised that in all he had heard about this particular agent, no one had ever mentioned the imposing size of the man or the look of threat about him. He'd be damned if Harrison didn't look more dangerous than the men they sought.

Extending his hand, Hobbs offered, "Jake Hobbs."

Harrison accepted his hand. "Garrett Harrison."

Hobbs's discomfort increased as they sat, but he knew it had little to do with the man across from him. Two long days of frustration had worn heavily on his customary composure. He was not at his best because he had not *done* his best. The Chesney woman had made a fool out of him. She had eluded him as easily as she would have eluded a novice, and the thought rankled, especially when faced by Harrison's somber stare.

Hobbs broke the silence abruptly. "We're going to be working together."

Harrison's expression did not change. "That's right."

Hobbs studied Harrison intently. Deciding to forgo pleasantries, Hobbs said directly, "All right, what do you want to know?"

"I want to know everythin' you know about the woman you were followin', and her connection to Forbes. I want you to tell me everythin' you've done since McParland put you on the case."

"That's easy. I don't know anything about her other than the fact that she's been showing up in the reports of agents who have been investigating the robberies Forbes's gang has been involved in."

"What do you mean, 'showin' up'?"

Pausing to unlock the case he still held in his hand, Hobbs withdrew a folder and tossed it on the table. "Here, read them for yourself. It seems every time we hear that the Forbes gang is in a particular area, this woman is nearby."

"No one ever saw her with the gang?"
"No."
"That connection is pretty slim."
"It's valid as far as I'm concerned."
"Are you sure it was the same woman every time?"
"It was the same woman all right. There's no mistaking Lila Chesney once you've seen her."
"Do you have a photograph?"
"No."
Harrison's brows knotted tighter. "Tell me more."
"She works as a dealer in the best saloon in whatever town she happens to be working in at the time. She travels around a lot."
"Whose woman is she. Forbes's?"
"I don't know."
"Where was she goin' when she got on the train?"
"I don't know."
Harrison's jaw turned to granite. "What *do* you know?"
Hobbs felt the prick of anger. "I know her ticket said her destination was Cheyenne. That's why she surprised me when she got off here in Denver."
"She must've known you were followin' her."
Hobbs drew back defensively, professional pride rising. "She might've known *someone* was following her, but she didn't know it was me. I'm sure of that."
"What makes you so sure?"
Meeting Harrison's challenging stare, Hobbs replied coldly, "I'm sure."
The antagonism between the two men a sudden, palpable force in the silence of the room, Hobbs awaited Harrison's next move. The superior size of the fellow didn't intimidate him. He'd gone up against bigger and tougher men than Harrison before and had come out on top.

Harrison's eyes held his without blinking and Hobbs suddenly realized that the menace he had read in that hard, unsmiling face went clear through to the man's soul. Hobbs's gaze narrowed as the bigger man sat forward.

"I want to hear it all, from the minute you got on the train."

All right. Strictly business. That was fine with him.

Hobbs began. "I was already seated and ready for her when Lila Chesney got on. There wasn't a man in the car who didn't snap up to attention when she walked down that aisle. I was sitting a short distance away from the seat she took, and she . . .

Garrett listened intently as Hobbs talked, his mind as much on the facts his new partner was relating as it was on the man himself. As much as he hated to admit it, Hobbs was probably right. His disguise was too perfect for a nonprofessional like Lila Chesney to see through it. As small and wiry as Hobbs was, he appeared to have been born to that flashy suit, stiff white shirt and tie he wore, and that bowler looked as if it had been made for his balding head. That small mustache was the perfect touch. Garrett paused speculatively. Something had happened to cause Lila Chesney to change her plans. He wanted to know what it was.

Hobbs's recitation came to an abrupt halt. Reacting sharply, Garrett questioned, "That's it? She just got off the train, walked away, and you never saw her again?" Garrett stared with open disbelief. "How in hell could you lose sight of a woman dressed in a red dress and a plumed hat! She didn't even try to look inconspicuous!" Hobbs's clean-shaven face colored hotly as Garrett pressed, "You only had to keep an eye on her. How difficult was that?"

"That woman's smarter than any of us thought she was. I don't know how she did it, but she just disappeared."

"That's impossible, and you know it."

"She did it!"

"Disappeared without a trace . . ."

"Without a trace! I didn't take my eyes off her for a minute from the moment she got on the train. I was grinning like the fool I wanted her to think I was right up until she got off here in Denver. I followed her to the station house and waited outside where I could see both the front and back entrances. But, damn it, Harrison, she never came out!"

"You questioned everybody in the station house . . ."

"Everybody saw her go in, but nobody saw her leave."

"What about the windows?"

"She couldn't have climbed out through a window. They were all in full view!"

"You asked the clerks if they sold her another ticket?"

"I sure did."

"Well?"

"They didn't."

"You checked the livery stables?"

"I'm not an amateur, Harrison."

"No one saw a woman travelin' alone who fitted her description."

"No."

"You checked the—"

"I checked, I checked. I did it all! I've been going around in circles for two days. She disappeared, I tell you! Right into thin air."

Garrett's eyes narrowed. When he spoke again, his words were slow and deliberate.

"No, she didn't, and until we find out what she *did* do, we're goin' to keep on goin' over this. Now, let's take it again, from the beginnin'—from the minute she got on the train. What did she do?"

Hobbs's narrow face slowly stiffened. "Let's get one thing straight, Harrison. I only have one boss in this agency. I don't take orders from you or anybody else."

The sudden drop in Hobbs's tone as he echoed the same sentiment he himself had expressed to McParland a short time earlier brought Garrett back from his mindless anger with a snap. He was impressed. He stood almost a foot taller than Hobbs, he outweighed him by at least seventy pounds, and he knew damned well the fellow wouldn't stand a chance against him in a fight—but he could tell from the look in Hobbs's eyes that none of that meant a thing to him. Hobbs wasn't afraid of him. He wasn't afraid of anybody.

Garrett almost smiled. It looked as if McParland knew a good man when he saw one.

Garrett's inner smile faded. Besides, Hobbs wasn't the enemy here.

Breaking the long silence between them, Garrett stated flatly, "You're right. I'm not used to havin' a partner."

Extending his hand toward Hobbs, Garrett saw the flicker of surprise in the smaller man's eyes. He also saw the budding of a new respect, one he had unexpectedly come to share as Hobbs accepted his hand.

Peace reestablished between them, Garrett pressed, "All right, so let's go over it again . . . from the beginning."

* * *

The bottle on the table was half empty when Garrett and Hobbs stood up at last. A satisfied look flashed between the two men before they shook hands and Hobbs turned toward the door.

The sound of Hobbs's progress toward the rear staircase slowly faded from his hearing as Garrett mulled over their intense speculation of the last hour. During that hour he had come to realize that Hobbs had a keen mind and a true dedication to his work. Hobbs and he would work well together.

Garrett moved restlessly and glanced at the newly fallen darkness outside the window. He chafed at the realization that with each passing hour, their hope of finding Lila Chesney became more dim.

Elizabeth's fair face flashed unexpectedly before Garrett's eyes, blending with the sober images of his parents to raise a familiar rage. His jaw tight, Garrett pulled his muscular frame erect. He didn't want to think anymore tonight, not about Hobbs, the job, or even the mysterious Lila Chesney. He wanted to forget for a little while.

Standing on the open staircase overlooking the crowded saloon, Garrett searched for a familiar female face. Lulu's gaze met his and she started toward him in immediate response, shaking off the arm and the protests of the man beside her. The door marked with the numeral 4 closed behind them moments later. Lulu's warm flesh was against his and there was no talking, no foolish games, no pretense that what passed between them was anything more than it was. He had learned to depend on that particular brand of honesty because he knew in his heart that there would never be anything more than this for him.

Three

It wasn't easy being Modesty. As a matter of fact, if she had known how difficult it would be . . .

That thought echoed again in Lila's mind. The afternoon sun was warm on her shoulders as she stood on a rise of land overlooking the modest Bar WK Ranch—a bit too warm. The air was sweet with the scent of spring wildflowers—a bit too sweet. But the man standing beside her . . .

"It really isn't much of a ranch . . . not yet." Lila turned as Luther Knox's voice penetrated her distraction. She squinted up at him in silence. The uncertainty in his deep voice touched an unexpected chord inside her, as did the honest emotion in his eyes and the rasp in his voice as he whispered more softly than before, "But I want you to be happy here. I want you to be as happy as I am that you finally consented to come."

Lila couldn't see him very clearly with the buffer of Modesty's small, wire-rimmed spectacles perched on her nose, but she had peeked over them whenever possible during the previous two days, and she did not have to see him now to know that Luther Knox was a handsome, thoroughly appealing man. She had felt his touch often enough during that time to know that his large, calloused hands were gentle. She had sensed his gaze upon her and felt warmed by it. She had heard the concern in his voice as she heard it now when she failed to respond, and she had regretted the discomfort she caused him.

Because, damn it, Luther Knox was *nice!* He was too nice for the deceit she practiced.

His expression mildly apologetic even as his eyes glowed with pride, Luther stretched out his arm in a sweeping gesture meant to encompass the land. "This ranch is going to be something special someday. I'm going to make sure of that."

Following the wave of Luther's hand with her gaze, Lila flicked the annoying spectacles lower on her nose and peered over them in an attempt to see what he saw . . . to feel what he felt. Somehow, it seemed the least she could do.

The ranch lay spread out before her, nestled snugly within protective hills, reminding Lila of a huge green tapestry that had hung on a wall at home. That home now seemed to be from another lifetime, and the tapestry did no more than stir memories better left unremembered.

Damn it all, she didn't belong here! There were no streets, or even broad, rutted roads that shuttled a constant line of traffic beneath her window. None of the familiar, reassuring sounds were present here—the rattle of wagons moving along the street, the hoorahs of cowboys riding into town, the ring of the blacksmith's hammer throughout the day, or the buzz of conversation that never ceased beyond her window. The rumble of a piano from the floor below her was missing, as were the shouts of raucous laughter that echoed through the night, the grunts and groans of the dancehall girls down the hall as they plied their trade, and the musical jingling of spurs as the traffic occasionally grew heavy there—the sounds of life at every level as it streamed by.

Those sounds had become a part of her life, a life she had painstakingly earned, where she depended on no one and nothing but her own quick mind and her nimble fingers to make her way.

Lila strained her mind to find the right word to describe this place where chance had delivered her. She strained harder. Vast . . . virgin . . . majestic . . . beautiful?

No.

Silent.

The hills were silent, except for the rustle of trees and the rush of the spring breeze. The pastureland was silent. She could almost hear the grass grow. The only sounds that occasionally interrupted that silence were the calls of birds flying overhead . . . the lowing of cattle in the meadow . . . a whinny from the barn beyond. The silence was an accusation that rang over and again in Lila's mind, reminding her that she was an outsider here, pretending to share this man's dream.

Suddenly aware that Luther awaited her response, Lila strained for the right words. The trouble was that Luther was right. It really wasn't much of a ranch. By his own admission, he hadn't even made a dent in the work he had set for himself to do. It would take months, years—a *lifetime* to accomplish all those things, and she knew within her heart that he wanted her, Modesty, to tell him that she was ready to spend that lifetime working beside him.

Lila looked up at Luther once more. He had such a nice face. More important than that, she had come to learn from the letters packed at the bottom of Modesty's bag, as well as from their few days of acquaintance, that Luther's niceness went deeper than the surface.

Could she stay here with him as he wanted?

Her answer was simple.

No.

Lila's adamant mental response halted abruptly with sudden realization. But Luther wasn't asking *her* to stay. He was asking Modesty. And it wasn't *her* life that would be at risk if she left here before it was safe. It was Billy's.

Lila swallowed tightly. She had done many things she did not care to remember over the years in order to support Billy . . . to protect Billy. She knew staying here and deceiving this good, generous man would not be the exception.

But she didn't like herself for it.

"LUTHER!"

A short, clipped, and heavily accented voice echoed up from the ranch house below, interrupting Lila's thoughts. That voice had become only too familiar in the past two days.

Someone else didn't like her, too.

Frowning, Luther turned toward the broad female outline in the distance. She felt him stiffen as the voice called louder.

"LUTHER! BRING DER WOMAN DOWN. IS WORK TO DO IN DER KITCHEN!"

An appropriate response to the woman's command sprang to Lila's mind, but she withheld it as Luther turned back to her with a grimace.

"I'm sorry, Modesty. Aunt Helga hasn't much tact."

"She doesn't like me."

Luther's grimace turned into a coaxing smile. "Aunt Helga doesn't like many people. She changed after Uncle Herman was killed a few years ago. Sometimes I think she doesn't even like me." His expression going suddenly serious, he whispered more softly than before, "Y-you know, her presence here is only temporary. We won't have need for a chaperon after we're married."

"Luther, I don't know . . ."

"I'm not trying to rush you, Modesty. I'm willing to wait as long as you need to be sure it's right between us. But I want to tell you now . . ." Luther's voice dropped to a huskiness that sent a tremor up Lila's spine. "I know you're the woman for me. You're everything I thought you'd be . . . and more. I fell in love with you from your letters, and now that I've come to know you, I love you more. And you're beautiful, Modesty."

"I'm not."

"You are. The picture you sent didn't do you justice. I didn't expect you to be beautiful."

"But you wanted me anyway?"

"I wanted you for the woman I knew you were, the woman on the inside who's warm and kind and loving. You're just shy."

"I'm not . . ."

Luther grasped her hand. "Give it a chance, Modesty. I think I know what's inside you. I think I've come to know you better by your letters than I ever could have come to know you by simple courting." Pausing, Luther continued more softly than before. "I know you're innocent and inexperienced, and you're uncertain because of it. I'm not as inexperienced as you are." His face colored unexpectedly. "I'm thirty-one years old. I've led a full life, but in all honesty, I never knew a woman I wanted to make my wife until I came to know you. I trust that instinct, Modesty, and I'm going to ask you to trust it as well."

"Luther . . ."

"Just give it a chance—a few weeks . . . a few months. You'll get over your shyness. I'll make you love me, just as much as I love you."

Lila attempted a smile. "I hope you'll be patient if I'm more cautious than you." Luther's face fell and Lila rushed to add, "Oh, I don't mean that I'm disappointed in you. I'm not! You're everything I expected and more. But this wilderness is—"

"It's not really a wilderness, darling." Hardly seeming to realize he had used an endearment, Luther continued. "I saw the way you were looking around you as we rode out here. There's little threat from Indians, if that's what you were thinking, and there're more and more people moving out here every day. As a matter of fact, I'm thinking that we'll soon be wishing for the times when neighbors were fewer and farther between."

Lila shook her head. "No, not me."

"I promise I won't press you for marriage." Luther's smile melted her. "You can tell me when you're ready . . ."

Lila paused, then spoke directly into his eyes. "And if I decide to leave?"

"You won't."

"If I do."

"Then I'll take you back to Deer Trail, put you back on the train, and you can set the West forever behind you."

Her throat unexpectedly tight, Lila whispered, "Thank you, Luther."

Luther's clean-shaven, sun-darkened cheeks creased into another heart-melting smile as he whispered, "I'll only ask one thing in return right now . . ."

Luther paused, again flushing. Unable to bear his silent discomfort a moment longer, Lila prompted, "Yes?"

"LUTHER!"

Luther's head snapped toward the call from below. He turned back a moment later, his expression strained.

"I'd like to kiss you, Modesty."

Lila's heart tugged lightly in her breast and she averted her eyes from his, her conscience nagging.

"Aunt Helga's watching."

Startled when Luther cupped her chin gently in his work-roughened hand and turned her face back up to his, Lila felt the tug grow stronger. He removed her glasses with an instinct keener than he realized, enabling her to see him clearly as he whispered, "I don't care. Do you?"

Luther's clear blue eyes caressed her, and Lila felt herself responding to him with full honesty for the first time.

"No, I don't."

He kissed her then. Gently, tenderly, his lips caressing and separating hers with surprising thoroughness. Sweeter than honey was his kiss, so comfortable and warm that it brought tears to her eyes. She didn't realize one had escaped until she heard Luther's distressed whisper.

"You're crying . . ."

Responding with instinctive honesty, Lila whispered, "No, I'm smiling."

Tears touching his eyes as well, Luther took her hand, a hand that she suddenly realized was trembling as he raised it to his lips.

"I love you, Modesty."

Lila hated herself for the tears brimming in her eyes then, for the tenderness they raised in this gentle man as he whispered, "The day you say those same words back to me will be the happiest day of my life."

Sliding his arm around her, Luther drew her along with him as he started back toward the ranch house below them. As they walked, Lila realized that the silence of the land was no longer an accusation. It had taken on an almost comforting sound . . . and a glow that was reflected in Luther's eyes.

The lights of the Golden Steer Saloon were glowing brightly although afternoon had not yet waned. Laughter and music spilled out through the swinging front doors onto the street as Billy Chesney guided his sorrel gelding up the street to the rail and slowly dismounted. Securing his horse there, he raised his sweat-stained hat and ran his hand through curly reddish-brown hair darkened with perspiration. The day had been unexpectedly warm for so early in the spring, and he'd had a damned hard ride. It occurred to him that the lengths a man would go to in order to please a woman were an astonishment.

Billy's eyes sobered. But Lila wasn't just any woman and he was damned anxious to see her.

Stepping up onto the board sidewalk, Billy brushed the dust of the trail from his clothes, then pushed his way through the saloon doors. He paused to allow his eyes to adjust to the light, then scoured the room for Lila's familiar face. Momentarily distracted from his search by an interested glance from a nearby saloon girl, he flashed her a smile. The effect of that smile was instantaneous, just as he had known it would be, but he was too accustomed to its reaction on women to give it more than passing thought. He was good-looking, and he knew it. Lila and he hadn't inherited anything but good looks and determination from their parents, and they both had learned to use their legacies to the best advantage.

Billy's smile dimmed. Lila's beautiful face and slim,

young body had been their only asset when they had been fresh from the orphanage, penniless and frightened of the world into which they had escaped. She had made those assets work for them both, and she had raised him up from a rebellious youth to a man who knew what he wanted and was determined to get it any way he could. Despite their closeness, that determination had become a bone of contention between them as the years had passed, but the knowledge that they could depend upon each other as they could no one else in the world had never been in doubt.

Billy's smile flashed again. He had used that smile often to charm and disarm the ladies, and they couldn't resist him. It was the steel behind that smile, however, that made him the man he was, and few who knew him forgot it.

Walking deeper into the noisy saloon, Billy squinted through the mist of tobacco smoke, his smile dimming. Damn it, where was she? He had ridden over a hundred miles to see her after getting her letter.

"Well, hel . . . lo." A syrupy voice at his elbow turned Billy to the buxom blonde standing there as she winked and slipped her arm through his. "My name's Ruby, honey. Is there anythin' I can do for you?" Encouraged by his smile, she added, "I bet you didn't know I've been waitin' for you all evenin'."

"You're right, Ruby. I didn't. I hate to disappoint you, but I'm looking for somebody else right now."

The blonde moved closer and smiled at him seductively. "Tell me who she is and I'll scratch her eyes out."

The steel behind Billy's smile came through with his whispered response. "No, you won't, because I wouldn't like that . . . not one little bit."

"Take it easy, honey!" Ruby was momentarily disconcerted. "I was only foolin'. Just tell me who you're lookin' for and I'll get her for you."

Billy's smile warmed. "I'd like that. I'm lookin' for Lila Chesney."

Ruby hesitated, obviously uncertain whether to be nervous or relieved as she shrugged her shoulders. "You're too late if you're lookin' for Lila. She left town a couple of days ago. She didn't tell nobody where she was goin', neither."

Sobering, Billy went momentarily still. "You must be mistaken. She wouldn't have done that. She was expecting me."

"Well, honey, I know *I* wouldn't have left town if I knew you was comin', but Lila sure did."

The significance of Lila's sudden departure struck Billy abruptly, and his hand snaked to the holster on his hip. His lean body tense, he surveyed the room with a narrowed gaze, slowly relaxing when he saw no visible danger.

Billy grasped her arm unexpectedly, and Ruby jumped with a start. She swallowed nervously as he flashed her an intimate smile and whispered, "On second thought, I'm thinking that you and me spending some time together tonight might be a good idea after all. It'll give us some time to talk."

His arm around her waist, Billy drew Ruby toward a nearby table. He pulled her closer as they sat. "You and me are going to get real friendly, Ruby honey. And when we do, you're going to tell me everything you know about what Lila did from the minute she started working here. Is that all right with you?"

When Ruby didn't respond, Billy leaned forward and nipped at the white skin of her neck. She smelled of sweat and cheap perfume, but that thought slipped from his mind as he pressed softly, "Is that all right with you, darlin'?"

Ruby's pale eyes were suddenly wary. "What's Lila to you?" She hesitated. "I don't want to get involved if you're out to get her or somethin'."

Billy whispered in return, "No, I'm not out to get her. I just want to find her, that's all. She's special to me . . . very special."

Ruby studied his expression in silence, then gave a short, relieved laugh. "Ain't that just the luck?" She moved closer. "But we'll make the most of the evenin' anyway, won't we, honey? And in the meantime, I'll tell you all I know."

Billy poured Ruby a drink. He could see it was going to be a long night.

The glow had faded.

It had faded an hour earlier, under the glare of Aunt Helga's disapproving gaze.

The clatter of dishes behind her turned Lila to look over her shoulder at the older woman, then at the kitchen around her. It wasn't any more or less than many other kitchens she'd seen. The fireplace that covered one end of the room had obviously been used for cooking at one time, but a large black stove now served the major portion of that purpose. The table at which she worked was small and hand hewn, as were the chairs. The sink, to which water needed to be carried from the well behind the house, was adequate.

But she had always *hated* kitchens.

Lila's mouth twitched. She would be the first to admit that her hatred of the kitchen was not entirely rational. Despite the passage of time, the memory of Billy's shrieking cries when she had been separated from him to work long hours in the orphanage kitchen still raised a painful lump in her throat. The sound of his pleas to join her still echoed in her mind. The week she had spent in that room where the cooking fire blazed unceasingly through the long, hot summer days had been the worst week of her life. Her work had been purposely poor there, and in the end, the matron had banished her to work in the laundry. That sentence had not turned out to be the punishment it was meant to be, for much of her work had been outdoors, where she had worked side by side with Billy for long hours, forging the bond between them ever stronger.

The kitchen, however, had been her enemy ever since.

Drawing herself back to the present, Lila gritted her teeth and attempted to clean up the flour she had dropped minutes earlier. Clumsy from vision distorted through Modesty's spectacles, she had spilled and stumbled her way across the kitchen for two days until her nerves were jangling and her temper short. She knew that if Aunt Helga said one more word . . .

"Der biscuits is all right?"

Turning toward the grey-haired woman behind her, Lila bit back the response that sprang to her tongue. Aunt Helga knew the biscuits weren't *all right.* Aunt Helga also knew from the experience of the past two days that the biscuits would never be *all right* with her making them.

Aunt Helga waddled closer. Her large, bulgy eyes popped as she looked at the floury mass on the board in front of Lila.

"Ach! What is dis?"

Helga's expression spoke more clearly than words, and Lila responded with what she hoped was a Modesty-like smile.

"They're biscuits."

"Nein." The woman shook her head emphatically. *"Nein."*

Lila forced her smile sweeter. "They're the only biscuits I know how to make."

The old woman's sagging jowls flapped as she shook her head harder. *"Nein."*

Lila's smile became strained. She wanted to tell this nagging old witch the truth. She wanted to tell her she could neither cook nor bake, and she was proud of it! But she wasn't Lila anymore. She was Modesty. As Modesty, she widened her eyes with an attempt at convincing bewilderment.

"I don't know what happened. They've always turned out well before."

"Nein! Was never biscuits!"

"Maybe it's the altitude."

"Nein! Was *never* biscuits!"

The urge for mayhem grew slowly inside Lila as Helga stared at her for long moments, suspicion rife in her eyes. With a wipe of her pudgy hand, the woman swept Lila's pitiful effort off the board and threw it into a nearby pail.

Working deftly with a new batch of flour and the crock of lard nearby, Helga began the irritating liturgy Lila had heard recounted too many times for comfort during the past two days.

"Der wife must work hard to be worthy of der husband."

Lila nodded.

"Der wife must keep der house clean."

Lila nodded again.

"Der wife must cook and bake."

Lila's nod was getting stiff.

"Der wife must be good and pure."

Lila's nod was weakening.

"Der wife must give der husband many children . . . many, many children."

Holding on to her Modesty-like personality by the tips of her fingers, Lila managed to nod again.

Helga flopped the biscuit dough over on the board and kneaded it with wide, experienced hands, never taking her eyes from Lila's face as the biscuits rapidly took shape.

"You tell Luther you cook and bake, but you do not cook or bake."

"I—"

"You tell Luther you sew and keep der house, but you cannot keep der house." Aunt Helga's eyes narrowed. "You sew?"

Lila swallowed uncomfortably. She had sewed on a button or two in the past few years.

"Ach! What *do* you do?"

Lila was tempted to tell her.

Deciding in favor of discretion, Lila gritted her teeth more tightly and averted her face. She had a feeling she knew what was coming.

"You do not cook. You do not bake. You do not sew. You can wash der clothes?"

Lila did not dare respond.

"You can wash der clothes?"

Lila's smile became a grimace.

"You can wash der clothes?"

Lila's hands were clenching into fists.

"You can wash der clothes?"

"YES! I CAN WASH DER CLOTHES."

"Ja? Dis is goot."

Her most fervent wish granted, Lila was out of the kitchen a short time later, but there was little joy in her escape. Her arms in hot soapy water up to the elbows, she grimaced as she looked at the mountain of dirty laundry piled on the ground beside her.

A familiar thought returned, never more intensely than before.

It wasn't easy being Modesty, damn it! It wasn't easy at all.

Dismounting, Luther Knox patted the neck of his bay, then turned toward the barn. His mind far from the long afternoon he had spent rounding up calves to ready them for branding, he quickened his step, drawing his mount behind him. He almost laughed. So anxious was he to return to the house to see Modesty that he was almost tempted to break into a run.

Reaching the stall, Luther slipped his mount inside and paused.

Damn. He was in love, all right.

Luther's expression became pensive as he recalled seeing Modesty for the first time. Slender and erect, dressed in somber brown, she had been obviously uncertain as she had stood on the station platform. He remembered thinking as she glanced left and right, then left again, her steps awkward and unsure, that she had looked like a little lost wren. She had stumbled several times in her nervousness. She had frowned at her clumsiness but had pressed forward, adjusting her spectacles on the bridge of her short nose in a way he had later come to realize was unconscious habit. He would never forget the moment when she had turned to face him fully for the first time.

Modesty was beautiful, but the feeling that had swelled within him had been far more than his reaction to physical appeal. It had been the sudden realization that he was seeing for the first time the woman who was to be his wife . . . and the abrupt realization that although he had never met Modesty before, he loved her.

His face flushing at the emotion those thoughts evoked, Luther loosened his horse's cinch and swung the saddle off his back. Removing the saddle blanket, he flopped it on the nearby rail and paused again. Granted, he had not met Modesty in a conventional way.

"Respectable young ladies willing to correspond with respectable young men for purposes of enlightenment and friendship, with an eye to the future and the possibility of deeper commitment."

The advertisement he had chanced to see in a newspaper from back East had been just vague enough to suit him. He had been somehow ready for it.

Having had enough of mending other men's fences and tending their cattle, he had come to the mineral-rich Colorado territory to make his fortune a few years earlier, but he had discovered something far more important than silver or gold. He had found land he wished to call his own. He had made a commitment to that land then and there, and to everything he wanted to build on it. He had not regretted that commitment for a single day since.

But he had gotten lonely. The company of his hired hand, Max Lipton, had not been enough to quell a growing restlessness that occasional trips to Deer Trail failed to alleviate. Modesty's name and address had been returned to him in response to that advertisement, and he had written her promptly. Her response had come just as quickly in return. She had intrigued him with her innocent candor in the first letter. Her obvious inexperience and curiosity had touched him in the second. A strangely protective emotion had begun rising in him by the fourth, and by the sixth letter, he had been smitten. In truth, he could not recall exactly when he had realized that it could be love.

Luther sighed. Who could help but love Modesty? She was such a dear, shy little thing. Admittedly, her cooking was a disappointment. Those biscuits. . . . He shuddered. But he was certain all blame for the culinary disasters she had worked in the past two days could be placed on an unfamiliar stove, a new atmosphere, and her unrelenting nervousness. He was certain it would all straighten out when she was finally relaxed enough to be able to walk a few steps without stumbling over her own feet.

Luther could not help but smile. Even Modesty's clumsiness had become endearing to him. It had become more difficult than she could possibly imagine for him to restrain himself from taking her into his arms to comfort her each time she stumbled. But then, the one kiss they had shared had proved to him that comfort was not all he had in mind.

The sudden tightness in Luther's throat was reflected in another part of his anatomy as well. It gave him pause to consider the scope of his feelings. He loved Modesty and he wanted her, but he knew she did not share those feelings . . . not yet. He would have to take it slow. He would have to take care not to frighten her. He would have to make her realize that living on a ranch in the "wilderness" did not mean a life of hardship and deprivation, and that he would devote his life to making all her effort worthwhile.

Those thoughts in mind, Luther started toward the house, only to stop abruptly in his tracks. His mouth dropped open at the long lines of laundry stretched across the rear yard, between which Modesty—her tidy bun no longer tidy, her sober grey dress water-stained, and her small face dotted with perspiration—stood wearily.

Luther groaned aloud, and Modesty's head snapped toward him. He saw the flicker in her eyes as he reached her side and took her hand in his. He groaned *inwardly* as he touched the chapped, abused skin, and whispered sincerely, "Modesty, I'm so sorry. I didn't bring you here for this. Aunt Helga should've known not to—"

Astonishing him, Modesty smiled. He could not help but believe she meant every word when she said, "I think Aunt Helga's discovered one of my few talents." Halting him when he attempted another protest, she said more softly than before, "Don't worry, Luther. There's nothing Aunt Helga can do to turn me against you." Again smiling, she added, "Besides, my laundry is much more acceptable than my biscuits."

Modesty glanced back at the billowing linens then, and Luther was stunned to see true pride reflected in the glowing beauty of her eyes. Speechless, he could not help but love her more.

Billy reached for his gunbelt and glanced behind him. The saloon below was silent and Ruby was sprawled on the bed in the corner of the small room, sleeping soundly as the first light of dawn glimmered against the drawn window shade. He had gotten all he needed and all he wanted from Ruby. It was time to move on.

So, Lila had run away because a Pinkerton agent had been asking questions about her. Billy frowned. Lila was going to be fit to be tied that he had gotten her involved in this mess. Damn, he was going to catch it!

Billy's frown turned abruptly into a smile. But Lila

was smart . . . too smart to let a Pinkerton get the best of her. She had slipped temporarily out of sight, and if he knew her at all, she was already in the clear and sitting pretty.

Billy consoled himself with the thought that Lila knew how to contact him. He knew she would, too, when it was safe.

But in the meantime . . .

Checking his gun once more, Billy picked up his hat, tipped it to the sleeping woman in the bed behind him, and slipped silently into the hall.

Four

Outside the Golden Steer Saloon, the main street of Salina, Kansas, bustled with afternoon activity. Wagons shuttled freight from recently arrived rail shipments to stores along the street while curious crowds gathered in active scrutiny of the new wares soon to be offered. From inside the saloon, Garrett observed the women gathering excitedly as a crated sewing machine arrived at the general store. His expression wry as he leaned casually against the bar, he also noted that the reception given the new shipment of beer barrels rolling through the saloon doors was not any less enthusiastic.

"Feelin' lonely, big fella?"

The piano in the corner of the room began another raucous tune in an effort to overwhelm the rumbling of the barrels and the scraping of chairs as a path was made for the new delivery. Ignoring the chaos underway, Garrett looked down at the redheaded woman who had stepped up beside him at the bar. She returned his assessment boldly, obviously relying heavily on the curves revealed in her gaudy gold dress to make an impression as she pressed herself against his side and spoke in a sultry purr.

"You look like you need some company, honey, and I think I'm just the girl you're lookin' for."

Garrett did not bother to smile. He had heard those words roll off women's tongues so many times that he'd lost count. For all the physical release those women had provided him, their names had long since begun to blur in his mind. Belle, Maggie, Lulu, and now . . .

"My name's Charlene, good-lookin'. What's yours?"

"My friends call me . . . Ace." Garrett slipped his arm around Charlene's waist. His voice deepened. "I take it you want to be my friend?"

"Ace, honey, when you look at me like that, there's nothin' I want more. As a matter of fact, you just pick up that drink of yours and we'll get us to that table in the corner so we can get ourselves some real friendly privacy."

Following Charlene's lead, Garrett allowed himself to be dragged toward a vacant corner table that served his purposes far better than Charlene realized. Moments later he was seated with his back to the wall as Charlene elbowed her way back across the crowded floor toward the bottle that awaited them at the bar.

Garrett settled back in his chair, his gaze wandering the room in silent judgment as a familiar tingle ran along his spine. Minutes earlier he had left the sun-drenched street to stand briefly in the doorway, the feeling in his bones that had begun the moment McParland had summoned him to his office growing stronger by the minute.

Admiration flickered briefly in Garrett's mind. McParland had been right. Jake Hobbs was a damned good man. The saloon was exactly as he had described it, down to minute details, including a description of the ornately framed mirrors on the far wall which allowed ample view of almost any quarter of the floor, the number of tables jammed into the narrow space between the mahogany bar and the gaming tables in the far corner, and the back entrance at the base of the staircase to the busy second floor.

With that thought in mind, Garrett also knew he would have no difficulty recognizing the Chesney woman when he saw her, for Hobbs's description had been more than detailed. Garrett gave a grunt of disgust. Hobbs had been almost salivating.

Continuing to peruse the crowded room, Garrett reviewed his mental picture of Lila Chesney. Light hair a soft shade of brown that was not quite blond or red; dark eyes, lashes and brows that Hobbs swore needed no artifice to enhance them; the fine features of a porcelain doll with clear, flawless skin to match, and a wide smile that flashed even white teeth and a fleeting dimple in her right cheek. She was a tall woman, according to Hobbs's standards, who stood over five feet six inches in height—and all of it pure woman.

Garrett shook his head. No, there was no one fitting that description here.

"I'm back, Ace honey." Charlene slid into the chair beside him. The obvious lines of dissipation marking her face deepened as she smiled and poured him a drink. She raised her glass.

"To our . . . *friendship.*"

"That sounds good to me." Garret tossed down his drink and poured himself another. "You new here? I don't remember seein' you the last time I was in."

"No, I ain't new." Charlene laughed. "I ain't new here or anywheres else. I must've been busy somewhere when you came in, that's for sure, because I know damned well I wouldn't have forgotten *you* if I had seen you before."

Charlene swallowed her drink with practiced ease and

Garrett poured her another, then glanced casually around the room. "There *is* somebody who's missin' here tonight, though—that faro dealer. I think her name was Lila."

Charlene stiffened as Garrett continued. "I'm not about to forget her. She took me for plenty, and I had a mind to get my money back. When's she comin' in?"

Suddenly sober, Charlene shook her head. "I don't know nothin' about Lila, and I don't want to know nothin'."

Charlene's reaction was unexpected. Equally unexpected was her sudden rise to her feet and her spontaneous step backward. "If you want to talk about Lila, you got the wrong person." Grabbing the arm of a buxom blonde as she passed, Charlene drew her forward, "This here fella's looking for somebody you know, Ruby."

The blonde turned toward Garrett. She flicked him an appreciative glance and responded wryly, "Don't tell me. Let me guess. You're lookin' for Lila."

Garrett's expression left no need for confirmation, and Ruby laughed shrilly. "I knew it! Every good-lookin' man that's come in here in the past two days has been lookin' for Lila!"

Instantly alert, Garrett made no protest as Charlene faded into the nearby crowd, leaving Ruby in her stead. Motioning Ruby into Charlene's seat, he filled the half-empty glass she had in her hand and offered companionably, "Somebody else lookin' for Lila?"

"Yeah, somebody else was lookin' for her." She grimaced. "And he damned near cut my throat when I made a little joke about her. I hope you ain't that touchy."

"That right? What was the fella's name?"

Ruby paused, looking at him speculatively. "He never did tell me his name."

"What *did* he tell you?"

"You ask a lot of questions, don't you, cowboy?" The dull blue of Ruby's eyes narrowed. "Look, I'm goin' to tell you the same thing I told him. If you're out to get Lila, I'm not answerin' any questions. I don't want to get involved in any of Lila's problems . . . and I sure as hell don't want that other big fella comin' after me." Ruby shuddered. "Hell, no, not after the look I saw in his eyes."

Garrett allowed a smile to quirk the corner of his lips. "The only thing I want from Lila is a chance to get some of my money back." He winked. "Besides, do I look like the kind of a fella who could *hurt* anybody?"

Ruby's response was another shrill laugh that grated along Garrett's spine. The echo was still reverberating in his ears when Ruby cocked her head and responded in a throaty voice, "Honey, you look like somebody who would do anythin' he needs to do . . . but I ain't goin' to get into that. I'll just tell you what I told the other fella. Lila left town . . . just like that. She didn't say where she was goin', and she didn't say if she was comin' back."

Garrett sneered. "I should've known nobody could be that lucky at cards without helpin' her luck along a little bit."

"Hey now, don't go gettin' that around!" Suddenly nervous, Ruby glanced toward the bar to see if they had been overheard. "You'll get me fired real quick if the boss thinks you got that idea from me. He prides himself in runnin' an honest house." Stealing a quick glance at the moon-faced, heavily mustached fellow standing at the end of the bar, Ruby continued more softly than before. "Lila didn't leave town in a hurry because of anythin' that happened here. She left because she had a Pinkerton on her trail."

"A Pinkerton!"

"That's right." Ruby nodded vehemently. "Charlie Peal, one of the regulars, recognized the fella when he was askin' questions about Lila in the livery stable. He hotfooted it over here and told Lila, and Lila didn't wait around for the Pinkerton to come avisitin'."

"A Pinkerton . . . What did he look like?"

"Don't know. I don't think Lila waited to find out, either."

"A Pinkerton . . ." Garrett shook his head in feigned amazement. "I've done a lot of things in my time that I don't like to talk about, but I've never had a Pinkerton on my trail. What did she do?"

"Don't know that, either. All's I know is that Lila's got more than one fella on her trail."

"You mean that fella the other night you were talkin' about? Was he a Pinkerton, too?"

"Hell, no!" Ruby's shrill laughter sounded again. "He didn't fool me. He was too damned dangerous behind that great big smile to be a Pinkerton." Ruby's lips twisted wryly. "Now you, you're different. You don't even bother to smile."

"I only smile when somebody gives me somethin' to smile about, darlin'."

"That so?" Ruby inched closer. "Maybe I can help you there."

Garrett concealed the unexpected sadness Ruby's response induced as he prompted, "Did you give that other fella somethin' to smile about . . . the one who was lookin' for Lila?"

"I did my damned best."

"Hummmm . . . well, maybe that fella and me are goin' to have somethin' in common after all."

Ruby laughed again and Garrett tipped the bottle once more. He knew his business. Another few drinks and Ruby would be talking easily, and a little while after that, he'd know all she knew.

It was all a matter of time and patience.

Garrett finished off another drink.

Advancing carefully, Billy guided his sorrel up the rugged hillside. The setting sun colored the new foliage surrounding him with glorious shades of red and gold, but he was oblivious to nature's artistry as he moved steadily forward. He had been on the trail too long. He was tired, and he had a driving need to bring his quest to a close.

But he was not too tired for caution.

His eyes narrowing into slits, Billy surveyed the raw terrain around him. The virgin forest grew thicker as he ascended the overgrown trail, and he strained to penetrate the lengthening shadows. The outline of a cabin appeared in the deepening twilight and Billy's heart quickened. He slid his hand toward the gun at his hip, the movement spontaneous as he drew his mount to a halt and sat motionless for long moments, acutely attuned to the silence. Hearing nothing amiss, he dismounted and secured the animal there.

Light flickered from within as Billy approached the cabin stealthily. Moving among the shadows, his gun drawn, he glanced carefully around him before stepping out into the open at last and approaching the door.

Breathing deeply, his heart pounding like a drum, Billy thrust the door open, the loud crack as it snapped back against the inside wall registering in his mind as he stepped inside.

The woman standing at the fireplace gasped sharply as she turned toward him. He saw the fear in her eyes the moment before her gaze met his.

"Billy!"

In a moment she was in his arms.

"What in hell happened to you?"

Jake Hobbs's sharp question cut the chill evening air as Garrett Harrison dismounted from his horse and turned toward him. Harrison was late. It was unprofessional to be late and Hobbs disliked unprofessionalism.

Harrison did not respond. The lights of Denver twinkled in the distance as the bigger man approached. Hobbs had not disagreed when Harrison had suggested upon their first meeting almost three days ago that they pursue different lines of investigation. It had made sense since it was imperative to pick up Lila Chesney's trail before it cooled completely. Recognizing the danger in being seen together, they had decided to rendezvous just beyond Denver's town limits by noon of that day.

Harrison maintained his silence, and a prickle of apprehension moved up Hobbs's spine. Something was wrong. Harrison was walking heavily, his step devoid of the smooth, animal-like grace with which the big man usually moved. Straining his eyes into the semilight of the campfire, Hobbs waited for the first clear glimpse of Harrison's face. What he saw answered his questions more clearly than words.

When Hobbs spoke again, his voice was wry.

"Seems to me like you're in need of a hair of the dog."

Harrison glanced up sharply. His bloodshot eyes confirmed the conclusion Hobbs had reached moments earlier as he snapped, "Seems to me that I don't need anybody's advice . . . most of all, yours."

"Oh, well, now . . ." Amusement beginning to replace his earlier annoyance, Hobbs restrained a suitable retort. Hell, he hadn't always been a Pinkerton man. He had come out West to make his fortune in his youth many years earlier. He had taken the time to sow some pretty spectacular wild oats, and in doing so had earned an education that was unrivaled by any school curriculum. He had joined the Army when the war started, and he had fought for a cause that, in the end, he could not justify when weighed against all the carnage he had seen. He had been left with a strange restlessness afterward, a sense of unfinished business that had plagued him until he had met up again with a Pinkerton agent he had met briefly during the conflict. That chance meeting had brought him his true vocation in life, and he had been dedicated to his work ever since.

Hobbs restrained a smile. That all seemed so long ago, but he was not so far removed from the high-living lifestyle of his youth not to remember the effects of unjudicious drinking and all it entailed . . . or the pallor that had greeted him in the mirror after his body had responded in long hours of spasmodic protest.

Hobbs snickered under his breath. Even in the poor light of the campfire Harrison's complexion glowed with that same revealing shade of green. Hobbs snickered again. He sure hoped it had all been worth it.

Unable to resist, Hobbs commented dryly, "I know what *I've* been doing the past few days. I've been retracing Lila Chesney's tracks up and down the line, just like we agreed. I was under the impression you were going to go back to Salina to get whatever background on her that I might've missed, but it looks to me like you took a detour."

Taking off his hat, Garrett rubbed a heavy hand across his forehead and then sat abruptly on a nearby log. He looked up, his expression black as he ignored the smaller man's comments and asked bluntly, "Well, what did you find out?"

Hobbs's amusement faded as the agitations of the previous two days returned. The frown on his face was reflected in his voice as he responded flatly, "Nothin'. Not a damned thing."

Harrison's black look darkened. "What do you mean, nothin'?"

"I told you, I didn't find out anything that I didn't know before. For all intents and purposes, Lila Chesney disappeared from the face of the earth after she walked into that station house. Nobody saw her, or anybody who looked like her, coming out. How did you do? Did you find out anything at the Golden Steer?"

"Yeah, I found out somethin', all right." Harrison's bloodshot eyes held his. "I found out that I made a mistake underestimatin' a blond dancehall girl named Ruby. Hell, she drank me under the table."

Not bothering to respond, Hobbs covered the few steps to his saddlebags, reached inside, and withdrew a half-empty whiskey bottle. Harrison groaned as he placed it in his hand.

"Another shot ought to set you to rights, or at least clear your head enough so we can talk." When the bigger man hesitated, Hobbs's expression tightened. "Take a drink. This Chesney woman got away from me once, Harrison. I'm not about to give her any more time so she can disappear for good."

Hesitating only a moment longer, Harrison tilted back his head and took a healthy swallow before shoving the bottle back into Hobbs's hand. The medicinal effects were obvious a few minutes later as Harrison responded in a more subdued tone.

"The trip to Salina wasn't a complete waste. Ruby had a hollow leg, but she also had a pretty good memory. She was there the day Lila Chesney first walked into the saloon lookin' for a job. She remembered that Lila reeled off a whole string of places she had worked before. Ruby said it sounded like a conductor reelin' off the stops . . . that Lila had worked at every town of a decent size along the line."

Hobbs nodded, his interest piqued. "You're thinking there's some reason she never stays too long in one place and never strays far from the railroad."

"Maybe. But I found out somethin' even more interestin'. Lila has herself a boyfriend . . . somebody who's tryin' to track her down."

"You're sure it's a boyfriend?"

"Ruby said he near to killed her when she said somethin' he didn't like about Lila."

"What's the fella's name?"

"Ruby didn't know, but she gave me a description that should make him easy enough to recognize. He's in his twenties, tall, about my size and weight, with green eyes and curly hair that's a shade short of red. She said he has a wide little boy's smile but that his eyes are cold as ice behind it, and that his hand springs to his gun at every sound."

"I'll be damned." Hobbs's heart began a rapid beating. "His size and coloring fit the description of the newest member of Foster's gang, all right. Looks like we're onto something. Did she tell you anything else?"

Harrison paused, his light eyes growing pensive. "Somethin' else she said has been running around in my head. She said this fella said Lila was expectin' him but that he didn't seem too upset when he found out she'd left because a Pinkerton agent was askin' questions about her."

"Damn! She ran out because of me!"

"Somebody recognized you and got to Lila before you did . . . but that's not important. What's important is that Ruby said the fella acted as if he didn't have to worry about how he was goin' to find Lila again."

"What's that supposed to mean? Maybe he didn't care."

Harrison shook his head. "He cared all right, but he wasn't worried about havin' missed her . . . as if they'd made plans on how and where they'd contact each other if he did."

Hobbs stared at Harrison, a familiar excitement pulsing through his veins as he pressed, "So, you're saying if we find Lila Chesney and just bide our time, this fella's going to come into the picture sooner or later."

"That's what I'm sayin', all right." Harrison's expression turned cold. "It's just a matter of time."

The ring of Harrison's voice was even colder than his words, and Hobbs felt a crawling sensation slither up his spine. It was true, all right, everything he had heard about Harrison. There was nothing professional involved in Harrison's feelings about his work. His feelings were personal. He'd seen vengeance like this in a man's eyes only once before. It hadn't ended well.

Seeing the end of it all for Lila Chesney and her mysterious boyfriend even more clearly than he could see Harrison's suddenly menacing visage, Hobbs unconsciously nodded. He also saw the commitment in Harrison's bloodshot eyes that made his statement take on the solemnity of a vow.

Right . . . it was just a matter of time.

* * *

"Real pleased to meet you, ma'am."

Hat in hand, Max Lipton stood in the ranch house doorway grinning broadly, and Luther silently groaned. Max had been following his orders, hunting up strays for the past week. He had just come in from the range. His boots were covered with mud and he smelled almost as bad as his horse, but his hair was slicked down neatly and his wrinkled, sun-baked face was clean-shaven. Luther knew his short, middle-aged hired hand had made a special attempt to present a favorable appearance, knowing he was to meet Luther's intended for the first time. He was touched at the effort, but he also knew that it had not been effort enough.

Luther turned to Modesty, uncertain. Her small face was sober as she squinted uncomfortably through her glasses at the grinning cowboy. Meticulously groomed as always, her hair was neatly bound, her grey cotton dress clasped tightly at the neck and her sleeves buttoned at the wrist despite the kitchen's heat. The white apron tied around her narrow waist was . . .

Luther almost smiled. Well, Modesty was Modesty, after all.

But the stains on Modesty's apron didn't truly concern him. Worrying him more intensely was the realization that Modesty had in all probability never been close enough to a real cowboy before to actually experience the grime or the smell of one. In his effort to make her believe that her life in this "wilderness" would not be any less civilized than the one she had led in the East, he had been careful to present himself at his best at all times with her. Despite his efforts, however, reality was now grinning directly into Modesty's beautiful face, and he wondered. Would she grin back?

Not realizing he was holding his breath, Luther watched as Modesty squinted more earnestly, then flicked her glasses down lower on her pert nose to peer over them as she often did when unsure. Her expression unchanging, he saw her take a breath . . . he was uncertain if he saw her wince . . . before extending her hand toward Max, a smile growing on her pink lips as she said with more earnestness than he had dared hope to hear, "I'm truly pleased to meet you, too, Max. Luther told me that you've been with him since he took possession of this land and that he couldn't have accomplished all he's done here without you."

Coloring unexpectedly, Max grasped Modesty's hand and shook it enthusiastically. Appearing unable to take his eyes from her face, he continued his energetic pumping as he returned, "Oh, it wasn't nothin', miss. The boss here's a right fine fella . . . one of the best I ever worked for, but he ain't got much of a way with words. He never did tell me how downright pretty you was."

The resounding "humph!" that came from behind turned all eyes to Aunt Helga's jowled face as she interrupted without hesitation.

"Ach! Foolish old man! Look at der boots on *mein* clean floor!"

"Aw, Helga . . ." Max relinquished Lila's hand and cast an appreciative glance at the roast beef that awaited cutting on the table, the potatoes heaped high in a plate nearby, and the fresh biscuits on the tray in Helga's hands. He winked and leaned toward the older woman with a smile. "I can't help the mud, you know. I don't work in town all day, but if it'll make you happy, I'll take my boots off and leave them by the door."

"Nein!" Helga waved a warning hand, then clasped her nose expressively. "You scrape outside."

The exchange between the two older personages continued, but Luther paid it little mind. Instead, he was intent on Modesty's unexpected reaction to their exchange. Her eyes sparkling, it was obvious that she barely contained her laughter. His heart did a crazy leap as she reached for his hand and squeezed it companionably before releasing it to walk toward her seat at the table.

Snapped from his bemusement, he saw Max heading outside to scrape his boots as Aunt Helga placed the last tray on the table. He was turning toward his seat as well when he felt Aunt Helga's hand on his arm. Her voice sounded softly in his ear in a tone of light command.

"In der kitchen, please."

Shooting Modesty a silent plea for understanding, Luther followed Aunt Helga into the kitchen. He took a defensive step backward as she turned to him, her eyes suddenly blazing.

"Dis woman is not what she say!"

"Aunt Helga . . ." Luther was at a complete loss. "What're you talking about?"

"Dis woman from der big city, is right?"

"Yes . . ."

"She work in der fine house . . . *fine* house, where she cook and clean, is right?"

"Yes. What are you getting at, Aunt Helga?"

"She work in der fine house but does not look at der mud on boots? She does not mind der smell of horses?" Aunt Helga wrinkled her nose, "Or other smells? She does not care?"

"So?"

"Der *lady* would care!"

Luther could feel a slow heat rise inside him. Controlling his anger with supreme strength of will, he replied softly, "Did it never occur to you, Aunt Helga, that Modesty reacted as she did, with courtesy and kindness to Max *because* she's a lady? After all, would a lady let Max see her distaste?"

Aunt Helga nodded. *"Ja."*

"Nein." Luther shook his head in confusion. "I mean, no. She wouldn't. Aunt Helga, you aren't being fair."

"I be fair!"

"You haven't given Modesty a true chance."

Helga raised her sagging chin. "I give her der true chance."

"Modesty is trying so hard to please you."

"Nein. She try to please *you."*

Luther smiled weakly. "Well? What's wrong with that?"

"She try to *fool* you, but you do not see! Max . . ." Helga humphed again, "Old fool . . . but Helga wait, and you see."

"Aunt Helga . . ."

"You see." Helga nodded stiffly. "Come. Eat."

Ending the conversation as abruptly as she had begun it, Aunt Helga turned and walked back into the dining room. Following her, Luther shot Modesty another silent appeal, which was interrupted by Max's reappearance in the dining-room doorway.

Luther jumped with a start as Helga's voice boomed, "Max, you scrape?"

"My boots are as clean as they'll ever be . . . and I'm mighty hungry, Helga."

Aunt Helga's expression flickered. Luther saw the flicker was not missed by Modesty as Aunt Helga then nodded abruptly.

"Come. Eat."

Relieved, Luther looked at Modesty once more. He was startled to see that she did not appear to be at all disturbed by Helga's discourteous behavior. Instead, she flashed Max a shy smile. As it did to Max, the sight of that smile rocked Luther down to his toes.

And Luther wondered. Could he help but love her?

Soft sounds, loving sounds, rent the silence of the night as Billy crushed the woman in his arms ever closer. Her sweet flesh was warm against his as he slid his lips down the column of her throat to bathe the fragile hollows at its base with his tongue.

Damn . . . he loved the feel of her, the heat of her, the way she moved beneath him. Slipping lower, he covered first one small breast with his mouth, then the other. He heard her sharp intake of breath as her fingers dug responsively into his back, and the gasping sounds she made as she clutched him against her. No woman had ever made him feel this way before. No woman had ever made him believe that she lived for the moment when she was in his arms, that she wanted him . . . *only* him.

His control tenuous, Billy raised himself to look down into her face. Eva . . . whose small dark eyes were notable only for the glow of emotion shining in their depths, whose common features, marred by the ragged scar on her cheek, were significant only for the pleasure they gave him as he worshipped them with his lips. To him she was beautiful. Her face was made to reflect the joy of their loving, her slender body born to fit his. He had ached for her, longed for her while they had been apart.

Swallowing her parted lips with his, Billy felt Eva's

long fingers slide into his hair, then move to trace his face caressingly as she urged the deepening of his kiss. He heard her murmur softly and he drew back, his breathing uneven as he looked into dark eyes brimming with love.

Eva's voice emerged shakily in answer to his unspoken question, the sound carrying the emotion of her words as she whispered, "I love you, Billy."

Those words again.

"I'll always love you."

The solemn rasp of Eva's voice raised a thickness in Billy's throat as he covered her mouth again with his. But it was not enough. Emotion rising beyond his control, Billy drew back with a soft curse, fitting the swell of his passion against her. His eyes closed briefly at finding her moist and waiting and he plunged deep inside her.

A blinding jubilation rose in Billy's mind as Eva rose to meet his voracious thrusts. He reveled in the sweet rhythm of their joining as their bodies met again and again, as the rhythm accelerated to loving abandon, as it soared higher, wilder . . .

Culmination came abruptly, sharply, rapturously.

The ragged pounding of Eva's heart echoed his own as he lay silent and replete upon her. Raising himself above her, he kissed the lashes that were dark crescents against the burnished gold of her cheeks. Her eyes remained closed and he kissed her again . . . remembering their first meeting.

Leadville's streets had been crowded with Saturday shoppers as he had ridden into town. He had been out of sorts when he had turned through the doorway of Walker's General Store and approached the front counter. It had been hot . . . uncomfortably so. Not a breath of air had been moving in the stifling emporium, a situation that had been further compounded by customers milling in narrow aisles cramped with towering piles of merchandise and the long line awaiting service at the counter. Annoyed with the delay, he had moved to the back of the store to search out his purchases on his own. His search had come to an abrupt halt at the sight of a small, dark-haired woman attempting to drag a huge sack out of the storage room. Her faded dress had been ringed wetly under the arms, her forehead had been beaded with perspiration, and her neatly bound hair had begun to loosen. She had turned toward him then, and his first sight of her scarred cheek had caused him to wince. But something about her had struck a responsive chord inside him. He had immediately gone to her aid, only to be startled at her sharp rebuff.

"I can do it myself!"

Angry, he had been determined to let her try. He had watched as she struggled with the heavy sack, dragging it forward an inch at a time, perspiration running from her temples, her skin whitening until he was certain her next moment would be her last. He had snatched the sack from her then, only to have her intense, brown-eyed gaze rise to his with a fervent plea.

"No, please. Mr. Walker will fire me." Her expression had softened, and his gaze had been inexplicably drawn to the melting warmth of her smile as she had whispered, "I can do it, really I can."

He had submitted to her plea and allowed her to drag the sack a few inches more before stepping forward with a mumbled curse and swinging the sack up onto his shoulder. At the counter moments later, he had been conscious of Eva's quaking as he dropped the sack at the feet of the overweight proprietor in full view of his customers and commented with a smile, "I figured you had better use for this lady in your establishment than to have her drag fifty pounds of potatoes up to the front desk when you could be doing that yourself."

Surprising him, the old man had responded with a shrug. "She's a half-breed. They're used to hard work. It don't bother them none."

Suddenly seething, he had replied with tenuous control, "Maybe that's so, but it bothers *me*."

Old man Walker had motioned Eva behind the counter then, and he hadn't given the matter much thought until the following day when he had run into her on the street. Her distress had been apparent when she told him that she was no longer employed at Walker's General Store.

It had been all Eva had been able to do to hold him back, and he was as certain now as he had been that day that in doing so, Eva had saved the overweight proprietor's life.

But she had done more than that.

In the weeks following, Eva had taught him how to truly love. It had been an exquisite tutelage. He—

The sound of fretful whimpers from the cradle in the far corner of the room turned Eva's head toward the sound, exposing her scarred cheek fully to his eye. Lowering his head, Billy pressed his lips against the uneven flesh, only to feel her draw back, the shadows in her eyes darkening.

His heart sinking, Billy covered her mouth again with his, reveling in its moist sweetness as he slipped his tongue between her lips. At the sound of another cry from the cradle, he rolled to his back, allowing her to rise.

Eva slipped into the worn dressing gown at the foot of the bed, and Billy felt true remorse as her smooth flesh was hidden from his view. He watched as she walked to a bucket of milk in the corner of the room, filled a glass bottle from it, and attached a small rubber nipple. Drawing the coverlet up to his waist as she leaned over the crib and lifted the fretting baby into her arms, he watched as she returned to the bed and lay back beside him before putting the bottle to the anxious baby's lips.

Rubbing his fingertip against the babe's fair cheek, Billy then smoothed her wispy blond curls and smiled as her incredibly blue eyes turned to his. The babe's light coloring reflected her dead father's blood. He had never known the man, but it was somehow painful to him to know that the fellow had died before seeing the beautiful child he had sired.

Sliding his arm around Eva, Billy drew her closer. He saw the love in her eyes as she looked down at the healthy nine-month-old in her arms, and he felt the familiar prick of jealousy in knowing that the child who shared their bed was not his own.

Billy shook off his momentary lapse. There was no room in his life for jealousy, just as there was no room in his life for commitment that went beyond desire. He forced a smile.

"Christina gets more beautiful every day—just like her mother."

Tears welled unexpectedly in Eva's eyes, and Billy cursed aloud, drawing her closer.

"You *are* beautiful, Eva."

"No, I am not."

Lowering his head, Billy pressed his lips against her scarred cheek, his heart in his words as he whispered, "This means nothing. I don't even see it anymore."

"I was never beautiful." Her gaze moving over his face, Eva blinked back her tears. "*You* are beautiful. More important, you are as beautiful on the inside as on the outside."

Billy's short laugh was caustic. "Only with you, darling."

"Only with me?" Eva shook her head. "No . . ."

Billy paused in amendment. "And with one other person."

He saw the flicker in Eva's eyes. He heard the hesitation in her whisper. "This other person . . . she is a woman?"

Billy's smile was reassuring. "Yes, but she's no threat to you. She never will be."

Unwilling to say more, Billy relied on the nature of the relationship between him and this unusual woman to fill in the gaps he had purposely left blank. It was part of the pact he had made with himself . . . with anonymity the only protection he could give Lila against the danger he could bring her. He owed her that much, and he would not, he *could* not, sacrifice that pact, even for the woman in his arms.

Billy drew Eva closer. He hadn't wanted or needed Eva in his life, but she was there—and she had made her mark on him indeed. He almost laughed. Disbelieving his own actions after he had accompanied the willing Ruby to her room a few days earlier, he had carefully manipulated the situation until all they had shared was a bottle and some necessary information. He had known then, as he did now, that fifty or a hundred Rubys could not give to him what Eva gave him with one glance. He also knew that no matter how temporary the emotion between them, he would never love a woman more than he loved Eva at this moment.

Drawing Eva closer, Billy whispered into the black silk of her hair, "I can't stay very long this time." And when she protested, "I have to meet my friends in a couple of days. We have something to do."

"But you've been gone so long. I miss you, Billy.

Why can't I meet your friends? Why can't Christina and I go with you?"

"Because you can't." The thought darkened his expression into a frown. "It's impossible."

"I . . . is it because you're ashamed of me?"

"No." Billy's response was immediate and sincere. "I've done plenty of things I could be ashamed of if I let myself, but loving you isn't one of them."

"Then why?"

"Because you're safer here."

"I'm lonesome here."

"I'll be back as soon as I can. I'll leave you more than enough to live on while I'm gone. You don't have to worry. No one will dare bother you. I've made sure of that."

Eva's dark eyes grew darker. "I'll miss you. I'll think of you every minute you're away."

Eva's heartfelt words registered deep in Billy's heart as he whispered words he never thought to hear himself say.

"I'll miss you, too, more than you know. And I'll think about the time we were together." He paused, his voice deepening. "I wear my memories out thinking about them over and over. I guess the best thing we can do for ourselves now is to make more memories, enough to last as long as we're apart." He glanced at the child, grateful she had drifted back to sleep as he looked into Eva's flushed face. "Lots more."

Eva was unable to refuse him.

And the loving began anew.

Five

The train whistle blasted loudly behind him as Garrett stood on the station platform, looking scornfully at the pitiful town of Deer Trail. A railroad station, a few stores, a saloon, and unimpressive houses strung along both sides of the railroad track . . . another in a series of whistle-stop towns with which he and Hobbs had become only too familiar in the past few days.

Slipping into the shadow of crates piled carelessly nearby, Garrett raised his hat and wiped his forehead with the back of his arm, then ran his hand through his perspiration-soaked hair. A gust of wind cooled him, briefly relaxing the stony set of his even features, but the relief was temporary.

Garrett's jaw tightened. He was in a damned vicious mood, and he knew it. Hobbs and he had been riding for hours with the sun beating relentlessly on their heads before arriving in town at noon. He was hot, tired, and thirsty, but he was also frustrated and determined to put an end to the dead ends that had plagued them.

The conductor's call was simultaneous with another blast of the whistle as the train prepared to depart, but Garrett paid it little mind, intent as he was on the short, unkempt fellow exiting the station house and walking toward him.

With several days' growth of beard on his chin and his hair protruding in uneven strands underneath an oversize hat with a yellowed snakeskin band, wearing a faded shirt and stained pants that had seen more wear than they should and sporting his gun low on his hip, Jake Hobbs was totally unrecognizable as the drummer he had first met in Denver over a week earlier. He had heard it rumored within the agency that Hobbs's ability to totally change his appearance was an asset McParland recognized and counted heavily on in the conduct of investigations. During the course of their association, however, Garrett had begun to wonder which of the men—the meticulously dressed drummer he had first met, the professional, casually dressed fellow he had rendezvoused with outside Denver a few days earlier, or the unkempt saddle bum walking toward him—was the true Jake Hobbs.

Garrett gave a low snort. He knew Hobbs did not face a similar question in assessing him. The sheer size and breadth of him, reaching the mark of three inches or more past six feet, was difficult to disguise even if he had the propensity toward physical deception. But he did not. His talent lay in detective work that depended upon quick thinking, cunning, and the intelligent use of information received from the network of reward-eager sheriffs the Pinkerton Agency had established across the West. He couldn't count the times that descriptions of local outlaws, their associates, friends, hideouts, and even photographs sent to the agency by way of the Pinkerton state-to-state system had aided him in his quests. Informers recruited into the network grew more numerous every day, feeding the Chicago, Denver, and New York offices with a steady stream of information. Pinkerton policy was simple. Nothing was too trivial to report. It was the duty of men such as McParland to fit the scraps and bits of fact or gossip together and cross-index them to form a whole picture of the hard-riding gangs agents such as he sought.

Garrett's eyes narrowed. No, he needed no disguises to do his work. Intense motivation from within and the lethal aura it projected, with occasional help from the much-folded wanted poster bearing his picture that he carried in his saddlebag and the carefully established police record he could call upon at any time, was all he needed.

Hobbs sauntered closer, his step deliberately paced so he would not attract attention. Garrett saw in that caution the mark of the man Hobbs truly was. The differences between them were more marked than he had first realized. Hobbs was pure Pinkerton. He was pure fury. Hobbs's reality lay in the case at hand. His own reality lay in vengeance.

That need was never sharper than it was at that moment, when Garrett sensed that he was close . . . so close to finding the one person who could lead him to the men he wanted. That need added a sting to his tone as Hobbs neared and he addressed the smaller man pointedly.

"It took you long enough! What did you find out?"

Hobbs squinted up at Harrison in solemn appraisal. The cold, light eyes of the man, the set of his chin, and the rigidity of his muscular frame gave him sudden pause. This wasn't the same person who had ridden into his camp with bloodshot eyes and a heavy head a few days earlier. He had understood that man and had even liked him. But that man had vanished over the course of the days they had spent stumbling along the rail line in their attempt to pick up Lila Chesney's trail.

Hobbs's experienced appraisal deepened. This Garrett Harrison, this big man who was as handsome as hell with a soul apparently doomed to the same place, was pure menace. He recounted in his mind the outlaws rumored to have been captured with Harrison's aid, but he recalled other rumors as well—shots that had not needed to be fired, lives that had not needed to be lost, men who could have been brought to the bar of justice but who had met with Harrison's brand of justice instead.

Surprising himself, Hobbs felt the nudge of pity for their present, unsuspecting prey. Lila Chesney and her unknown lover had no way of knowing what was in store for them.

Harrison's expression darkened as Hobbs maintained his silence, finally snapping, "I asked you what you found out, Hobbs."

Hobbs's bony shoulders stiffened. "I still think you're wrong. The woman who got off at this stop that day was *plain*. There's no way Lila Chesney could ever look plain, I tell you."

"You checked with the clerk at the Denver depot yourself, didn't you? He told you he saw Lila Chesney come in. Hell, how could he miss her in that red dress and plumed hat! He didn't see her leave, but he did sell a ticket back East to a very plain young woman shortly afterward."

Hobbs felt his color rise. "She could've been anybody. Denver's a busy station."

"But if she wasn't just anybody . . . if she was a woman who had changed clothes with Lila Chesney—"

"That's crazy!"

"If she was, then the woman who got off at *this* stop was Lila Chesney."

Hobbs shook his head, adamant. "Those two women didn't know each other when Lila Chesney got on that train, I tell you. I'll stake my career on it!"

"What difference does that make?"

"Damn it, Harrison! Think about it. What could possibly induce a perfect stranger to take the kind of chance that woman would've taken if she had agreed to help Lila Chesney throw a Pinkerton off her trail?"

"Don't be a fool! There's always the common denominator."

"What's that?"

"Money."

Hobbs paused to reconsider, then shook his head. "No . . ."

The flash of fury that lit Harrison's light eyes set Hobbs back a step as the bigger man snarled, "Look, you can believe what you want. Just tell me where the woman who got off at this stop went from here. I'll check it out myself."

Hobbs shook his head. "You're making a mistake. While you're wasting time chasing shadows, Lila Chesney's trail will be getting colder."

"It'll never be colder than it is now if I'm wrong and you're right, so I'm askin' you one more time. Who was that other woman, and where did she go from here?"

Hobbs paused a moment longer. "Her name is Modesty Parkins. She came here to marry a rancher named Luther Knox. His place is a few miles due west from here."

Harrison turned without a word. He was halfway to his horse when Hobbs growled, "Wait a minute. I'll go with you."

But Harrison didn't wait. He was already pointing his mount due west when Hobbs scrambled to mount.

Digging his heels into his bay's sides, Hobbs cursed aloud. He was struggling to catch up with Harrison moments later when the thought crossed his mind that Lila Chesney didn't know it, but the devil was on her heels, breathing hard.

It *really* wasn't easy being Modesty!

Lila squirmed uncomfortably on the hard wooden seat as the wagon bumped along a rutted trail to nowhere. She looked up at the silent man seated beside her, at his profile etched against the midafternoon sky. She felt the pressure of his muscular thigh against hers, her gaze lingering on the corded muscles in his arms as he guided the wagon over the uneven terrain. She had become increasingly drawn to Luther Knox in the time she had spent at the ranch, and she knew that this ride he had suggested so unexpectedly had been a result of the undeclared state of war that existed between Aunt Helga and her back in that hot little kitchen.

Damn! The woman was unrelenting. There was no pleasing her.

Lila sniffed with annoyance. Granted, her efforts had been less than satisfactory on most fronts. She could not cook or bake, and the truth was that she'd be damned before she'd let that woman teach her. She was inordinately clumsy because of the ridiculous glasses she was forced to wear, a fact that aroused a tenderness in Luther that she could not comprehend, while inciting Aunt Helga to extreme agitation. But she had tried—oh, how she had tried—to compensate in other areas of household responsibility, if only to make matters easier for Luther.

Nothing worked. The lines were clearly drawn and she had begun to believe that nothing could worsen the situation she was forced to endure until that morning's fiasco had proved her wrong.

Lila glanced up to watch the flight of a hawk as it glided gracefully in the cloudless blue sky overhead. She trailed her gaze to the brilliant sun that baked the rough trail ahead of her, unconsciously following its rays down to the grassy valley, fresh with the new green of spring, through which they rode. Nestled between pine-covered bluffs, it was snug and protected, with natural grazing for the great herd of cattle that Luther had confided he would someday pasture there.

It was verdant, peaceful, quiet, extraordinarily beautiful . . . but she saw none of it. She saw instead the huge pot on the kitchen stove that had started the whole disastrous affair with Helga a short hour ago.

How was she supposed to have known? It had *looked* like a laundry pot. It had *smelled* like a laundry pot. And after she had finished dumping Luther and Max's muck-stained pants into it to boil, it had *been* a laundry pot.

No one had ever told her that cabbage smelled just like boiling laundry!

Lila silently groaned. And no one had told her that stuffed cabbage was Aunt Helga's specialty—or that those particular heads of cabbage she had been boiling were the last of those Aunt Helga had carefully stored and brought with her from her root cellar at home in Deer Trail.

A smile flickered across Lila's lips. Under other circumstances, she might've laughed at the old woman's expression when she had returned to the kitchen and found her stirring the pot with a laundry stick. The truth was, however, that Aunt Helga's howl had set her hair on end. It had also brought Luther into the kitchen on the run, and within minutes he had decided that another tour of the ranch was in order.

Poor Luther.

Turning back to study the strong line of Luther's jaw, Lila acknowledged that her feelings for this man grew deeper each day. In silent moments, she had even found her mind wondering how it would have been if circumstances had been different . . . if she wasn't the person she truly was . . . if her first loyalty wasn't to Billy . . . and if she wasn't certain that if Luther knew who she really was that he wouldn't want her at all.

Turning unexpectedly toward her, Luther caught Lila's scrutiny. She read the desire in the clear blue of his eyes and the pure, manly appeal of him set her heart to pounding.

Modesty, you fool . . .

But she was not Modesty, and she was not a fool.

Struggling to keep that thought in mind, Lila felt a peculiar breathlessness assault her as Luther's gaze dropped to her lips. It held her strangely immobile as Luther reined the wagon to a halt, dismounted, and swung her down beside him. It kept her silent and unmoving as Luther removed her glasses and took her into his arms. It closed her throat against denial of his husky whisper.

"I want to kiss you, Modesty."

Luther's broad, gentle hands stroked her back as he awaited her reply. One strayed to the bun at the back of her neck and tangled in the tightly bound hair there as the other moved to cup her chin. His mouth only inches from her parted lips, Luther whispered again, "I'm going to kiss you, darling."

Lila sighed her acceptance of Luther's lips as they met hers, of his arms as they slid around her to crush her close, of the pure, virile strength of his body as it enveloped her.

Oh, damn, he felt so good . . .

"Modesty . . ."

That name again . . .

Lila stiffened, the beauty of the moment paling as she was reminded of her deception. Suddenly as angry with herself as she was with Luther for the unwelcome emotions he had stirred, Lila attempted to draw back, but Luther refused to allow her withdrawal. An almost debilitating weakness assailing her, Lila felt frustration soar.

Why hadn't she met Luther years earlier, when she had been more like the person she pretended to be? He would have protected her then. He would have left her less vulnerable to the man who had stirred her passion and promised her love, but who had delivered only heartache. He would have granted the security she hadn't been able to give Billy or herself, and he would have guided Billy away from the path he had taken as she had not been able to do.

Luther would have made everything right. She knew he would have.

But everything was wrong. She hadn't met Luther years earlier, or anybody like him. She had made her way as best she could. And Billy, dear Billy—with the sadness in his eyes that only she could see, claiming he didn't care, trying to make up for things over which he had no control when she knew he never could—had suffered. Dear Billy, the only person she felt safe in loving because she knew Billy only felt safe in loving her.

Yes, everything was wrong. Only Luther was right . . . but not for her.

"I can make it all better for you, Modesty. I can

make all the unpleasantness go away. I can do all that by loving you, if you'll let me."

Luther's uncanny intuition pushed a tear to flow from Lila's welling eyes. Her throat too choked for response, she remained silent as he wiped it gently from her cheek. She saw him swallow thickly and she heard the emotion in his deepened tone as he whispered, "Don't you want me to love you?"

Another tear followed the trail of the first. "I . . . I don't know."

Doubt entered Luther's intensely serious gaze. "I want you to tell me the truth. Do you think you could love me . . . someday?"

Lila managed a smile. That truth was easy. "I know I could."

"Then let it happen." Luther's voice was a low plea. "You won't regret it."

Lila searched Luther's sober face. "I . . . I think I would."

"I promise you, you won't."

"Don't promise me anything, Luther." Lila was never more ashamed of herself . . . never closer to confessing her deceit, than at that moment. She averted her gaze in an attempt to regain stability. What was wrong with her? She knew where her priorities lay. She had come here for a place to hide until it was safe to contact Billy. When she moved on, Luther would forget her . . . or forget the person he believed her to be. That was the way of men.

Sensing her withdrawal, Luther pleaded earnestly, "What do you want me to do, Modesty? Tell me, and I'll do it. I want you to be happy, darling."

"I . . . I want you to give me more time."

"Time . . ." The tenderness in Luther's smile melted her heart. "I've already promised that. I said I wouldn't rush you, but I didn't promise that I could stop wanting you."

"It's all right to want me. I want you, too . . . in so many ways." At the hope that sprang to life in Luther's eyes, Lila added, "But . . ."

"But you need time." He sighed. "All right." Leaning forward, Luther kissed her gently. Sensing her uncertainty, he drew back to search her gaze for a silent moment, then slipped his arms around her and kissed her again, more urgently than before.

More shaken than she dared admit by his kiss, Lila was trembling as Luther reached back to the wagon seat and retrieved her glasses. His gaze, never leaving her face as she slipped them on and squinted up at him, spoke the words he dared not say as he stroked a strand of hair back from her cheek with an apologetic smile.

"I messed your hair." And as her hand sprang to the bun at her neck, "No, don't fix it now. Let's just walk for a little bit. I know the sun's hot, but there's shade up ahead and I don't want to go back yet."

Lila's smile was reluctant. "Neither do I."

Taking her hand into his, Luther urged Lila to match his step, and Lila's heart quivered anew. His hand was so strong and comforting surrounding hers.

If only . . .

Lila continued walking, her smile slowly fading. The most difficult lesson of her inexperienced youth had been to learn that for men, passion was fleeting and not necessarily related to love. The second had been to finally accept the fact that wishing did not make things so.

Uncertainty raging, Lila took comfort in one fact. Here, in this deserted spot where no one knew her true name, she was . . . totally secure . . . for the first time in her life.

No one could find her. No one could touch her. Totally secure.

Lying flat on his stomach on a rise of land a short distance away, Garrett held his spyglass trained on the strolling couple. A strange intensity mounted inside him. The woman was Lila Chesney . . . he knew it was.

Garrett adjusted the glass, satisfaction growing. It appeared his luck had finally turned. Hobbs and he had been making good time in the direction of Luther Knox's ranch when they had spotted a wagon in the distance. They had drawn their mounts out of sight before they could be seen and climbed an outcropping of rocks to observe the conveyance more closely. He had seen it all, the entire, tender scene from the moment the wagon had drawn to a halt on the rough trail.

The couple made a subtle turn in his direction, and Garrett caught his breath as the woman's face came fully into view. A delicate, heart-shaped face with dark, heavily lashed eyes and incredibly dainty, almost fragile features. Hobbs's description had been accurate in every detail. But there was something Hobbs had not touched upon.

Silent, Garrett studied the woman more closely. She raised her eyes in the midst of earnest conversation, and then Garrett knew. He had never seen eyes as sensual as those she trained on the poor unsuspecting fool who had taken her in. He was instantly aware of what that look was doing to the man. He could tell by the way the fellow raised his hand to her hair, then slid his arm around her. But there was no resumption of the tender moments he had witnessed earlier, and Garrett grunted with reluctant admiration. The woman was controlling the fellow well. But then, she obviously had had considerable practice.

The woman reached back to the bun at the base of her neck and, with a subtle movement, released a shower of golden brown shot with copper highlights onto her shoulders. The silky strands gleamed in the sunlight, a shade not quite red, blond, or brown, and he was abruptly possessed with the desire to reach out and touch the glittering mass. A sharp emotion akin to jealousy tightened his jaw as Knox reached out to gather a handful of the vibrant locks in his stead.

More soft words were exchanged. Knox's hand dropped back to his side as the woman deftly gathered up her hair and confined it once more. Garrett's stomach twisted. No, this woman was not the virgin, mail-order bride Knox had been awaiting. It was only too obvious now what had actually occurred on that train when the two women had met. The virgin bride had changed her mind and had sent the escaping whore here in her place.

But there was no honesty in this whore . . . not in the way she had clung to the unsuspecting Knox and then drawn back to assume the role of the anxious virgin once more. Lila Chesney was playing a waiting game. She was manipulating Knox to her own end and was no doubt laughing inwardly at the knots into which she was tying the gullible fellow.

Garrett drew a deep, angry breath. The only thing Lila Chesney did not know was that the laugh was now on her.

Suddenly realizing he held the spyglass in a crushing grip, Garrett turned abruptly to the smaller man beside him.

"Here, take a look. Then tell me that woman is plain."

Snatching at the glass, Hobbs put it to his eye and adjusted it carefully. His stubbled cheek twitched.

"That's Lila Chesney all right."

"Damned right it is!"

The couple below turned unexpectedly and walked briskly back toward the wagon they had abandoned a short time earlier. Unexpectedly relieved that the couple's earnest conversation had not turned into a lover's tryst, Garrett slid back off the rock and drew himself to his feet. He turned toward his horse.

"What's the hurry, Harrison?" Hobbs's tone halted Garrett momentarily. "Seems to me Lila Chesney figures she's got herself the perfect hideout until she decides she doesn't need it anymore. She isn't going anywhere."

"Maybe not." Garrett's expression did not change. "But I'm not goin' to take any chances on losin' her again."

Mounting hastily, Garrett did not wait to see if Hobbs had mounted behind him as the wagon turned out of sight on a curve in the road. Annoyed, he spurred his mount into a surprised leap forward that left the animal off balance as he plunged down the rugged grade. The shaken gelding stumbled. Uncertain of the exact moment when he realized his horse was going to fall, Garrett jerked back roughly on the reins, but it was too late. The ground went out from underneath the animal's scrambling hooves and the protesting beast went down with a suddenness that left time only for Garrett's flashing realization that he was going down, too.

Tossed high into the air, Garrett hit the ground with a shattering crack before coming to a twisting and tumbling halt that left his head ringing. Stunned, the ringing still resounding in his ears, he recognized another, more frightening sound.

Garrett raised his head, straining to focus, his blurred vision clearing in time to see a coiled rattler the moment before it struck. His reaction spontaneous, Garrett raised his arm to shield his face. He gasped aloud as the snake's fangs sank deep into his forearm.

Shaking the clinging reptile off, gasping with pain as the venom burned deep, Garrett rolled to his back. He did not hear the crack of the gunshot that snapped the rattler in two. Nor did he hear Hobb's mad dash to his side or the fellow's artless comment as he leaned over him, then shook his head.

"Hell, you're in for it now."

Consciousness slipping away, Garrett saw only the image of Lila Chesney's face and heard only the echo of his own fading whisper. "I can't let her get away . . ."

Harrison slipped into unconsciousness and Hobbs felt the onslaught of panic. Harrison's arm was already swelling.

Scrambling back to his mount, Hobbs ripped a rawhide strip from his saddle. Back at Harrison's side, he tied it tightly around the bigger man's arm just above the swelling, then paused to collect his racing thoughts. He wasn't a doctor, but he'd had enough experience to know that either the fall or the snakebite could end up killing Garrett Harrison if he didn't do something quick. At a loss where to begin, Hobbs turned back toward Harrison's mount. The animal lay a few yards away, whinnying with pain as he struggled to rise. Wincing at the sight of the bone protruding from the horse's foreleg, Hobbs knew there was only one way to end the animal's torment.

The matter disposed of with one shot, Hobbs returned to Harrison's side, a knife in hand. He was poised over the grossly swollen wound when the rattle of an approaching wagon echoed around the bend.

Hobbs's heart stopped still. Damn! He should've realized that Knox would come to investigate the shots he had fired. If Lila Chesney recognized him, the investigation would come to an abrupt halt and all would be lost.

The sound drew closer and Hobbs made a quick decision. Springing to his feet, he ripped his gun from his holster and pushed it into Garrett's limp hand. Taking Garrett's gun, he jammed it into his own belt and raced to his horse. Leaping into the saddle, he spurred the startled animal into a run, not daring to look back until he was safely hidden in a copse of trees nearby.

Breathless, he awaited the wagon's appearance.

A knife poised over the swollen arm of the unconscious stranger lying in front of him, Luther studied the puncture wounds a moment longer. He had had no difficulty in determining what had happened. The wounded man's horse had stumbled and thrown his rider right into the rattler's path. It was a mystery to him how the fellow had managed to shoot the sidewinder, tie off his arm, and take care of his suffering horse before blacking out completely, but he did know that if he didn't do something quickly, this fellow wouldn't live to tell the story.

Taking a steadying breath, Luther made one sharp cut and then another at the site of the punctures. He allowed the gashes to bleed freely for a few moments before clamping his mouth over the wound to draw out the venom. He repeated the process several times, Modesty's presence behind him forgotten until he spat out the last of the bitter fluid and saw the canteen she held out to him. He accepted it gratefully, turning back to the unconscious man when he had rinsed his mouth clean.

Her expression devoid of the panic he had expected to see reflected there, Modesty leaned over his shoulder, speaking for the first time since they had heard the gunshots echoing across the meadow.

"He doesn't look good to me." Moving closer to the man's side, she leaned forward to raise his closed eyelid. "I saw a man take a fall like this once before, and I've seen snakebite a few times. It's not good."

Surprise registered in Luther's mind at Modesty's response to the unexpected situation. Her former temerity a thing of the past, she placed her palm against the stranger's forehead, then, examined his skull, frowning at the lump at the back of his head before exploring his neck and shoulders with equal concern. She showed no trace of embarrassment as she continued her inspection down his chest and hips, then cautiously ran her hands down the length of the fellow's legs before carefully straightening them.

She was still frowning when she looked back up.

"His temperature is already rising, but I don't think he has anything broken—not on the outside, anyway. I think we should get him back to the ranch as soon as we can."

Luther nodded in full agreement. Drawing the wagon up alongside the prone stranger moments later, he dismounted and struggled to draw the big man to a seated position. Beside him in a moment, Modesty helped to raise the unconscious man to a point where Luther could swing him over his shoulder. A moment later she was in the back of the wagon, waiting to receive the fellow as Luther lay him down.

Negotiating the uneven trail with as much speed as he dared, Luther glanced back to the rear of the wagon and his passengers there. Her fine features seriously composed as she held the stranger steady against the jostle and sway of the wagon, Modesty had lost all trace of the uncertain young woman he had held in his arms a short time earlier. Surprised as he was, Luther could not help but feel proud. He was also relieved. His gaze fixed back on the trail, Luther knew that Modesty's reaction had eliminated his only doubt as to her suitability to this raw frontier.

Luther smiled. Modesty had what it took to be a rancher's wife, all right, but he had sensed it all along, hadn't he? Modesty had been born to be his wife. Now, more than ever, he knew he could not let her get away.

Cradling the stranger's head in her lap, Lila attempted to shield him from further injury in the roughly swaying wagon. Her heart pounded at the unnatural heat flushing the man's sun-bronzed skin, and her throat tightened. Yes, she had seen snakebite before. She had also seen a man die from a fall from a horse. That man had been her pa, and she would never forget it.

Her screams of protest when her father had been left to lie where he had fallen until the doctor came to tend to him still echoed in her mind, but she knew now the wranglers had done their best to help him. The doctor had finally arrived and she had watched in horrified fascination as he had examined her pa. That scene had run over and again in her mind during the years since, until she had become as familiar with the finer points of the doctor's examination as the doctor himself. She knew the bloodshot condition of this stranger's eyes indicated that his head injury was serious, and even if she had not detected any broken bones, she knew the possibility of deeper damage was very real.

The wagon jumped wildly across a rutted expanse, and Lila clutched the stranger closer. He winced with pain, his dark brows furrowing. His eyes opened, catching hers briefly with startling impact, and Lila shuddered as an unexpected tremor ran down her spine.

Her throat tight, Lila studied the unconscious man more closely. His features were strong and even beneath his growth of beard, and the thick hair that lay against the collar of his faded shirt was as black as a raven's wing. The marks of his fall did not disguise an appearance that was intimidating, despite his unconscious state.

But there was something else . . .

The unconscious man's breathing grew more ragged. The wagon sank into another rut, and Lila winced as his arm, grotesquely swollen, slapped against the side of the wagon. This time he gave no reaction at all, and Lila looked up toward the driver's seat to meet Luther's concerned gaze. Their silent exchange set her to quaking. The stranger's time was running out.

Suddenly angry, Lila stared down into the unconscious man's face. Speaking in a soft, intimate hiss, she whispered into his unhearing ear, "You're not going to die—not in my arms, you're not! Live, damn you . . . live!"

"Ease him onto the bed carefully. That's it."

His wiry grey brows knit in a concerned line as he struggled under the weight of the injured man, Max nodded at Luther's instructions, waiting until the fellow's head was resting against the pillow before swinging his feet onto the bed as well. No one had to tell him that this stranger Luther and Miss Modesty had found on the trail was in serious condition. He stepped back, allowing Luther and his bride-to-be full access.

At a sound in the doorway behind them, Max turned to see Helga standing there. Luther turned as well.

"We need some help here, Aunt Helga." When his aunt did not react, Luther repeated, "Aunt Helga . . ."

The older woman took an unexpected step backward, shaking her head, her eyes wide with trepidation.

"Nein. I do not help." She stared at the man's rapidly ballooning arm. "Der schnakes I do not like . . ."

Luther was momentarily incredulous. "This man didn't bite the snake, Aunt Helga. The snake bit him."

Luther's reply had no effect on the shaken woman as she took another step backward.

"Nein . . . I do not touch."

As startled at the old woman's reaction as the two beside him, Max looked at Helga's white face. Damned if he didn't think she was going to faint!

Grasping her arm, Max steered Aunt Helga toward the living room and the battered settee there. She sank appreciatively down onto its softness without speaking a word, her pale lips trembling and unexpected tears rising to her eyes.

"Der schnakes I do not like."

"Aw, come on now, Helga, don't cry." Deeply affected by the woman's distress, Max leaned solicitously over her and patted her shoulder with a grimy hand. "There's not everybody who can stand the sight of an injured man, most especially delicate, sensitive ladies like yourself." He smiled, a gold tooth flashing. "We men understand that, and we don't hold you to account for it."

The sound of rapid footsteps raised Max's head toward Modesty's slender figure as she exited the bedroom and turned toward the kitchen. He heard the splash of water and saw her return a moment later, all trace of her former clumsiness gone as she returned to the injured man's bedside with a basin, a bar of soap, and a toweling cloth.

Helga's face blanched whiter.

A slow ache started inside Max's chest at the distress so obvious on Helga's expression. The truth be known, he had a real soft spot for the old biddy. There was something about her that made his calloused heart go pitty-pat more than the sight of a pretty young thing like Miss Modesty.

Silently swearing he'd die before he'd let her find that out, Max continued. "Now don't you go gettin' yourself all upset, Helga. There's some that have one kind of talent, and there's some that have another. Miss Modesty is a natural-born nurse, while you're a natural-born cook—just about the best cook I ever knowed."

His compliments had no affect at all on the woman's stricken expression as she whispered through trembling lips, "Der schnakes take away *mein* Herman."

"Is that so!"

Max's eyes widened at the unexpected revelation, his sympathy for the distressed woman growing. Sitting beside her, he took her hand and patted it gently. His old heart stirred again when Helga turned her pale-blue eyes on him and continued in a quaking voice. *"Mein* Herman chop der wood but der schnakes is waiting." She blinked almost comically. *"Gott in Himmel,* I bury him der next day!"

Helga's hand still in his, Max whispered, "You did all you could do. I'm thinkin' Herman knows that, wherever he is right now, and I'm thinkin' you should know that, too."

Helga's pale eyes blinked again. *"Ja,* you think?"

"Yes, I think." Max's gold tooth flashed once more. "I'm also thinkin' you treated your man real good while he was alive, 'cause I remember him. He was big and round . . . like he was eatin' better than any man I knew."

"Ja." Helga's lips hinted at a smile. *"Er* was."

"And he smiled a lot, like you was treatin' him good in other ways, too."

Helga's pale skin flushed, but she nodded determinedly. *"Ja, er* did."

Wistfulness touched Max's lips. "Yeah . . . well, you got no cause to go feelin' like you let your man down. Like I said, you did all you could. No man could ask for more."

A sound from the bedroom beyond raised both their heads. Her color deepening, Helga stated more strongly than before. *"Nein.* I do not help."

Shaking his head as the old Helga began to return, Max sighed. "You done the best you could then, and you can't do nothin' more than the best you can now. So I'm thinkin' if you get right back into the kitchen and get somethin' ready for supper, the boss'll be appreciatin' it more than anythin' else you might do." Max assessed Helga cautiously. "You can do that now, can't you?"

Helga drew herself shakily to her feet. *"Ja.* I do."

Rising beside her, Max accompanied Helga as far as the kitchen doorway. Smiling, he could not resist, "By the way, what're you makin' for supper, Helga? I . . . I'm thinkin' the boss might like to know."

Her composure almost fully restored, Helga responded proudly, "I make der stuffed cabbage."

Max gulped, a vision of that morning's laundry pot returning vividly to mind. He managed a weak smile as Helga turned back to the kitchen.

Max returned to the bedroom doorway. Luther looked up, his expression chasing all other thought from Max's mind as he ordered, "Get the doc, Max. Tell him if he doesn't get here fast, he'll be wasting his time coming at all."

Mounting his horse moments later, Max turned him toward town. He was racing down the rough trail when he was struck with a sudden thought. It looked like he might miss supper.

He almost grinned.

Now wasn't that a damned shame . . .

Six

It wasn't going well.

Standing in the darkest corner of the room where she might draw as little attention to herself as possible, Lila watched as Deer Trail's only doctor entered the room. Her heart plummeting to her toes, Lila assessed the man's unkempt appearance, his blotchy complexion, the small broken veins on his rather large nose and puffy cheeks that gave his unshaven face an unnaturally ruddy glow—not to mention the paced deliberation of his step. The explanation for the abnormally long time he had taken to arrive at the ranch was suddenly obvious.

The doctor was drunk.

A new panic besetting her, Lila stared at the stranger. No one had to tell her how precarious a hold he presently had on life. His temperature continued to soar, and it did not take a practiced eye to determine that he had slipped into a deeper unconsciousness than before.

Lila studied the trembling of the physician's hands as he examined the wound and his unsteadiness as he drew himself upright. The revealing slur of his voice twisted her lips with disgust as he looked around him and then bellowed, "Where in hell's my bag? I put it down somewhere. Who took it?"

The wounded man twitched spasmodically, and Lila felt her tension rise. The damned fool was wasting precious time!

Looking toward Luther where he stood on the opposite side of the bed, Lila sent him a pleading glance that went unseen, and her stomach twisted more tightly. Why wasn't he doing something?

"Where's that damned bag, Luther?" Doc Bennett turned to scour the room with his wavering gaze. "We're wastin' valuable time here!"

Unable to stand it any longer, Lila stepped out of the shadows and moved silently to the doctor's side. She picked up the medical bag he had kicked under the bed with one of his faltering steps and placed it on the coverlet beside the stranger's swollen hand. Her heart skipping a beat as she looked into the unconscious man's flushed face, she reached out spontaneously to touch his forehead, hardly restraining a gasp at the burning heat there.

"That's right, this man is burnin' up." Doc Bennett squinted at Lila. "Who are you?"

Luther responded in her stead. "This is Modesty Parkins, Doc. She's my . . . she's visiting."

Doc squinted more closely. "Visitin', huh?" And then to Lila, "Just answer me one question. How's your stomach?"

"My stomach?"

"Yeah, your stomach. Truth is, this stranger here caught me at a bad time. I ain't at my best and I'm in need of a steady hand right now. So answer the question. How's your stomach?"

"Now wait a minute, Doc!" Luther took a step forward. "Modesty's been real good in helping out, but I'm not going to ask her to—"

"You don't have to ask her. I will."

"But—"

"Do you want this man to live or not?" Doc Bennett did not wait for his response. "I got a second sense about these things, drunk or sober. I say this woman's got what it takes to handle things for me better than you can." Directing his next words to Lila, he demanded, "So, what do you say? We can't go wastin' any more time here."

Modesty nodded.

"Good!" Dropping himself down into a nearby chair as if he could not have maintained his balance another moment, Doc shook his head, then said abruptly, "If I fall asleep, kick me and tell me where I left off." At her wary expression, Doc gave a short snort. "Don't worry . . . Modesty. That's your name, ain't it? Don't worry. Just do as I say. Ready?"

Lila nodded again.

"All right. First, there's some packets of white powder in my case. Dissolve one in water and make the patient drink it."

Lila was momentarily taken aback. "He's unconscious. How can I make him drink?"

"Wake him up!"

"But—"

"Come now, Modesty." Doc Bennett managed a lopsided smile. "Why do you think I wanted you to take over for me instead of Luther? If I don't miss my guess, this big fella'll respond better to a woman's voice than a man's. Just use your instincts. I got the feelin' you'll find a way."

Lila moved to the injured man's side, the glass in her hand. She slid her arm under his neck and raised his head. His heat scorched her arm and her anxiety soared. Damn! How did she get herself into this? She didn't want to be responsible for this man's life. She had problems of her own. She—

The stranger's still face twitched and panic touched Lila's senses. Dismissing her silent protests, she held the glass to his lips and shook him gently.

"Wake up. You have to drink this medicine."

There was no response.

"Come on, wake up. You have to drink this if you want to feel better."

Still no response.

Panic bit deeper and, steeling herself, Lila shook the unconscious man again. His head flopped against her breast, momentarily startling her. A confusing rush of feelings ensued as she tightened her arm spontaneously to cradle his head. His mouth rested against the fullness of her breasts, separated from the soft flesh by the thin fabric of her dress, and Lila took a steadying breath as she tried a more forceful approach.

Leaning down, she whispered directly into his ear. "Wake up! I don't know who you are or where you came from, but I'm not going to let you slip away. Wake up!"

The injured man remained unmoving.

Reacting in anger as frustration soared, Lila turned her back so the others in the room would not hear her as she grated once more into his ear, "Do you call yourself a man? A man fights for what he wants. You're going to have to fight for your life if you want to keep it! You're going to have to drink what I'm giving you, and you're going to have to do it now!"

When there was no reaction at all, Lila hissed, "Wake up . . . wake up! If you don't, you're going to die. Don't you care? Well, if you don't, I do! I'm not going to let that happen, so wake up!"

Suddenly realizing she was trembling, Lila looked at the man whose face was so close to hers. She did not know his name, this man whose head rested against her breast, whose body heat scorched her, whose light-eyed gaze had stung her as it had touched her only briefly, but she knew she could not let him die. She would *not* let him die.

Lila's next words were a furious, whispered growl meant for his ears alone. "You're not going to die in my arms! I told you that once before and I meant it! I won't let you do that to me! Wake up!"

The stranger's heavily lashed eyelids moved briefly before becoming still once more. Regaining her voice, she whispered in a heated rasp, "Open your eyes! Open them!"

Pausing, hope beginning to wane when he did not respond, Lila commanded sharply, furiously, "Open your eyes, damn you!"

Another silent moment passed before the stranger's heavy lids moved again, before he slowly opened his eyes.

That voice . . . low and melodic, sharp and demanding, angry, and then profane entered Garrett's shadowed world. He knew that voice.

Straining, he fought the visions that flashed through his heated dreams. The fire was burning again, hotter than before. The flames licked angrily at him, scorching him as he called out their names. Elizabeth! Mother! But they were nowhere to be seen. He struggled through the flaming debris, stumbling, falling. . . . The smoke choked him, burning his lungs, blinding his eyes, but he fought his way deeper into the fire.

He saw something then, lying on the ground, almost indiscernible in the shifting smoke. It was his mother's rounded form, and his heart began a wild beating. He struggled to reach her, but the flames flared higher. He strained to call her, but the words would not leave his scorched throat. He cried out aloud in agonized protest as a torrent of flames fanned out to consume her.

She was gone!

He heard Elizabeth's cry echo his pain from somewhere within the dense flames, but the fire roared louder. It swallowed her protest, consuming all sound.

Except the sound of that voice.

The voice grew louder. It whispered into his ear with pleas that changed to angry demands. It railed at him, challenged him, commanded him.

It cursed.

A spontaneous anger touched Garrett's wandering mind. Struggling against the heavy weight of his eyelids, he forced his eyes open at last, his blurred vision registering on the female face so close to his. He could not see it clearly, but he felt the brush of a faint, fragrant breath against his cheek, the touch of warm lips against his ear. He heard that voice again.

"Good. Now drink."

He felt a glass pressed against his lips and he struggled to elude it, only to hear the female voice harden.

"Drink, I said!"

The hint of steel in that thin voice was compelling. He strained to see the woman more clearly as he obediently opened his mouth and drank the bitter liquid.

"Drink it all."

Garrett complied and the blurred shadow of the woman slipped from his sight. He protested vocally, but no one heard him. A strange thickness in his throat worsened. The pain swelled. He was sick . . . nauseous, but no one helped him. He was being consumed by it all, his strength waning. He was being overwhelmed—

The voice echoed in his ears.

"Do you call yourself a man? A man fights for what he wants. You're going to have to fight for your life if you want to keep it!"

Anger negated pain.

"Damn you!"

Consciousness slipped away, but in the darkness that swallowed him, anger remained.

"Are you awake?" Lila turned toward the chair where Doc Bennett sat observing. She caught his peculiarly squinting stare.

"Of course I'm awake! My eyes are open, ain't they?"

Lila's cheek ticked tensely. "Barely."

"Well, barely is enough! Did he drink it all?"

Lila held up the empty glass.

"Good. That ought to help with the fever and the infection."

"What should I do now?"

"I was gettin' to that."

The old sot dragged himself to his feet and Lila reached out spontaneously as he swayed. At his side in a moment, Luther drew an angry protest as Doc Bennett shouted, "I'm not so drunk that I can't stand! Get your hands off me. I have an examination to perform."

Luther's uncertain gaze touched hers and Lila inched closer to the swaying physician. The old man surprised her by snorting impatiently, "I never was one to object when a pretty woman tried to get close to me, young lady, but I do object to your motives. I said I could stand. Now get out of my way so I can do what I have to do."

Having no choice, Lila gave the swaying doctor a wider berth. She watched closely as his trembling hands moved over his patient with instinctive skill. His expression was relieved as he turned and again sank into the chair.

"I don't find anythin' broken, but it looks to me like this fella has a hell of a concussion along with that snakebite. He ain't goin' no place too soon, that's for sure." He shrugged. "If he makes it."

"If he makes it . . ." Lila swallowed against the sudden lump in her throat. Luther's hand closed supportively on her arm as she questioned harshly, "What do you mean?"

"What do you think I mean?" Doc Bennett eyed her assessingly. "This fella ain't out of the woods yet, by any means. We have to cleanse that wound again and try to draw out the rest of that poison. Then we have to do whatever we can to get that fever down from the outside while the medicine is workin' on the inside. And even then, I ain't promisin' nothin'." Doc Bennett paused, adding, "He does have one thing on his side, though. If size and muscle tone is any indication, he's a healthy bastard."

Luther's hand tightened on Lila's arm. His voice was sharply edged. "I'd appreciate it if you'd watch your language, Doc. You're in the presence of a lady."

Doc's eyes darted back to Lila and she felt his scrutiny deepen. "Yeah, I forget myself sometimes, but even so, I think this young woman can handle it. I got the feelin' she can handle just about anythin' she sets her mind to. In any case, we ain't got time for conversation." He addressed Lila directly. "Are you ready?"

Lila nodded.

"Then uncover that wound and let's get goin'."

Crouching in the foliage outside the bedroom window, Jake frowned. It had been a long, difficult afternoon, and he had spent the major part of it in this difficult hidden posture as he had followed the conversation within. He was taking a big chance, and he knew it.

Rubbing the bristles on his unshaven cheek, Jake turned again to survey the immediate area around him with a keen, professional eye. He was tired and stiff, but he was damned proud of his ingenuity. Who else but he would've thought fast enough to turn a situation with such disastrous potential into one that suited his own ends?

Jake smiled briefly. Because of his quick thinking, Harrison was firmly ensconced on the *inside* now. He had Lila Chesney just where he wanted her. Nothing would get past him.

Provided he lived.

That variable had made Jake more uncomfortable than he cared to admit. It had made him so uncomfortable that he had abandoned one of his own cardinal rules by sacrificing the professionalism that would have demanded he maintain a safe distance from the house to protect his own position and conduct a tight surveillance. That would have sufficed. He would have kept apprised of Harrison's condition just as easily that way. After all, they'd have to carry Harrison out to bury him, wouldn't they?

Jake's professionalism had faltered there. It had suffered the assault of a purely human failing—anxiety.

As a result of that anxiety he had risked everything

by hiding his horse a safe distance away and making a stealthy approach to the house. The frantic activity within had aided his cause, but despite the risk he had taken, he had learned no more about Harrison's condition than he had known before. If he were to believe the drunken old fool Knox had called in to tend to Harrison, Harrison's condition could go either way.

The sense of helplessness he experienced at that thought increased Jake's discomfort. In any case, the die had been cast. He had no choice but to wait to see what color it turned out.

The sound of an approaching wagon startled Jake from his thoughts, forcing him to slip back into the lengthening shadows of evening as the old cowpuncher who had been identified as Max returned. One look at the cargo the old fellow carried in the back of the wagon and Jake groaned.

Harrison's saddle.

So, he wasn't so smart, after all . . .

Staring at the saddlebags bouncing against the sun-bleached wood of the wagonbed, Jake envisioned Harrison's cold, accusing stare.

Damn, he had slipped up, all right. He just hoped that Harrison hadn't slipped up, too, by carrying anything in those saddlebags that would identify him to Lila Chesney. Because if he did . . .

The old cowboy drew the wagon to a halt and, dismounting, walked back to the wagonbed. He swung the saddle down and turned toward the barn, and a seed of hope took root inside Jake. It was crushed beneath the heel of Max's mud-caked boots a few moments later as he exited the barn with Harrison's saddlebags slung over his arm and returned to the house.

His mind racing, Jake inched back up to the window

and listened as the old cowboy's unmistakable voice sounded in the silence of the sickroom.

"I picked up the saddle like you told me to, boss. Here's the fella's saddlebags."

"Put them on the chair."

"Is there anythin' else I can do for you?"

"Not now, Max." Knox sounded distracted. "We're pretty busy here right now. Why don't you go get something to eat. Aunt Helga has supper ready."

The brief silence following Knox's suggestion was broken by Max's hesitant response.

"Ummm . . . no . . . ummm. I mean, maybe not. I . . . I ain't hungry."

"You're not hungry?" The note of incredulity to Knox's tone was unmistakable. The incredulity turned to suspicion moments later as Knox pressed in a softer voice, "What's Aunt Helga cooking?"

"Ummm . . . stuffed cabbage."

"Oh."

"I'll be outside if you need me."

Again retreating footsteps, then the sound of a quick catching of breath. He heard Knox's voice again.

"Are you all right, Modesty?"

The woman's voice was shaken. "His arm . . . it looks so bad."

"It's goin' to look worse if we don't get some cold compresses on it right away." The doctor's voice was less slurred than it had been when he arrived. It sounded almost normal when he instructed, "We ain't got no more time to waste. Make yourself useful, Luther. Get us some cold water and some large cloths. I've got the feelin' it's goin' to be a damned hard pull bringin' this fella back."

Heavier footsteps signaled Knox's departure. Silence

reigned for long moments before Lila Chesney spoke again in a tone just above a whisper.

"D-do you think he'll make it, Doctor Bennett?"

"Your guess is as good as mine right now. I'd say whatever you whispered in his ear a while back got his attention at some level of consciousness. I'm not about to ask what you said, but I'd say that if you want to help him, you'd do well pursuin' the same course."

Turning at the sound of approaching footsteps, Jake jumped back into the shadows just as Max turned the corner of the house. He remained motionless until the fellow had again passed from view before releasing a tense breath.

Surrendering to the danger of his position a moment later, Jake faded back into the darkness surrounding him. Tomorrow was another day.

If Garrett Harrison lived to see it.

The night was crisp and clear. A full, luminescent moon rode the crest of the hill to the north, lending a glittering coat of silver to the verdant valley below. The sounds of night swelled in cadence, in vivid contrast to the silence that reigned within the ranch house nestled there.

A brisk night wind gusted, stirring the shadows beyond the open bedroom window and rattling the crystal teardrops of the hurricane lamp beside the injured man's bed. The delicate sound awakened Lila. Momentarily disoriented, she glanced around the dimly lit room. Log walls, carefully mortared, a simple bedroom chest, table and chair, a large bed . . .

The unmoving form in that bed caused Lila to jump with a start, returning the long, tense afternoon in total recall. Beside the bed in a moment, Lila frowned down into the face of the unconscious stranger. He was so still. His skin was grey and beaded with perspiration and his breathing seemed pathetically weak. Swallowing tightly, Lila placed a palm against his forehead. His fever was again mounting.

Looking through the bedroom doorway into the next room, Lila saw Doc Bennett sleeping soundly on the lumpy settee there. Luther was asleep in a nearby chair. Like herself, Luther had not left the injured man's side throughout the long ordeal, but Lila somehow sensed that although he worried about the stranger's survival, his greatest concern was for her. That concern had been written in his close scrutiny of her, in the way he had touched her and drawn her close to lend his strength when it had appeared that their patient might not survive.

Lila paused at that thought, her eyes on Luther's face. She was unaccustomed to such concern. She was ill at ease with it.

The injured man twitched spasmodically, and Lila was drawn from her thoughts as panic nudged her senses. The fever frightened her, but she knew waking Doc Bennett would do little good. The old physician had been totally sober, completely exhausted, and not particularly optimistic when he had left the room a few hours earlier with a short, "I'm goin' to lie down before I fall down. Give him another powder if you think he needs it, but I don't know how much good it'll do. Don't wake me up unless he stops breathin'."

Another powder if she thinks he needs it?

Lila looked down at the stranger's arm. It didn't look good.

Lila removed another packet of powder from Doc's bag and dissolved it in water. Sliding her arm under the injured man's head, she raised the glass to his lips, only to find that this time no manner of coaxing or threat seemed able to penetrate his unconsciousness. The sharp edge of panic cutting deeper, Lila stared down into the face of the man whose head she still cradled against her breast. She remembered those steel-grey eyes she had glimpsed only briefly. Strangely, she did not think she'd ever forget them.

Who was this man? How could she reach him if she didn't even know his name?

Her gaze darting to the saddlebags she had moved from the chair earlier, Lila lowered the stranger's head back to the pillow and placed the glass on the nearby table. She picked up the saddlebags and unbuckled the closure, her hands trembling unexpectedly.

Toilet articles—a razor, a bar of soap, a brush—a pencil, a pad of paper, liniment, a half-filled bottle of whiskey. Disgusted, Lila unbuckled the other bag. A change of clothing, a few miscellaneous articles, an envelope containing a small photograph.

Her throat tightening, Lila studied the young blond woman in the picture. She was standing in a stiff pose commonly used by many frontier photographers. She was smiling broadly, her appearance unremarkable in any way, except for that smile, which shone with youth and joy.

A familiar sinking began inside Lila. The woman's smile also shone with an innocence that she herself had shed so many years earlier that she could hardly remember its loss.

A hot flash of jealousy curled Lila's fingers tightly around the edges of the photo. She steeled herself against crushing it in her palm. Realizing the absurdity of her reaction a moment later, Lila raised her chin in an unconsciously defiant gesture. She had learned long ago that a person could do no more in life than play the hand she was dealt. Her own cards had not been particularly good, but she had become more skillful in handling them with every passing day. There was no room in her life for envy, especially of a woman she didn't know.

In control once more, Lila turned the picture over. Her stomach knotted as she read the short message written in elaborate script.

To Garrett, with all the love in my heart,

Forever,
Elizabeth.

So, his name was Garrett . . .

Slipping the picture back into the envelope, Lila returned it to the saddlebag and turned back to the bed. Her heart pounding, she slipped her arm under the stranger's neck and drew him so close that her lips grazed his ear as she spoke.

"Garrett, can you hear me? You have to wake up now. You have to take your medicine. Garrett . . ."

Not a flicker of response moved the big man's features, and Lila was suffused with a sudden fury. She was not the innocent young Elizabeth whose eyes had shone with love and joy, but she was determined. She would not let this man die.

"Garrett! Wake up! I know your name now and you can't hide from me. Wake up and drink your medicine, damn you, or I swear I'll—"

Garrett's eyelids flickered, and the annoying thickness returned to Lila's throat. Grasping the glass on the nearby table, she held it to his lips.

"Drink. You have to drink this, Garrett."

Garrett's eyes opened unexpectedly. They looked directly into hers, and Lila gasped. They were so cold.

Lila ordered again, "Drink. You have to drink all of this."

Garrett's full lips parted obediently. Withdrawing the glass when it had been emptied, Lila held his icy stare in silent challenge.

Garrett's eyes closed as abruptly as they had opened. Strangely drained, Lila lowered his head back to the pillow. Weary to the bone, Lila collapsed back into the chair and closed her eyes.

So his name was Garrett . . . damn him . . .

Seven

Outside the small cabin, birds chirped noisily as an early-morning breeze stirred the trees. Shafts of brilliant sun danced against the forest floor, the scent of aspen and spruce mingling with the fragrance of fresh coffee, fried bacon, and warm bread wafting through the open doorway of the modest dwelling. Within the cabin, Eva shook a heavy skillet with an expert hand, immune to the sights and sounds around her as the eggs sizzled and popped. Her concentration was intense.

But it was not food that was on her mind.

Billy was leaving.

Her eyes misting, Eva indulged memories of the last few nights in Billy's arms. Ah, yes . . . Billy's arms were ribbons of steel that held her heart captive . . . his eyes were brilliant, sea-green pools wherein she saw herself as she had always wished to be seen . . . his lips were a solace beyond compare—but it was the strong, masculine strength of him as it enveloped her with exquisite tenderness that had been the key to total surrender, the touch that had finally brought her home.

Home. Eva shivered against the thought that had previously brought her only pain. A half-breed had no home—not the Apache camp of her mother that she could not remember, not the mining camp where she had lived with her father before the fever finally brought him down, and not the towns where she had wandered aimlessly afterward, despised for her mixed blood.

A familiar sadness returned. One man had not despised her. Olaf Nielsen, with greying gold hair, brilliant blue eyes, and fair skin that contrasted vividly with her own coloring, had been more than twice her age and the kindest person she had ever known. He had taken her in when she was ill and unable to care for herself. To her amazement, he had proposed marriage after she recovered, and for the four short months of their married life, he had shrugged aside the contempt of his fellow miners and had treated her with respect and gentleness.

Eva unwittingly raised a hand to her cheek. It had all ended too soon. A suspicious fire in the middle of the night and she had been alone again, this time scarred and carrying Olaf's child.

Christina, beautiful, golden-haired, and blue-eyed, had been born afterward in a temporary haven she had been forced to flee when the childless matron who had taken her in became determined to make the babe her own. She had begun a frightened, headlong flight then that had not ended until she was safe in Billy's arms.

Eva smiled. Olaf's memory was dear to her, but she had felt no shame in the realization that she had never experienced with her husband the overwhelming passion she had found with Billy. Instead, a sense of well-being had settled over her, and she had gloried in the beauty of the love Billy and she shared.

But she suffered. Doubt was her constant companion and fear was an ever-darkening cloud over her head.

Eva's hand rose to her scarred cheek again. Did Billy

really love her? And if he did, why? Despite Billy's insistence, she knew she had never been beautiful. Her eyes were small and a common brown in color, and, although heavily lashed, were too deeply set above the sharply sculpted cheekbones common to her mother's people. Her brow was high and clear, but straight hair as black as midnight bespoke her origins too plainly for most to see beauty there. Her father's blood had tempered the even tone of her skin, but its color was still too sharp a divergence from that of her child's to be accepted. And if Billy truly loved her despite it all, if his love made him blind to the person others saw in her, would that mist of love clear one day, stripping her naked before him?

Her throat so tight she could hardly breathe, Eva fought back her tears. Most disturbing of all, if Billy truly loved her, why didn't he trust her?

Oh, Billy . . . Billy . . .

Eva despaired, realizing she knew nothing about the man she loved except his name and the simple truth that in this time and place, he wanted her. She did not know where he came from or where he went when he left her, and she was never certain when or *if* he would return. There was one thing of which she was certain, however. Having learned what it was to truly love, having given herself to Billy so completely that her spirit had become intertwined with his, she would never be totally whole again if he should leave her.

A sound behind her alerted Eva to Billy's return to the cabin the moment before his arms slipped around her waist. Silent, she welcomed his touch as he drew her back against him, as his hands roamed her soft flesh, claiming her breasts. She sighed as he trailed his lips across her shoulder and up the column of her neck in tender, loving bites. She felt his tongue trace the shell of her ear as he whispered, "I'm hungry, darling."

At the familiar huskiness in Billy's voice, Eva slid the pan off the fire and turned to face him. The rock-hard rise of his passion as it pressed against her was as revealing as the glow in his clear eyes. It left her breathless as he whispered against her lips, "I'm hungry for *you*."

His words igniting a fierce, responsive hunger within her as well, Eva slid her arms around Billy's neck and pressed her mouth to his. The first touch of his lips set her heart singing and she moved urgently closer. She gasped as his mouth left hers to scorch the skin of her throat. She spoke soft, unintelligible words of encouragement as he jerked the string of her shift free and pushed it to her waist. She cried out aloud as his mouth closed over her naked breast. She crushed his head against her, aiding his assault, then extended her arms high over her head, groaning her pleasure as he laved the tender flesh with his tongue. The sweet torment soon more than she could bear, Eva stepped back. She noted the passionate narrowing of his eyes, her gaze promising him more as she quickly stripped away her shift and pressed herself against him. Billy's trembling hands grazed the moist flesh of her breasts as he fumbled with the buttons on his shirt. Her own hands trembled as well as she worked feverishly at his belt, then the buttons on his trousers. Slipping her hand inside the closure the moment it was freed, she caressed him lovingly, each shudder of his strong body, each gasp, each mounting groan, raising her own passion higher. Still clasping him tightly, she lifted her mouth to his. She trailed her tongue across his lips, tasting his gulping breaths as his passionate shudders deepened. She was almost beside herself with wanting him when he stepped back and swept her up into his arms. The bed against her back moments later, she begrudged the moments it took him to strip away the rest of his clothing and welcomed him hungrily as his hot, eager flesh met hers fully at last.

Billy was inside her again, and Eva sobbed aloud at the ecstasy of their joining. Unaware of the tears running down her cheeks, she slid her hands, fingers splayed, against the smooth skin of his back. Exalting at the play of tightly corded muscles beneath her palms, she clutched him closer. Meeting his thrusts, she spoke loving encouragements, giving herself to him ardently, without restraint, wanting, needing, reveling in the knowledge that Billy wanted and needed her as much at that moment as she did him. Waiting, trembling at the brink, swept with emotions too myriad to contain, Eva rasped Billy's name. With a sharp, spontaneous cry of response, Billy joined her as her joy soared to consuming flame.

Then it was done.

In the silent aftermath of their lovemaking, Eva sought to control her gulping sobs. She felt Billy's gentle touch on her cheek. The concern in his voice forced her to look up as he whispered hoarsely, "Eva, what's wrong?"

Her moist eyes meeting his, Eva whispered in return, "It's just that I love you so . . ."

There it was again, that woman's voice . . .

Drifting in a painful world of semilight and sound, Garrett struggled to identify the persistent, nagging call. It had summoned him, penetrating the shadows. It had coaxed him, rebuked him, and then it had threatened him, forcing him to struggle against the currents dragging him ever downward. Angry, he had fought his way to the surface. He had opened his eyes, and he had seen her.

She had been as angry as he.

Garrett heard her voice again.

"Wake up, Garrett. Come on. Wake up!" A moment's silence, and Garrett heard a note of despair. "He doesn't hear me."

"He should be wakin' up by now. His arm's lookin' better this mornin' and his fever's down, so I don't think that's the problem." The gravelly male voice paused. "If we can't get him to wake up soon, I'm thinkin' the reason might be that his head injury's a lot worse than I thought."

Another man's voice. "What're you saying, Doc?"

"I'm sayin' he should be conscious now. I'm sayin' that if we don't get through to him soon and if he don't start takin' fluids and nourishment, he's goin' to start havin' problems of another kind, and that's one thing this fella don't need more of—problems." Another pause. "What did you say his name was?"

"Garrett . . . that's all I know."

The gravelly voice addressed him sharply. "Garrett . . . wake up!" It paused. "Wake up, goddamnit! Oh, hell, it ain't no use me tryin'. You try again, Modesty."

The woman's voice grew sharper.

"Did you hear what Doc Bennett said, Garrett? He said you have to wake up now or you might not be waking up at all." The voice drew closer. It brushed his ear, growing softer, more taunting. "Or is that what you want? Are you afraid to wake up because you're in pain. Is that it, Garrett? A real man doesn't hide from pain, Garrett. He faces it and he conquers it, and then he goes on. Or maybe you're not a real man. Maybe you only look like a real man, Garrett, but inside you're a frightened little boy who hides when the world is too tough to face. Is that it, Garrett? Tell me . . . is that it?"

Anger mounting, Garrett fought the heavy shadows oppressing him. Damn her! Who was she? How did she know his name?

"Do you want me to leave you alone so you can hide forever, Garrett? No, I don't think I'll do that. I don't like cowards."

She had called him a coward.

"Are you angry?" The female voice paused. "No, I don't think you are. You don't have the gumption to get angry. You'd rather lie back and let your life drift away. It's easier that way, isn't it? Cowards always take the easier way."

Who was she?

Coward . . .

Damn her!

Coward . . .

Enough!

Garrett forced his eyes open. His mind was burning, his head throbbing. The world around him was bathed in an eerie haze . . . and *she* was leaning over him. His vision cleared.

Face of an angel . . . tongue of a devil.

Coward . . .

Garrett released an angry bellow that emerged as a hoarse hiss.

"Coward . . . ?"

The woman blinked but she did not move back. Her dark eyes held his. "You heard me? Answer me!"

"I heard you." The pounding in Garrett's head deepened. "I heard everythin.' You'll eat those words."

Surprise flashed briefly in the woman's dark eyes the

moment before her angelic face drew closer and her fresh breath brushed his ear.

"Not a chance."

Realizing he could not hold on to consciousness much longer, Garrett forced a furious, slurred response.

"We'll see . . ."

"What did you say?" The woman was again taunting. "I can't hear you."

Forcefully widening his eyes, Garrett looked into the woman's gaze in weak but direct challenge. "I said . . . we'll see!"

The light faded, but Garrett's words remained, reverberating in his mind as ardently as a vow.

Her heart pounding, Lila drew back from the bed. She looked up at Doc Bennett and then at Luther, realizing that she was trembling.

"He's unconscious again."

Doc Bennett nodded, then glanced at Luther. "This is some woman you got yourself, Luther. She looks like a real shy little bird, but when she gets to whisperin' in a man's ear, she's somethin' else again."

Still shaken, Lila pressed, "But he's unconscious again."

"I ain't worryin' about that no more, not now that I know you can draw this Garrett fella out whenever you want. We'll just let him rest for a little while longer." A smile tugged at Doc Bennett's lips. "I gotta admit, the curiosity's got to me. Just what did you say to that big fella to make him snap awake like he did? I couldn't hear what he said to you, but there wasn't no doubt he knew what he was sayin'."

Feeling the weight of Luther's gaze, Lila averted her eyes in Modesty-like fashion. She brushed a loose strand of hair back into her bun and reached self-consciously for the glasses she had discarded earlier. She adjusted them carefully on her nose before responding softly, "I . . . I said he had to fight in order to get well." She paused, then added, "I think he thought I called him a coward."

"Oh, ho!" Doc Bennett's laughter boomed. "If I don't miss my guess, that big fella ain't the kind to take somethin' like that lightly. You're goin' to have some pretty fast explainin' to do when he gets on his feet again."

"Modesty won't have to explain anything." Luther's voice was steady as he slipped his arm around her waist. "If he's too much of a fool to realize what she's done for him, you can depend on me to call it to his attention."

"Well, now." Doc's eyebrows rose expressively. "Look at that, little lady. Seems like you got two fellas fightin' over you, and one of them ain't even half conscious! Now, ain't that somethin' for a shy little Easterner like you!"

Luther's arm tightened, and Lila looked up as he responded, "Modesty may be shy, but she's more of a woman than most of the others I've known. But even she needs a rest now and then." Turning her toward him, Luther whispered with obvious concern, "I want you to sleep for a while, dear. You were up most of the night." Lila glanced at the bed, only to have Luther insist, "He'll be all right. Doc and I'll take care of him." Luther's voice dropped a note softer. "Don't worry about him. Doc isn't leaving yet."

Suddenly weary, Lila nodded. Confusing emotions warred dizzyingly inside her mind. Luther was right. She needed rest and to put this situation in its proper perspective. She had been so caught up in this angry stranger's life-and-death struggle that she hadn't given the threat that hung over Billy and her a thought in almost twenty-four hours.

"Yes, maybe you're right. I think I will rest for a while." Then to Doc Bennett, "I . . . if you need me . . ."

"If I run into a problem with this big fella, I'll just call you in to set him straight." Doc laughed. "I'm not so sure Luther and me could handle him, but I know *you* could."

Unwilling to chance a reply, Lila nodded and left the room. A few steps outside the bedroom door, she stopped. Where was she going? The stranger was sleeping in *her* bed.

"Modesty . . ."

The hair on the back of her neck stood at attention at Aunt Helga's clipped pronunciation of her name behind her. Steeling herself, Lila turned around slowly, realizing that she had almost forgotten the woman's existence, so scarce had Aunt Helga made her presence in the sickroom.

"Yes?"

Aunt Helga raised her chin. Her sagging jowls swayed as she stated flatly, "I do not like der schnakes."

Lila was momentarily at a loss for a reply. "Der schnakes? Oh, the snakes . . ."

"*Ja* . . . der schnakes. I do not go near them."

"Oh." Lila was still confused.

"Der schnakes is for me what der kitchen is for you—no goot. Is right?"

Slow realization began dawning.

Aunt Helga took a fortifying breath. Holding Lila's eye, she extended her broad, plump hand. "Is friends?"

Astounded at the woman's unexpected about-face,

Lila accepted Aunt Helga's hand, only to be startled further as the older woman then grasped her arm and drew her along with her toward the kitchen. Lila was stunned into speechlessness when Aunt Helga clucked like a mother hen and shook her head. "You eat. Too thin. Luther like big woman." At Lila's questioning glance, she gestured, "Big woman."

Lila watched the full sweep of Aunt Helga's hands. Her brows rose as she gestured expressively in return. "Big woman. You mean a fuller-bodied woman?"

"*Ja,* like me."

Doubting the older woman's claim even as she realized its sincerity, Lila was seated at the kitchen table moments later. She blinked as Aunt Helga placed a plate in front of her. Smoked ham, potatoes, and biscuits in servings of monumental proportions. She smiled weakly as she picked up a biscuit, uncertain if the new Aunt Helga would end up posing a greater problem than the old.

Despite her lack of appetite, Lila took a generous bite. The biscuit was as light as a cloud.

"Is goot? Eat."

Unexpected approval rang in Aunt Helga's tone, and as Lila looked up, she was again startled, this time by the sight of Aunt Helga's smile.

Comprehension dawned. With that first bite of the biscuit, Lila had sealed the truce between herself and this difficult woman.

Lila's relief was short-lived as the image of the injured stranger returned before her mind's eye. An instinct older than time warned unexpectedly that the greater enemy still remained, and that the stranger . . . Garrett . . . was enemy enough for any woman.

* * *

Billy tied his bedroll to the back of his saddle, then checked the supplies he had carefully secured behind it. Satisfied, he turned to survey the heavily forested area beyond the clearing once more. Caution had become second nature to him, even in this place where he had found only love awaiting him.

The babe's short cry drew his attention back briefly to the cabin he had exited only moments earlier. Eva returned to mind—coal-black hair spread across the pillow, golden skin gleaming in the sunlight filtering through the cabin window, eyes intently loving, focused on him alone.

A conscienceless part of him, never long dormant when Eva was near, surged to life. Damn, he hated leaving her!

Annoyed at the realization that each separation from Eva grew more difficult, Billy scanned his surroundings critically. It was quiet here on this hillside, yet untouched by man's greed. He was only too aware, however, that in the gulch below them, shielded from their view by a virgin stand of trees, man's impact was only too apparent. Giant sluices littering the streams, great gouges in the earth where veins of gold and silver had changed lives and countryside, and mushroom towns, spread across the landscape like an ever-expanding fungus, abounded. Men and women of all types and persuasions roamed the streets below, seeking their fortunes. Rich one day and poor the next, they continued their search. He had seen many of them die in that pursuit, leaving little behind them. He had determined long ago that he would not be one of those. There was an easier path to fortune, and this time *he* would not be the victim.

For the pain remained . . .

He was a child of eight years again. Pa was dead

and he was frightened. Strangely, he had believed Nellie's grief was real when she had stood over Pa and cried until she could cry no more. He had been angry when Lila said Nellie was glad she was free. It had not occurred to him that Nellie had been pretending when she said she loved his pa. He could not believe she had lied when she said she loved Lila and him, too. But most of all, he had never, in his wildest dreams, imagined that she would desert them.

Strangely, Nellie's image was as clear to him now as it had been the day she sent Lila and him away. Young Nellie, pretty Nellie, with curly blond hair, blue eyes, and a ready smile. Her eyes had been red-rimmed when she said, "I can't take care of the ranch all alone, and I can't take care of you. You'll only be at the orphanage for a little while. I'll send for you as soon as I can and we'll all be together again."

In hindsight, his gullibility was almost laughable. Despite Lila's warnings, he had believed every word Nellie had said. He had continued to believe her, growing more rebellious at the orphanage as weeks became months, and months became years. Finally, Lila and he had run away. It had been difficult to convince Lila to go back to the ranch, and it was only after they reached it that he knew why she had not wanted to return. The ranch had been sold and Nellie was gone.

He had learned difficult lessons that day. He had discovered that his sister's love was the only love that was constant. He had realized that for others, love was merely a tool, a means to an end. In the time since, he had come to realize those truths held true, and that the word "friend" was loosely used and rarely served.

Despite his resolution, his revenge on the world that had treated him badly had been poorly organized. It had been filled with little satisfaction and minor brushes with the law . . . until he had met Bart Forbes.

A familiar agitation knotted Billy's brow as Forbes returned to mind. He was going to be late. Forbes was expecting him and he didn't like being kept waiting.

The sound of movement from within the cabin turned Billy toward the doorway as Eva stepped into sight carrying Christina. The babe's head rested against her shoulder, a patch of pure gold against the raven-black silk of her hair. Slim, graceful, and silent, Eva was a creature of the woods surrounding them, different from any person he had ever known. Yet he and she were alike, for although Eva's scars were visible for the world to see, his were deeply hidden behind his smile.

Eva neared and Billy reached out instinctively to gather her into his arms. The musky smell of her sent his pulse racing. He felt her breath against his throat as her question became a whispered plea.

"You must leave today, Billy?"

Billy drew back as he felt himself weakening. He forced a cocky smile. "All good things come to an end, darlin'."

Eva's eyes held his. "I don't want you to go."

"I'll be back soon. You have more than enough supplies to last until I do, and enough money to—"

"I'll miss you."

Billy's smile gradually faded. "My life doesn't begin and end in this cabin."

"Mine does."

Billy forced his voice harder. "That might be a mistake."

Christina took that moment to protest her inactivity, drawing Eva's attention, but not before Eva's stricken expression registered in his mind. Silently cursing, Billy took the fretful child and swung her up into the air.

The babe's response was a happy gurgle that almost succeeded in restoring her mother's smile. Encouraged, he spoke in a mock whisper into the tiny ear close to his lips as he propped the babe against his shoulder

"That's right, Christina, show your mother how to smile. You're not worried about my coming back, are you? That's because you believe me when I say I will."

"I believe you, Billy." Eva's voice was strangely harsh. "I believe you'll come back . . . if you can."

Billy stiffened. "Meaning?"

"I wish I knew."

Taking the protesting child from his arms, Eva stepped back. "Goodbye, Billy."

Billy was suddenly angry. "Just like that?"

Eva became visibly distressed. "You're confusing me, Billy. What do you want from me?"

"I'll show you what I want." Snatching the babe from her arms, Billy placed her on a cushioning of leaves nearby. Turning back, he slid his hand into Eva's hair and jerked her close. Holding her gaze intently, he then crushed her mouth with his, only to find her lips parted, waiting. His kiss settled there, tasting her, wanting her, consuming her. Her response promised more . . .

Drawing back abruptly, Billy gave a short laugh, more shaken by the brief exchange than he dared admit.

"Oh, no you don't. I'm leaving . . . now." Sweeping the child back up into his arms, Billy kissed her smooth cheek and placed her back in her mother's arms. Suddenly sober, he ordered tightly, "You have everything you need here. Don't go down into the camp unless it's necessary. I'll be back as soon as I can. If everything goes well, I'll get you away from this place to somewhere safer soon."

Eva nodded.

"Bolt the door at night. The gun I left you is loaded. Use it if you have to."

Eva nodded again.

He hesitated, then added, "If anything should happen, you can reach me at Denver Post Office Box Number 23. Can you remember that? Number 23."

"Number 23."

Forcing himself to turn his back on Eva's solemn stare, Billy mounted up. His sorrel pranced nervously as he restrained him a moment longer, repeating, "Remember what I said."

"I'll remember."

Spurring his horse into motion, Billy started down the hillside trail. Cursing himself as much for what he had said as for what he hadn't, he refused to look back.

There was a sound, a sudden crash, and Garrett came awake with a snap. His vision blurred, he looked around the small room, the realization dawning that every muscle in his body ached becoming more pronounced with every moment. His head was faintly throbbing and his memory was faulty, but a strange sense of agitation emerged vividly clear.

His vision unclouding, he scanned the log walls, the chest nearby, the table beside the bed in which he lay. Where was he?

He attempted to move. His arm was a deadweight causing him agonizing distress, and memory returned abruptly, vividly. His horse was stumbling, falling . . . The ground rose to meet him with a sickening crack as he rolled over and over down the grade to a gradual stop. That sound. A rattler! He raised his arm to shield his face!

Garrett closed his eyes, trembling weakly. At a sound

close by, he opened his eyes again to see a woman kneeling in the corner of the room. She was mumbling under her breath as she wiped the floor with a cloth. He strained to see her. She stood up unexpectedly and turned toward him, her attention focused on the cloth in her hand. His breath caught in his throat. It was her!

"Modesty? I thought I heard something fall."

Garrett closed his eyes as an old man appeared in the doorway.

"I dropped the glass of medicine. I'm going to have to mix another one."

He knew that voice.

The old fellow responded, but Garrett heard only the familiar ring of the woman's clear tones.

Coward . . .

Garrett trembled with anger.

Do you call yourself a man?

Fury . . .

A real man fights for what he wants.

Rage . . .

Coward . . .

Determination.

Garrett waited. The voice drew closer.

"I'll give it to him. You can finish eating, Dr. Bennett."

An inestimable length of time passed before Garrett heard the sound of a step close by. He felt a slender arm slip beneath his shoulders to raise his head. Waiting until it became firmly fixed, he opened his eyes abruptly and grasped the woman's free arm. He held it tightly, drawing her closer. Eyes as black as midnight widened with shock as he rasped, "So I'm a coward . . ." His grip tightened and the woman's face blanched. "I told you you'd eat those words . . ."

"Let me go!"

The woman wrenched her arm from his grasp, and

Garrett cursed the weakness that allowed her to slip her other arm free as well. His head flopped back against the pillow with an impact that set off a new round of painful vibrations and he groaned aloud. His uncertain consciousness began drifting away as the woman's voice sounded once more.

"Are you all right? Answer me. How do you feel?"

He felt bad. Damned bad.

"Here, drink this. It'll help the pain."

Garrett struggled to open his eyes. When he did, he found those dark eyes close to his once more. He murmured a low, emphatic epithet.

"Don't swear at me, damn you! Just do what I say! It's for your own good."

He fought to clear his head. "No."

"Don't be a fool. It'll help you feel better."

"So, you want to help me . . ."

"Damned if I know why I do."

"Because you're expected to."

The woman's lips tightened. "Maybe."

"You don't like it."

The dark eyes narrowed. "I don't know what you're talking about."

"Don't you?"

"I've had enough of this. Just drink this medicine and go back to sleep."

"No."

"You're going to drink it anyway. And you know why? Because you're too damned weak to fight me."

"Bitch . . ."

"Bastard . . ."

"Take it away!"

"Drink it!"

Garrett could feel himself weakening physically as he rasped, "You're not going to give up, are you?"

"No."

He cursed. "Give me that damned stuff."

Parting his lips as she held the glass to them, Garrett forced himself to swallow. Wincing at the bitter taste when it was done, he muttered, "Get out. Leave me alone."

"Ungrateful bast—"

"Is something wrong, Modesty?"

Her head snapped up toward the big man in the doorway. Her furious expression changed immediately to a shy smile. "No, nothing's wrong. I was just helping our patient take his medicine."

"It looks like he's asleep again. Why don't you go outside and eat. Aunt Helga has something ready for you."

"No, that's all right. You go ahead. I'll stay with him a little longer."

"But—"

"Please, Luther. I'm fine."

The man turned back out of sight, and Garrett opened his eyes. "Damned fool . . ."

The woman's eyes snapped back to his face. "What are you talking about?"

"He doesn't really know you at all, does he?" His head pounding, Garrett grasped the woman's wrist once more. He felt his grip slipping as he rasped, "You know what I'm talkin' about. You aren't foolin' me." Reading the sudden panic in her eyes, Garrett gasped, "My saddlebags . . . inside my other shirt. Don't let them see it. If I go down, I'll take you down with me. I swear . . ."

Keenly aware of the risk he was taking despite his debilitating weakness, Garrett rasped again, "Find it . . . hide it. Don't let them see it."

Unable to hold on any longer as those unfathomable

dark eyes continued to stare, Garrett felt consciousness drifting away.

And then it was dark.

Lila stared down into the face of the injured man, her heart pounding. Taking a step back from the bed, she placed the empty glass on the table nearby and rubbed her aching wrist. She was somehow unable to take her eyes from his face.

Those eyes . . . as cold as ice and just as impenetrable. He looked at her as if he hated her.

Suddenly realizing she was trembling, the big man's threats resounding in her mind, Lila glanced at the saddlebags lying on the floor close by. What had he been talking about? Had he seen her before? She had thought she was safe here.

Beside the saddlebags with a few quick steps, Lila picked them up and rested them on the chair. Glancing toward the doorway to make certain she was indeed alone, she unbuckled the flap and reached inside. She pulled out the carefully folded change of clothing.

Inside my other shirt . . . Don't let them see it.

Her hands trembling, Lila shook out the worn shirt and snatched up the folded sheet that fell to the floor. She unfolded it, her breath catching in her throat as a blurred picture of the man in the bed stared back at her.

WANTED—$500 REWARD
BANK AND TRAIN ROBBERY
GARRETT HARRISON

No. This couldn't be!

Her heart pounding, Lila glanced again toward the door. Garrett Harrison, or whoever he was, was right!

She couldn't let anybody see the poster. The last thing she wanted was to get involved with the sheriff. She needed to stay here a little longer, until she could write to Billy and get a letter in return.

Folding the sheet carefully, Lila slipped it inside her dress. Quickly refolding the shirt, she stuffed it back into the saddlebag and turned back to the bed. He was no threat to her now, with a wanted notice bearing his name in her safekeeping.

Recalling the coldness in his eyes and the contempt in his voice, Lila steeled herself against flaring anger. Whatever he knew or thought he knew, he was nothing more than a thief . . . a wanted man who sought to play judge.

"Modesty . . ."

Looking up as Luther reappeared in the doorway, Lila forced a shy smile. She turned away from the bed and walked toward him. His arm slid around her as she reached the doorway, raising a genuine warmth that contrasted sharply with the wrath stirred by the man in the bed behind her.

Lila's smile deepened. Garrett Harrison thought he had her where he wanted her, but he was a fool because the reverse was true.

No, he was no threat to her.

She dismissed him.

Eight

"What in hell kept you?" Bart Forbes's thin, unshaven face drew into angry lines as Billy dismounted and tethered his horse on a nearby tree. The sounds of twilight rang in the silent camp as Forbes took an aggressive step forward, his tall, whipcord-slim body tense. His voice was heavy with threat as he rasped, "I told you we'd be meetin' at noon today. You're late. I don't like bein' kept waitin'."

Billy glanced around the small clearing. Eaton, Picket, and Ricks were sprawled by the campfire in deceptively casual postures. Their bedrolls had been set up for the night, but the remains of their evening meal had not yet been discarded. Their silence in the face of Forbes's fury was a warning for caution that Billy did not ignore.

Forbes's eyes were narrowed and intent. He was vicious when in these moods. He had been known to whip a horse to death after it stumbled and threw him, but Billy knew Forbes's viciousness wasn't confined solely to animals. The sight of a fireman being thrown from a racing Illinois Central train they had robbed a few months ago still lived in his mind. Forbes said he had done it to teach the man a lesson. Whether that fellow had lived to learn that lesson or not made little difference to Billy, but *he* had learned a lesson that day. He would not forget it.

Billy remained silent, reading in Forbes's livid expression the danger of his weakness for Eva and the harsh price he might be forced to pay for those last few hours with her. No, he didn't like Forbes, but he *did* like having more money in his pocket than he needed for the first time in his life. More importantly, the excitement that pumped hotly through his veins when he rode with the gang had blurred the edges of bitter memories until he was finally able to look back on the past with a sense of repaying an old debt in full.

Knowing that satisfaction was worth any price he might pay, Billy forced a smile. "Looks like I kept you waiting all right, but I wasn't wasting my time." Noting the further narrowing of Forbes's eyes, he continued with deceptive ease. "My horse threw a shoe on the way here. I had to stop at a ranch a few miles back to reshoe him, but what do you suppose I saw prancing around in that fella's corral while I was doing it?" Forbes's chin rose a notch from his intimidating stance, and Billy's confidence mounted as he went on. "That fella, Buck Howell was his name, had six mares waiting to be shipped back East. They were fat and sassy . . ."

"When's he goin' to ship them?"

"Next week."

"No, he ain't." Forbes's chin came up another notch. " 'Cause he's goin' to wake up real soon and find that corral empty. And you're goin' to have them horses attached to your lead and ready when the boys and me get that shipment from the Denver bank a couple of days from now."

Relieved to have evaded Forbes's savage bent, Billy

nodded and started toward the campfire, only to be stopped unexpectedly by Forbes's growl.

"You ain't off the hook yet, Chesney!"

Again on the alert, Billy moved his hand into an uncompromising position where it would be as easy to reach his gun as to scratch his head.

"Don't even think about it, Chesney, unless you're contemplatin' an early demise."

"Think about what?"

"You ain't as good as you think you are." Forbes laughed harshly the second before he snaked his gun from his holster in a lightning move. A shot rang out before Billy had time to react, creasing the tip of his boot as he jumped a step backward.

Walking toward him, his gun leveled squarely at Billy's midsection, Forbes stopped a few feet away and laughed again. "Don't go sweatin', boy. I ain't about to shoot you . . . not this time. You're too good a hand with horses and I ain't got time to find somebody else to replace you. But I'm givin' you a few words of advice that I'm hopin' you'll take. Don't keep me waitin' again, not for any reason. And the next time you think of drawin' on a man, make sure your hand moves quicker than your eyes. You damned kids are all alike. Your eyes are a dead giveaway."

Slipping his gun back into his holster, Forbes snapped, "Sit down! We ain't got no time to waste, 'cause we're goin' to Denver tomorrow."

"Tomorrow!"

"That's right, boys. We're goin' to open an account in the Denver bank, and then we're goin' to spend some time watchin' and waitin' until our money gets put into that express car like it should. The only trouble is, we're goin' to be usin' our guns to withdraw it, right along with the rest of the cash. While we're waitin' in Denver,

Chesney here's goin' to get them horses he was talkin' about so we'll have nice fresh mounts ready for us when we make our getaway. Hell, we don't want no sheriff and his posse outrunnin' us, do we?"

Turning back toward Billy, Forbes smirked. "Relax, Chesney. Give us one of your great big smiles. And then make sure you listen real close while I explain exactly what I want you to do, 'cause I ain't goin' to be acceptin' any more excuses from you . . . horses or no horses."

Billy walked slowly toward the fire. He sat beside the other men, and Forbes sat, too. But Billy didn't smile. Forbes was a bastard all right, but he was a little crazy, too. So he'd listen, like he was told, and he'd remember, like he was told.

Yeah, he'd remember . . .

Old Doc Bennett was as sober as a judge as he paused by the open front door, and Lila assessed him silently. Clean-shaven, his shirt freshly laundered by Aunt Helga's meticulous hand, he looked almost respectable, even if his eyes had not lost their bloodshot appearance and his bulbous nose still retained an unnatural glow. Surprising herself, she had gained a healthy respect for the man, in sharp contrast with her feelings when he had first arrived. As incredible as it seemed, he was almost as good a doctor drunk as sober, and that was saying a lot for any man.

Effectively reading her thoughts, Doc smiled. "Well, now, Modesty, if I ain't mistaken, I see a genuine spark of affection in your eye when you look at me." He looked up at Luther, who stood beside her. "She didn't like me much at first, you know. Not that I blame her.

I ain't the most appealin' man when I've got a snoot full."

"You're not the most appealing man without a snoot full, either, Doc, but you're the best we've got, so I guess we'll have to put up with you."

Luther's response, delivered with a wry smile, turned Lila toward him with surprise.

"Now don't you go defendin' me to your intended, Modesty. He's got a right to his opinion, especially since I know he don't mean it." Doc winked, then turned to Aunt Helga as she walked toward him with a carefully wrapped package. She handed it to him without explanation.

"What's this, Helga? A present?"

"Is ham and biscuits. You eat on der way back to town . . . *before* you go to saloon."

"What makes you think that I'll . . ." Doc paused, and laughed. "Hell, what's the use of pretendin'. I can hardly wait to walk through them swingin' doors. There's no way around it. I feel at home wherever I am once my foot is propped on a bar rail and I've got a glass in my hand and a smilin' lady beside me. Besides, I'm mighty thirsty."

Lila's smile grew sad. She had seen too many men like Doc Bennett. The only trouble was, not many of them were half as good as he was, drunk or sober.

"There you go lookin' at me all misty-eyed again, Modesty. You keep that up and I just might speak up for you myself."

"Ach, foolish old man!" Aunt Helga shook her head, her jowls flapping. "Modesty is young. You are old."

"I'm only old on the outside, Helga dear . . ."

His practiced leer fading, Doc looked back at Luther. "It's been a pleasure spendin' time in your fine house, my friend. I would've said it was almost like a holiday if it wasn't for my uncooperative patient in there."

Following the line of Doc's gaze, Lila glanced back toward the bedroom door, frowning.

"Don't you go worryin' about that fella, Modesty. The worst is over for him, although I'm thinkin' it ain't for you, since you're goin' to have to keep him quiet and in that bed for as long as you're able. You just keep givin' him them powders when he needs them and don't let him get you down. He's a strong fella. He'll be on his feet and almost as good as new in a week or so. If you have any trouble, just let Helga—"

"I don't like der schnakes!"

Three heads jerked toward Helga at her sharp interjection, in time to see her turn abruptly and head back to the kitchen. Luther's expression was apologetic as he looked at Lila.

"Aunt Helga won't go near that room until that fella's arm is healed. I'm sorry. I'll do what I can to help you, but the calves are penned for branding. I can't put it off anymore, and Max—"

"Don't worry about me, Luther."

Lila's words of reassurance emerged convincingly despite her inner uncertainty. Actually, despite the nudge of panic she had experienced at the thought of Doc's leaving, she was relieved. She still hadn't had a chance to find out what Garrett Harrison meant when he had said—

His gaze gentle and sincere, Luther interrupted Lila's swelling uncertainties. "But I do worry about you."

"Listen to the lady, Luther." Doc winked again. "Like you said, she's a real woman behind them silly little eyeglasses and that shy smile. She'll handle it, and if she don't, you send Max for me and I'll come back and give that fella hell."

"Doc . . ."

"Yeah, I know. I'll watch my language if you'll go see what's holdin' Max up with the wagon." Withdrawing his watch from his pocket, Doc shook his head. "It'll be damned near dark by the time I get back to town at this rate. I've got Millie Hargus's rheumatism to check on yet, along with John Stern's knife wound and little Bobbie Miller's broken leg."

"I'll see what the problem is."

Lila stepped out into the yard beside Doc as Luther strode toward the barn. She looked up at a touch on her arm. Suddenly serious, Doc held her gaze intently as he spoke.

"I wanted to talk to you alone for a minute, Modesty. I know this whole thing ain't been easy on you, with that fella in there givin' you a hard time like he has."

"He hasn't given me a hard time. He—"

"Now, now, don't go fibbin' to me, dear. I've been around too long not to recognize a hard case when I see one. It's my thought things are goin' to get worse before they get better, and if they do, I want you to promise you'll send for me. I'll drag that fella back to town so fast that he won't know what hit him. I'll keep him in my office until he's able to get back on his feet, and I promise you, he won't enjoy a minute of it. Another thing, my dear . . ." Doc paused, his bloodshot eyes searching hers. "I just want to say that Luther's a fine man, one of the finest I ever met, but if he ain't the man for you . . ."

Lila took a spontaneous step backward. "I don't know what you mean, Doc. Luther—"

"Yes, you do, dear. Luther's in love. Just make sure you love him as much in return before you make any decisions, or it won't be fair to either one of you."

"Doc . . ."

"And another thing." Doc was suddenly frowning. "Get rid of them glasses!" Snatching off her glasses unexpectedly, Doc folded them and slapped them into her hand. "You don't need them worth a damn. You do more stumblin' around when you wear them than when you don't!"

Too startled to reply, Lila felt her heart jump nervously as Doc looked at her keenly. His eyes narrowed thoughtfully. "You know, without them glasses in the way . . ." He shook his head. "Right from the first I had the strangest feelin' that I met you somewhere before."

"That's just wishful thinking, Doc," Luther interrupted, leading Doc's wagon as he approached. "Modesty came straight from back East and we didn't spend more than five minutes in town when I picked her up at the train, so you couldn't have met her before. But since you're so reluctant to part from her, I just might bring her to town next week to visit you." At Lila's surprised glance, Luther smiled. "Would you like that, dear? You could do some shopping and—"

"And I could post a letter I've been wanting to write so everyone back East will know I'm all right."

Luther appeared momentarily confused. "That's fine, of course, but I thought you said there wasn't anybody there you'd miss."

Lila felt her face flush. Modesty had tripped her up again.

"See now. You've embarrassed the lady, Luther. And they call me a fool."

Turning to place his package on the wagon seat, Doc faced them again with a lopsided smile. "You just make sure you come visit me when you come to town, you hear. You don't want to disappoint an old man." He paused, adding with a revealing flick of his wiry brows,

"You can leave that Garrett fella behind, though, unless you feel the need to get rid of him. If I never see him again, it won't be no loss."

Succumbing to impulse, Lila stepped forward and kissed Doc's wrinkled cheek. "You're a nice man, Doc. I'm going to miss you."

Surprising her, Doc flushed. "I thank you for that kiss, dear lady, and I don't mind sayin' that I'm goin' to miss you, too." He sighed elaborately. "Damn my old bones . . ."

Lila turned back to the house as the dust of the trail obscured Doc's wagon from sight, realizing even more clearly than before that Doc was an unusual man. She walked toward the bedroom doorway. As for his comment about Garrett Harrison being difficult, a real hard case, he didn't know the half of it.

His eyes slitted as he pretended sleep, Garrett watched Lila Chesney walk back into the room. He didn't feel well, but he hadn't needed to overhear that drunken quack's opinion to know that he'd soon be on his feet. His fever was down, and although his arm was a deadweight, he was able to move his fingers without pain. His head still pounded every time he moved, but he could think more clearly . . . clearly enough to realize the enormity of the risk he had taken when he had asked Lila Chesney to remove the wanted poster from his saddlebag.

Contempt surging anew inside him, Garrett watched the slender imposter move around the room. She was such a drab little dove with her awkward glasses, tightly bound hair, and that hideous grey dress. Her shy glances and uncertain manner were so well done that he might have believed them himself if he was that poor fool, Luther Knox.

But he wasn't Luther Knox.

Waiting until she stepped closer to the bed, Garrett opened his eyes abruptly.

"Did you find it . . . Lila?"

Lila Chesney gasped as her gaze snapped up to his. Garrett felt a surge of pure satisfaction as she paled with her whispered response.

"What did you call me?"

"You can drop your act, Lila. I know who you are." Garrett paused, realizing he had gone too far to turn back as he continued. "The only thing I can't figure out is what you're hopin' to gain pretendin' to be somebody you aren't." He gave a short laugh. "I can't believe you want that Luther fella so much that you're tryin' to trap him into marryin' you."

Her colorless cheeks suddenly hot with color, Lila took a step closer. She glanced nervously toward the door. "Be quiet, damn you!"

"That's more like it . . . the true Lila Chesney."

A revealing flicker of her dark eyes did not escape Garrett's notice as Lila questioned tightly, "How do you know my name? Who are you?"

"You know who I am."

Lila sneered. "I know *what* you are, and I know what the wanted notice says your name is."

Garrett paused in response, gritting his teeth against a painful spasm that stole his breath, finally rasping, "Where'd you put the poster?"

"I put it away for safekeeping."

"What's that supposed to mean?"

"It means you'd better watch what you say from now on or you're in big trouble."

"As much trouble as you're in?"

The dark eyes looking down into his narrowed. "What do you know about the trouble I'm in?"

"Nothin' much. I just know you're pretendin' to be somebody you aren't, and that you're doin' a real good job of pullin' the wool over the eyes of that Luther fella. The damned fool looks at you like you can walk on water."

Lila took an angry step closer. "Watch what you say about Luther. He's worth ten of any man like you."

"I wouldn't go makin' broad statements like that if I were you. You don't really know me."

"I know all I want to know."

"Yeah?" Garrett fought a wave of weakness. "That's too bad, because I figure we're goin' to get to be good friends before we leave this place."

Lila stiffened. "What makes you think I have any intention of leaving?"

Garrett allowed the full measure of his contempt to show through. "Lila Chesney . . . dancehall girl, faro dealer, and whatever else happens to appeal to her at the time. That kind of woman would die of boredom on a ranch like this."

"You don't know what you're talking about!"

"Don't I? The Golden Steer's a real nice saloon, isn't it? And that Ruby . . . she's real good company, otherwise you can be sure I would've taken a closer look to see what all those fellas crowdin' around your faro table found so fascinatin'."

"You were never in the Golden Steer! I would've remembered you."

"Honey, your memory's not as good as you think it is."

Satisfaction soared anew when Lila raised her chin defensively. "What do you want from me?"

Garrett's hard laugh was filled with the menace of his thoughts, despite its weakness. "What can I get?"

"Nothing!"

"Oh, no, I'm goin' to get more than that."

"Bastard!"

"That's sounds more like Lila Chesney."

"You think you're so damned smart." Lila's face flamed and Garrett was momentarily stunned at the power of her furious beauty as she rasped, "But you're too stupid to realize that I'm in control here."

"Only for a little while."

"Longer than you think. You won't be getting out of that bed for at least a week."

"I'll be on my feet tomorrow."

"Not a chance."

Garrett could feel true anger rise. "That's the second time you said that to me. I don't like it."

"I don't care what you like."

"You will."

Lila sneered again, adding with great deliberation, "Not a chance."

Fury overwhelming caution, Garrett attempted to rise when pain sharper than a knife momentarily darkened the room around him. When the light returned, Lila was at his side.

"Are you all right?"

Catching her wrist with a fury that lent him unexpected strength, Garrett ignored the pounding in his head that began anew as he rasped, "No, I'm not all right, but I'll tell you this. That wanted poster had better be somewhere safe or your little masquerade is goin' to be over faster than you can blink an eye."

"Let go of me!"

"When I'm ready."

"Arrogant bastard!" Lila jerked her arm free of his

weakening grip. "You have the nerve to give *me* orders? You can't move. You can't even raise your head without passing out. You're dependent on me for everything now that Doc Bennett's gone."

"That's where you're wrong."

"Oh, no, I'm not wrong."

"Yes, you are." His fury building despite his rapidly weakening state, Garrett demanded, "Look at me Lila . . ." He paused until she met his gaze. Never more fervent than he was at that moment of passionate fury, he continued. "Do you really believe I'd let *you* control me?"

Lila blinked under the heat of his gaze, but her response was unyielding. "You don't have any choice."

His energy waning, Garrett managed with a weakness of tone that did not disguise his strength of purpose, "We'll see . . ." He closed his eyes. "Get out and leave me alone."

"Bastard . . ."

His response a contemptuous laugh, Garrett allowed the hovering darkness full reign.

Shaking with frustrated fury as Garrett closed his eyes, dismissing her, Lila drew back from the bed and glanced toward the doorway. Realizing her rage was so intense that she would not be able to conceal it should the need arise, she slipped into the shadows of the corner and pretended to busy herself there. Despite herself, she felt herself turning to stare at the silent man in the bed once more.

"Bastard . . ."

Suddenly disgusted with herself, Lila breathed deeply in an attempt to regain control. No, this would not do. She was playing into Garrett Harrison's hands . . . allowing him to manipulate her. She was behaving as if he had the upper hand, just as he claimed, but she knew nothing could be further from the truth.

Testing her mettle, Lila walked back to the side of the bed. Her sleeping adversary was frowning in his sleep, unconsciously perpetuating the aura of threat he exuded while awake. Despite herself, doubts rose in her mind. Harrison was right. She didn't really know him. Too many aspects of his past remained a mystery for her to adequately assess the danger he posed.

Cursing her stubborn streak and the spot deep in the core of her that would not permit her to bow to the dominance of any man, Lila knew it would be far easier for her if she played along with the egotistical bastard and allowed him to think he had cowered her. Luther had already promised to take her to town. She had no doubt Billy had already gone to the Golden Steer looking for her, and finding her gone, would check his post office box in Denver for her letter. She also knew that if he didn't get one soon, he'd begin worrying.

A hard smile touched Lila's lips. It would serve Billy right to worry a little.

Lila's gaze traveled Garrett Harrison's still face. His features were strong, resolute, evenly drawn beneath the heavy bruising and fresh growth of beard. She gave a scoffing laugh. She could imagine the interest he stirred among the girls when he walked into a saloon with that hair as black as pitch, those light eyes that seemed to see right through you, and that deep voice as smooth as velvet. She knew the size and breadth of him alone was enough to set the girls buzzing. There were not many men who were his match. Her gaze lingering, she wondered if there had been a time in this big, angry man's life when emotions other than hatred and contempt had shone from those clear, hard eyes.

She wondered if Elizabeth was able to make him smile.

Lila's lips curled with silent derision. Sweet, innocent Elizabeth, who had given "all the love in her heart, forever," to a thief.

Finding that thought somehow too uncomfortable to retain, Lila realized that the week Doc Bennett had estimated it would take for Garrett Harrison to get back on his feet, would probably be one of the longest in her life.

Bowing to impulse, Lila leaned closer to her patient and whispered harshly into his unhearing ear. "I'm going to take real good care of you. Oh, yes, I'm going to make sure you get well as fast as possible and get strong enough to ride out of here and never come back."

Lila's expression hardened as she drew back. But if Garrett Harrison thought he was going to get away with anything on this ranch in the meantime, he had another thought coming.

She'd shoot him herself if she had to.

And she wouldn't bat an eye.

His foot resting on the rail, a glass in his hand, and a smile on his face as the bustle and buzz of the Red Slipper Saloon grew gradually louder, Doc Bennett was home at last.

Tilting his glass, Doc drained it dry, then wiped his full mustache with the back of his hand as he caught the bartender's eye and crooked a knobby finger.

"You come right over here and fill this glass again, Willie. And fill it to the top this time. I'm in need of strong fortification. I had a long, hard ride today, and

I still got a ways to go before my doctorin' duties are done for the day."

"Sure, Doc, anythin' you say." Filling the glass to the brim, the corpulent bartender grinned. "Any fuller than that and you'll be lappin' that redeye up off the bar."

"I've been known to do worse than that on occasion, my boy." A twinkle in his eye, Doc Bennett drained the glass once more."

"Whoa, Doc!" Willie raised a hairy brow. "You ain't goin' to see any more patients tonight if you keep emptyin' your glass like that."

"I'd say that I'm a better judge of my capacity than you, my friend." Doc Bennett's bloodshot eyes narrowed. "I'm the doctor here."

"Did I hear you say you're a doctor?"

Turning toward the opportune interjection, Doc Bennett eyed the small man standing at the bar a few feet from him. He appraised the fellow's grip on the beer in his hand and the look in his eye, and responded accordingly.

"Don't tell me you're in need of my professional services. You don't look sick to me and you don't look like nothin' could pry that beer away from you, even if you was. So why are you askin'?"

The small fellow's unkempt mustache wiggled. "Well, I came damned near to needin' a doctor on the way ridin' into town today. Damned if I didn't have a close call!"

Doc's curiosity was piqued. "That right?"

"Sure enough. There I was, ridin' along just as easy as I pleased, dreamin' of how good a nice cold beer would feel slippin' down my throat . . ."

"I know the feelin' . . ."

". . . when all of a sudden stretched across the trail

was the biggest damned rattler I ever seen! Scared the hell out of my horse, too. Before I knew it, I was flat on my back in the dust with that rattler starin' me in the eye."

"You don't say!"

"Lucky thing I still had my wits about me. I scrambled out of that big fella's range and plugged him one for good measure. He won't be scarin' any more unsuspectin' riders, I'll tell you that."

Doc appraised the small man some more: faded clothes stained with sweat, dust-caked boots, and a hat that had seen many summers, all draped on a short, skinny frame without a muscle in sight, yet he had done better against a rattler than that big, hard-nosed fella back at Luther's ranch.

Doc had to laugh.

The little fella looked puzzled. "What's so funny, Doc?"

"You don't know how lucky you are. I just came back from treatin' a fella that didn't fare as good as you did in a face-off with a rattler."

"That so?"

"Yeah, a big fella. He cracked his skull when he hit the ground and the rattler got him, but he still managed to split the viper in two."

"Well, I'll be. Dead, huh?"

"No." Doc frowned and shook his head. "I'd say that fella's too damned mean to die, although I have to admit that there was a point where I wasn't sure he'd make it. He's all right now, though, aside from a real bad headache and a stiff arm that'll take a while before he can handle a gun again."

"Hummm . . ."

"With a little luck he should be back on his feet in a week."

"Don't like the fella too much, huh?" The stranger grinned. "Guess it must be tough takin' care of somebody you can't cotton to."

"That ain't my problem no more. If I'm lucky, I won't never see that big fella again. But he'll be all right. I left him in dainty, very capable hands."

"You left a woman to take care of him! If that fella's as bad as you say, that wasn't exactly the gentlemanly thing to do, was it?"

"Oh, no?" Dock snickered, truly amused. "You ever see a sparrow go after a hawk?"

"Well . . ."

"It gets right on that hawk's tail and it don't let up until that big bad bird's been taught some manners, and then some."

"So, you got yourself a feisty little sparrow to take care of your hawk, huh?"

"Sure enough do."

The little fella's grin widened. "Well, I'll drink to that! I might even hang around a week to see if that big bad hawk comes into town with some of his tail feathers missin'."

Doc laughed again. "It might be worth the wait."

"It might, at that."

Emerging through the swinging doors of the Red Slipper Saloon a short time later, Doc paused and rubbed his chest in a satisfied gesture as he glanced up and down the street. He had warmed his belly with a few shots of Willie's redeye, and he had warmed his heart recounting his own version of the sparrow and the hawk. He kind of hoped that little fella . . . what had he said his name was? Damned if he could remember. Well, he kind of hoped that little fella hung around for a few days. He was good company, even if he could've used a bath and a change of clothes. That hat with the yellowed snakeskin band had to be older than he was.

Oh, hell, what did he care, anyway? It was time to check little Bobbie Miller's broken leg.

"Open your mouth."

Garrett glared into the dark eyes of Lila Chesney, a familiar agitation growing. He had suffered her fussing around him most of the day since their angry exchange earlier. She hadn't spoken one word more than necessary, but she had been so damned solicitous that she was making him wary. He didn't trust her one damned bit.

Propped with two pillows behind his back and a clean cloth spread across his chest as Lila Chesney held a spoon a few inches from his mouth, Garrett glared as Lila spoke again.

"I said, open your mouth."

"I'm not hungry."

"Don't bother to lie. I can hear your stomach rumbling."

"I don't need anybody to feed me."

Lila Chesney glared in return. "You're a stubborn jackass. Your arm's still numb. You couldn't pick up a spoon if you tried."

"You think so?" Garrett all but growled. He couldn't wait until he was in condition to put this nasty little piece in her place.

"I know so. Open your mouth. The sooner you're done eating, the sooner you'll get rid of me."

"Is that a promise?"

Lila's gaze dripped ice. "You're asking me for a

promise? I didn't think you gave dancehall girls that much credit."

"I don't."

Lila's color flared, and Garrett knew he had hit the mark again as she snapped, "Open your mouth or I promise you I'll pour this plate in your lap!"

Garrett reluctantly opened his mouth. The spoon clattered against his teeth and he choked as the hot soup slipped down his throat.

Lila's tone held an acid twinge. "Oh, dear . . . did that go down the wrong way? We'll just have to be more careful from now on, won't we?"

"If *you* know what's good for you, we will."

Holding Lila's gaze intently as she guided another spoon toward his lips, Garrett adequately conveyed his thoughts with his gaze. After two more careful spoonfuls, he allowed himself to relax. His stomach was reacting gratefully to the warm liquid, and his appetite was returning with unexpected enthusiasm.

"Take it easy. I won't take the plate away before you're finished." Lila grimaced. "Or maybe I will . . ."

"You'd like to do that, wouldn't you?"

Lila stared him straight in the eye. "Yes, I really would."

Realizing she meant it, Garrett taunted, "Why don't you, then?"

"I thought you had that figured out already."

"No." Garrett held her dark eyes imprisoned with his gaze. He wanted no opportunity for deceit.

"The answer's simple. I want you on your feet and out of here as soon as possible."

"Afraid I'll spoil a good thing for you?" Garrett sneered. "I suppose I'd be afraid, too, if I were you and I had a Pinkerton on my trail."

Lila gasped. "How did you kno—"

"How did I know a Pinkerton's after you? I stopped back to see Ruby a few days ago. She told me the whole story. How you ran out when one of your 'friends' told you a Pinkerton was askin' questions about you. What did you do to get a Pinkerton on your trail, anyway?"

"That's none of your damned business!"

"I think it is. We're in this together, remember?"

"We're not in anything together . . . not a damned thing!"

Lila's unexpected fury lit a familiar spark in her dark eyes, and Garrett could not help but respond to the fire there, despite his debilitated state. Resenting his reaction to the pure womanly power of her, Garrett snapped, "Wrong again, Lila."

"Don't call me Lila!" She glanced up anxiously toward the doorway. "Luther is due to come back anytime. If he hears you—"

"If he hears me, you can claim I'm delirious . . . Lila."

"I told you not to call me Lila!"

"Try to stop me."

Her eyes widening with barely controlled rage, Lila stood abruptly. Snatching the cloth from his chest, she then ripped the pillows out from behind him. His head smacked the mattress with a resounding snap, stimulating another round of pounding as Lila glared down at him.

"You're *finished* eating . . . and I don't think you're going to be hungry again until your delirium clears."

Garrett's stomach took that moment to react vocally, and Lila gave a sharp laugh. "Sounds like your stomach's delirious, too."

She turned on her heel as he growled after her. "I'll

be on my feet tomorrow. Then we'll see who has the upper hand."

Lila disappeared through the doorway as he called out deliberately, "Lila . . ."

Her step halted abruptly outside the doorway, and Garrett felt satisfaction soar. When it continued on moments later, he realized that satisfaction would do little to fill his empty stomach.

And he burned.

"What was dat? Dis Garrett calls *Lila?*"

Lila silently cursed as she placed the half-filled bowl on the kitchen table and averted her gaze from Aunt Helga's curious stare.

"I think he's a bit delirious."

"Ach! The fever comes back?"

"Just a little. I . . . I'll give him another powder and he'll be better."

Aunt Helga nodded, her jowls dancing as she looked approvingly into Lila's eyes. "You take goot care of der Garrett."

Lila's smile was weak. "No, I—"

"Ja, you do goot." Aunt Helga paused. "You take care of Luther der same way, and dat be goot, too."

Lila looked into Aunt Helga's sincere expression, the irony of the situation strong. This difficult woman was praising her—now, when she had just left a sick man hungry and helpless in the next room. Aunt Helga was offering her acceptance now, when she had never in her life felt *less* worthy.

Oh, damn. It was too much!

"Excuse me, Aunt Helga."

Lila brushed past the older woman and left the room, but not before she saw Aunt Helga's look of concern.

She closed the door of the bedroom she temporarily shared with the older woman just as Luther's step sounded in the room beyond. She heard their whispers through the closed door.

"What's wrong with Modesty?"

"Too much work. No sleep . . . and der Garrett is delirious."

"Delirious?"

"Modesty gives him powder."

"I'd better check and see."

Footsteps left and returned moments later. "He's sleeping. I felt his head. It's cool."

"Is goot nurse."

A silence lingered before Luther prompted, "You've changed your mind about Modesty, haven't you, Aunt Helga."

Lila could almost hear Aunt Helga shrug in the silence that followed before she finally responded. "She does not cook. She does not bake. She does not sew."

"But—"

"But she washes der clothes and is goot nurse. I cook. I bake. I sew. You do not worry."

"I never did, Aunt Helga."

"Is goot."

The sound of Aunt Helga's retreating footsteps ended the conversation, and Lila felt tears well. She didn't want Aunt Helga's approval, and she didn't want Luther to feel encouraged. She needed to get out of here, as soon as she could.

Between the devil and the deep blue sea . . .

The deep blue sea was Luther's eyes, filled with love, and the devil . . .

* * *

His boots echoing hollowly along the board walk, Jake Hobbs emerged from the Red Slipper Saloon and looked down Deer Trail's main street.

Starting down the walk, his gaze intent on the station house at the end of the street, Jake lifted his hat and wiped his arm across his sweaty forehead. The odor that permeated up from his armpit brought a grimace to his unshaven face. He needed a bath, a shave, and a change of clothes. But at least he was now sure that Harrison would recover.

A wry smile jerked at Hobbs's overgrown mustache. The hawk and the sparrow, huh?

Hobbs's smile faded. The only thing Doc didn't know was that the sparrow was really a brilliant peacock in disguise.

Pushing his way through the station-house doorway minutes later, Hobbs walked up to the desk and addressed the fellow seated there. "I'd like to send a wire. Can you do that for me, my friend?"

Drawing himself slowly to his feet, the fellow slapped a paper and pencil down in front of him. "I ain't your friend."

Hobbs tipped his hat with a twist of his lips. "Must've been mistaken."

Pencil in hand, Hobbs ignored the fellow's scowl and leaned over the sheet with deep concentration as he printed in awkward block letters far different from his usual educated script:

To JAMES MCPARLAND
16 MAIN STREET
DENVER, COLORADO
HAVE LOCATED MISSING SHIPMENT. WILL KEEP YOU INFORMED.

HOBBS

Hobbs slapped the pencil back down onto the counter. "Whew! I'm glad that's done. I ain't at my best when I'm writin'. How much will that cost me?"

The balding fellow mumbled a reply and Hobbs counted out the required coins. He was outside on the street moments later, the realization that he need return to the Knox ranch house before nightfall wearying him.

Hobbs scowled as he started back down the street toward his horse. Another night on the hard ground, watching and waiting, while Harrison played hawk and sparrow with the beautiful Lila Chesney. He had to admit that his curiosity was piqued after hearing that old doc talk. Knowing Harrison, he couldn't believe he'd come out of an encounter with anyone, not even Lila Chesney, with his tail feathers plucked.

That thought only momentarily amusing, Hobbs knew that something had to happen quickly. Forbes and his men were wild spenders. If he didn't miss his guess, they would be planning another robbery soon. They might even be planning it right now while he and his partner awaited Lila Chesney's next move.

Lila Chesney's beautiful face returned to mind, and the stiff lines of Hobbs's face momentarily softened. Forbes and his men were thieves and murderers. Too bad a beautiful young woman like her had to pick a man who was no good. He had the feeling she could've done better.

Dismissing that thought as he reached his horse, Hobbs mounted with a sigh and headed due west.

The sounds of clicking silverware and smacking lips filled the silence hanging uneasily over the dining-room table as Lila toyed with her food. Glancing up, she noted with surprise that all eyes were on her.

"Food no goot?"

Lila managed a weak smile. "No, it's fine, Aunt Helga. I'm not hungry, I guess."

Aunt Helga shook her head with vigorous disapproval. "Must eat."

Realizing the same sentiment was reflected on Luther and Max's faces as well, Lila forced her smile brighter. "I'm all right, really I am. It's just . . ."

It's just that I can't eat knowing that Garrett Harrison, bastard that he is, is lying in bed hungry because of me.

"It's just that you're worrying about that Garrett fella, ain't that right, Miss Modesty?" Max's eyes were filled with sympathy. "A sweet young thing like you shouldn't be troublin' yourself if that fella don't want to eat. He's plenty big. He can go for a while without eatin'. It won't hurt him."

"Doc Bennett said he has to eat." Lila was feeling worse with every word she spoke.

"Modesty . . ." The compassion in Luther's gaze deepened Lila's inner misery as he continued. "It was only yesterday that we thought he might not live. We can't expect the fellow to have an appetite so soon."

"But—" Suddenly unable to bear the solicitous talk another moment, Lila stood up abruptly. "Excuse me, please."

Lila had only gotten a few steps across the parlor before a touch on her arm stayed her. Enfolded in Luther's arms a moment later, she felt the warmth of him, the touch of his hand on her chin as he raised her face to his. She saw the love in his eyes as he kissed her briefly, then wrapped her more tightly in his embrace.

"I'm so sorry about all this, Modesty. It's been one

trial after another since you came here. I didn't intend it to be this way."

"It's not your fault." Lila burrowed closer. She had never known anyone as comforting as Luther, as genuine, as gentle, as compassionate . . .

"Oh, yes it is. You're not used to this kind of life. I knew that when I asked you to come out here. I should've been able to shield you from all of this. I wouldn't blame you if you packed your bag and walked out of here right now." Luther drew back a step, his voice dropping in timbre as he questioned softly. "You wouldn't do that, would you, Modesty?"

Her throat so thick at that moment that she could not speak, Modesty averted her gaze.

"Would you?"

"Oh, Luther . . ." Lila struggled to avoid a direct response. That damned Modesty had been a fool, running away when she could have had this good, handsome, appealing man for her own. She'd never find another man like him. He was one in a million.

"You can't answer that question, can you, because you're not certain if you want to stay."

"I want to stay . . ." And then at the sudden leap of hope in Luther's eyes, "I . . . I just don't know if I can."

"You mean you don't know if you can tolerate a life this difficult."

"No . . . yes, I mean—"

"But you haven't seen the best of life out here, darling. You've only seen the worst. You have to give it more time. Once this Garrett fella is off our hands and the branding is out of the way, I'll be free to spend more time with you. If you think you can manage a day on horseback, you can even ride out with me and Max then. If you see the land up close and really get the feel of it, I know you'd grow to love it just as much as I do."

Despite herself, Lila glanced toward the bedroom doorway behind them, and Luther frowned.

"I know. You're thinking it's easy for me to tell you about tomorrow while you still have to make it through today."

Lila could stand this good man's misplaced sympathy no longer. Taking a deep breath, she took a backward step for courage and locked his gaze with hers.

"Luther, I haven't been really truthful with you. The fact is that I'm not—"

"MODESTY . . ."

Lila's breath caught in her throat at the sound of a weak summons from the bedroom. Uncertainty caused her heart to race as the summons sounded again.

"MODESTY . . ."

Disengaging herself from Luther's embrace, Lila walked to the doorway. She stood there hesitantly, feeling Luther at her back as Garrett Harrison rasped hoarsely, "I'm thirsty."

Beside the bed in a moment, Lila filled a glass half full of water. Turning back to her patient, she saw Garrett Harrison's eyes were clear and watchful as she approached. She slipped her arm under his head and he drank obediently, but the look he raised to her face when he was through was dark with warning.

She was mesmerized by that silver gaze when she heard Luther's step behind her. She looked up to see him smiling down at the injured man.

"It looks like you're feeling better."

Garrett Harrison nodded, his expression stiff. "A bit."

"Do you feel like eating something? Aunt Helga has some pretty good food cooked up."

"That sounds good."

Lila turned toward the doorway with the realization that the situation was slipping out of her control. "I'll get some soup."

"I'll help you."

Behind her as she moved through the doorway, Luther drew her out of sight, his gaze searching hers. "He's feeling better already, darling. He'll probably be off your hands in a few days. Do you think you could try sticking it out?" At her hesitation, Luther whispered, "Please . . ."

"Oh, Luther . . ." Lila could not refuse him. "Of course I'll try."

Unprepared as Luther drew her abruptly into his arms, Lila was equally unready for the passion in his kiss. Her heartbeat rose to thunder as she was crushed against the hard length of him, as his hands caressed her seekingly and his hungry mouth devoured hers. Her arms were wrapped tightly around his neck and she was lost in the comforting strength of him when a sound from the dining room snapped them apart the moment before Aunt Helga stepped into sight.

Glancing between them, Aunt Helga shook her head in self-disgust. "Ach . . . I belong in kitchen."

Luther gave a short laugh. "That's all right, Aunt Helga." The arm he slipped around Lila had a proprietary feel as he urged her along with him toward the dining room. "Modesty's patient is feeling better. He'd like something to eat."

"Goot. He eat. Modesty eat."

Lila was walking back toward the bedroom minutes later, a plate in her hand, wondering . . .

"That was a touchin' scene . . ." Garrett's whispered comment stopped Lila in her tracks as she walked through the bedroom doorway, but Garrett did not heed her hesitation as he continued with unconcealed scorn. "What did you think you were doin' out there with Knox?"

Rigid, Lila hissed in response, "Let's get something straight, once and for all. What I was doing out there or anywhere else is none of your business."

"You were going to tell Knox about me when I interrupted you, weren't you! Do you really think I'd let you go on with your little masquerade if you did? You couldn't be that much of a fool!"

Lila sneered with contempt as she came closer to the bed and placed the plate on the nearby night table. "I told you, your secret's safe with me as long as you behave yourself."

"It didn't sound that way a few minutes ago."

"I don't care what it sounded like."

"You'd better start to care, because I'm the only person in this house you can count on right now, whether you realize it or not."

"You?" Lila gasped, then laughed. "You're telling me I can count on you? I really would be a fool if I believed that!"

Garrett took a steadying breath. He felt weaker than he cared to reveal, but he hadn't needed to see the scene being played out just beyond his bedroom door a short time earlier to know that Lila had been in Knox's arms. She had obviously felt she had the besotted fool wrapped around her finger. He had sensed that he needed to act quickly or he would lose control of the situation. He couldn't let that happen. He was too close to getting Bart Forbes to lose him now.

Summoning all his strength, Garrett boosted himself up a few inches in bed and affixed Lila's gaze with his. He saw her eyes narrow expectantly as he rasped,

"You can count on me, all right . . . for one good reason. It's to my advantage to protect you if you're protectin' me in return. You'd be a damned fool if you thought you could tell Knox about yourself without havin' him check out your story. That means he'd have to talk to the sheriff about you."

"Luther wouldn't do that."

"Oh, wouldn't he?" It was Garrett's turn to sneer. "Why wouldn't he? You've been lyin' to him from the beginnin', haven't you? You came here misrepresentin' yourself as someone else. You've been pretendin' to care for him. You've even been pretendin' to consider marryin' him. Do you really think he wouldn't be angry to have been played for a fool? What makes you think he'd be able to believe your confession . . . or even *want* to believe you when he finds out you're not the woman he thinks you are, and that you're bein' chased by a Pinkerton agent, too?"

"Because . . ." Lila raised her chin. "Because he cares for me."

Garrett's short laugh cut like a knife. "That's the biggest joke of all. He doesn't even *know* you! He's in love, all right. That's easy enough to see by the way he looks at you. But you seem to forget, he isn't seein' you. He's seein' the person you're pretendin' to be—Modesty, a plain, shy woman who's sincere and innocent. Lila Chesney couldn't be any further from that person if she were on the other side of the world."

Lila's jaw tightened. "You *are* a bastard."

"Yeah," Garrett nodded his pounding head. "But I'm right."

"No, you aren't."

"Yes, I am." Garrett refused to release Lila's gaze as he concluded, "But even if there's a possibility that I'm not, can you afford to take the chance?"

His weakness getting the best of him, Garrett closed his eyes momentarily, missing Lila's revealing blink and the spasmodic reflex in her throat. His strength rapidly fading, he opened his eyes to Lila's rigid stance and growled, "I'm tired of talkin'. Just do what pleases you, but I don't want to hear you cryin' when the sheriff shows up to take us both away."

Lila's lips twisted. "I'm not the weepy type."

"Oh, yeah . . ." Garrett's eyes were silver ice. "I know what type you are."

"You bastard . . ." Lila took an aggressive step forward. "For two cents I'd—"

"What would Luther say then?"

"Let's settle this once and for all!" Surprising him with the venom in her tone, Lila snatched up the cloth on the night table and spread it across his chest. She then jerked the nearby chair closer to the bed and sat down. Picking up the plate of soup, she leaned closer. "You're not telling me what to do. Not now . . . not ever. It's in my best interest to protect you right now, so I'll do it, but as soon as you're well, I expect you to get out of that bed and onto your horse, and I expect you to ride out of here without looking back. Is that understood?"

Garrett forced a smile. "I told you before. I'll leave this house when I'm good and ready."

"You'll leave when I tell you to."

"Or you'll do what?"

Lila paused, her dark-eyed gaze fixed on his. "I'll do whatever I have to do."

Holding that gaze, feeling the heated intensity that came from deep inside the beautiful woman so close to him, Garrett had no doubt she would. But he also knew that he would do whatever he had to do to get Bart Forbes. If that meant taking this surprising, stirring woman down with Forbes, he would do that, too . . . any way he could.

"You're wasting your time with Knox, you know." Garrett allowed his gaze to roam the fragile planes of Lila's face. Lingering on her mouth for long moments, he felt the stirring inside him deepen. His voice dropped a notch lower.

"Knox could never be man enough for you. I can do more for you than he can."

Garrett sensed the shock his words raised in the woman sitting beside him. His admiration for her grew, despite himself, as she calmly dipped the spoon into the bowl and guided it to his lips. His gaze did not leave hers as he accepted it and the next few spoonfuls that followed.

Finally responding to his comment, the concise phrase she used both explicit and familiar, Lila spoke in a voice that was steady and distinctly clear.

"Not . . . a . . . chance."

The shadows of night had fallen across his room as Garrett awakened, his head throbbing and his arm taking up its cadence. Uncertain exactly what had disturbed his sleep, he suddenly recalled the face that had been floating in and out of his dreams. He frowned at the recollection and Lila Chesney's image frowned in return.

His exchange with Lila Chesney earlier had not ended well, and he was annoyed with his poor handling of the situation. The reason behind his constant tormenting of the woman when he should be trying to gain her confidence was a complete mystery to him.

Oh, no, it wasn't . . .

Garrett's discomfort increased. The mental picture he

had gotten of Lila in Knox's arms as they had stood just beyond his doorway had somehow been more than he had been able to tolerate. He had silently cursed Lila for the woman she was—a woman who would go to any lengths to protect a worthless criminal who was her lover, even so far as playing with another man's emotions.

Garrett's anxiety deepened. He had meant every word when he had said that Knox could never be man enough for a woman like Lila Chesney. Lila needed a man who wasn't afraid to treat her the way she treated others . . . someone who would use her as she used others . . . someone who would wipe that sneer off her beautiful face and replace it with a smile by the sheer force of his loving . . . someone who would make her toe the line and make her love doing it. Knox could never be that man.

Perhaps Lila Chesney's unknown lover was that man.

No, Garrett somehow knew he wasn't.

Who was?

Who else?

No!

Yes!

Garrett gave a harsh laugh. He *was* delirious. He had been suffering that same delirium when he had told Lila Chesney he could do more for her than Knox. Lila Chesney already had two men. She didn't need a third.

And he didn't need her. What he did need was to get Bart Forbes.

A familiar hatred washed over Garrett, reminding him that while he lay helpless, the deeds of that terrible day in Lawrence, Kansas, still lay unavenged. Forbes was still free to roam, rob, and kill as was his desire. How many other innocent lives would Forbes take before his murderous career was brought to an end?

Where was that conscienceless killer now? What was he doing? Did he have fresh blood on his hands or was he merely in the planning stages of shedding more? Was Forbes asleep now, or was he awake, talking to his men, saying . . .

"Do you have that straight now?" Bart Forbes swallowed the last of his coffee, then wiped his arm across his mouth, his narrowed gaze never leaving the men sitting across the fire. Agitated by their silence, he snapped, "Well, do you?"

The first to respond, Will Eaton shrugged his broad, beefy shoulders. Too long a layoff between jobs and too much money in Eaton's pocket had added a solid ring of poundage around his waist, and Forbes didn't like it. They had both been younger, much younger, when they had ridden with Quantrill, but he remembered Eaton had drawn his admiration for being one of the fastest, coolest men among them. Eaton was no longer one of the fastest of his men, but he was still one of the coolest as he demonstrated by meeting Forbes's gaze with his own.

"We understand, all right. You've gone over every angle of the plan five times already. I don't know about the rest of the boys, but I'm about ready for some sleep."

"We'll get some sleep when I'm satisfied everybody knows their part." Forbes surveyed his men more closely. Thin and long limbed, Picket nodded, his slitted eyes appearing ready to close. Ricks scratched his matted hair, then turned to spit a wad of tobacco out onto the ground behind him. He wiped the excess spittle from his beard with the back of his arm before turning dutifully forward again.

Forbes hesitated in his assessment, his eyes narrowing. Then there was Chesney. . . . Clear-eyed, clean-shaven, and intent, Chesney watched him closely. Somehow uncomfortable with the intensity of that gaze, he addressed the youngest member of his gang directly.

"You look like you're the only fella around here that ain't half asleep, Chesney. How about tellin' these fellas how we're goin' to hit that train this time."

"Me?" Chesney pulled his lean frame up an inch or two in deference to the direct question.

"That's what I said."

Chesney shrugged. "That's all right with me. It goes this way. You, Eaton, Picket, and Ricks are going to be waiting for the train at the foot of Swanson's Hill. When it slows down to make the grade, you're going to climb onto the hind end of it and make your way across the top until you get the drop on the engineer and fireman. You're going to get the engineer to stop the train, and Ricks will uncouple the rest of the cars, leaving only the express car attached while Picket keeps an eye out for trouble. Then you're going to get the engineer to take you all a mile or so up the track. I'll be waiting there with the extra horses and the powder to blast the express car open if we need to. We'll take what we want and leave everything else behind us. We'll ride back to the hideout, wait there a couple of days until it's safe to split up the money, and go our separate ways until next time."

Forbes nodded. "Did you get that, boys?"

"Yeah, yeah."

The men's weary chorus turned Forbes back to Chesney.

"You're a clever fella, you know that, Chesney?"

Chesney smiled. "Yeah, I know it."

Forbes felt his gun hand itch as he smiled thinly in return. "I like clever fellas. You know that, too?"

Chesney's gaze grew cautious. "Yeah, I suppose."

"I like 'em just as long as they don't think they're too clever to take orders, 'cause if they get too smart, they're out . . . one way or another. You know what I'm sayin', Chesney?"

"I know." Chesney smiled again . . . one of his big, wide grins, but Forbes saw through it as Chesney continued. "You don't have anything to worry about there. I'm too smart to get *that* smart. I like things just the way they are right now." He gave a short laugh. "Besides, I've seen you draw, remember?"

"That's right, you have at that." Suddenly intensely serious, Forbes ordered, "All right, let's get some sleep. We'll be headin' for Denver tomorrow."

Lying down, Forbes closed his eyes and waited for the sounds of camp to still. Opening them again when silence reigned, he stared across the fire to the spot where Chesney lay. The young fella's chest was rising and falling in steady breaths. He was already asleep.

Forbes stared at Chesney a few moments longer. There was something about Chesney that made him uneasy . . . a sixth sense that told him the fella was trouble. Maybe it was the feelin' that he was lookin' back at himself seventeen years ago when he first met up with Bill Quantrill. Or maybe it was something else . . .

Forbes shook his head and forced his eyes closed. Hell, maybe he was just getting old.

And maybe he wasn't.

The light of a full, silver moon shone through the bedroom window as Lila tried to sleep. Shadows played against the far walls, their shapes ever-changing as a brisk night breeze whispered through the trees with a gentle, undulating rhythm that clashed harshly with

Aunt Helga's even, grating snore. Consistent, the abrasive sound had counted out wakeful minutes that had stretched into hours as Lila's mind had whirled with confusion.

What *had* she intended saying to Luther in the moment before Garrett Harrison had interrupted? Now, a distance from the emotion and guilt of the moment, she could not quite believe she had intended to reveal her true identity and throw herself on Luther's mercy.

Damn that Garrett Harrison! In his offensive, revolting way, he had been partially correct. He had saved her from making a mistake she was certain to have regretted. As sick as he was, Harrison had assessed the situation well enough to see as clearly as she that Luther was truly in love . . . with Modesty Parkins. But Harrison had been dead wrong in another way. Luther not man enough for her? Lila gave a harsh laugh. If anyone wasn't man enough for her, it was Garrett Harrison!

I can do more for you than he can . . .

Lila shuddered as a chill ran down her spine. She had learned the hard way, a long time ago, to stay away from men as dangerous as Garrett Harrison. It was a lesson she could not afford to forget.

I can do more for you than he can . . .

No . . . never.

She shuddered again.

Not a chance!

Nine

Lila awakened abruptly from a fitful night's sleep. A glance toward Aunt Helga's bed revealed the older woman had already arisen although dawn had barely creased the morning sky. Driven by a second sense, she donned the drab grey cotton dress she alternated with Modesty's other drab grey cotton, twisted her hair into a quick knot, and walked swiftly down the hallway to Garrett Harrison's room.

She paused in the doorway. Her second sense had not been wrong.

Anger flaring, she snapped, "What do you think you're doing!"

Clothed only in long-underwear bottoms, Garrett Harrison was sitting on the edge of the bed. His bare chest was heaving and wet with sweat as he struggled for the strength to stand.

Lila rushed to his bedside. Growing more furious by the minute as he pointedly ignored her, she hissed, "Don't be a fool! Doc Bennett said—"

"I know what he said!" Unembarrassed by his semi-nakedness, his face pale beneath the dark stubble covering his cheeks, Garrett shot her a deadly glance. "I'm gettin' up."

"You have a concussion, not to mention your arm. It's still swollen! The poison—"

"Don't tell me about snakebite. I've been bitten before."

"I don't care how many times you've been bitten." Lila gritted her teeth. "Lie back down in that bed . . . now . . . or I'll knock you down, damn it!"

Garrett's grey eyes, sharp shards of ice, met hers in frigid warning. "Don't try it."

"You know I will if you don't—"

"What's the matter, Modesty?"

Turning at the sound of Luther's voice, Lila released a tense breath. Clean-shaven, his hair wet and freshly combed, Luther was an oasis of unfailing calm in the icy storm that was Garrett Harrison. She had never been happier to see him.

"This fool thinks he's going to get up and walk!"

Luther switched his attention to Garrett, his even tone brooking no argument. "You won't be getting up for another day or so. Doc Bennett left strict instructions, and even if he hadn't, it should be pretty plain to you by now that you're too weak to get up."

"I'll make it."

"No, you won't." Closing the distance to the bed in a few easy steps, Luther pressed the bigger man back against the pillow with the flat of his hand. It was incredibly easy, and Lila realized it would not have been as difficult as she had anticipated to follow her threat through. Garrett Harrison's bravado had been all bluff. He was as weak as a kitten.

As if in response to her thoughts, Garrett rasped, "Don't fool yourself into thinkin' I'm back in this bed to stay. I've had enough of it. I'll be on my feet today, one way or another."

"What's your hurry?" Pulling the coverlet back up

to Garrett's waist, Luther suddenly smiled. "Look, let's start all over again. It occurs to me that you've been in my house for three days now, and we haven't yet been formally introduced." Luther extended his hand. "My name's Luther Knox. My friends call me Luther. I know your name is Garrett."

Lila watched with considerable surprise as Garrett accepted Luther's hand and shook it briefly.

"Garrett Harrison . . . from Kansas City." Lila listened as he continued tightly. "I thought I'd try my luck out here for a while, but it looks like I ran out of luck before I got started."

"You're on the Bar WK, in case Modesty hasn't already told you. I own this spread. Modesty's visiting for a while. I'm hoping she'll decide to stay. The other two people in this house are Aunt Helga and Max." Luther shrugged. "You won't be seeing her until you're back on your feet and you've recuperated from your injuries. She 'don't like der schnakes.' "

Luther grinned at that, and Lila felt the warmth of his grin spread through her. Looking back at Garrett Harrison, she saw his expression had not changed. Her withering glance went totally ignored as Luther continued.

"The fourth person here is Max, my hired hand. I don't know how much you recall, but Modesty and I found you on the road and brought you back here. For a while we thought you weren't going to make it." Luther's expression suddenly sobered. "I'm telling you all of this because I want you to know where you stand in this house. All of us here had a hand in getting you to this point of good health, and your care is up to us. Max and I are busy with branding and, until we're done, Modesty's going to be the person you'll be seeing the most of here. So, I'd like you to remember something. You're sick and you don't really know what's good for you right now. We do, and we're not going to let you hurt yourself. But neither am I going to let you give Modesty a difficult time." Luther held Garrett firmly in his gaze. "So, you'll be staying in bed for another day, at least. If you feel better tomorrow, I'll help you up. Do we understand each other?"

Lila held her breath as she glanced between the two men. It was foolish, she knew. Luther was strong and in perfect health, and her reluctant patient was as weak as a child, but she still—

"Yeah, we understand each other."

Lila released her breath as Luther continued. "Is there anybody you want us to get in touch with for you . . . anybody who's expecting you somewhere?"

"No."

Luther slid his arm around Lila's shoulders and drew her against his side. "Well, I don't know if you realize it or not, but you're a lucky man, Garrett. Not only did you cheat death a few days ago, but you ended up in Modesty's care. That's almost worth the pain of it all."

Lila sensed a hidden meaning in Garrett Harrison's unexpected response. "Yes, I suppose it is."

Appearing pleased, Luther nodded, then released Lila and addressed her directly, "Why don't you go into the kitchen and see if Aunt Helga has breakfast ready for our friend here, while I see if there's anything I can do for him now."

"But I can take care of him."

Luther hesitated. "I think it would be better if *I* took care of some things for him."

"O-oh!"

Luther's meaning abruptly clear, Lila took a quick step backward. She turned toward the doorway and was a few steps beyond when she heard Luther say, "As you can probably tell, Modesty's very inexperienced in some ways. I don't want her to be embarrassed, so if you need—"

Modesty's very inexperienced in some ways . . .

Lila continued on toward the kitchen. The extent of her deception was never clearer to her than at that moment when she knew Garrett Harrison was inwardly laughing in Luther's face.

Disliking herself and despising Garrett Harrison for his contribution to her discomfort, Lila raised her chin. Garrett Harrison could laugh all he wanted now, but she'd be damned before she'd let him get the last laugh on either Luther or her.

Stepping into the kitchen, Lila met the silent question in Aunt Helga's gaze with a brief reply. "Our patient's better today—almost too feisty, but Luther took care of it."

"Ja, Luther is strong man . . . goot man." Aunt Helga looked closer. "Something wrong? Ach, is too much work taking care of dis man. I tell Luther—"

"No, Aunt Helga, I'm fine."

A sound at the back door turned both women toward Max as he appeared in the doorway. His whiskered smile was almost a leer.

"Good mornin', ladies!" Max's leer deepened as he looked directly at Aunt Helga. "That ain't Johnnycakes I smell cookin', is it, Helga?"

Aunt Helga nodded stiffly. *"Ja,* is Johnnycakes."

Max sighed. "I ain't had Johnnycakes in so long, my tongue almost forgets what they tastes like."

"Today it remember." Aunt Helga's gaze dropped to Max's feet, her expression suddenly souring. "You don't walk on *mein* floor like dat! You scrape!"

Max disappeared obediently and Aunt Helga turned

back to Lila, her scrutiny acute. "I tell Luther dis man too much work for little woman like you."

"No, I'm fine . . . just hungry, that's all."

"Hungry? *Ja?*" Helga's face lit up like a candle as she whipped the cloth off a mountainous pile of Johnnycakes on the stove. "You get Luther. We eat."

Grateful to escape Aunt Helga's observant eye, Lila hurried to obey. Hesitating outside the bedroom doorway, Lila called, "Is it all right . . . I mean, may I come in?"

"Of course." At the doorway in a moment, Luther drew her inside. "Garrett and I had a good talk. Everything's going to be fine."

Lila looked at Garrett. His expression was blank.

"Aunt Helga has breakfast ready."

"Fine, let's eat."

"You go ahead, Luther. I want to fix Garrett's bed first."

Luther nodded and left the room. At Garrett's bedside the moment Luther was out of hearing, Lila looked into the icy grey eyes returning her gaze.

"What did Luther mean, you had a good talk?"

"I'll tell you what he meant. He talked and I listened . . . and as soon as he's out of the house, I'm gettin' up."

"Over my dead body."

Garrett Harrison's gaze captured hers. "I wouldn't like that. I have better plans for us."

"If you do, you're more of a fool than I thought you were."

Garrett paused in response, his voice dropping to a soft purr. "No, Lila darlin', I'm not a fool."

Garrett's intimate tone startled Lila. It held her strangely immobile as he took her hand, then raised it to his lips. His mouth was warm against her palm the moment before he nudged the delicate hollow with his tongue.

Lila snatched back her hand as if she had been stung. Her face flamed.

Forcing up her chin, Lila turned toward the doorway without comment. She left the room, the sound of Garrett's soft laughter lingering behind her.

"Luther . . ."

Luther turned from his saddlehorse to see Modesty walking across the yard toward him. The soft morning sunlight glowed on the coppery silk of her bound hair, and the intense emotion that was never far from the surface in Modesty's presence flamed to life inside him. He longed to see that shimmering mass freed as he had seen it briefly only once before. He wanted to feel its softness streaming through his fingers, to wrap his hands in it, and bind her to him with its length. He hungered to hold her close, so close to him that she would never want him to let her go. He wanted . . .

A closer look at Modesty, and Luther's anxieties rose. She had been unnaturally silent at the breakfast table after returning from Harrison's room. As she neared, his fears were confirmed.

"What's wrong, Modesty?"

Modesty hesitated in response. "I . . . you said you'd take me into town for a visit. I'd like to go soon, Luther."

"Why, darling? What happened to upset you?" Luther felt her resistance to the arm he slid around her waist as he attempted to draw her closer.

"Nothing. It's just that . . . well, I'd like to post that letter."

"Oh." Barely subduing a flash of jealousy, Luther

prompted, "There *is* someone special back home, then . . . someone you didn't tell me about."

"No." Modesty's expression pleaded understanding. "I wouldn't have done that to you. I mean . . ." Her eyes suddenly filled. "I don't really know what I mean. I just want to send a letter to a friend . . . a dear friend who's always been like family to me. It would console me to write the letter and to know it's off in the mail. I guess I'm more homesick than I expected to be out here." Modesty took his hand. "I hope you're not too disappointed in me, Luther."

"Disappointed?" Luther overrode her minimal protest as he drew her into his arms. "How could anyone be disappointed in you? If I could, I'd give you the world, but the truth is, I can't even promise you that visit to town until the end of the week. Max put a lot of time into getting the calves ready for branding. I know it sounds unreasonable for me to put branding before your convenience, darling, but all our work will be wasted if we don't get the job finished quickly. I'll be getting new bulls in a few weeks, and we still haven't finished preparing for—"

"You don't need to explain." Modesty averted her gaze. "It's all right."

Modesty attempted to draw back, but Luther pressed. "No, I do have to explain, and someday I'll explain everything more completely. I'll tell you all the things I'm trying to accomplish here, like improving my stock with different breeding procedures, and about my plans for fencing off special areas so we can accomplish it. I have so many things that I want to share with you, but the truth is that all I can think about right now is how much I love you and want you to love me. I—"

Halting abruptly, Luther was suddenly ashamed. "No, I'm not being completely honest with you." At Modesty's confused expression, Luther continued softly. "Everything I just said about the branding and my plans for the ranch is true, but I wasn't thinking about any of that when you said you wanted to go to town to mail a letter. All I was thinking about was that you were missing someone you left behind and you wanted to make arrangements to leave."

"No, it's not like that." Modesty's expression was stricken. Luther's guilt expanded as she continued softly. "I . . . I just want to post a letter, that's all."

Luther made an abrupt decision. "Have you written the letter yet?"

"No."

He forced a smile. "Write it, then. I'll take you into town as soon as I can straighten out a few things with Max."

"Luther, I . . ." Modesty hesitated, then whispered, "Thank you."

"Don't thank me, darling. But while you're writing that letter, I want you to remember this."

Drawing her into his arms, Luther guided her mouth to his. His fingers slipped into the warm silk of her hair as he held her fast, kissing her until her lips separated under his, until the sweetness of her mouth was his to taste and probe and consume. Modesty slid her arms around his neck, and Luther's heart leaped to a wild pounding. Tearing his mouth from hers, he trailed heated kisses across the smooth line of her jaw to the fragile shell of her ear, whispering ragged words of love as he searched the delicate hollows with his tongue. He nibbled at the pink lobe, suckled it greedily, the sweet intimacy raising his hunger for more. His mouth slipped lower, touching the fluttering pulse in Modesty's throat. It was pounding wildly, as wildly as his own heart as he met with the frustration of the lace-trimmed neckline at the base of her throat. He was freeing the small buttons there with shaking fingers, his anticipation soaring, when he suddenly froze in realization. They were standing in the open, in full view of the house . . .

Damn!

Taking a firm hold on his racing emotions, Luther stepped back. He saw the surprise in Modesty's eyes as he released her, then an abrupt flash of realization the moment before the rise of grateful tears.

His voice gruff, Luther instructed softly, "Go back into the house and write that letter, darling. We're going into town and we're going to forget this ranch for today. It'll be just you and me, and we'll talk . . ."

"Luther, I—"

"Don't worry about Harrison. Max will take care of him while we're gone. And don't take too long with that letter. I'm suddenly looking forward to this trip to town as much as you are."

Modesty's eyes brimmed. "I'll hurry."

Modesty started back toward the house at a pace just short of a run. Luther followed her slender form with his gaze, his sense of loss overwhelming when she disappeared from view.

Realization was sharp and swift. He loved Modesty . . . really loved her. He would do anything he had to do to keep her.

Luther's jaw slowly hardened. Anything . . .

The morning sun was hot on his head as Billy rode at a comfortable pace across the low, grassy hills with Picket at his side. Picket and he had spoken little since starting out, and he knew part of the reason was that Picket wasn't particularly pleased that Forbes had sent him along to help with the horses. Billy felt a familiar tug of annoyance. The pecking order had been firmly established, and he was at the bottom of it. Picket resented sharing that spot with him.

Billy glanced toward Picket in guarded assessment. Picket's gangling form absorbed the jolt of the uneven terrain with the skill of a natural rider, but Billy knew that other, less admirable traits were inborn in this deceptively quiet fellow as well. Picket was a crack shot who did not hesitate to use his gun. He was slow to anger, but not above any dirty trick in the book when in a fight . . . and he was a fellow who never gave up a grudge. He had seen the man pursue a dancehall girl who had mocked him through three different towns, making her life a misery until she had satisfied him by begging his forgiveness. He had bragged about other ways he had made her satisfy him, too, and he had laughed the loudest when he had related how he had humiliated her by throwing her out into the street afterward. Billy remembered most clearly, however, the look in Picket's eyes when he had said he owned that woman now, that he could have her anytime he wanted her.

But, in truth, it wasn't Picket's resentment that disturbed him. The look in Forbes's eyes as they parted had confused him almost as much as Forbes's unexpected animosity toward him. Lifting his hat from his head, Billy rubbed his hand against his perspired scalp, then jammed his hat back in place at the thought of the man's parting warning.

"Make sure you get them horses without any trouble, smart fella. And make sure you find someplace to hide them until we need them. We're going to be dependin' on them, and I tell you this, smart fella. If there's a one of us who don't make it because of them horses, you ain't goin' to make it, either."

Billy didn't like threats, especially when he was on the receiving end of them . . . and especially when he knew the person issuing them wouldn't hesitate to carry them through. Forbes had something stuck in his craw. The situation puzzled him . . . put him on edge. He had been with the gang for over a year. He hadn't given Forbes's increasing scrutiny of him much thought until it had erupted in the bullet that nicked the tip of his boot, but he had given it a lot of thought since. Whatever Forbes was thinking, it wasn't good and he knew there was only one way to clear the air. He'd talk to the man and he'd set things straight as soon as this job was over. But until then, he'd bide his time and make sure there weren't any slipups.

Billy's frown darkened as tension prickled up his spine. Forbes wasn't his only problem. He still didn't know where Lila was, and too much time was passing for him to be comfortable with the thought. Then there was Eva. He was worried about her, and he didn't like worrying. Neither did he like the subtle way thoughts of Eva had begun intruding into every aspect of his life. He didn't like it at all.

"How come you ain't smilin', Chesney?" Picket's unexpected interruption of his thoughts snapped Billy's head toward him as Picket gave a short laugh. "Well, hell, I guess I wouldn't be smilin', either, if I had Forbes on my tail like he is on yours. You sure ticked him off showin' up late like you did. I'd watch myself from now on if I was you. Forbes's goin' to be waitin' for you to make a mistake and then he's goin' to—"

"Forbes isn't going to do anything, because I'm not going to let him."

"Well, now . . ." Picket's thin face creased in a broken-toothed smirk. "Brave talk when Forbes ain't around to hear it."

Billy forced a smile he did not feel. He continued in a congenial voice that he did not feel as well. "You got me wrong, Picket. Forbes is the boss and I'm happy to let it stay that way. He's the man with the experience, and I've got a lot to learn."

"Only if you live to learn it."

Billy's smile slipped, momentarily revealing the steel behind it. "I'll live. Don't you worry about it."

Bringing an abrupt end to their conversation, Billy glanced up to assess the position of the sun in the cloudless sky overhead. It was a few hours before mid-day. With any kind of luck, Buck Howell and his hired man, Luis, would be out riding the fences and he would be able to get the horses without any problem. If not, he would be forced to wait until nightfall. In any case, he knew that getting the horses wouldn't be as great a challenge as managing to keep them. It hadn't taken him long to read in the lines of that old rancher's face a determination and skill that would serve him well when it came to tracking his horses down.

Billy's boyish countenance hardened. But he'd get those horses, and he'd keep them . . . one way or another.

The sound of a baby's wail broke the silence of the cabin, and Eva turned toward it. Smiling for the first time since she had awakened that morning and realized she was alone again, she approached the railed bed Billy had made for the babe. It had been laboriously constructed with little expertise, but in it her beautiful daughter was able to pull herself to her feet as she smiled and gurgled for attention, and in it she was safe while Eva tended chores outside the cabin. It had been a labor of love . . . Billy's love for her that went expressed in so many ways except in words.

Her round blue eyes sparkling, Christina reached out for her as she approached, and Eva marveled anew at her child's beauty. A supreme sadness overwhelmed her as Olaf's image briefly returned. She mourned her husband's loss in her heart, despite the intimate part Billy had come to play in her life. It had been Olaf who had given her a home when she had been wandering, food for her body and for her soul with his generosity, and respect when she had believed it was beyond her. But most precious of all, he had given her Christina.

Lifting her child into her arms, Eva held her close, chanting a soft, nameless song that came from the shadows of her childhood, from the lips of a mother she barely remembered. The strains of that song had held a soothing magic for her when the warmth of her mother's arms was gone. It had often worked the same magic for Christina, but she was well aware as her daughter began a determined squirming that the beloved chanting was no substitute for dry linens and a full stomach.

A bottle readied moments later, Eva sat in a nearby chair to rock her child as the babe drank her bottle greedily. A familiar sadness overwhelmed her. Her own poor physical condition after Christina's birth had left her unable to nourish her child from her own body. Christina had barely survived, but her resulting guilt had not been the worst of it. Both she and her child fully recuperated a month later, Eva had found her inability to nurse the child used as a weapon against her with the accusation that the babe was not really hers.

Recalling her headlong flight during the darkness of night as the result of that claim and her frightened wandering until the day she had looked up to see Billy watching her in Walker's store, Eva felt her throat thicken. She stroked her child's smooth, light-skinned cheek. Eyes as blue as the sky . . . hair as bright as gold, Christina would be a beautiful young woman one day, for whom she had great plans.

Christina suckled noisily as Eva recounted her dreams. Christina would go to a real school as her mother never had. She would learn to read books, and she would learn to write in a beautiful, flowery hand unlike the simple block letters her mother was able to scrawl. She would wear proper clothes. She would grow up to be a lady and she would meet a handsome young man who would marry her and give her a fine life where she would never be criticized for the mixed blood that ran in her veins.

Eva's daydreams halted abruptly. Such fine dreams for a woman to dream for her child when she was still without the certainty of what the next day would bring, and without a man who would say he loved her.

Oh, Billy . . .

Tears falling freely, Eva indulged the image of Billy that appeared before her eyes. In her heart she knew something was wrong. The secrecy . . . the time that passed without explanation before Billy returned to her. Then there was this other woman who "was no threat to her" . . .

Realizing she was as powerless against this unknown woman as she was against the tenderness of Billy's touch, the magic of his smile, and the wonder of his loving, Eva attempted to strike the thought from her mind. She knew she would wait a lifetime with the thought that Billy would someday walk back through that door and take her again into his arms.

Christina moved restlessly, snapping Eva from her wandering thoughts as she drained the bottle dry. The knowledge that her babe had consumed the last of the milk she had stored in the icy creek sent a familiar apprehension down her spine. Despite Billy's warnings, she would have to make another trip to the mining camp below to buy milk from old lady Greer.

All trace of softness left Eva's gaze. Down there she would face the censure and uncertainty anew, and she would relearn a difficult lesson that did not grow easier with time. But as so many of her mother's people before her, she would face that enemy bravely, in stoic silence. She would grow stronger, and she would become prepared for the day when she feared . . . *when she knew* . . . Billy would not come back.

Her hand trembling, Lila folded the hastily scribbled note and slipped it into an envelope. She sealed it carefully and addressed it, raising her head from the task for the first time since she had left Luther in the yard and had come into the bedroom. The rattle of the wagon echoed through the open window, and Lila felt her heart begin a new pounding.

Lila clutched the letter tightly. Her message to Billy had been brief, almost curt. She had told him where she was, that he was in danger, and that she needed to hear from him as soon as possible. She knew Billy would feel the coldness she hoped to convey.

That thought giving her less consolation than she had hoped, Lila sat back and rubbed an anxious hand across her forehead. She knew full well why she was suddenly so anxious to put an end to her present situation. The touch of Garrett Harrison's lips against her palm and the darting pressure of his tongue against the moist hollow was suddenly as vivid as it had been earlier, and she gasped aloud.

Lila stood up, her heart pounding. What was wrong with her? She was no innocent, as Garrett Harrison did not hesitate to remind her. She had known all types of men, and except for a single instance when she had been outmatched by a man more experienced than the girl of seventeen she had then been, she had emerged unscathed. Why then, when she had just left Luther's arms and the incredible sweetness of his loving, could she not strike from her mind the touch of an abominable man who was no more than a liar and a thief?

The hypocrisy of her thoughts struck Lila sharply. Garrett Harrison a liar and a thief? Was she any better than he, living on Luther's hospitality, deceiving him, and taking advantage of his goodness and misguided love for her? She became more like the man she despised with each day she spent at the Bar WK, but that was not the worst of it.

Lila unwittingly rubbed her palm where the touch of Garrett Harrison's lips still burned. She remembered the tremor that had shot up her spine as his warm tongue had flicked against her skin. His light-eyed gaze had held hers and she had been shocked into sudden panic at the abrupt realization that, at that moment, she would have been incapable of denying him.

Lila briefly closed her eyes. Somehow . . . some way, with each hour that passed, she became more drawn to Garrett Harrison. Bastard that he was, he sensed her attraction, and as physically weak as he was, he was still capable and despicable enough to take full advantage of that attraction.

Suddenly furious, Lila walked stiffly to the washstand. She stared at her reflection for a long, silent moment. The former Lila Chesney was gone, almost without a trace. Devoid of paint, her face was pale, with little of the beauty Luther claimed to see. Her crowning glory confined in a neat bun and the appealing curves that turned men's heads disguised by the dull rag she wore, her reflection held no more appeal than a colorless prairie mouse, whose actions she had been emulating too closely for comfort with her panic of the past few hours.

Well, she had had enough of it!

Carefully pouring water into the bowl, Lila worked up a lather with the fragrant soap and washed her face fastidiously. She then dried her face and smoothed back her hair before slipping the hated eyeglasses into place and putting on Modesty's simple grey bonnet. She tied it under her chin, silently noting that she could not look any less like Lila Chesney if she tried. Snatching up her reticule, Lila slipped the letter inside, along with the envelope that had previously been addressed, and turned toward the door.

She had taken only two steps into the parlor when she heard a familiar call from the bedroom a few feet away.

"MODESTY . . ."

Lila's determined step froze.

"MODESTY . . ."

When she refused to respond, she heard an exasperated rasp. "I know you're there. Damn it, *Lila . . .*"

Lila stepped into the doorway, her expression tight. "What do you want?"

Garrett Harrison's eyes narrowed as they assessed her attire. "Where're you goin'?"

Lila returned his stare. "To town . . . to see the sheriff."

"You're lyin'!"

"You can't be sure, can you?"

Garrett's gaze burned her. "Yes, I can be sure . . ." "Modesty . . ."

Lila turned abruptly as Luther walked into sight and advanced toward her. "The horses are hitched to the wagon and waiting. Are you ready?"

"Yes, I'm ready."

Stepping into the doorway beside her, Luther addressed Garrett directly. "We're going into town. We probably won't be back until nightfall, so Max'll be stopping in to take care of you during the day." Slipping his arm around her, Luther smiled. "Are you ready, darling?"

Lila nodded, glancing back at Garrett long enough to catch his icy glare. Turning deliberately, she smiled up into Luther's loving gaze in return. "Yes, I'm ready. You are a dear man, Luther."

They had taken only a step away when Garrett spoke again.

"Could you give me a drink of water before you go?"

Modesty hesitated and Luther shrugged. "Go ahead. I'll get the list of things Aunt Helga wants me to buy in town."

Unable to do else, Lila turned back to Garrett's room. She was holding the glass to his lips when he grasped her wrist unexpectedly and smiled.

"I saw you outside with Luther . . ."

Lila stiffened. "So?"

Garrett's smile grew mocking. "I told you I can do more for you than he can . . ."

"Arrogant bastard!"

Snatching back the glass so quickly that the water lapped over the side onto his chest, Lila watched with unconscious fascination as a few beads followed the dwindling row of dark hair that disappeared beneath the coverlet at his waist.

Lila's gaze jerked back to Garrett's as he whispered, "No, that's a promise, Lila darlin' . . ."

"MODESTY . . ."

Lila's head snapped up at Luther's summons. Turning stiffly, she placed the glass on the nightstand without response. She climbed onto the wagon minutes later, despising herself at the realization that she was not truly leaving Garrett Harrison behind her.

Agitation overwhelmed Garrett's distress as the rattle of the wagon faded from his hearing. His head pounding and his arm throbbing, Garrett's frustration soared. Lila Chesney was riding off and he couldn't do a damned thing about it!

Not for the first time, Hobbs returned to mind and Garrett cursed aloud. His invisible partner. . . . He gave a scornful laugh that only succeeded in elevating his pain. McParland had chosen well.

A greater agitation returning, Garrett recalled the scene he had witnessed through the rear window earlier. Had he not known better, he might have believed the scene was staged for his benefit. He had been unable to hear the exchange between Lila and Knox, but it had been obvious by the expression on Knox's face that Lila had been convincing in whatever she had said. The damned fool had believed every word and had been totally deceived by her feigned response to his lovemaking.

Garrett's stomach knotted tightly. The sly little witch had that besotted dunce dancing to her tune. The only problem was that he wasn't sure what the tune was, and if she had finally decided to take the opportunity to escape a situation that became more complicated each day.

But that wasn't the worst of it.

Garrett gritted his teeth with self-disgust. The sight of Lila in Knox's arms had stimulated so hot a rush of jealousy that if he had been able, he would've jumped through the window and ripped her out of his grasp. Disturbing him even more was the realization that his true concern had nothing to do with the injustice of an unsuspecting man being taken for a fool by a wily, determined dancehall whore, or the fact that Lila Chesney was his only lead to a man he had been chasing for more years than he cared to count. Instead, he had had one thought in his mind, to—

Garrett halted that thought before it was complete. He was sicker than he thought. His mind was rambling and his emotions were running so high that he wasn't sure what he would be thinking next. He—

"You all right, there, fella?"

Garrett looked up at the sound of Max's voice. He frowned at the old cowboy.

"Yeah, I'm all right. What do you want?"

The old fellow looked surprised. "It ain't what *I* want that's the point. I'm your new nursemaid. The boss gave me orders not to wander too far from the house until he comes back with Miss Modesty in case you might need somethin'." He paused. "Do you need anythin'?"

Garrett's frown deepened. "Nothin' *you* can get me."

Max smiled, unexpectedly amused. His gold tooth glinted as he shook his head, "You sure are a hard case, ain't you? Of course, it could be that you ain't at your best because you're hurtin', but somehow, I got the feelin' your bein' sick don't have nothin' to do with it. No wonder Miss Modesty wanted to get to town for a while. I'm thinkin' she needed a break from your smilin' face."

Garrett did not bother to respond, and Max laughed

aloud. "Well, you just give a call if you need anythin'. I'm goin' to be in the kitchen for a while. Helga's got some of them Johnnycakes left over, and I ain't about to let them go to waste. Just give a call, you hear?"

"Yeah . . . yeah . . ."

The old cowboy disappeared from sight, and Garrett's frustration soared anew. Determined, he boosted himself up higher on the pillow, and with a supreme effort, pulled himself to a seated position in bed. A moment later he had thrown back the coverlet and had slid his legs over the side. He was going to get up and walk, damn it, if it was the last thing he ever did.

"Psssst! Harrison!"

The hissing summons from the direction of the window turned Garrett's head with a snap that sent the room temporarily reeling. The balding head that peeped over the windowsill raised his brows with surprise.

"Hobbs?"

"Who else would be sneaking up to your window?"

"What're you doin' out there?"

"I'm doing my job!"

Weakness regaining control, Garrett leaned back against the pillow and slid his legs back onto the bed. Again steady, he rasped, "If you were doin' your job, I wouldn't be in this damned bed right now."

"That's the thanks I get! If it wasn't for me you would've met your maker already!"

"Is that so . . ."

"Yes, that's so! Who do you think tied off your arm after you got snakebit?"

"I have no idea, since you've been nowhere around since I came to."

Hobbs's head peeked up higher. "You didn't expect me to take the chance of Lila Chesney's recognizing me, did you? I heard them coming after I tied off your arm and I figured they'd take care of you."

"You figured. . . . So you just took off and left me lyin' there."

"That's right. Besides, you can thank my quick thinking for getting you inside the house. You'll never get closer to Lila Chesney than this."

Garrett glowered. "Remind me to do the same for you some day."

"Look, we don't have time for any of this." Hobbs glanced around him, the professional in him emerging past his disreputable appearance and ridiculous posture. "We're both working toward the same end and we both know how important it is. I'm taking a chance being here, but I figured it was the only opportunity I'd get to check in with you since both Knox and Lila Chesney are out of the way and that other fella's in the house where I can keep track of him. I wanted you to know that I've been in touch with McParland. I told him we found Lila Chesney."

Garrett's jaw hardened. "If you keep hangin' around outside this window, we just might lose her again. She's playin' that Knox fella for everythin' she can. She got him to take her into town today." Garrett's stomach tightened as he added, "And I'm not sure she's comin' back."

Hobbs's eyes narrowed. "You're not? I admit to being surprised. I thought you'd have the situation in hand by now."

Garrett frowned. "If you're serious, you aren't as bright as you're painted to be. But I'll tell you one thing. *If* she comes back, I'll have her just where I want her."

"If . . ."

"Yeah, *if.* So you'd better get movin' and follow

them." Garrett flicked a disparaging glance over Hobb's face. "If you're worryin' about her recognizin' you, believe me, she won't, even if she sees you. I hardly did. You look like hell."

"I'd say neither of us is at his best right now. I only have one more thing to say." Hobbs's expression was direct underneath its sweaty, stubbled exterior. "You do your job on the inside and I'll do mine on the outside. I promise you, Lila Chesney won't get away from me a second time."

Hobbs was gone before Garrett could reply, his departure timely as Max's footsteps sounded outside the doorway. Entering the room to stand a few feet away, the old cowboy belched loudly before announcing, "There's a few of them Johnnycakes left. Helga wants to know if you want 'em."

"No."

Appearing genuinely amused, Max gave a short laugh and turned toward the door. The sound of his voice trailed over his shoulder as he stepped out of sight.

"A real hard case . . ."

The thought occurred to Garrett as he slid down further in his bed and closed his eyes that Max was right. The only thing was, none of the people in this house knew how hard a case he could be.

Allowing himself to drift off to sleep, Garrett consoled himself with the determination that Lila Chesney would be the first to find out.

The makeshift boardwalk of the mining camp sagged under Eva's feet as she walked briskly along the street. Plainly dressed in a dark cotton dress, her hair bound neatly at the back of her neck, she clutched Christina tightly as she adjusted the blanket that shielded the babe's fair hair from view. The banks of silver-laden Clear Creek, scarred from years of abuse, were visible in the distance, but Eva did not spare them a glance as she stepped past the mix of full-bearded miners, bullwackers, an occasional Indian, and the newly arrived with their anxious expressions, crowding the walk. She gasped as a swaying miner emerged unexpectedly from the canvass saloon to her right and careened directly into the wooden horse trough beside her. She did not join the laughter that ensued as amused bystanders dragged the man out and dumped him, sodden, onto the ground. Instead, she crossed the street, dodging a lumbering freight wagon, her gaze intent on the small cabin at the end of the street.

"Hey now, sweetheart, what you got there?"

Halting as an unsteady miner stepped into her path, Eva looked up into the fellow's flushed face. Heavily bearded, wearing clothes that reeked of sweat and filth, he strained to focus bloodshot eyes on her face. He gave a surprised laugh.

"You're an Injun, ain't you?" He grasped her chin with a calloused hand and turned her scarred cheek toward him. "Looks like somebody thought you was too pretty for an Injun and decided to change your looks . . ." His eyes strayed to Christina as the babe turned wide blue eyes toward him. "That baby ain't yours, is it?" He shook his head. "No, couldn't be." His expression tightened unexpectedly, turning ugly. "Where'd you get it? Did you steal that kid, goddammit!"

A familiar fear rose inside Eva. She was saved the need for response as a smaller miner, his face familiar, stepped up and pulled the drunken man's arm.

"Leave her alone, Ned. She's that half-breed from up

on the mountain. She's got a man who won't take kindly to your abusin' her."

"I don't give a damn about her 'man.' Any fella who'll take up with an Injun ain't much of a man, anyways." The drunken miner attempted to jerk his arm free of his friend's hold. "Take your hand off me! That ain't her kid! Some poor woman's probably cryin' over losin' her baby right now because of her! I'm goin' to—"

Taking advantage of the opportunity provided by the miner's well-meaning friend, Eva stepped quickly past them and continued down the street at a pace just short of a run. She was breathless, shaking visibly when Mrs. Greer's cabin door opened unexpectedly. She gasped, clutching Christina tighter as the old woman demanded, "What the matter? You look like you seen a ghost."

"No . . . no ghost." Eva glanced behind her. The drunken miner was walking unsteadily in the opposite direction, his friend at his side, and she released a shaken breath. "I . . . I came to buy milk."

Old lady Greer's faded blue eyes were knowing. "Somebody's been askin' what you're doin' with a light-haired baby again. That's it, ain't it?" The old woman shook her grizzled head, her lips tightening. "Your man's gone again, too, ain't he? No, don't bother to answer. If he wasn't, you wouldn't be down here alone."

"I had to come down. Christina needs milk."

"That child won't miss her milk as much as she would miss her mother."

Eva stiffened. "What do you mean?"

"I'm sayin' that you're goin' to meet the wrong person walkin' on that street some day if you don't watch out, and then you're goin' to end up losin' that baby."

Eva took a quick step backward. "Christina is mine."

"That don't mean nothin'! There's too many who've lost their babes to this hard country and who look on the likes of you as unfit to raise a white child."

"Christina is mine. She has my blood."

"She don't look it."

Eva's eyes grew hard. "Christina is mine."

"Look, don't go gettin' your Injun blood up with me." The old woman's voice was sharp. "I'm only talkin' for your own good. I spoke to that man of yours a while back when he came for milk. He don't want you down here when he's not around."

"Billy's gone." Eva raised her chin. "I don't know when he's coming back."

The old woman's eyes narrowed. "Or *if* he's comin' back, is that it?"

Fear nudged at Eva's senses. She could feel herself pale. "He's coming back."

"Yeah." The old woman opened the door wider. "Come on in. I just finished milkin' Julia and Hettie. The milk's real fresh." Waiting until Eva complied, the old woman closed the door behind her and walked toward the metal containers in the corner of the room. She turned abruptly. "That man of yours leave you money to pay for this here milk?"

Eva nodded. "I have money."

"Let me see it."

Eva's lips tightened at the uncaring affront. She dug into her pocket and pulled out some coins. The woman took them from her hand and counted them carefully. She looked up, appearing suddenly uncomfortable. "I'm an old woman. I have to look out for myself." She paused and continued more kindly. "You ain't bad-lookin' in spite of that scar, you know. My advice would be to find yourself a young fella you can depend on to take care of you. You might even be better off goin' back to your own people if you can't find a white man. At least there you won't have to worry about losin' the baby."

Eva's gaze did not flicker. "I *am* with my own people."

"No you ain't." Slipping the coins into her pocket, old lady Greer held her gaze steadily in return. "There ain't no law in this town except your man's gun when he's walkin' beside you, and you ain't safe down here unless he is, so you listen to what I say. I've lived a long time. I seen and heard it all. You take that milk and you go back to that cabin of yours, and don't come back down until your man is here to protect you."

Eva assessed the old woman's lined face. Seeing true concern behind her harsh manner, she nodded. Withdrawing a handmade sling concealed in Christina's blanket, she walked quickly to the nearby table and laying the babe down, slipped her inside. Christina on her back moments later, Eva picked up the heavy milk container and turned toward the door. The old woman spoke again as her hand touched the latch.

"You look even more like an Injun carryin' that baby like that." With a few steps, the frowning woman was beside her. She covered Christina's fair hair with the blanket and tucked the corners down firmly into the sling. Her parting words were heavy with weariness. "And don't come runnin' back here if you're needin' help. There ain't nothin' I can do for you. I learned a long time ago that a woman's got to look out for herself. You'll do well to learn the same."

The heat of tears heavy under her lids, Eva saw the misery in the poor woman's eyes. Mrs. Greer was old and alone, with no one to look to for help. Was she seeing herself a few years from now . . . when the time came that Billy did not return?

That thought too painful to be retained, Eva nodded a wordless reply and slipped quietly back out onto the street.

Lila sat stiffly beside Luther as the carriage rattled down Deer Trail's main street. The object of curious stares, Lila felt her heart begin a heavy pounding. Silently cursing, she realized she had failed to take into account that a town the size of Deer Trail would pay astute attention to all newcomers, most especially a newcomer straight from the East who was rumored to be marrying one of the area's most eligible bachelors.

Lila's lips twitched as she reminded herself that she no longer bore even the slightest resemblance to Lila Chesney, that in the simple, unbecoming garments she wore, she would not have stirred a single, interested glance had it not been for her presence beside Luther.

"Well, we're here." Luther's deep voice broke into her thoughts, snapping Lila's eyes open as he smiled down at her with open pleasure, "Where do you want to go first? Would you like to get something to eat? You must be tired. It's been a long ride."

"No, I'm not tired." Lila forced a smile despite her weariness. "I think I'd like to walk around a bit first . . . just to stretch my legs."

"That sounds like a good idea."

Drawing up the wagon in front of the general store, Luther dismounted and reached up to swing her to the ground beside him. He accomplished the effort easily, obviously reluctant to release her as her feet touched the ground. "You're as light as a feather. I don't think I want to let you go."

Noting the attention they had drawn from two women

passersby, Lila whispered, "I think you'd better or you'll have the whole town talking."

Luther appeared amused by her comment. "I wouldn't blame them for talking. There hasn't been anybody like you thinking of settling in this area in longer than some of the folks here can remember."

Lila hesitated. "Like me?"

"Young and beautiful . . ."

Lila grimaced. "I'm not beautiful."

Dismissing Luther's protest, Lila slipped her arm through his and fell into step at his side. She sighed. There was something good about walking beside this man . . . feeling his warmth surrounding her, feeling the protection he afforded, and knowing that while he was with her, she was safe from . . .

Lila's smile faded. She was thinking like a fool. Luther could not hold her safe from the threat that hung over her, because he was ignorant of that threat, as ignorant as he was of who she truly was. That realization effectively dissolving her former haze of well-being, Lila pushed her eyeglasses down on her nose and assessed the town.

A hot, dusty street that grew hotter and dustier as the sun reached its zenith, a single line of buildings on either side with the railroad tracks and station house visible from every door, Deer Trail had not grown in luster in the short time since she had first seen it. Her gaze intent, she searched the drab false fronts of the buildings with a discerning eye. The general store, a barber shop, a bakery shop, a restaurant, a small hotel, a saloon, a livery stable, a blacksmith's shop . . . the sheriff's office . . .

"If you're looking for the post office," Luther's voice held a more sober note, "it's in the general store.

Horace Nealy's the storekeeper and the postmaster, too." He paused. "Do you want to go there first?"

Lila did not smile. "Yes, I do."

The bell on the door of the general store jangled noisily as Luther pushed it open and ushered Lila inside. Lila paused as all eyes turned in their direction. Two women at the counter buzzed noisily as the rotund storekeeper smiled.

"Well there, Luther. I ain't seen you in here in a while. I was thinkin' you were becomin' a hermit out there on that ranch of yours, but now I can see that I was wrong. Who's that pretty lady on your arm?"

Luther led Lila forward. His voice held a note of pride as he said, "This lady is Modesty Parkins. She's visitin' with Aunt Helga and me for a while."

"Visitin'? I thought—"

Luther cut the storekeeper short with a forced smile. "Modesty's visitin', just like I said." Tipping his hat, Luther turned to the two matrons standing silently nearby. "Mrs. Wilson . . . Mrs. Newsome, I'd like you to meet Modesty Parkins."

Nodding to the women's brief pleasantries, Lila felt her discomfort grow. She hadn't thought about this . . . about the added humiliation Luther would suffer after having introduced her to his friends. She studied the women's faces briefly, her heart sinking. She knew nosy biddies when she saw them. They couldn't wait to get back to their sewing circle and spread the news that they had met Luther Knox's intended. She knew she would be described in detail, with little generosity, and that when the truth came out about her a short time from now, these women would handle it the same way—with great excitement and little generosity.

Poor Luther . . .

"Modesty?"

Modesty came back to the present with a start. "Yes?"

"Horace will take that letter for you now."

"No . . . I mean, that's all right, I'll wait until he's finished taking care of these ladies."

Responding in Luther's stead, the heavily mustached storekeeper waved his hand. "Don't you worry about these two ladies, Miss Modesty. They ain't finished shoppin' yet . . . are you, ladies?" Not waiting for their reply, he motioned Lila toward a smaller counter in the corner. Winking, he added when out of the two women's sight, "They don't get into town as often as they'd like and they enjoy making a day of it. They'll be wandering around for another hour or so. I'm thinkin' you and Luther'll be seein' them just about everywhere you go."

Lila's smile was weak. "That's nice."

"No, it ain't." Horace's eyes sparked with amusement, "but don't blame the poor souls too much. They ain't got much to talk about."

Knowing the two women would soon have more gossip to spread than either Horace Neely or Luther realized, Lila remained silent as Horace slipped behind the counter and popped an official-looking cap on his head. "All right, ma'am, what can I do for you."

Glancing toward the front counter where Luther was engaged in conversation with the two women, Lila released a relieved breath. She withdrew the two envelopes and placed them on the counter. "I'd like to send this letter home." Lila inwardly groaned, knowing that the first envelope addressed to a fictional address back East and containing a blank sheet of paper was another deceit—a ploy to fool Luther in the event the postmaster was talkative. She added as if in afterthought, "And I'd like to send this other one to Denver."

"Home, huh?" Horace studied the first envelope carefully. "New York . . . this where you hail from?"

Lila nodded stiffly. "Yes."

Horace picked up the other letter and perused it just as closely. "W. Chesney, Denver Post Office Box 23 . . ."

"It's a letter to a lady I met on the train on the way out here . . . Wilhelmina Chesney. She told me to drop her a line and I thought I would." Lila forced a Modesty-like smile. "I know so few people out here, and she was so kind."

"Was she now . . ." Horace nodded. "But I suppose she couldn't help bein' nice to such a sweet young thing like yourself."

Lila averted her gaze, glancing back as the letters were carefully weighed. The price paid and the letters noisily stamped moments later, Lila adjusted her glasses and turned back toward the front counter. She tripped clumsily, righting herself as Luther grasped her arm. He hesitated, then said softly, "It seems to me you trip more often when you're wearing those glasses than when you're not. Are you sure you need them as much as you think you do, darling?"

"Darling? Did I hear you call this dear girl 'darling'?" Beside them in a rush, her small eyes sparkling and her lined face flushed, the smaller of the two women shoppers pressed, "You said Modesty was just visiting. Are you hiding something from us, Luther?"

"Hiding something?" Luther's smile was forced. "It would be impossible to hide anything from you, now wouldn't it, Mrs. Wilson?"

Tipping his hat politely, Luther gripped Lila's elbow more tightly. "I think it's time to leave."

Luther's determined strides brought them to the doorway just as the door was suddenly thrust open, forcing Lila to take a quick step backward.

"Oh, sorry, ma'am!" A ruddy-complexioned fellow with a handlebar mustache grasped her arm to steady her, and Lila caught her breath. The star on his chest glinted in the modest light of the store, and she fought the urge to shake off his touch as he glanced up at Luther and smiled.

"Luther! Well now, is this the little lady I've been hearin' about all over town?"

Luther was obviously chagrined. "Yes, I suppose it is. Modesty Parkins . . . Sheriff Dan Barker."

"Pleased to meet you, ma'am." Sweeping off his hat to reveal a heavy mane of grey hair, Sheriff Barker smiled broadly down at her. "You sure enough do add a pleasant touch to the scenery in this here town. With the exception of the ladies in the Red Slipper Saloon down the street, we haven't had a pretty new face around here in a long time."

Luther smiled. "Seems like that's the general opinion around town."

Sheriff Barker squinted, scrutinizing her more closely. "I can see why that would be so. A pretty face like yours would be hard to forget, Miss Modesty." He paused, his scrutiny deepening. "It sure would . . ."

An annoyed voice interrupted their exchange unexpectedly from Sheriff Barker's rear.

"What in hell's the holdup in this doorway? A man can't even get inside to buy himself a new shirt when he has a mind to!"

Sheriff Barker stepped aside obligingly to reveal Doc Bennett's unsteady figure.

"Well, I'll be damned!" Doc Bennett grinned broadly as he took Modesty's hand and raised it gallantly to his lips. "I didn't expect to see you so soon, dear lady, but it sure is a pleasure." Glancing at Luther in afterthought, Doc added, "You, too, Luther."

"Well, thank you, Doc."

Doc ignored Luther's wry response as he questioned Modesty directly. "Tell me, is that big stranger givin' you any more trouble back there at the ranch?"

Sheriff Barker frowned. "Trouble . . . with a stranger?"

Doc shot him a backward glance. "A stranger who got bit by a rattler. This lady did a damned fine job of takin' care of him while I was . . ." Doc paused for effect. "A trifle indisposed."

Sheriff Barker nodded, a smile quirking his lips. "I suppose I've seen you indisposed a time or two, too, Doc."

"This here young woman took over for me like she was born to the task." Doc patted Lila's hand, his bloodshot eyes gleaming. "If you was a man, I'd invite you down to the Red Slipper for a drink, but since that ain't the case . . . and I'm not sayin' I'm sorry . . . I think I'll invite you and Luther over to Flossie's Restaurant for one of her specials instead."

"Well, I don't know, Doc . . ." Luther looked tentatively at Lila. "We were kind of planning—"

"Don't go tellin' me you're goin' to refuse my offer, goddamnit!"

Luther's brows rose expressively. "Doc . . ."

"Excuse my colorful language, dear lady." His expression anything but apologetic, Doc added, "But I was never known for my tact, so tell me here and now. Are you goin' to eat with me or not?"

Aware that Sheriff Barker was still standing beside them, studying her intently, Lila responded in a high voice totally unlike her own, "I'll be pleased to spend time in your company, Doc."

Taking her arm, Doc slipped it under his with a stiff nod at Luther. "See! Women just can't resist me." Dragging her along with him, Doc offered brightly, "See you later Dan. You comin', Luther." And then, mercifully, when out of Sheriff Barker's range of hearing, "What's wrong with your voice, Modesty? You don't sound nothin' like yourself with that pitiful squeakin' you were doin'."

About to respond, Lila pulled back instinctively as Doc's hand moved toward her face. Snatching her glasses off her nose, he folded them and stuffed them into his pocket. He looked up at Luther as the younger man fell into step beside them and appeared about to object.

"I'm the doctor here, and I say that Modesty don't need them glasses worth a damn . . . ah . . . *darn.* She just hides behind them when she gets nervous, but she don't have no need for them now with two big men walkin' beside her. Ain't that right, Modesty?"

"Doc, I—"

Doc squinted purposely into Lila's face. "Ain't that right, Modesty?"

Suddenly realizing Sheriff Barker was far behind them, Lila felt her gratitude to the unpredictable physician at her side swell. Her smile was genuine as she replied, "You're the doctor, all right."

Turning to slide her other arm through Luther's, Lila experienced a brief, bittersweet pang that threatened to destroy her smile. True affection on one side, and a patient and growing love on the other. She was a lucky woman.

Or she would've been, if her name was really Modesty.

Watching the threesome from the saloon doorway across the street, a beer in his hand and his eyes intent,

Hobbs scratched his stubbled face with a grimy hand. He grimaced with discomfort as Doc Bennett and Luther Knox vied for the opportunity to open the door of Flossie's Restaurant for the shy little dove between them. He shook his head at the recollection of how close he had come to running his horse into the ground as he had raced to catch up with Knox's wagon after his talk at Harrison's bedroom window. Harrison's uncertainty as to Lila Chesney's plans had unleashed a near panic inside him. He had followed the wagon closely without being seen and had arrived in town in time to watch through the store window as Lila Chesney posted two letters. He had then observed as the clever young woman had wrapped four grown men around her slender finger, and he had made a firm determination. Clever or not, she would never make a fool out of him again.

Hobbs drank deeply from the glass in his hand as Lila Chesney and the two men settled at a table near the window. They would soon be busy eating and he would take a leisurely walk to the general store, where he would engage the talkative storekeeper in a conversation about the pretty young woman he had just seen drive into town. It wouldn't be difficult to get the fellow to talk. Nor would it be difficult to discover the destinations of the two letters Lila Chesney had been so determined to mail.

Hobbs smiled. He was becoming comfortable with the situation as it now stood. Harrison would be on his feet in a day or so, and, judging from the expression on his face, he was damned determined to make up for lost time.

If he didn't miss his guess, Knox and Lila Chesney would be back at the ranch by sundown. That suited him fine.

Things were going well.
It was just a matter of time . . .

Sinking beyond the distant mountain in a blaze of glory, the setting sun cast a crimson glow across a pastoral scene that stretched as far as the eye could see from Buck Howell's cabin window. Billy smiled, knowing his smile could not be seen behind the neckerchief that shielded the lower half of his face. He glanced at the man beside him, similarly masked, then at the two men tied and gagged on the cabin floor behind them.

"Make sure you tied them tight." Billy's voice was curt. "We don't want either of them coming after us until we've had a chance to take care of the horses."

"I don't take orders from you! Check them yourself if you're so worried!" Picket's patience had expired after spending the hot hours of afternoon in the sun, waiting for the opportunity they had sought. He had been ready to pick Howell and his hired man off with his rifle, but Billy had known the killings would be sure to get a posse on their trail. Forbes wouldn't have liked that, on edge as he was.

Unwilling to test Picket's mood any further, Billy leaned over to check the hired man's bonds, and then Howell's. He caught the old man's eye, and he knew the fellow had recognized him. The realization was momentarily amusing. The old man was probably cursing the day he had let him reshoe his horse there. His generosity had cost him six fine mares.

Billy drew himself up straight, his gaze still holding Howell's. Well, maybe the old man had finally learned the lesson that he himself had learned a long time ago . . . that if you let yourself get played for a fool, you got everything you deserved.

Tipping his hat to his bound host, Billy signaled Picket. Within minutes the two men rode off into the approaching darkness, trailing the mares behind them.

The rapidly descending night was spreading its dark cape across the sky as Lila and Luther drove steadily homeward. Lila heaved a sigh. It had been a long, often tense, but somehow enjoyable day.

With a brief smile, Lila recalled her difficulty in reclaiming her eyeglasses from Doc Bennett upon leaving. Finally surrendering them, he had ignored Luther and instructed tightly, "I don't want to see you wearin' these damned things again when you come to town, you hear me?"

She had protested, only to have her claims that she could not see well without them openly scorned.

"They're a crutch, that's what they are. They'll make you damned cross-eyed . . . whoops, pardon my French . . . if you keep on wearin' them." He had then turned to Luther with a frown. "You're not to let her wear these things again, you hear?"

Desperate to change the subject, Lila had brought Garrett Harrison into the conversation. She had only succeeded in raising Doc Bennett's ire when she had stated, "He's determined to get up even though he's too weak to stand. I told him what you said and he—"

"And he told you that he was goin' to get up anyway." Doc gave a low snort. "So let him! Damned hard-head. He'll just fall flat on his face and he won't try it again too soon."

But she had been somehow reluctant to part from the old man, despite the fact that she suspected Doc was beginning to see more than she wanted him to see.

The spark of true affection in his eye had warmed her heart.

As for Luther . . .

Lila glanced at the man beside her. Catching her eye, Luther slid his arm around her. They had dallied on the road a while back and Lila knew that had she not been so acutely aware that she was playing a part, she might have succumbed to the soul-stopping tenderness of Luther's touch. Even now she wished she were free to—

Luther lowered his head to touch his lips to hers. She felt his control straining as he drew back with a husky whisper.

"Did you have a good time today, darling?"

"Oh, yes, I did."

Luther drew her closer, then laughed. "Doc sure made a pest of himself."

"A nice pest."

"You like him, don't you?"

"Yes."

"Better than you like me?"

"Oh, Luther . . ." Lila's smile deepened. "I don't like anyone better than I like you."

Suddenly realizing those words were sincere, Lila whispered, "I wish . . ."

Luther urged, "You wish . . . ?" He waited, then pressed, "Tell me what you wish and I'll make it come true."

Lila's smile wobbled. "I wish . . . I wish you could."

Suddenly sad, Lila leaned against Luther's shoulder, allowing the strength of his arm around her and the steady rocking of the wagon to soothe her troubled heart and dull the realization that her dearest wish at that moment could not possibly come true.

* * *

The rattle of a wagon outside the window awakened Garrett with a start. Pulling himself up on the pillow, he strained to see into the deepening twilight as the wagon came into view around the side of the house. He saw Luther dismount and lift Lila to the ground. He saw the familiarity with which Lila leaned against Knox's side and the spontaneous warmth between them as they walked slowly back to the house.

And he burned.

The sound of voices in the kitchen alerted Garrett to Lila's entrance minutes before Knox and Lila appeared in the doorway of the room.

His arm slung casually around Lila's shoulders, Knox inquired, "How are you feeling? Max said you were the ideal patient . . . that you didn't give him any trouble at all."

Garrett sneered. "Max is a liar."

Knox laughed. "You sound like you're feeling better."

"Yeah, I feel great."

"LUTHER . . ."

Luther turned at Aunt Helga's summons.

"COME INTO THE KITCHEN, PLEASE."

Luther excused himself and, realizing Lila was about to follow, Garrett gave a sharp gasp and clutched his arm. Lila was beside him in a moment.

"Are you in pain? Should I call—"

Garrett caught Lila's arm in a viselike grip. Realizing he grew stronger by the hour, Garrett gave a hard laugh. "No, you don't have to call anybody. I have the medicine I need right in my hand." Lila struggled to free herself as Garrett hissed, "So, you came back after all."

All trace of her former tranquility gone, Lila replied hotly, "You see me, don't you?"

Garrett pulled her closer. "Did you talk to the sheriff?"

"As a matter of fact, I did. He thinks I'm a pleasant addition to the scenery."

"You're that, all right."

"The only thing he doesn't know is that the scenery is going to be changing soon."

"Not before I'm ready to let it change."

With a sudden yank, Lila freed herself and stepped back. "You don't have a damned thing to say about it."

"Oh, yes I do. Listen to me, Lila." Garrett's voice dropped to a husky whisper. "Whether you're willing to admit it yet or not, we haven't gotten started yet together, but when we do—"

"I told you . . . that day will never come!"

"I'll be on my feet tomorrow."

"You'll never make it."

Garrett's gaze hardened. "I'll be on my feet tomorrow."

"And off this ranch within a week!"

"Only if you come with me."

Her eyes widening, Lila's lips parted, but no words emerged. They snapped tightly closed again, a moment before she turned on her heel and left the room.

Following the sound of her step, Garrett heard her go into her room and close the door behind her. Knowing full well that if he were able, he would have been on his feet in a minute and that the barrier of the closed door would not have stood between them, Garrett finally faced the full scope of his feelings for Lila Chesney.

He wanted her.

Garrett stared out the bedroom window as darkness fell. Yes, he wanted Lila Chesney, but he wanted Bart

Forbes and his gang of cutthroats more. He also knew he was not above using one to get the other.

Darkness fell outside the cabin walls as Eva checked off the last minute details of the day. Sagebrush, her pa's old burro and the only thing he had left her upon his death, had been fed and watered where he was tethered behind the cabin. The fire in the cooking stove had been banked for the night, the milk stored in the creek, and the beans for the next day were soaking.

Taking a moment to check on Christina where she was safely asleep in her bed, Eva undressed quickly, slipped into her nightshift, and removed the pins from her hair. She picked up the new brush Billy had bought her, and with great care, stroked her hair free of snarls as Billy's voice echoed in her mind.

Your hair is like heavy black silk, darling. I've never felt anything like it. I'll never get tired of touching it . . . of touching you . . .

Her throat filling with an emotion she dared not indulge, Eva extinguished the last lamp and lay back against her pillow as the sounds of night stirred memories to life.

She saw Pa, the silent man who had protected her and kept her safe from the torments of others. She glimpsed again the sadness she had always seen in his eyes when she asked about her mother, and she recalled reading there his determination to tell her no more about the graceful shadow in her mind than the name she was given by her people—One Who Waits. Like her mother, she had waited for the day when she would learn more, but that day had never come.

Pa's image faded unexpectedly, yielding to Olaf's.

Kind Olaf, so like her father, who had slipped from her life as suddenly as her father before him.

The faded blue eyes of Mrs. Greer appeared unexpectedly before her, and Eva felt the thickness in her throat tighten. The old woman's bed was as empty as her own. The old woman's heart was as heavy as her own, and the old woman's future was as uncertain as the future that lay before Christina and her.

Billy's image returned, supplanting the old woman's sad-eyed gaze, and Eva felt hope stir within her breast as she berated herself for her despair. Billy had said he would return, hadn't he? He had held her in his arms and loved her with all the fervor in his strong, lean body, and she had returned the loving in kind. And she knew . . . how certainly she knew . . . that no loving could be more beautiful, more sincere, more fulfilling than what they had shared.

Eva's breath caught with a sob. But she knew something else, as well. She knew there were times when Billy wished himself free of responsibility for her and Christina, and she wondered if resentment would overcome his undeclared love in the end.

As if in answer to her question, Billy's handsome image became clearer . . . so clear that she could almost feel his breath against her cheek, could almost feel the touch of his lips against hers, could almost hear his impassioned whisper in her ear. With a sudden certainty, she knew that the time had not come . . . not yet. Billy would return . . . if he was able. Billy would—

A sound of movement outside the cabin window brought Eva's wandering thoughts to an abrupt halt. She froze, her senses acute. Fear raised the hackles on her spine as she listened more intently than before.

There it was again . . . the sound of a step, barely

distinguishable above the loud chorus of night sounds beyond the cabin walls.

Reaching for the gun lying on the table beside her bed, Eva slowly rose to her feet. The handle was heavy and cold as she gripped it tightly, moving quickly and silently to stand beside Christina's bed. Her finger stretched to curve around the trigger at the sounds of fumbling at the cabin door. She heard a low cursing as the barred door refused to yield, and she jumped with a start at the sudden pounding there as a slurred voice demanded, "Open up, Injun girl! Come on. It'll go hard on you if you make me wait!"

The voice was familiar. It brought to mind the face of the drunken miner who had stopped her on the street earlier that day. Eva responded harshly.

"Go away! This is *my* cabin!"

"That's where you're wrong! Injuns don't have no right to nothin' in this camp . . . most especially to a white woman's kid. Open up! I'm takin' that baby back to its mama."

Eva glanced to the bed behind her where Christina slept on, miraculously oblivious to threat. Her voice caught in her throat.

"I'm Christina's mother!"

"No you ain't! Don't go lyin' to me! Open up!"

Eva took a steadying breath. "Go away. I have a gun!"

"If you do, you'd better put it down right now, 'cause there won't be no way out for you if you fire on a white man. You know what I'm sayin' is true, so let me in!"

"No! Go away!"

The low laughter that followed was harsh. "I ain't goin' nowhere but inside . . . *now!"*

Her throat tight with fear, Eva stiffened as the barred

door bulged against a crashing assault. She gasped as the crashing sounded again, as the weakened bar snapped and the door popped open with a sudden thrust to reveal the miner's shadowed figure in the doorway.

Grasping the gun with two hands to steady it, Eva shouted over Christina's sudden, piercing wail, "Don't move! If you take one step into the cabin, I'll shoot!"

"No you won't, 'cause you know you can't get away with shootin' a white man." The miner's voice was a feral growl. "I'll get to you first, anyway, and if you make me mad, then what I'm goin' to give you before I leave with the kid ain't goin' to be too pleasant." He took a confident step forward. "Put that gun down . . . now!"

"Don't . . . don't take another step."

"Put the gun down!"

A second sense allowing her a moment's warning, Eva gasped as the miner lunged forward. Her finger tightened spasmodically on the trigger once . . . twice . . . three times! Her eyes widened as the bullets struck the man, his body jerking once . . . twice . . . three times with the impact before he fell heavily to the floor.

Frozen, arms still outstretched in front of her as she clutched the gun, her finger on the trigger she had pulled moments earlier, Eva stared at the shadowed form on the cabin floor. It did not move, and Eva knew with a sudden certainty that the man would never move again.

Eva slowly lowered her arms. Strangely calm despite her shuddering, she reviewed in her mind what the miner had said. It was true . . . she would never get away with shooting a white man, whatever the cause. They would take Christina away from her and put her in jail.

No.

Eva lowered the gun and put it on the table beside the bed. She turned to comfort her crying child, knowing what she must do.

Her burro loaded with her meager belongings and as many supplies as he could carry, Christina asleep and secure in the sling on her back, Eva took the animal's lead as the first shafts of dawn rent the night sky. Turning onto the trail Billy had taken a few days earlier, she drew the animal along behind her. Her mind worked feverishly.

How long would it take for the miner's body to be discovered? Someone would remember his interest in her when he did not return to his claim, and someone would eventually check the cabin. She had a few days . . . a week at the most.

She would be gone by then. She would go where no one could find her. No one. Not even Billy . . .

Eva's breath choked on a sob. Oh, God . . . not even Billy . . .

Ten

The smoke thickened. The fire burned brighter. Garrett cried out against the scorching heat, his protest impassioned as he fought to elude the bonds that restrained him. The voice calling from within the blaze sounded again, and panic grew to frenzy.

He must reach her. He must!

He struggled to his feet and took a lurching step just as a slender figure appeared in the blinding smoke. Surrounded by flame, the woman staggered toward him, her arms outstretched. He strained to run . . . to walk . . . to inch forward, but he was rooted to the spot by his weakness. He could do no more than watch as she emerged from the swirling smoke, flames licking at her clothing. Her figure became clearer, her torment more real, when he realized that the hair that streamed out behind the woman was not blond . . . that the eyes were not light. Instead, the hair was of a coppery hue, the accusing eyes dark!

Garrett's throat tightened as he relived a familiar anguish. He had failed to save her before. He was failing again . . . again . . . again . . .

Snapping awake with a start, Garrett gasped aloud. The semidarkness of the bedroom in which he lay was suddenly clear. The fire was gone, consigned to the dark caverns of his mind, but the anxiety remained. It crawled along his skin, torturing him, allowing him no respite.

Shuddering and dripping with sweat, Garrett attempted to draw his emotions under control. The familiar terror of his dream had taken a frightening twist that he could not seem to comprehend. The subdued copper of the woman's hair . . . the accusing darkness of her eyes . . . the apprehension . . . the panic . . .

Abruptly determined, Garrett turned up the lamp beside the bed and threw back the coverlet. He swung his legs over the side and drew himself upright, battling the resulting lightheadedness with all his strength. Feeling the floor under his feet, he paused cautiously before forcing his weight down and standing at last.

Damn, he was weak . . . almost giddy. He closed his eyes.

The flames licked out once more to consume him, and Garrett snapped his eyes open. Resolution firm despite the pounding in his head and the resurgence of pain in his arm, he took one wobbling step forward, then another. Standing at the washstand moments later, leaning heavily against it for support, he poured water into the bowl with a shaky hand and bent down to splash the tepid liquid on his face. Immediately relieved, he then leaned over the stand and poured the remaining contents of the pitcher over his head. Snatching up the cloth hanging on the rack as water streamed down his bare chest in shiny rivulets, he rubbed his hair and face as briskly as he could manage and wiped the remaining moisture from his chest.

Glimpsing his shadowed reflection in the washstand mirror, Garrett grimaced and raised a hand to his stubbled cheek. He looked at his saddlebag in the corner before turning toward it resolutely. In a few staggering steps he reached it and withdrew his razor. A few unsteady steps back to the washstand and he paused as the hovering darkness threatened to consume him.

Unwilling to submit to weakness, Garrett worked up a lather with the soap nearby and spread it on his face. His arm a leaden weight, he raised the razor to his cheek and scraped at the coarse hair there. A cursory job accomplished, Garrett carefully rinsed his blade and patted his face dry.

Again weak, Garrett closed his eyes briefly, relieved to see the fire behind his closed lids did not return. The unexpected twist in his dream continued to disturb him. He could not overcome the thought that it had been a warning . . . that time was slipping away . . . that he need act fast before it was too late.

Too late . . . but for what? He was not sure.

Garrett glanced down at his arm appraisingly. Some swelling remained but mobility had returned. His legs had been as wobbly as a child's, but they had supported him. He had proved to himself that, although still weak, he was no longer totally incapacitated.

He would go forward from there.

Sounds of activity within the kitchen grew louder as Lila walked quickly out of her room. A glimpse out the window a few minutes earlier had revealed that Luther and Max's horses were already saddled although daylight was still reaching lazy fingers across the sky. Despite her effort, Lila was once again the last to arise.

Annoyed, she slid her palm against her freshly bound hair, then ran a hand against the bodice of her grey cotton dress. She had assumed Modesty's appearance and personality without a break in stride, with one exception. The clock within her, accustomed for many years to the late hours of saloon work, continued to resist early risings. She was strangely embarrassed by that lapse on this ranch where all pulled their weight without complaint and silently expected the same of others. She was even more embarrassed by the realization that Luther did not fault her for that shortcoming when, indeed, he should.

Lila gave a short sigh. But then, Luther was in love. She knew instinctively that he had a great capacity for love . . . unlike the hard man whose room she was approaching. She also knew instinctively that Luther would be a warm, generous, and thoughtful lover, while Garrett Harrison would rely solely on passion to carry him through.

A tremor coursed down Lila's spine. She had felt that passion. It had shaken her deeply, increasing a sense of awareness of Garrett's every glance, every touch. She—

Suddenly realizing the direction her thoughts were again taking, Lila forcibly ejected them from her mind. She paused outside Garrett's bedroom doorway, recalling her departure the night before and steeling herself against the inevitable confrontation.

Raising her chin, Lila turned into view of the bedroom and gasped. Bare to the waist, wearing only his trousers, Garrett Harrison was standing beside the washstand! Her throat suddenly thick, Lila realized she had been unprepared for the towering size of him, for the breadth of muscular shoulder and chest, and for the sense of power he exuded despite his obviously weakened state. He turned sharply toward her and she was startled to see that he had managed to bathe and shave. Free of the dark stubble of his beard, his face was sober, intense, and pale as he studied her stunned expression, but the dark circles under his eyes and the bruising on the side of his face did little to alter his innate virile appeal or her realization that he was a heartstoppingly handsome man.

Garrett's silent scrutiny intense, he suddenly swayed. Startled from her immobile state, Lila moved instinctively toward him.

Glowering, Garrett halted her advance with a single glance. "I don't need your help."

Torn as his unsteadiness became more apparent, Lila took another step.

"I said I don't need your help. I'm all right."

Anger moving hotly to her aid, Lila flared, "I suppose you'd prefer for me to wait until you fall so I'd have to struggle to get you on your feet again . . . or so I'll be punished with another round of nursing you back to health!"

Garrett's grey eyes hardened. "If I fall, I'll get myself up."

Rushing toward him as his swaying step faltered and the nearby chair toppled under his grip, Lila slid her shoulder under his arm and gripped him firmly for support. She felt him resist and she snapped, "Don't be so damned stubborn! You've already made your point! You're on your feet, just as you said you'd be."

The bare flesh of Garrett's back was warm against the arm Lila had slid around his waist to support him. Her skin tingled where it touched his, raising a breathlessness that settled in the pit of her stomach as he towered over her. Determined not to allow him to realize she was so affected, Lila urged him back toward the bed. In a moment he was sitting, his eyes almost even with hers as he returned her stare.

"Satisfied now?" Garrett's gaze returned to familiar

ice. "Now that you have me where you want me again?"

"If I really had you where I wanted you, you'd be off this ranch and miles from here by now."

"And if I had *you* where I wanted you . . ."

The smoldering heat that sparked to life within those silver shards of ice completed Garrett's statement more clearly than words, and Lila's heart began a suddenly rapid pounding.

"You really are a bastard, aren't you!"

"I'm bein' honest."

Lila made a low, scoffing sound. "You've never had an honest day in your life."

Garrett's eyes became pinpoints of intense grey light. "I wouldn't talk about honesty if I were you. At least you know who and what I am. That fool Knox doesn't have the faintest idea who and what *you* are."

"Who . . . and *what* I am?" Lila's lips curled with contempt. "At least I make an honest living."

"Sure, that's why a Pinkerton's after you."

"I've never done anything illegal in my life!"

Garrett's gaze grew mocking. "You don't have to defend yourself to me, darlin'."

"I'm not defending myself to you!"

"It sounded like that to me."

"Well, you're wrong!" Lila stiffened. "Let's get one thing clarified here. *You're* wanted by the law. I'm not."

"All right. Anythin' you say." Garrett glanced toward the window, dismissing her agitation with arrogance. "I see Knox and Max are already saddled up. That means they'll be ridin' out right after breakfast. That suits me fine . . ."

Lila was immediately suspicious. "If you think you're going to get away with something here while they're gone—"

"The only thing I'm goin' to do is to get up and get around a little bit."

Lila stiffened and took a short step back. "Do what you want. You will anyway, and the sooner you're on your feet, the sooner you'll be off my hands."

"Don't count on it."

Allowing Garrett's gaze to lock with hers, Lila stated flatly, "You don't know how much I'm counting on it."

"Then you're makin' a mistake." His hands snapping out to lock on her shoulders with surprising strength, Garrett drew her closer, continuing in an intimate whisper. "Because I promise you there's no way you're goin' to get away from me, Lila Chesney . . . not one second before I'm willin' to let you go."

The throbbing rumble of Garrett's words reverberated within Lila with unexpected intensity. Her response was short and grated from between stiff lips.

"Let me go."

Garrett did not comply. Instead, he drew her gradually closer until his lips were only inches from hers. Unwilling to give him the satisfaction of a struggle, and uncertain if she was capable even if she had tried, Lila remained unmoving as Garrett closed the final distance between them. With sheer strength of will, she allowed Garrett's heady plunder of her mouth as she remained rigid in his arms. She struggled to retain conscious thought as he crushed her breathlessly close, to deny the onset of ragged emotions hovering dangerously near, to steel herself against the rise of languorous warmth that threatened her rationality. She was clinging to frigid control by the tips of her fingers when Garrett drew back abruptly, his expression thunderous.

"You're lucky this isn't the time or place to take this any further, or you wouldn't be gettin' away with the act you just put on. But listen to me, darlin', and listen good, because I'm makin' you a promise. The next time I take you into my arms, things'll be different. I won't be lettin' you go until things are the way they were meant to be between us and you admit to me that you want me as much as I want you . . . just like you're wantin' me right now, though you're afraid to show it."

"I'm not *afraid* of anything!"

"You're afraid of wantin' me."

"You conceited ass! You see what you want to see!"

Garrett released her unexpectedly, and Lila fell a step backward, her knees wobbling unexpectedly. He gave a short laugh, and her temper soared.

"It would serve you right if I marched out of here and turned you in!"

"But you won't."

The confidence in Garrett's tone thrust Lila's chin belligerently forward. "Maybe I won't, but it won't be for the reason you'd like to believe."

"Darlin', you can tell yourself anythin' you want, but I know the truth . . . and it's goin' to give me great pleasure to make you admit it."

"MODESTY . . ."

Lila's head turned with a snap at Helga's summons. She forced a normal tone.

"YES, AUNT HELGA?"

"BREAKFAST IS READY. LUTHER COMES INTO DER HOUSE NOW."

"I'LL BE RIGHT OUT."

"That's right, Luther's comin'." Garrett's voice was a contemptuous sneer. "You have to go out and play your part."

"Bastard . . ."

"But you won't be playin' a part with me."

Suddenly shuddering, Lila turned abruptly and

walked to the doorway. She slipped into the hallway and did not look back at the sound of Garrett's bed creaking under his weight because she knew he had settled back against his pillow once more. She knew he would lie back and wait—for her to return . . . to regain his strength . . . and for all that would follow.

Watching as Lila slipped through the doorway out of sight, Garrett leaned back against the pillow and closed his eyes. His head and his heart were pounding, but he knew his physical distress did not stem from the injuries he had sustained. Silently cursing, he also knew that despite his desire to the contrary, he had been too weak to carry through when he had held Lila in his arms minutes earlier.

The thought rankled.

During those moments, he had forgotten the stiffness in his arm, the nagging ache in his temples, and the fact that he had been barely able to hold himself upright during his angry exchange with Lila. He had been overwhelmed by the desire to draw Lila's womanly warmth ever closer, by the sweet scent of her that filled his nostrils, by the taste of her lips, intoxicating, more compelling than any he had tasted before.

With one exception.

A fair, youthful female image returned vividly before Garrett's mind's eye. The glow of her light skin and the loving innocence in her eyes renewed a familiar pain and Garrett gave a short, convulsive laugh. The emotion Lila Chesney stimulated in him was as different as night and day from his love for Elizabeth. There was none of the wonder, of the sense of sweet purity that struck him with her every glance, of the selfless emotion that had made Elizabeth's life more important to him than his own, of the sense of knowing that he had become one with her so completely that a part of him had been consumed in the fire along with her, never to revive again.

Lila's vibrant, dark-eyed image supplanted Elizabeth's pale beauty in his mind and the heat returned. No, Lila Chesney appealed to an emotion in him that was far more base than love. Despite her denials, he knew she was as drawn to him as strongly as he was drawn to her, that it had taken all her control to walk away . . . and that through it all, she was as repelled by that attraction as he.

But he would change her mind.

Garrett's smile became caustic. He would use Lila Chesney in the same way she was using Luther Knox. And when he was done, he would walk away from her the same way she intended to walk away from Knox.

Poetic justice . . .

Garrett's smile faded as Lila's image became vividly clear. His drawn face hardened.

Justice . . . and a little bit more.

Branding smoke curled upward, hot and pungent with the odor of singeing hair. Luther turned his head to the side, his eyes watering as Max applied the brand to the squirming calf's side. Releasing the rope from the animal's hooves with a flick of the wrist, Luther stood up and watched as he scrambled to his feet, shaking his head and bawling for his mother.

Luther looked up at the blue sky overhead as the sun neared the summit. The morning had grown hotter and the branding fire was sweltering. Sweat ran from his face and trickled down his spine, and every muscle in his body cried out with strain. A glance at the holding pen behind him revealed that although Max and he had been working since sunrise, a full day's work still lay ahead of them.

A look at Max as the aging cowboy adjusted the irons at the fire and stretched stiffly revealed that he was also dripping with sweat. A quick scanning of the freshly branded calves informally grouped behind them, however, confirmed that, despite his age, there was nobody handier with a branding iron than Max. He had seen too many smeared brands and hair-branded calves in his day, and he was keenly aware that calves so branded showed no sign of a brand in three months time and were easy prey to rustlers. He could not afford to lose a single head that way, and he was certain that as long as Max was working with him, he never would.

Luther sighed. But the problem remained. Long hours of roping and tying frightened calves had made his arms feel like leaden weights, and he knew Max was feeling the strain even more. He also knew that the calves still penned behind him awaiting branding were only the second batch of the season. He was not certain how many more Max and he would find tucked away in the corners of the ranch when this group was completed, but he did know that at least another hard week's work lay ahead of them before the chore would be completed.

But that would not be the worst of it.

Luther frowned. The new Hereford bulls would arrive within two weeks time. If he kept to the schedule he had set for himself before Modesty's arrival, that also meant new fencing need be raised to separate the first-calf heifers from the rest of the herd. Then would come the careful scattering of bulls, the Mexican bulls to the first-calf heifers to ensure smaller calves, and the Herefords to the prime breeding stock in a selected breeding procedure that had worked well in other portions of the country and which he was determined to undertake.

Luther mentally adjusted his scheduled workload in his mind, coming to the same conclusion that had been bedeviling him the morning long. Weeks of work that stretched from sunrise to sunset lay ahead of him—too much work for two men, even under normal circumstances. Nagging at his mind was the realization that since Modesty's arrival, circumstances had strayed far from the norm.

Damn!

Watching as Max straightened up, his face creasing into a myriad of weary lines as he glanced revealingly at the penned calves, Luther felt frustration soar. No one had to tell him that he was rapidly coming to a turning point with Modesty. He had seen the uncertainty in her eyes when she looked at him. He had felt the hesitation in her response to his lovemaking. Without a shred of conceit, he knew her hesitation was not due to a lack of feeling for him on her part.

A familiar stirring inside him, Luther recalled the parting of Modesty's lips under his and the warmth of her slender body pressing against him. The spark was there, waiting to be fanned into passion. But, damn it all, he needed time—time to introduce Modesty to passion . . . time to help her discover the beauty of the dream he wanted her to share . . . time for Modesty to come to know him well enough to trust him with the rest of her life.

Time . . . with fifteen-hour workdays staring Max and him squarely in the face and with no end in sight.

"What do you say, boss?" Luther turned as Max continued. "Are you ready to take on that ornery bull calf in the corner of the pen? When we have him out of the way, the rest will be easy."

Max was smiling, but the upward turn of his lips was weary, and Luther felt affection for the old cowboy rise. Max would work himself into the ground before he'd let him down, but he knew even that sacrifice wouldn't guarantee him the time he needed with Modesty.

There had to be a way.

The sudden gleam that entered Max's eyes tightened his smile into a grin. "Somethin' tells me you ain't thinkin' about them calves right now, and if you ain't, to my mind there's only one other thing . . . or person . . . you'd be thinkin' about."

Luther's brows rose. "You're sure of that, are you?"

"I sure am. I ain't that old that I don't have some feelin's in a similar direction myself."

Luther's mouth dropped open with surprise. "Well, I'll be. Are you tellin' me you're thinking of taking yourself a woman?"

Max flushed like a boy. "Well, not exactly . . ." He hesitated, then continued, his flush darkening. "I suppose what I'm tellin' you is not to let the opportunity to get yourself a good woman pass . . . not if you don't want to find yourself a lonely old cowpoke someday with his youth behind him, empty tomorrows stretchin' out in front of him as far as his mind can see, and nothin' much more to offer a woman than a pair of calloused hands and a ready smile."

"Come on now, Max." Luther gave a short laugh. "Seems to me you're painting the picture kind of black. I know a few ladies at the Red Slipper who find your ugly old face real appealing."

"That's right, I reckon, as long as I can jingle two coins together in my pocket. But that don't mean too much when a man has his heart set on more." His gaze direct, Max continued without a trace of a smile. "I guess what I'm tryin' to tell you is that Miss Modesty is one in a million. If I was you, I wouldn't let her get away."

"Don't worry. I don't intend to."

"Well, if that's the case," Max's grin suddenly returned, "I guess we'd better be gettin' back to work so we can finish with these critters before sundown."

"Yeah." Luther could not help but add, "So you think Modesty's the right woman for me."

Max's gaze became unexpectedly thoughtful. "All I know is that Miss Modesty's more woman than anybody would think at first glance. Underneath that pretty face and them shy ways, she's got true grit and a lovin' heart. Them things ain't easy to come by, and it pays to remember that when that pretty face ain't so pretty no more, the grit and that lovin' heart will still be there to keep a man happy."

Luther nodded. "You're right."

"I know damned well I am." Max pulled himself suddenly erect. "Well, which calf will it be?"

Luther did not hesitate. "The ornery one . . . and keep those irons hot. I just decided I'm going to watch the sun set with Modesty tonight."

"Sounds like a fine idea."

Luther leaned over to pick up the rope.

Yes, there had to be a way.

The bed sagged under Garrett's weight as he drew himself to a seated position, creaking loudly, and he cursed under his breath. He glanced at the doorway, half expecting Lila to spring into sight there despite the fact that she was presently involved in washing a mountainous load of laundry in the backyard.

Garrett was momentarily amused. Lila Chesney,

reigning queen of the faro table, elbow deep in a laundry tub!

Garrett's brief smile faded. He had to give the resourceful witch credit. Except for elimination of the true Modesty's glasses, which had posed her a problem, Lila Chesney had maintained her disguise with the expertise of a professional. Quiet and shy at all times in the presence of others, she played her part especially well with Luther, but he knew he should not have expected anything else. Handling men skillfully was part of Lila Chesney's chosen profession.

That thought eliminating his temporary amusement, Garrett planted his feet firmly on the floor and drew himself slowly erect. Standing in his bare feet, wearing only the pants he had donned earlier, he waited for the onset of dizziness that had accompanied his former efforts to stand. Satisfaction flashed when nothing more than a dull throbbing in his head ensued. The throbbing rapidly fading to a dull ache, Garrett reached for the shirt that lay on a nearby chair. Taking the time to rip off the itchy bandage he no longer needed, he slipped his arm into the sleeve, the effort raising a fine veil of perspiration on his brow as he strained to slip the other arm in as well.

Unwilling to expend any more of his limited strength on dressing, Garrett dispensed with the thought of boots and started slowly toward the bedroom doorway. He had not needed any further contact with Hobbs to know that his "partner" was maintaining a surveillance on the ranch house at that very moment. It was not in Hobbs's nature to give up, but it was time for him to start pulling his own weight in this investigation. There were too many intangibles to make him feel secure doing anything else.

Emerging from his room, Garrett paused to appraise

the small parlor and connecting dining room, making special note of the visible entrances. He looked around him, mentally counting the rooms—two bedrooms, a parlor and dining room, and beyond that . . .

Garrett started uncertainly forward. Sounds of activity emanated from the room beyond a dining area furnished with a wooden plank table and some much-abused chairs. He noted in passing that the windows throughout were equipped with shutters but were bare of curtains, and that the house was totally lacking in a woman's touch.

A sharp, bittersweet pang tightened in his stomach as he recalled the small, warmly decorated farmhouse of his youth. He had brought Elizabeth home to that house as a bride with the thought of remaining there until a parcel of land became available nearby. Elizabeth had made the room they had shared as man and wife their own in subtle ways that had warmed him to the heart. She had done it out of love and out of a desire to set a seal of permanence to the life they had begun together.

A familiar pain returned, setting the planes of Garrett's face into harsh lines. But there had been no permanence beyond that black day, not for his mother and father, who had devoted their lives to the bit of land on which they were buried, and not for Elizabeth, whose chance had never come. Nor had there been permanence for him, except in a quest that had turned more bitter with the years.

A crash of pans was accompanied by a low grunt from the kitchen as Garrett neared the doorway, acutely aware that he needed to dismiss the past to attend the present and familiarize himself with the layout of the house before too much more time elapsed. Lila had made an effort to contact her lover. The uncertainty of what that contact would bring this unsuspecting household had begun haunting him. He would not have a repetition of the tragedy of Lawrence, Kansas, here at any price.

His eyes coldly reflecting that resolution, Garrett straightened his shoulders and stepped into the kitchen doorway.

Moving efficiently in the warm familiarity of her nephew's kitchen, Helga turned to the pot on the stove beside her. Picking up a fork, she gently stabbed the beef cooking there, knowing that in a few more hours and with a few more spices, her family would be eating her special sauerbraten.

Her full cheeks drawing up into an unconscious smile, Helga turned back to the table and the potatoes awaiting her. She picked up the grater, her mind skipping ahead to the picture of golden-brown potato pancakes she would later heap on a platter, to be garnished by applesauce she had prepared earlier in the day. The scent of cooking apples still lingered in the small room, mingling with the rich beef aroma. The scents revived warm memories, imparting a familiarity to a home that was only temporary and consoling her with the thought that although long hours of work would produce a meal that would be consumed in a fraction of the time it had taken to prepare, the meal would not be easily forgotten.

The loneliness that had beset her when Herman had passed from her life returned briefly, raising the mist of tears. Cooking was her special gift, which she was happy to share with these people who had given her so much. Luther did not fully realize that his need for her presence in the house had given her a renewed sense of worth. With no children to give her life purpose, she had looked upon Luther as the son she had not been able to bear her dear Herman, and she had been jealous of the woman who had come to take her place.

Helga's uneven grey brows furrowed. *Ja,* she had been unfair.

Regret tightened Helga's frown. It was true. Modesty did not cook. She did not bake. She did not sew. She did not keep house as a true *hausfrau* should, but inside she was strong. *Ja,* stronger than she . . . better than she, who could not help an injured man for the memories that stood in the way. But they were bad memories . . . memories of a terror that froze rational thought until she was—

Turning at a sound behind her, Helga went suddenly rigid. The injured man stood unsteadily there. He was tall—so tall that he filled the doorway with his height, so broad of shoulder that he stole her breath as he stared at her with light eyes that were darkly ringed. Black brows arched strongly against his ashen skin, and his expression was harsh.

He was silent—cold, pale, expressionless, staring at her as Herman had stared at her with lifeless eyes on that last day.

Helga's heart pounded wildly as her gaze jerked to the tall man's arm. Peeking from beneath the torn shirt were the marks where fangs had bitten deeply.

Reacting instinctively with remembered terror, Helga gave a sudden, blood-curdling shriek.

"Nein! Go away! Is death!"

The man did not move from the doorway as Helga stumbled backward, her round face blanched of color as she shrieked once more, "Is death der eyes!"

The sound of running steps at the outer door did not

budge Helga's terrified gaze from the specter staring at her with unblinking, lifeless eyes. She was shuddering, screeching her protest when Modesty appeared suddenly at her side. Within minutes slender, surprisingly strong arms were around her, and Modesty's voice was demanding, "What's wrong, Aunt Helga? What happened? You look like you've seen a ghost!"

"Nein, no ghost! See!" Raising a thick, trembling arm, Helga waved at the apparition in the doorway. "You see what it is. Is death dere . . . in der eyes!"

Modesty attempted once more to comfort Helga before turning sharply to address the specter in a voice totally unlike her former shy tone.

"What are you doing here? Can't you see you've frightened Aunt Helga? Damn it, get out of here! Go back to your room and lie down before you fall down."

Long moments passed before the specter turned and obediently disappeared from sight. Freed from his pale-eyed gaze, Helga turned stiffly to meet Modesty's concerned expression. Still trembling, the thought growing stronger in her mind with each passing minute, Helga whispered to the younger woman in a quivering voice, "Must take care! Is death in der eyes. Must take care!"

Reading compassion in the dark eyes that returned her gaze, Helga read disbelief as well.

And her fear grew.

Reaching the bedroom with sheer strength of will, Garrett collapsed onto the bed, the echo of the old woman's shrieks resounding in his mind. Her unexpected reaction to him had unnerved him, but it had not deterred him.

Relegating the woman's hysteria to the back of his mind, he had assessed the kitchen carefully, noting the access from the rear of the house, the location of the windows, paying particular interest to the trapdoor which obviously led to a storage cellar of some kind. He had stored the information in his mind for the time when it might become necessary to devise a defense against attack.

Disturbing him far more than the old woman's reaction to his appearance, however, was the accusation in Lila's eyes. She had defended the older woman against *him,* but it was *she* who could bring the world down around everyone in the household as he never could.

A cold smile slowly curved Garrett's lips at the memory of the old woman's words. She had said she saw death in his eyes. The old *hausfrau* had read him well. There was death in his eyes and in his heart. *Who* would die was yet to be determined.

Garrett nodded and closed his eyes. He would wait and see.

The sky above Eva, barely visible through the leafy cover of trees overhead, was striped with the gold of the afternoon sun beginning its descent from the noon apex. The wilderness around her, rich with foliage so thick that it was occasionally impossible to see more than a few feet in front of her on the seldom-used trail, rang with silent sounds heard by Eva alone as she continued onward as she had since first light. Sleeping in the sling on her back, Christina breathed evenly, the sound a sweet song of reassurance that overwhelmed the pain of burden.

The voices trailing relentlessly through Eva's mind

had grown louder as weariness took its toll. Nagging intermittently had been Mrs. Greer's gruff tone . . .

Find yourself a man you can depend on. Go someplace safe. You might do better to go back to your own people, if you can't find a white man to take care of you.

Olaf had spoken to her, too, his halting accent thick as he had repeated the words he had spoken so prophetically a week before he was killed.

Remember to protect yourself first when I'm no longer with you, Eva, young love of my heart. Keep yourself safe . . . and love our child. When you love her, you'll be loving me, and I'll be with you . . . forever . . .

Insistent had been Pa's low, firm tone as she heard his voice speaking words he had never spoken to her before.

Remember who you are, Eva. Rely on the instinct that comes from deep inside you. Your mother's people were one with the land, and if you close your eyes you'll hear the echo of their voices guiding your way.

She had closed her eyes, and the voices had stirred her heart.

But loudest of all through her long, uncertain hours had been Billy's voice as his passionate words of departure had resounded in her ears.

You're beautiful, Eva . . . really beautiful. I'll be back as soon as I can. If all goes well, I'll get you to someplace safer soon.

But it was too late to be safe.

If anything happens, you can reach me at Denver Post Office Box 23. Can you remember that? Number 23.

Number 23.

Staggering onward through the long day, Eva had

made a decision. She would eventually make her way to Denver, but first she must hide . . . hide. . . . She knew that at that very moment, someone might be starting off after her. Even if they were not, someone would discover the miner's body in her cabin sooner or later. Someone—perhaps the miner's short friend who knew where she lived on the mountain and who would remember the confrontation in the street. When he came, he would find his friend's body where he had fallen on the cabin floor, because she had had neither the time nor the inclination to bury him.

She needed to be as far away as possible by that time.

Perhaps as far as Denver . . .

A whimper from the sling on Eva's shoulder announced Christina's awakening and Eva stopped abruptly. Sound echoed in the forest. It could resound, alerting those even miles away of her location. She could not allow Christina to cry.

A nippled bottle filled moments later from the precious container of milk secured on her burro's back, Eva sat with Christina in her arms. A little corn meal mixed into a thin paste would settle her child's hunger as well as her own, and she would continue on until darkness made it impossible for her to go any farther. And if her tired muscles screamed their protest in the time between, she would hum the haunting chant sung by the mother she barely remembered. She would find consolation there, and she would find the strength to go on.

As for happiness . . . safety . . . she would find them only in one place: Billy's arms.

If she found them at all.

Denver's busy street rang with the sounds of revelry

as night fell and flickering lights of the city came to life. Raucous music and shouts of drunken revelry mingled with the sounds of heavy traffic that had not yet waned as Billy rode along the saloon-lined street amidst a populace seemed bent on celebration. Billy glanced behind him. As he had most of the day since they had left the horses at a nearby ranch where no questions were asked if the price paid was right, Picket traveled a few feet to his rear. Uncertain of Picket's reason for that position, he had become increasingly annoyed. He would set Picket straight after he smoothed things out with Forbes.

Billy's gaze settled on a saloon midway down the street, his jaw hardening. The Palace, the best saloon in the city, was the spot where he would find Forbes carefully seated with his back to the wall, watching the door as he made his way through a bottle of red-eye. Soon he would be seated beside him, and they would talk. He would tell Forbes that he—

"I can almost hear your mind tickin' Chesney." Surprising him, Picket urged his mount up alongside him and smiled snidely. "You're goin' to find Forbes and tell him what a good job you done gettin' them horses, and how he can depend on you to be right there with them horses when the time is right. Then you're goin' to buy him a drink or two, maybe three, and worm your way back into his good graces."

Billy could not help but laugh. "Looks like you got a window right into my head, Picket. I'm going to do just that, because if there's one man I don't want looking at me out of the corner of his eye, it's Forbes."

Picket nodded. "As long as you don't take all the credit for the job we just done, it's all right with me, 'cause I'm goin' to keep my distance. I don't want none of Forbes's bad feelin's for you rubbin' off on me."

Having made his position clear, Picket spurred his horse into a faster pace. He was already tying his horse off at the hitching rail when Billy dismounted. Dallying so Picket had the time he wanted to enter the saloon ahead of him, Billy felt his lip curl with contempt. He took a moment to adjust his gun securely on his hip, then pushed his way through the swinging doors and scanned the room.

A glance at the bar revealed Picket had already joined Eaton and Ricks there. A quick perusal of the perimeter of the room failed to reveal Forbes's location. He was about to step up to the bar when a voice at his shoulder turned him to Forbes's narrowed gaze.

"Well, well. I was beginnin' to think Picket had come back without you. I wouldn't have liked that."

Billy forced a smile. "Picket had a heavy thirst. He came to life when the Palace came into view. I'd have had to race him down the street to get here ahead of him. I figured that wasn't necessary, seeing as how we have the whole night ahead of us."

Making no verbal comment, Forbes motioned Billy over to a corner table where a bottle lay waiting. He smiled. "This table's mine for as long as I want it, and there ain't nobody in this saloon who's goin' to challenge me for it. Sit down. We got things to talk about while Picket's quenchin' that thirst." Taking only a moment to fill two empty glasses, Forbes looked up, his gaze intense.

"So, how did it go?"

"I got six of the prettiest mares you've ever seen waiting for us at Rondo's ranch. We can pick them up on the way out of town, and as soon as you choose the spot, I'll tuck them in, nice and tight. We didn't have any trouble, either, but there's going to be two fellas who're going to be mighty mad when they finally manage to untie themselves."

"You didn't do no shootin', did you?" Forbes's expression was suddenly tight. "I don't need no posse with blood in its eye chasin' after us before I'm ready."

"We never fired a shot."

Forbes nodded, his eyes traveling Billy's face in a way that set the hairs on the back of his neck up straight before he offered in a softer voice, "The boys and me have been pretty busy, too. We've been makin' ourselves real familiar with the Denver Bank, and it looks like that shipment's goin' out about a week from now."

"A week?" Billy frowned.

"Yeah. Why?" Forbes's bloodshot eyes were suddenly cautious. "You got somethin' better to do?"

"Come on, Forbes." Picket's interjection from behind him was unexpected, turning Billy at the sound of his voice. Sliding his lean frame into a nearby chair, Picket continued in a mocking tone. "You ain't that old that you can't recognize a fella who's got a yearnin' for his woman."

Forbes's eyes lit with unexpected interest. "That right, Chesney? You got yourself a woman?" He gave a short laugh. "Well, if you did, you're more of a fool than I thought you was. Hell, look around you. A man can have his choice in this place, and in just about every saloon along the street. What would you want to saddle yourself with one woman for, anyway?"

Somehow sensing it safer not to deny Picket's observation, Billy shrugged. "This woman'll do me for a while . . . until I take a fancy to another."

Forbes nodded, suddenly thoughtful. "You know, I had me a girl when I was about your age. She was damned pretty, too, and as sweet-talkin' a woman as I ever did know."

"What happened to her?"

Forbes's eyes narrowed. "She ran off with one of the fellows in my outfit and I never seen her again."

"Your outfit?"

"Yeah, when I was with Quantrill."

Billy controlled a grin at the unexpected turn the conversation had taken. Realizing he couldn't have asked for more, he urged, "I've heard a lot about Quantrill. He was some man."

"Damned right!" Forbes's face tightened with pride. "He knew a good man when he saw one, too. I remember the time . . ."

Billy sat back as Forbes slipped into a recitation he had heard several times before. Feigning acute attention, he downed the contents of his glass, poured himself another drink, and prepared himself for a long siege. Picket flashed him a brief, broken-toothed smile that was tinged with relief before he got up and sauntered back to the bar. Picket knew as well as he that before the night was over, Forbes and he would no longer be at odds.

Billy's inner smile grew. Yeah, he was smart, all right. A smart man kept track of the weaknesses of others, and Forbes had only one.

And slowly Billy's inner smile faded. The only trouble was that he knew his own weaknesses as well, and there was one that posed him a threat. It was called by the name of Eva, and it felt better than anything else in his arms.

"Ain't that right, Chesney?"

Meeting Forbes's gaze without missing a beat, Billy responded, "Yeah, they're still talking about Quantrill's raids. There wasn't another Confederate leader like him."

"Damned right!"

"Yeah, damned right." Forbes lapsed off into another tale as Billy emptied his glass again and poured another . . . as in the corner of his mind, Eva's dark eyes beckoned.

The sunset hour was behind him, dinner had been eaten, and the sounds of cleanup filled the kitchen as Luther walked with a barely noticeable limp toward Garrett Harrison's bedroom door. It had not been an easy day. That ornery bull calf that Max had been eyeing had proved the greatest challenge of the day, and the spot where the animal's hind leg had darted out and caught his thigh was still throbbing.

But it wasn't pain that knotted Luther's brow with an uncharacteristic frown as he made his resolute way forward. That quick, well-aimed kick had slowed him up just enough so that the sun was already setting when the ranch house came into view after the day's work. His plans for the evening Modesty and he would share had come to an abrupt end with the setting of the sun, and it appeared they were not about to be revived, if the silence around the dining-room table had been any indication.

Recalling Max's puzzled expression throughout the meal and the old fella's concerned glances toward an unnaturally subdued Aunt Helga, Luther made a mental note to tell him about Helga's encounter with Harrison earlier in the day as Modesty had related it. But, first things first.

Pausing unnoticed at Harrison's bedroom doorway, Luther watched as the big man sat propped up in bed, struggling to eat the food on the plate in front of him. Luther controlled a smile. He recalled Lila's annoyed frown as she had cut Aunt Helga's sauerbraten into bite-size pieces before delivering it to the room, and he had observed the tight set of her lips when she had returned. At his questioning glance, she had responded, "I told him his fingers are still too stiff to handle a fork well, but he says he can feed himself."

It had taken Luther only a moment's observance to see that Modesty had been right. He had the feeling, however, that Garrett Harrison would starve before he'd admit it.

"Looks like you're having a little trouble there." Harrison looked up as Luther continued easily, "Modesty tells me you've decided to feed yourself." He paused. "She really wouldn't mind doing that for you for a little longer. Modesty's a generous young woman, she—"

"I don't need her help anymore." Harrison paused, his expression unchanging as he stated flatly, "I appreciate what you've done for me, but I'm well enough to take care of myself. Another few days and I'll be as good as new."

"You think you'll be on your feet that soon?"

"I *know* I will be."

Luther nodded. "Modesty told me what happened today." Harrison's eyes narrowed defensively. Surprised at the man's reaction, Luther smiled. "It seems we owe you an apology."

Leaning slowly back against the pillow, Harrison scrutinized him intently. "You do?"

"Yes." Luther searched for the right words. "Aunt Helga's very set in her ways and there isn't much anyone can do when she gets something into her head. You probably know her husband died from a rattlesnake bite a few years ago." Harrison did not respond and Luther continued, "She's never gotten over the shock of finding him dead. He was bitten on the arm, and I guess seeing you come in here the same way was just too much of a shock. I understand she reacted hysterically when you walked into the kitchen today."

"It's all right."

"She'll get over it."

"I said, it's all right."

Those cold grey eyes were still assessing him, and it occurred to Luther that he couldn't really blame Aunt Helga for being startled when she turned and saw this big fellow standing in the doorway behind her. He could be a damned intimidating sight.

But he also could be the answer to his prayers.

"So, you're thinking you'll be on your feet in a few days."

"That's what I said."

"What are your plans?"

"Why do you want to know?"

Becoming more sympathetic with each passing minute to the hardship he had foisted upon Modesty in caring for this difficult man, Luther responded candidly. "Your horse is dead, and if you don't mind my being frank, you don't look like you've got the money to spare to get another, even if one was available out here."

"So?"

"Have you ever done any ranch work?" Luther glanced at Harrison's hands. "Those callouses make me think you're no stranger to hard work."

"I know my way around a ranch."

"Are you interested in some temporary work?" Harrison did not reply immediately, allowing Luther to continue, "This is a busy season for Max and me here. My herd's starting to build up and we've got more work than we can handle right now, what with branding and putting up new fences."

"New fences?"

"I'm getting some new bulls. I'm going to try out a breeding procedure that's worked pretty well up in Wyoming for the past few years. I'm thinking that it'll put me ahead of the crowd if I can get a jump on things, but that means I'll have to pick out the best of my stock and separate them. That'll take time, and time's running short. The bulls are due to arrive soon."

"I won't be able to do a decent job for you for another two or three days. Isn't there somebody from town who can start helpin' you right away?"

"There isn't much help to spare around here . . . not that's worth a damn, anyway. Well, what do you say?"

Harrison did not immediately respond. "What about your aunt? I make her uncomfortable. Will she object?"

"Aunt Helga's had her say already. Besides, I make the decisions here."

There was another prolonged silence before Harrison nodded. "All right. I'll take the job."

"You haven't asked what I'm going to pay you."

"I'll work off the price of another horse. It doesn't matter. I owe you."

Smiling fully for the first time, Luther extended his hand. "It's a deal, then."

Harrison grasped it with a small wince of pain. "A deal."

Harrison's clasp was hard and firm despite his weakness, and Luther was silently impressed. "I'll leave it to you to let me know when you're ready to sit a horse." Luther looked at Harrison's plate again. "You're sure you don't—"

"I'm sure."

"Yeah . . . well, I'll tell Max his life is going to be a little easier in a few days."

Back through the doorway a moment later, Luther was startled to see Modesty waiting outside of the room. Her expression was strained. He took her arm with concern.

"Is something wrong?"

"I . . . I heard what you said in there. Are you sure you want him to stay? H-he isn't a very pleasant fellow."

"It's not his personality I'm concerned with, Modesty. Harrison said he's going to be in a good enough shape to ride in a few days, and I think he means what he says. I think he'll work out."

"But I . . ."

Modesty hesitated, then shook her head, and Luther urged, "But you . . . what?"

Her somber gaze rising to his, Modesty continued with obvious hesitation, "I . . . I don't like him very much."

Modesty was obviously uncomfortable putting those thoughts into words, and Luther slipped his arms around her. He drew her close, suddenly realizing that he was relieved to hear them. Damned if he hadn't been the slightest bit jealous . . .

Tipping Modesty's face up to his, Luther brushed her lips with his. She tasted good . . . too good. He forced himself to draw back.

"Harrison will stay only a few weeks, long enough to help Max and me over the hump. Besides, with him here, I'll be able to get back to the ranch at night before I'm too tired to do anything but eat and fall asleep." Luther's face sobered. "I'll have a little more time to spend with you, darling."

Her eyes filling unexpectedly, Modesty whispered, "I

guess I'll be able to bear it, then." Surprising him, Modesty stood on her toes and pressed her mouth lightly to his.

His voice noticeably husky, Luther whispered, "Come outside with me and try that again."

Lila hesitated only a moment before taking his hand and leading him toward the outer door.

Luther's heart took wing.

The sound of the outer door snapping shut was simultaneous with Garrett's low curse as he slammed his fork down onto his plate in sudden fury. Realizing he was shaking, he took a deep breath.

Oh, he was wise to Lila Chesney, all right! She had done it purposely. She had kissed Knox and accepted his invitation to go outside with him because she had known he could hear her. She wanted to torment him . . . to show him he couldn't control her.

But she was wrong.

Garrett's strong features hardened. Lila Chesney hadn't proved anything to him except that he had been right in believing she had no conscience. What she didn't know was that he was as ruthless as she herself, and that he'd make her pay for every moment of torment he suffered while imagining her in Knox's arms.

And he'd enjoy every damned minute of it.

Enfolded in Luther's strong arms, the light of a million stars illuminating the black velvet sky above them, Lila raised her mouth to his. At the first touch of his lips, she slid her arms around his neck and drew him closer, kissing him fully as she had never kissed him before. She heard the groan of his passion and separated her lips further, indulging the delicate play of his tongue against hers, wishing . . .

Damn!

Drawing back abruptly, Modesty looked up at Luther.

"What's the matter, darling?"

"Nothing . . . nothing . . ."

Lila was suddenly ashamed. Why was she leading this good man on when the touch of his lips did no more than evoke the picture of cold grey eyes and the memory of lips that had touched hers briefly, without any tenderness at all?

Stupid question. She knew why.

Sliding her arms back around Luther's neck with new determination, Lila raised herself on tiptoe once more and slanted her mouth against his. Luther's kiss could not erase the memory of Garrett's, but while she was in Luther's arms, she was safe from arms that would be more demanding than his. She was behaving selfishly, perhaps even cruelly, but she would give Luther pleasure . . . as much as she could manage with a few brief kisses . . . and she would hope that he would forgive her one day.

You can't rely on the protection of Luther's arms forever . . .

The nagging voice in her mind grew louder as Luther's kiss deepened, and Lila groaned. The sound, misinterpreted as passion, stirred Luther to greater loving assault.

What will you do when other arms reach out for you and draw you close?

Lila trembled. What would she do?

What *could* she do?

Lila shuddered again.

Eleven

A train whistle echoed in the distance as puffs of black smoke curled upward to dissipate against the descending twilight. Holding their horses rigidly in check a few miles up the line, four men were concealed in the foliage along the tracks. Long duster coats flapped against their horses' sides as the animals snorted and sidestepped nervously in an anxious silence that was broken by a low, angry command.

"Hold on to that horse, Picket, and make sure he don't bolt. I thought you said you could ride anythin' with four legs!"

"How in hell was I supposed to know that this damned mare was only half broke? Damn it! I'll get Chesney for this."

Grating uneven teeth, Picket pulled back sharply on his mount's reins. The animal whinnied loudly in protest, causing Forbes to rasp, "You queer this job for us, Picket, and there'll be hell to pay, I'm tellin' you now. Get that animal in hand or I'll drop him right here, on the spot!"

Paling, Picket moved his protesting animal a few steps to the rear as Forbes continued tightly, "All right, remember. Eaton—you stick with me like always. We get movin' as soon as the engine hits the bottom of the grade. Ricks—you and Picket stay right behind us and keep up with the train. When we reach the engine and stop it, you uncouple everythin' but the express car. Picket—you shoot anythin' that moves while we're pullin' away. As soon as it's safe, you set your horses loose and get on the train. You all understand?"

The low chorus of assent from the men around him turned Forbes back to the sight of the approaching train as a familiar excitement raced through his veins. He laughed aloud. Hell, it was only at times like this when he felt really alive! It had been a damned long week while he had waited for this shipment to be sent. The truth be known, he'd be doing this even if there wasn't the kind of money in that express car that he knew was there waiting to be taken.

Forbes paused at that thought. Maybe that was why his portion of the haul always slipped through his fingers so easy, bringing the jobs closer and closer together as he got older.

His eyes becoming fixed on the approaching train, Forbes recalled a time when he was young . . . no more than twenty . . . when he rode for the first time with Quantrill and discovered the thrill of holding lives in the palm of his hand and of using his gun at will as the hate boiled out of his pores. The exhilaration had been greater than any he had ever experienced.

But that had been war—Quantrill's war. This war was his own, and was more determined. It was a war against the scum who had looked at him like he was trash after the South had surrendered. It was a war against the life that had been taken away from him and left him nothing. It was a war against losers, those who had knuckled under, behaving like beaten animals while they worked from dawn to dusk as if they had never ridden high wearing the Confederate grey. If he had let them, they'd have made him just like them, but that would never be. Them dumb fools would never know the thrill of taking what they wanted from life, of winning against the odds, of being alive just for the fun and challenge of it, and of knowing that they were one step ahead of everyone else because they were willing to risk it all.

A hard smile touched Forbes's lips. There was only one thing he held precious. Power. Without it a man was nothing, and with it he was everything. A gun gave a man power, and when he wasn't afraid to use it, his power increased. He remembered the fear he saw in men's eyes when they looked up the barrel of his gun, and the rush of an emotion, closer to ecstasy than any he had ever known, in realizing that with one twitch of his finger, they would see no more.

The blast of the train whistle echoed in the stillness, closer than before, and Forbes's heart began a rapid pounding. In a few minutes, he'd be making his way across the top of that train, knowing that the prize awaiting him when he reached that engine was as much a sense of triumph as it was the gold that was waiting in the express car immediately behind.

For gold was also power, and he used it well. Just as he used the damned fools who followed him. Aside from Eaton, there was only one other man in the group worth a damn. Yeah, he saw himself behind Chesney's grin, all right, and he—

The train whistle blasted into the twilight once more, close—very close—and Forbes's heart leaped. He glanced at the man beside him, seeing in Eaton's eyes a glow he had seen there countless times before.

The train rushed by, and Forbes caught his breath. He grinned as it began its laborious climb up the rise of the hill, waiting only until the rear car had passed him before spurring his horse into a sudden leap forward.

His head tucked down into his shoulders, the wind rushing at his face, Forbes felt elation surge anew as his galloping mount gained steadily on the train. Jumping, he caught the rear car. He swung himself aboard and was climbing onto the roof when he heard Eaton jump aboard behind him. He smiled—a bone-chilling sight for the evil it displayed as he made his way forward.

Twilight was falling as Garrett looked up from his plate and scanned the faces around the dining-room table. His head down, Luther was eating enthusiastically, obviously anxious for the meal to be over. Garrett controlled a scornful snort. He supposed he'd be anxious to be through, too, if he could count on a long walk in the darkness with Lila afterward.

Seated to his right, Lila was eating with limited enthusiasm, as she had most of the week since he had assumed a place at the table as a part of the crew. He had moved out of the bedroom in the house and into the bunkhouse with Luther and Max several days earlier, and it had not been easy during the long nights that had followed, knowing Lila was lying in the same bed where he had lain, alone and doubtless as restless as he. The witch that she was, she had managed to cut off all but the barest of contact with him in the time since. He was frustrated and annoyed, and determined to—

The sound of a heavy step coming from the kitchen turned Garrett to Helga's arrival with a fresh plate of biscuits. She caught his eye and her gaze froze. She didn't like him, and she made no secret of it. She watched him like a hawk whenever he was near, frustrating his efforts to get Lila alone so completely that he knew he would be tempted to tie and gag the woman if he thought it would help.

But it wouldn't, because wherever Helga was, there was always Max. Smiling Max. Congenial Max. Max who was spending more and more time in the kitchen, his favorite room of late.

Cutting another mouthful off the thick slab of roasted beef on his plate, Garrett shoved it into his mouth and chewed vigorously. His appetite had returned full measure. The headaches had not bothered him for the past few days and full mobility had been restored to his arm. He had been functioning well as one of Knox's hands, and had even gotten a chance to talk to Hobbs, looking seedier than ever, in his concealed position a distance from the ranch. It had consoled him to know that Hobbs was able to slip into town to maintain regular contact with McParland during the evening hours, and that his silent partner never let Lila out of his sight during the day when he was otherwise occupied. Something was due to break soon. They could not take a chance of losing her again.

That thought turned Garrett back to Lila as she toyed with her meal, the feeling that time was slipping away too quickly growing stronger. His gaze lingered, touching on the soft brilliance of her hair. It was too tightly bound for his taste. It called out for the touch of his hand to ruffle it into the gleaming waves he had seen once before. He could almost feel the heavy strands slipping through his fingers. He could almost smell its warm scent.

As if sensing his perusal, Lila glanced up, and Garrett's heart began a slow pounding. Her cheeks were lightly colored from the sun. The color enhanced the creamy perfection of her skin. He had dreamed of caressing that flawlessness with his lips.

Wariness sprang into Lila's heavily lashed eyes, and Garrett ached for the chance to foster a more potent emotion there. The fine line of her lips tightened and twitched, and Garrett longed to cover them with his own, to make them warm and pliable with his kisses. He would teach her what loving was about then, and he would make her see that—

Suddenly realizing that his body was reacting revealingly to his erotic thoughts, Garrett looked back at his plate and continued eating. But the food was sawdust in his mouth, his appetite diminished, and he knew it would be harder than ever before to watch as Knox took Lila's hand and drew her out into the moonlight when the dishes were done.

Helga's voice raised Garrett's head from his churning thoughts to see the old woman's grey brows were knit with concern as she addressed Lila.

"You do not eat. Der meat is no goot?"

"It's fine, Aunt Helga." Lila raised a tentative hand to her forehead. "I . . . I have a little headache, that's all."

"Doctor Bennett leave powders. You take."

"No, that won't be necessary. I think I got a little too much sun today."

"Ja." Helga nodded. "Too much work in der garden. You rest after dinner. I do dishes."

"No, that's not necessary!"

"Aunt Helga's right, Modesty." Luther's frown deepened. "You're working too hard."

"That's right, Miss Modesty. Don't you worry about Helga. I can help her in the kitchen tonight."

Max's addition to the chorus of concern suddenly

more than he could stand, Garrett slammed his fork down on his plate and stood up abruptly. All eyes turned toward him as he stated flatly, "I've had enough . . . to eat."

Not bothering to look back, he walked directly to the door and stepped outside. He took a deep breath of night air and attempted to still his agitation. It made him sick . . . the fawning everyone did over the lying little witch. If they only knew . . .

Feeling a need for isolation, Garrett turned toward the bunkhouse. He was walking briskly past the window when Knox's concerned voice trailed out into the rapidly falling darkness.

"You look a little flushed, Modesty . . ."

Lila's reply was soft, disturbed. "M-maybe you're all right. Maybe I should lie down for a while. Excuse me, please."

Playing her role to the hilt . . .

Garrett's frustration soared. Lila Chesney had everyone in that damned household dangling from strings which she jerked and manipulated at will. He scowled. If he were to be honest, he would have to admit that Lila was manipulating him just as firmly, but in a different way. He didn't like it, and if something didn't happen soon . . .

Pushing open the bunkhouse door minutes later, Garrett took another deep breath. He had no choice but to wait and see where Lila Chesney would lead him from here. Too much was at stake.

More than he had originally anticipated.

Much more . . .

Anticipation crawled along Billy's spine as he waited, hidden in a ring of trees alongside the tracks as the sound of the approaching train drew closer. Peering out from his concealment, he strained his eyes into the rapidly falling darkness. The train drew closer, traveling at a revealingly slow speed, and Billy counted. The engine and *one* car. Forbes had done it! It was all clear!

Withdrawing a box of matches from his pocket, Billy struck one and lit the lantern hanging from his saddle. He pulled his neckerchief up to conceal the lower half of his face as the lantern flickered to life and rode out into the open, waving it in a prearranged signal. A spontaneous laugh escaped his lips as the engine slowed to a halt almost directly in front of him. His shout of welcome died on his lips as a shot rang out unexpectedly and the engineer fell from the cab. It did not take more than a glance to see that the man was not moving . . . that he would never move again.

"Never mind him!" His voice muffled behind the neckerchief that masked the lower half of his face, Forbes stepped into sight within the cab and directed gruffly, "Get back to the express car and keep your gun drawn. We're not in the clear yet."

Following instructions, Billy drew his gun and moved cautiously toward the express car. He noted out of the corner of his eye that the dead engineer was dark-haired and young, appearing to be in his early thirties. He took his place beside Picket.

The sound of footsteps turned Billy to the sight of Forbes and Eaton approaching, guns drawn. The fireman stumbled ahead of them.

"You know the men in that express car?" Forbes poked the fireman with his gun. "You know their names?" The fireman nodded. His soot-stained face was ashen, and Forbes pressed with a snarl, "I didn't hear you . . ."

"Y-yes, I know them."

"If you don't want what happened to your friend to happen to you, you'd better tell them right now to throw out their guns. They don't have no choice nohow, because we got enough powder to blow the door off if they don't cooperate."

"But . . ."

"Tell them!"

Visibly shuddering, the fireman shouted in a quaking voice, "WINTERS—BLAKE—OPEN THE DOOR AND COME OUT. THESE FELLAS HAVE POWDER AND THEY'LL BLOW THE DOOR OFF IF YOU DON'T."

"Tell them what happened to your friend—what's goin' to happen to you if they don't . . ."

"THEY'VE ALREADY KILLED O'NEIL. THEY'RE GOING TO KILL ME, TOO, IF YOU DON'T."

There was no response and Forbes's sneer turned to a rage that emerged in a rumbling shout.

"I DON'T HAVE TIME TO WAIT HERE. I'M GOIN' TO FIRE TWO SHOTS. THE FIRST WILL BE INTO THE GROUND. THEN I'M GOIN' TO COUNT TO FIVE, AND THE SECOND WILL BE THROUGH THIS FELLA'S HEART. IT'S UP TO YOU . . ."

His mouth dry, Billy saw Forbes lower his gun and fire into the ground at the trembling fireman's feet. He saw Forbes laugh the second before he shouted, "ONE . . . TWO . . ."

Billy glanced nervously around him. Eaton's gaze was intense, emotionless. Ricks' bearded cheek twitched, and Picket's heavy lips were parted, his narrow face expressionless.

"THREE . . . FOUR . . ."

Billy's throat was thick, his flesh crawling. He watched Forbes raise his gun.

"FI—"

"DON'T SHOOT. WE'RE COMIN' OUT!"

The express car door slid open slowly.

"WE'RE THROWIN' OUT OUR GUNS."

Two rifles hit the ground.

"THROW OUT THE REST OF THEM!"

Two handguns followed.

"COME OUT WITH YOUR HANDS UP!"

One figure appeared in the express car doorway, then another, and Billy released a tense breath. Suddenly realizing he was shaking, he started back toward the horses.

The moneybags loaded a short time later, Forbes shouted, "Get mounted! Time's awastin'."

Holding his mount carefully in check as Forbes mounted, Billy saw Forbes turn and raise his gun toward the three bound-and-gagged men lying on the ground. Their eyes bulged as Forbes gave a short laugh, then cocked the hammer.

"What're you doing, Forbes?"

Forbes turned sharply toward Billy. "What do *you* care what I'm doin'?"

"They didn't do anything. They haven't even seen our faces."

"I'm the boss here!"

Billy hesitated. Intensely aware of the risk, he pressed, "They can't hurt us. Why don't you leave them be . . . *boss?"*

The tense moment's silence that followed was broken by Forbes's unexpected laughter.

"You're a clever fella . . . you know that?" Forbes laughed again. "Seein's how you asked so nice . . ."

Forbes holstered his gun unexpectedly, then wheeled his horse around to direct Billy a pointed glance void of any trace of amusement. "Just remember not to get *too* clever . . ."

Within a moment it was all behind them.

* * *

Lila paced nervously in her room, the scene at the table a few minutes earlier playing over and again in her mind. Halting at the washstand mirror, she glanced at her reflection and questioned through stiff lips, "What's the matter with you?"

Seeing no answer forthcoming, Lila briefly closed her eyes, wondering how much more she could take. She resumed her pacing, cursing the day she had first met the shy Modesty Parkins.

Well, how was she supposed to have known that Modesty's betrothed would turn out to be more than any woman had a right to expect in a man? How was she to have known her guilt at using him would end up vying with anxiety for Billy's safety in her mind? How could she ever have foreseen that Garrett Harrison, bastard that he was, would arrive to haunt her, awake and sleeping, that he would recover from his injuries only to continue harassing her with a presence she could not seem to dismiss . . . with glances that raised a trembling so intense inside her that she feared she would shake apart . . . with a knowledge that he wanted her with every fiber in his body, and that she . . .

Lila's anxiety increased. She couldn't stay here any longer. She knew if she did . . .

Frantic, Lila searched her mind for a solution. Billy would get her letter soon. Possibly he already had and was on his way here. She couldn't leave. She had to warn him. She'd move into town. That was it! She'd tell Luther that she needed some time away from him to think things over. He had noticed her tenseness during the last week. He had commented on it on their nightly walks. He had noticed that she had begun to draw away from him when his ardor became intense. He'd believe her, and he'd let her go. He wanted what was best for her.

Damn it . . . he was so good . . .

Lila nodded, relieved at her decision. She'd tell him now . . . before another minute passed.

Taking a moment to splash some water on her burning cheeks, Lila dried her face carefully and smoothed back her hair, startled to see a hesitation entirely uncharacteristic of her strong personality in the mirrored image.

Furious at that hesitation, Lila raised her chin and turned toward the door. Within minutes she was in the kitchen doorway. Aunt Helga and Max turned toward her as she managed in an even voice, "Where's Luther?"

Max smiled. "I'm mighty happy to see you're feelin' better, Miss Modesty. He went outside. He'll be glad to see you ain't too tired for a nice little walk after all."

Lila turned toward the door. A nice little walk . . .

Outside in the yard, Lila glanced around her. A light flickered in the bunkhouse. She shook her head. Oh, no, she wasn't going anywhere near Garrett Harrison. Another light flickered in the barn. Heaving a relieved sigh, she started toward it.

Reaching the barn doorway, Lila paused. The shadowed interior was dark and she hesitated.

"Luther, are you in there?"

In answer to her inquiry, the tall, male silhouette moved into view. Luther did not respond, and Lila felt her throat tighten. She had told so many lies to this man. How could she tell him another?

Lila proceeded toward Luther, dread growing stronger with each step she took. He did not move, allowing her to walk deeper into the shadows as she whispered, "Oh, Luther, I'm so sorry. It seems I'm always apologizing to you, or asking you to understand. And now, when I've already asked for so much, I have to ask for more. Luther dear, please try to understand what I'm saying now, but—"

"You're wasting your breath, Lila . . ."

Lila gasped aloud at the sound of Garrett's voice, as his strong hands snapped out to clamp onto her upper arms and she was suddenly whirled around and thrust into the darkness of the corner. Pinned against the wall with the hard, male length of Garrett's body, Lila rasped, "Let me go, damn you! Wh-what are you doing in here, anyway? I thought you were in the bunkhouse?"

"You were wrong."

Garrett crushed her tighter, effortlessly subduing her struggles as he whispered against her lips, "You're not foolin' me. I know what you've been doin' with Knox. You've been tryin' to use him to put me out of your mind, but it's not workin', is it, darlin' . . ." Garrett did not wait for her response as he continued hotly, "It's not workin' because every time you're in Knox's arms, you think of what it would be like if *I* was holdin' you instead. Every time he kisses you, you think of what it would be like if *I* was kissin' you instead, and every time he touches you . . ."

Garrett cursed low in his throat the moment before he closed the tantalizing distance between their lips. His kiss was angry and demanding, and unexpectedly soul-shattering as it surged relentlessly deeper. It seared Lila's mind and body with brilliant, blinding colors that left only the sensation of Garrett's warm breath against her skin and the male taste of him in her mouth as he laved the hollows there with increasing ardor. He was consuming her with his passion. The weight of his muscular strength moving against her womanly softness was silk against steel, an ecstasy just short of pain. She was losing herself to the kaleidoscoping emotions warring inside her as Garrett tore his mouth from hers at last, his voice a ragged whisper.

"Now you know what it's like to be in *my* arms, but you don't feel one damned bit better, because a taste has only whetted your appetite for more. And it's drivin' you crazy, isn't it, darlin' . . ."

Garrett's eyes were hot pinpoints of light as he gave a harsh laugh. "How do I know all this . . . ?" He laughed again. "Because, damn you, the same torment's been makin' my life a livin' hell every time you slip off into the darkness with that sanctimonious bastard . . ."

Grateful for the sudden anger that drew her from her mindless lethargy, Lila stiffened. "Luther isn't sanctimonious! He's good and kind and decent—but you couldn't possibly understand a man like that!"

"If Knox is as wonderful as you say, why don't you call him to come and save you from me? Are you afraid I'll tell him the truth about you?" Garrett's voice dropped to an insidious whisper. "Would I do that to you, darlin'?"

Garrett traced her trembling lips with his tongue. His breathing was uneven as he responded harshly to his own question. "You know I would, because if Knox threw you out, I'd be the only person left to help you hide from whatever you're running from."

"I don't need your help. I don't need anybody's help. I can take care of myself."

"Funny, I remember sayin' the same thing to you a little while back, but it didn't do me any good, did it?" Garrett's body pressed tighter against hers, stealing her breath, raising a hunger in her she fought to deny as Lila gasped again.

"You're hurting me . . ."

The pressure instantly lessened, but Garrett's voice lost none of its sharpness as he whispered against her mouth, "Just like you hurt me every time you respond to Knox's touch with a smile . . . every time you take his hand . . . every time you go out that damned door into the darkness with him for 'a little walk.' "

Garrett cursed again. His fingers splayed against the smooth skin of her cheeks, holding her firmly in place as he covered her mouth with his once more. He drank slowly, so deeply, of the welling emotions within her that she was powerless to resist him as he trailed his lips to her ear to whisper with startling gentleness, "But I don't want to hurt you, darlin'. I want to make love to you. I want to kiss you and touch you and caress you until you cry out for more, and then I want to give you what you're wantin' because it's what I'm wantin', too . . . what I've been wantin' since the minute I opened my eyes and saw you leanin' over me."

Panic surged inside Lila at the unexpected change in Garrett's tone, at the stirring timbre of his voice as he brushed the curve of her cheek with his lips, as his mouth found hers for another mind-drugging kiss.

Damn him! He was a master of the game . . . a spellbinder, destroying her will to resist him as he whispered, "You want me to love you, too. You know you do. Let me show you how good it can be between us. Let me do that for you, Lila. Let me prove to you that I can give you pleasure you've never had before . . . that I can make you feel what you've never felt before . . . that I can make you love as you've never loved before." The grey velvet of his eyes holding hers, Garrett rasped, "As you've never loved before . . ."

A lazy warmth began assuming control of Lila's emotions. An inclination to slide her arms around Garrett's neck grew stronger as his mouth renewed its loving assault, as his hand stroked her intimately . . . as her body responded with growing heat to his touch. Oh, yes, he was right. She *wanted,* more than she had ever wanted before. She *needed,* more than she had ever needed before. She longed to—

No!

Coming abruptly to her senses, Lila began struggling wildly, her clenched fists pounding at Garrett's shoulders as she twisted and turned in a frantic effort to break free.

"Stop that, damn it!" Garrett's whispered command was harsh. "You know I'm not going to let you get away."

Grasping her wrists in one strong hand, Garrett thrust them high over her head, pinning them to the wall above her as he held her lower body motionless with his.

"Don't fight me, Lila. It'll be right between us. I know it will."

"Let me go." Lila's grip on reality began slipping away again as Garrett's free hand trailed past her shoulder in a gentle caress. It lingered on her rounded breast and her voice escaped in a final, whispered plea.

"Let me go . . . please . . ."

The flickering shadows played against Garrett's face as he drew back slowly, far enough to slant an unreadable gaze down into her eyes.

"Don't beg me, Lila."

"Beg?" Sudden humiliation touched Lila's mind. "I wasn't begging! I wouldn't beg you for anything! I'm *telling* you to let me go. I—"

Garrett's mouth closed over Lila's once more, swallowing her protests, making a mockery of her words as he devoured her with his hunger, as he infused her with his need, as he slowly, meticulously, eliminated all thought of denial from her mind.

Her lips gradually yielding of their own accord as her softness melded to the rock wall of his frame, Lila felt her aching arms settle around Garrett's neck. Her hands slid into the heavy thickness of his hair to clasp him closer. She was drowning in the bittersweet pain of desire, in the need to be made a part of this man, even as he pulled back unexpectedly and rasped, "Come away with me, now, darlin'. I want—"

"MODESTY, ARE YOU IN THERE?"

The sound of Luther's voice snapped Lila abruptly back to reality. She looked up into Garrett's shadowed face, humiliation welling in the moment before she wrenched herself free.

Forcing a stability to her voice that she had not thought she could manage, Lila called out in reply, "YES, I'M HERE."

Hatred for herself as well as for the man who stepped back and away from her with a contemptuous sneer burned deep inside her as Lila slid a cautious hand to her hair and tucked in a straying wisp, then hastily straightened her dress. She walked quickly toward the barn doorway, meeting Luther there. She continued with a lightened tone, "I was looking for you. Max said you had come outside. I saw someone in here and I thought it was you." She grimaced pointedly as Garrett emerged into Luther's view. "But it wasn't you."

"I went to the bunkhouse for something." Luther took her arm, dismissing Garrett's presence behind her with a nod, raising an inner sigh of relief within Lila as he continued, "I'm glad you're feeling better. Why were you looking for me?"

Lila slid her arm through Luther's, as grateful for the limited light of the yard that shadowed her unnatural flush as she was for having been saved from herself as she responded, "I . . . I just wanted to be with you for a while." Speaking more to the man behind her than to the man whose arm she held, she gave an exaggerated shudder. "There was a rat in there. A big one. It was so close to me . . ." She paused. "My flesh is still crawling."

"I thought you looked upset. I'll see what I can do about that tomorrow, darling."

The heat of Garrett's eyes bored into her back as Lila slid closer to Luther. Suddenly realizing she was safe from Garrett and from herself only with Luther beside her, Lila clutched his arm tighter.

She did not look back as she walked away.

The sounds of night encircled her as Eva adjusted the wick of the lantern resting on the forest floor beside her. She was conscious of the need to conserve the limited fuel, of the threat in the darkness that would settle around her like a fluttering black cloak without it. She glanced to the spot a few feet away where her burro was loosely tethered, noting that he seemed to feel none of her apprehension as he munched contentedly on nearby foliage.

Eva looked up at the cover of trees that defused the moon's meager light into flickering shadows, then to the spot a few feet away where her beautiful, fair-haired child slept on the blanket she had spread there.

A shiver passed down Eva's spine, but she knew it was not due to the damp chill of the forest, and she stirred, her back aching and her muscles protesting the prolonged, difficult trek she had sustained throughout the day. She shivered again, apprehension rising. She had traveled without pause from dawn to dusk, but she knew she had not traveled far enough. She had escaped immediate danger, but she knew she was not yet safe. She knew she must make a plan more definite than to follow the drumming voice in her mind that whispered Billy's name, but she was presently incapable of the task.

Eva released a trembling sigh. She was exhausted to the bone.

Crawling the few feet to the blanket where her child rested, she curled up beside the sleeping infant and wrapped the blanket around them both, sealing them in a cocoon of fragrant, familiar scent. She breathed the scent deeply, seeking consolation as a soft lament arose in her mind.

She had thought she was through with wandering. She had thought she was through with fear. She had thought she had found a home.

Eva closed her eyes, shutting out the night sounds that grew persistently louder. She drew her child closer. Denver was so far away, and it was difficult to hide when you could make yourself walk no farther. She needed peace . . . for a little while.

Billy's image sprang before her mind's eye, and Eva smiled. The rhythm of a familiar Indian chant began in her mind, and she indulged it. She allowed herself to drift off to its calming cadence as smiling green eyes held her warmly entranced, as they brought her to the edge of sleep.

A sound in the darkness!

Eva's eyes snapped open. She drew herself abruptly

erect. She heard it again . . . a rustling within the trees, then shuffling footsteps . . . a horse's whinny.

Her heart pounding, Eva blew out the lantern and reached for the gun lying nearby. Her hand closed around the cold wooden handle as the rustling grew closer.

An Injun can't get away with killin' a white man . . .

Eva's chin rose in response to the remembered taunt.

"SHE'S GOT TO BE AROUND HERE SOMEWHERE, WALLER!"

The call of a slurred male voice rent the silence, echoing in the surrounding darkness. It sent a remembered horror slithering down Eva's spine as she heard the shouted response.

"SHE COULDN'T HAVE GOTTEN MUCH FARTHER. WE'LL GET HER, ALL RIGHT!"

Eva's finger curled around the trigger as the shifting shadows of darkness closed around her and the sounds drew ever closer. She had somehow known this time would come. She had killed a white man and she did not regret it. She would kill again to keep her child.

"PETE! OVER HERE! OVER HERE!"

The sound of crashing footsteps close by . . . a shot in the darkness . . .

Eva's breath caught in a gasp of pain . . .

The lonesome midnight howl of a wolf, eerie and prolonged, awakened Garrett from a restless sleep. Momentarily disoriented, he squinted into the shadows of the bunkhouse, into a darkness alleviated only by the pale light streaming through the rough window covering nearby.

A small potbellied stove, resting for the season, occupied the center of the small structure. Around it, four cots were grouped, only three of which were presently occupied. A table and four chairs in the corner, a washstand and bowl, and an accumulation of miscellaneous articles that had found their way into neglected piles, filled the limited space between. The beamed ceiling over his head was draped in countless lacy webs that he knew had not been disturbed since the roof had been secured years earlier. The ventilation was poor, the air close, and the wooden cot on which he lay was a far cry from the comfortable bed in which he had lain while recuperating. Over it all rang the sounds of Knox's steady breathing and Max's loud, persistent snores.

A familiar knot tightened in Garrett's stomach. But his unrest was no reflection on physical discomfort, and he knew it. A picture of Lila and Luther, walking slowly off into the yard as he had watched from the barn doorway earlier that evening, returned to haunt him. Lila's scent had clung to his senses as their footsteps had ceased. He had strained to see into the shadows, but the effort had been to no avail. His agitation had soared, and, disgusted with himself, he had turned back into the barn to fix the split saddle strap that had brought him there in the first place.

Cursing and silently railing, he had finished the chore a short time later and started back to the bunkhouse. He had heard Lila's whisper in the shadows and Luther's soft response as he walked past, and he had discovered a new level of pain.

Damn her for the conscienceless witch she was, leading an unsuspecting man on, encouraging his arms about her, letting him believe his patience would be rewarded with a gift of herself, when she had other, very definite plans!

A new burning began inside Garrett. He wondered how many other men Lila had led on in a similar way, how many others she had allowed to hold her, how many others had tasted the sweet delights he had only sampled briefly. He wondered if she had fought the others as she had fought him, if her nameless lover, for whom she seemed willing to risk so much, had raised the same response in her that he had sensed to his kiss.

Refusing to indulge his nagging jealousies any longer, Garrett closed his eyes, but it was no use. The warmth of Lila's arms around his neck returned once more to haunt him, as did the searching touch of her fingers as they had wound through his hair. He recalled the way she had clung to him, separating her lips to welcome him in, the way she had moved instinctively against him, the way she had—

Loud, choking snorts from Max's gaping mouth snapped Garrett abruptly back to the present. Jerking bolt upright in his bunk, he shot the sleeping man a deadening glance as the snorting lapsed back into the maddening seesawing sounds that had penetrated his restless dreams. Garrett raked his hand through his hair, agitated beyond recall as he threw his feet over the side of the cot. Standing up, he grabbed his pants, was dressed and turning toward the door when a deep voice questioned unexpectedly from the darkness, "Something wrong?"

"Nothin's wrong that stickin' a sock in Max's mouth wouldn't cure. I'm goin' to sleep in the barn."

Snatching his blanket off the cot, Garrett walked silently out the door to the sound of Luther's subdued chuckle.

Garrett disappeared into the shadows of the barn moments later, knowing it would soon be his turn to laugh. Spreading his blanket on a pile of hay in the corner, he walked cautiously out the rear door and turned toward the house.

The tenor of Lila's disturbing dreams was changing. The harried agitation, the anxiety that would not end was turning to slow warmth. She allowed the warmth to encompass her, reveled in its glow, resisting the insistent murmur that brushed her semiconsciousness.

"Lila. Lila, open your eyes, darlin'."

That voice . . . she knew that voice . . .

Awakening to the semilight of her room, Lila gasped, her spontaneous outcry muffled by the hand that clamped across her mouth.

"No, you don't want to do that." Garrett's voice was a soft warning she could not ignore as he slowly removed his hand. Curving his lean, muscular length toward her as he lay beside her, he held her prisoner with the wall of his body and the strength of the arm he slipped around her as he whispered, "No, you're not dreamin' . . . not this time . . . not any more than I'm dreamin'. I'm here, darlin', lyin' beside you where I belong, and this is where I'm goin' to stay."

"No, you're not!"

Lila attempted to rise, only to have Garrett restrain her with the flat of his hand against her breast. She was intensely conscious of that warm, broad palm pressing against the thin cotton of her nightdress, and even more aware of her heart's pounding against the soft flesh beneath as she rasped, "You're crazy coming here! If Luther—"

"Hush . . . don't talk, darlin'." Garrett's tone softened to a husky whisper. "I don't want words to get between us . . . not now. The torment's over, darlin'. It's endin' tonight because we're goin' to have what we've both been wantin' and needin'. I'm goin' to make sure of that."

"No, I don't want—"

Swallowing her protest with his kiss, Garrett slid his hand up to tangle in the unbound length of her hair. His fingers tightened there, holding her fast. The bittersweet pain heightened the sweet shafts of ecstasy shooting down her spine as his kiss deepened, seeking, demanding the response that rose despite her efforts to restrain it. Her lips were parting of their own accord. Her tongue was meeting his, joining in its erotic play as the heated core of her expanded slowly, sending white-hot spears of desire coursing through her veins.

It was sweet . . . so sweet, good . . . so good . . .

Escape . . . escape . . .

The warning voice sounding briefly within Lila's mind was overwhelmed by the beauty of Garrett's mouth against hers, the intoxicating taste of him, the trembling of his massive body as he crushed her closer. Shuddering in return, she was not certain of the exact moment when her nightdress was separated and pushed from her shoulders, or when Garrett's lips touched the warm swells beneath for the first time. She knew only the wild singing that began in her mind, the breathlessness that assaulted her as his mouth closed over the aching crests awaiting him, as he suckled and drew from them with increasing fervor. The nagging voice in the back of her mind grew more faint as he worshipped her tender flesh, as he murmured indistinct words of love, as he relinquished his ardent task to whisper against her parted lips, "This is what you wanted, isn't it, darlin'?" He paused, his gaze holding hers with a strange intensity as he asked again, "Isn't it? Answer me, darlin'."

Struggling to retain her failing resistance, Lila fought

the gaze of grey velvet eyes seeking to draw her in. She managed a gasping whisper. "No, I . . . this is wrong . . . a mistake."

"It's right." The grey velvet grew strained. "Nothin's ever been more right than this, and I want to hear you say it. Tell me you want me, Lila."

Withholding the response Garrett sought even as her body ached for the wonder of his loving, even as her mind shouted in wild contradiction of her silent dissent, Lila saw the tensing of Garrett's shadowed face. His gaze never leaving hers, he resumed the sweeping caress of her naked flesh. He cupped her breasts lovingly, gently, pausing to stroke first one swollen crest and then the other with his calloused thumb. A soft whimper of protest rose in her throat, but he stopped it with his mouth, pausing to trace the trembling line of her lips with his tongue as his caresses slid lower still. Her impassioned gasp was halted by a deepening of his kiss as Garrett found the tight curls resting between her thighs. He drew his mouth from hers as his fingers sought the moist female delta below, as he found the delicate bud of her desire and stroked it gently.

Tremors of incredible pleasure shook Lila, growing steadily stronger, stimulating a shuddering which she was helpless to restrain. A new hunger surged to life within her, bright and golden. She basked in its warmth as it spread through her like the rays of the sun, glowing, burning, threatening to consume her.

"Talk to me, darlin' . . ." Garrett kissed her again, tearing his mouth from hers to rasp breathlessly, "Do you feel warm inside? Do you feel the heat growing? Tell me what you feel. I want to make you happy, darlin'. Tell me what you want."

"No. I—"

"Talk to me, darlin'." Garrett stroked her more

boldly, and Lila felt a new moistness between her thighs as her shuddering heightened. His voice throbbing with the passion of his touch, Garrett demanded once more, "Tell me . . ."

"Garrett, please . . ."

"Look at me, Lila."

Seared by the heat of his gaze as her eyes were drawn to his, Lila struggled to retain a last scrap of restraint as Garrett whispered, "Tell me you want me to love you."

"No . . ."

"Tell me you want me as much as I want you."

"Garrett . . ."

"Tell me you need me as much as I need you."

Lila managed a brief shake of her head. She couldn't say those words. She couldn't commit to her weakness. He was asking too much.

The stroking grew more sensuous. "Tell me, Lila . . ."

"Garrett, please . . ." Lila's voice was a breathless whisper. It was so hard to resist him. The strength had left her limbs. The will had left her heart. All that was left was need, a need that—

"Tell me. . . . Say the words!"

Lila gasped a final, desperate denial. "No, I—"

Rolling away from her, Garrett stood up abruptly. Stunned at his sudden withdrawal, Lila was silent and quaking as he stood over her for long, furious seconds.

"Damn you for the witch you are!" Garrett gave a harsh laugh as he began unbuttoning his shirt. "No, I'm not leavin'. You're mine tonight. You don't have to say it. Your body speaks for you. I'll accept that for now because I'm beyond waitin', and so are you."

Naked, his broad form glistening in the meager shaft of moonlight slanting through the shade, Garrett lowered himself slowly upon her. Gasping as their flesh met, Lila heard the sound echo in Garrett's throat as well. Did she want Garrett? Oh, yes, she did. Did she need him? Oh, yes, she did. Her arms slowly rising of their own accord, slid around his neck to draw him down upon her. Her parted lips welcomed him in as his mouth met hers. The swell of his passion was taut and firm against her and she reveled in its strength. She felt him seeking, and she opened herself to him. He entered and she gasped at the joy of it. She was beyond conscious thought when Garrett's whispered demand brushed her lips.

"Open your eyes, Lila."

Gritting his teeth against the emotions he held so tightly in check, Garrett commanded as her gaze met his, "Say my name."

Confused at his anger, Lila sought to draw Garrett down upon her, only to have him resist as he commanded again, "Say my name . . ."

"Garrett . . ."

"That's right . . . Garrett!" Breathing heavily, his restraint failing fast, Garrett rasped, "It's *Garrett* who's making love to you. It's *Garrett* who's inside you now, and it's *Garrett* who's going to take you where you've never been before with any other man. *Garrett* . . . Say it again!"

"Garrett . . ."

Garrett plunged inside her. "Again . . ."

"Garrett . . ."

"Again."

"Garrett . . ."

He plunged deeply once more. "Again. Oh, God—"

His hoarse cry echoed her own as she joined him in shuddering culmination, as she returned his clutching embrace, never wanting to let him go.

Shaken by the unfamiliar emotion Lila slowly opened

her eyes. Garrett still lay intimately upon her as reality slowly returned.

What had she done?

Knowing a sudden need to be free, Lila moved beneath Garrett's weight, only to have him cup her cheeks with his palms and raise her face to his. His gaze searched hers, reading the sudden panic there. His response was a gentle whisper.

"No."

Panic nudged more sharply than before. "I . . . I want to get up."

"I said, no."

"Let me up!"

Surprising her, Garrett brushed her mouth with his. His eyes were warm, his tone tender.

"It's too late to deny what happened between us, darlin'."

"N-no! I was almost asleep! I wasn't responsible . . . I didn't realize—"

"You knew." Tense lines began muting the former softness of Garrett's expression. "You knew I was making love to you. You knew I was inside you and you—"

"No!" Lila slipped from beneath Garrett. The bed creaked loudly as she jumped to her feet and grasped the wrapper lying on the nearby chair.

Garrett was standing beside her in a moment, the powerful naked breath of him sending tremors down her spine.

"It's too late for modesty, Lila." Garrett's short laugh at the unintended pun was void of mirth. "Modesty . . . You were never Modesty to me. The woman I just made love to was you—Lila. And the man you loved back was *me.*"

Garrett reached for her, but Lila avoided his touch. "No, this is wrong."

"Why is it wrong? Because of Knox? He's in love with a fantasy, a woman who doesn't exist."

"No, not because of him."

"Because of someone else?"

"No."

"You're lyin'."

"I'm not!" Lila took another step back, hardly believing the sudden shift in emotions between them as a slow rage began to build in Garrett's eyes. "I didn't invite you here! I was asleep . . . dreaming. I didn't realize what was happening!"

"You knew, and you loved every minute of it!"

"No!"

Snatching the wrapper from Lila's hand, Garrett threw it on the floor. He took her by surprise as he scooped her up effortlessly into his arms, then lowered her onto the bed to pin her there with his weight. His smile was cold, his voice colder, as he whispered, "You'll know who it is this time, darlin', because I don't intend leavin' you tonight until you admit what you feel for me . . . until you call out my name again and again and you—"

Panic exploded within Lila and she was suddenly fighting Garrett with all her might! She would not . . . she *could* not give in to this man! She—

"MODESTY . . . YOU ARE ALL RIGHT?"

The sound of Aunt Helga's voice outside the bedroom door brought Lila's struggles to an abrupt halt. Her face flaming, she looked up at Garrett, silently imploring as she managed through quivering lips, "I . . . I'M ALL RIGHT, AUNT HELGA. IT WAS JUST A BAD DREAM. I COULDN'T SEEM TO WAKE UP . . ."

There was a short silence.

"YOU WOULD LIKE SOME MILK?"

"NO. THANK YOU. I JUST WANT TO GO BACK TO SLEEP."

"YOU WILL CALL IF YOU ARE SICK?"

"YES. I WILL."

Another silence.

"GOOT NACHT . . ."

"GOOD NIGHT, AUNT HELGA."

Trembling, Lila looked back up at Garrett as Aunt Helga's footsteps faded away. At the click of the old woman's bedroom door, she whispered shakily into the silence between them.

"You must get out of here!"

Gently wiping Lila's cheeks free of tears she had not realized she had shed, Garrett whispered huskily, "I don't want you to cry, Lila."

"Then go . . . now. Please."

"I can't." Garrett touched his mouth to hers. "I can't, darlin', not yet." He kissed her again, his arms sliding around her, his mouth exploring hers caressingly until she was weak with the wonder of it. Drawing back at last, he whispered against her lips, "I can't because I don't want to . . . and because you don't want me to, either."

As Garrett shifted his weight, the bed creaked loudly. Lila stiffened responsively, her gaze darting to the wall separating Aunt Helga's room from hers, and Garrett frowned. A moment later he rolled off her and stood up again. An ache began inside her the second before he spoke in soft command.

"Get up."

"What?"

"Get up."

Standing, Lila stepped back as Garrett slid the mattress off the bed and onto the floor. With an unexpected sweep of movement, Lila found herself lying beside

Garrett upon it. His solemn whisper shook her to her soul as his mouth met hers.

"You're mine, darlin'. You know it and I know it, and I'm tired of talkin'."

A sixth sense plucked at Garrett's sleeping mind, stirring him. He shifted uneasily, his arm tightening around the woman lying beside him.

Lila . . .

Her back was to him and he drew her into the curve of his body, fitting her nakedness against his with a contented sigh. Her firm buttocks pressed warmly against his skin. Her rounded breast filled the curve of his palm. The temptation too great, he turned her gently toward him. The first glimpse of Lila's sleeping beauty halted him, stealing his breath. Silky strands of hair generously tinted with red curved around delicately formed features appearing too perfect to be real. But he knew they were real. He had explored every inch of that face with intimate wonder. The heavy brush of her lashes had stroked his lips as her eyelids had fluttered under his kiss. The short, straight bridge of her nose, the rise of her magnificent cheekbones, the slope of her cheek, and her mouth—he had tasted them all.

Garrett's throat tightened. But it wasn't solely Lila's beauty that had touched him. Garrett drew her closer. There was something about this difficult, enigmatic woman that turned him inside out with longing. He wanted . . . he needed . . . he ached to keep her close within the circle of his arms where the world could not touch them, where her shadowed past and the mystery of her present could not make inroads into his mind. He longed to thrust aside all he knew about the true reason for her presence at this ranch. He did not want to recall that her blind devotion to a lover who was a thief and murderer made her no better than the man himself.

That thought too painful to sustain, Garrett sought the only escape he knew. Fitting his mouth over hers, Garrett nudged her lips apart. His heart took wing at the spontaneity of her response, first subtle and then warming as passion stirred. He remembered the sound of her voice as she had sighed and gasped in response to his loving . . . as she had clutched him close when he had whispered incoherently into her ear all the wonders he had felt in loving her. He had known she felt them, too.

He remembered that culmination had been mutual and powerfully fulfilling, yet it had left him strangely uneasy. He wanted . . . he *needed* more.

"Lila . . . darlin'."

Lila's eyes fluttered open. They were dark, fathomless in the limited light of the room in the moment before she glanced toward the window and the gradually lightening sky there. Sudden anxiety flashed in her gaze and in her voice as she spoke in a quaking whisper.

"It . . . it's almost morning. Luther will wake up soon. You have to go . . . please! I don't want him to find you here."

A heated emotion sharper than a blade slashed Garrett sharply.

"I don't give a damn about Luther!"

"I do."

"No, you don't!" Garrett cupped Lila's face with his palm, holding her fast as he whispered, "Come away with me, darlin'. We'll leave this place and everybody in it behind us. We'll go somewhere where we can be alone, somewhere where we—"

"No, I can't! I have to stay here."

"Why?" Garrett's fingers left angry marks on her

cheek, before he slipped his hand into her hair. His grasp tightened on the silky strands. "Why can't you go with me?"

"I . . . you're wanted by the law!"

"So are you!"

"No I'm not!"

"It's because of Knox, isn't it."

"No."

"Because of someone else?"

"Garrett, please . . ."

"Tell me who he is."

"I can't."

"Tell me, damn you!"

"All right!" Lila's eyes were suddenly as hotly angry as his. "I'll tell you about that 'someone else' if you'll tell me about Elizabeth."

Elizabeth!

Garrett went suddenly still.

"What do you know about Elizabeth?"

"I know enough."

A slow shaking began inside Garrett. "Tell me what you know."

Lila did not respond.

"Tell me!"

"All right! I saw her picture in your saddlebag. I know you carried nothing personal with you except that picture and that she signed it 'with all the love in my heart, forever.' " A harsh laugh escaped Lila's lips. "Does Elizabeth know how short *forever* is for you, Garrett? Does she know you're with me right now? What would she say if she did?"

A sudden rage enveloped Garrett's mind. "You could never understand a woman like Elizabeth—all innocence and purity. You're nothin' like her . . . nothin' at all."

The heat that flushed Lila's face was visible even in

the limited light as she raised her chin and smiled mockingly. "Is that so? Is that why you're in *my* bed right now, instead of hers?"

Garrett froze. Releasing Lila abruptly, he drew himself to his feet. He looked at her coldly as she stood and grasped the wrapper he had discarded earlier. Reaching for his clothes, he dressed within moments, picked up the mattress and slid it onto the bed, then turned back to Lila where she stood watching him.

"You're right . . ." Garrett's voice was harsh in the unnatural silence. "Askin' you to come away with me was a damned fool idea."

All trace of her former anger gone, Lila's face was expressionless as Garrett drew a smile from deep inside him. He forced it to his lips as he gave her a jaunty salute and dipped his head in a gesture of mock courtesy.

"Thank you, ma'am, for a real pleasant few hours. You've done a lonely cowhand a true service."

Feeling little satisfaction as Lila paled, Garrett turned to the window. Within moments he was walking rapidly toward the barn. He was lying on the blanket he had spread hours earlier when he heard Knox enter. He drew himself to a seated position as the sound of Knox's heavy footsteps neared.

"Did you have a good night's sleep out here?"

Garrett shrugged. "Not really."

"Too bad, because we've got a full day's work ahead of us."

Garrett stood and brushed the straw from his clothes. He watched as Knox left as abruptly as he had appeared.

Yeah, it was too bad . . .

Twelve

Trapped . . . trapped . . . trapped!

The word sounded over and again in Lila's mind, keeping pace with the sound of her step on the freshly tilled earth and the steady beating of the sun on her uncovered head as she walked in the fenced garden to the rear of the ranch house. She was hot and uncomfortable. She had escaped to the garden earlier in the day and labored amidst the rows of plants, preferring physical labor to Aunt Helga's intense scrutiny of the past week. Long hours of work under the unrelenting rays had offered a release she had not been able to effect in any other way. She silently dreaded returning to the house to meet with Aunt Helga's open concern again. For all her good intentions, the woman was driving her crazy.

Halting abruptly, anger surging anew, Lila leaned down and jerked a solitary weed from the ground. She threw it over the fence with a vengeance, fervently wishing she could pluck Garrett Harrison from her life and toss him away just as easily.

The deadening ache inside Lila returned. It had been the bane of her existence since that night a week earlier when Garrett had slipped silently from her room. It expanded slowly into a familiar torment as the assault of memory began anew. Garrett's strong arms around her became vividly real, as did the sound of his deep voice whispering loving, almost incoherent, words into her ear. She felt the brush of his breath against her soft flesh as he had worshipped it with his lips . . . the taste of his mouth against hers . . . his gentle touch on her cheeks, her throat, the curve of her shoulders, her breasts. She recalled the intimate invasion of that touch and the wonder it had evoked . . . the soaring ecstasy when he had come to rest inside her. She—

Suddenly disgusted with herself, Lila cursed aloud. She attempted to empty her mind of the torturous thoughts. When that was to no avail, she forced the return of bitter memory. A sharp edge of pain cut viciously as she recalled the abrupt cessation of loving warmth in Garrett's eyes when she had uttered a single name.

Elizabeth.

A hot, uncontrollable flash of jealousy surged through Lila. What had Garrett said?

You're nothin' like Elizabeth. Elizabeth is good and innocent and pure.

She had reacted with spontaneous anger to those words. She had taunted him with a truth he had not been able to face, and Garrett had reacted just as spontaneously in return. She would never forget the look in his eyes the moment before he turned his back and slipped through the window into the lightening dawn.

One thought had plagued her all through the long week since that night. Bedeviling her, taunting her, making her life an endless misery, was the realization that he wanted her still.

More frightening than that, however, was the realization that despite all the bitterness that had been spewed between them, she wanted him, too.

Trapped . . . trapped . . . trapped . . .

The endless litany resumed as Lila moved to the next row and began pulling at weeds viciously. How much longer must she endure this torment? How much longer until she received word from Billy, until she was free to leave this place where she was torn between one man's love, another man's desire, and her own debilitating weakness?

Garrett's intense, brooding glances, the coldness that contrarily burned with an innate heat each time his gaze touched hers, was a daily torment that did not relent. She had not asked herself why he still remained at the ranch, because she knew the reason only too well. But she was determined not to allow herself to fall victim to that same defect. She would leave this place and all its tribulations as soon as she was able, and she would put it behind her forever.

"Lila . . ."

Startled, Lila looked up with a gasp. Luther's broad outline was etched against the brilliant, early-afternoon sky. His face was shadowed by the light behind him as he stood a few feet away from her in the garden, but she did not have to see his concern to know it was there. It was present in the sudden silence between them, in the aura of unexpressed discomfort that had grown steadily stronger as the week had passed.

Lila took an involuntary step back, her foot coming down uncertainly as it encountered the mounded earth behind her. Luther's hands snapped out to steady her, but she drew herself free of his touch with a forced smile.

"Oh, Luther! You startled me." Lila's uneasiness mounted as Luther searched her face for the words that went unsaid, as did her sense of guilt as his frown deepened.

"Did I? I didn't mean to. You were preoccupied. You haven't been yourself for the past week, Lila."

Lila was intensely aware that Luther no longer used the endearment "darling" when addressing her. She knew it was due more to her withdrawal from him than to a lessening of feeling for her on his part. She responded with silent irony.

"I haven't been myself for longer than I care to contemplate." She added tensely, "Don't worry about me, Luther."

"But I do worry about you." Luther took her hand into his. The callouses on his palm were rough against her skin as he raised her hand to his lips. "I worry that you're reaching a decision in your mind, and things aren't going in my favor. I don't want it to be that way."

Aching inside at her ever-deepening deceit, Lila strained against the desire to withdraw her hand from Luther's. She allowed him to take a step closer, discovering the error in that judgment when he took her tentatively by the shoulders, then slid his arms around her to hold her close.

The heavy pounding of Luther's heart rang against her ear as Lila rested her head against his chest. She closed her eyes, unable to bear the torment she had foisted on a man totally undeserving of such treatment. She opened her eyes a moment later and jumped with a start to see Garrett watching her from horseback a few feet beyond the fenced enclosure. His eyes were shadowed by the dusty hat pulled down low on his forehead, but she felt their coldness freeze her.

Luther glanced in the direction of her gaze as she drew back from him, then whispered apologetically. "I embarrassed you. I'm sorry. I didn't realize Harrison was there. We came back for a few things we needed. Max is probably in the kitchen, but it looks like Harrison doesn't have the good sense to realize he's intruding."

"I wasn't embarrassed. I just . . ." Lila paused abruptly. Lies, lies, lies . . . she was so tired of them! She wished she could tell this man the truth right now . . . that she never was and never could be the woman he thought her to be . . . that she was unworthy of his love because she had betrayed his confidence in so many ways . . . that the best thing he could possibly do would be to put her out of his mind forever.

But she could not.

Feeling the weight of Garrett's stare, Lila fidgeted uncomfortably.

Glancing back at Garrett, Luther called out abruptly. "I'll be with you in a minute. If you've already loaded that wire onto the wagon, you can get that length of rope we needed while you're waiting."

Garrett nodded and nudged his horse into motion. Luther mumbled a curse under his breath at what seemed Garrett's unnaturally slow pace and Lila was startled at his uncharacteristic lapse. She had never heard him curse before.

"I'm sorry, but there are times when that fella gets under my skin."

"Yes, I know." How well she knew.

"You never liked him, did you, Modesty? Is he the reason you've seemed so tense the past week? I'll tell him to leave if it'll make you more comfortable."

"No! I mean . . ." Lila heaved a heavy sigh. "I don't know *what* I mean, Luther. All I know is that it really doesn't make much difference if I like him or not if you need him until you can catch up on the work around here. That's the most important thing . . . that you should be ready for those bulls when they arrive."

"No, it isn't." His clear blue eyes sober and sincere, Luther glanced over his shoulder to make certain Garrett had indeed moved out of view, then turned back to stroke her cheek. *"You're* the most important thing."

"I don't want to be more important to you than this ranch. This ranch is your life."

"This ranch *was* my life."

"Don't say that!" Lila's throat filled with unshed tears. "I don't want the responsibility of those words."

"It's too late for me to say anything else, darling."

Darling. That word again. It cut like a knife.

"Luther, please . . ." Dangerously close to shedding her tears, Lila whispered, "I can't say what you want to hear. I can't!"

"Not yet."

Lila paused. She wanted to say the words she knew to be true: *not ever.* She wanted to tell this man that for all his goodness and honesty, she had allowed a wanted man who was no better than she in the deceit he practiced to get under *her* skin as well. She wanted to tell Luther that, despite herself, it was Garrett Harrison's image that filled her dreams . . . that it was he who made her heart race with every dark glance he sent her way. She wanted to explain that even knowing he loved another woman as much as his black heart was capable of loving, she could not get Garrett out of her mind, and that she had come to fear she never would. She wanted to confess to Luther that Garrett had marked her with his unexpected tenderness the night she had spent in his arms, with his loving homage, with the flame, however brief in his eyes, that had changed grey ice to grey velvet chains that still held her strangely captive. And she wanted to tell him that she intended to break free of those chains if it took the rest of her life.

Still staring at Luther, Lila wanted to beg his forgiveness and tell him that all the words in the world could not change the way she felt, and that all the regret in the world could not make her love him when she did not.

Billy's image returned before her mind, reminding Lila that she could say none of those things . . . not yet.

The sound of a horse's leisurely pace turned Lila toward Garrett's slow approach, and her heart stilled.

Luther again followed her gaze. His patience expired, he demanded, "What do you want, Harrison? I thought I told you—"

"I got the rope we needed from the barn. Max and I already packed the wagon with the extra wire. We're ready to go."

"Then *get* going! I'll catch up with you when I'm finished here."

"Max said you wanted to—"

"I don't give a damn what Max said! Get going!"

Lila could feel the slow stiffening of Luther's body when Garrett remained stubbornly still. Her heart pounding so loudly that she could hardly hear her own voice above its reverberation, Lila drew back from Luther.

"I . . . I find that I don't really feel too well after all, Luther." Her smile was forced. "I've been out here since noon. Too much sun, I guess. I'm going inside. I'll see you later."

Walking stiffly, her chin high, Lila left the fenced garden and walked directly toward the house. Keenly attuned to the silence behind her, she heard Luther's angry step. She walked faster, seeking to shut out the confrontation she was certain would come as Luther strode angrily toward the spot where Garrett still sat his horse.

The distance from garden to house stretched into miles and Lila felt momentarily weak. If it weren't for Billy, with his wide grin that touched her heart and the frightening bitterness inside him that gave her little rest . . .

Lila took a ragged breath. She had always known she was the only person who could save Billy from himself, but she had never realized how high a price she might be asked to pay.

Under control once more, Lila drew open the kitchen door. She consoled herself that Billy would get her letter and would come for her soon. But in her heart, she knew it was already too late.

Knox approached, his posture aggressive and his fists balled as Garrett silently sat his horse. A peculiar satisfaction drummed through Garrett as he maintained his casual posture, concealing the heat that had burned all rational thought from his mind when he had seen Knox holding Lila in his arms.

It had been a damned hard week, sheer hell as he had watched Knox fawn over Lila, as he had watched him pet and console her, as he had suffered a matchless torment each time Lila had looked up into Knox's face. He had questioned his feelings and had come up confused.

What in hell had he been thinking when he had asked Lila to run away with him? Had he really expected . . . had he really *wanted* her to agree? What would he have done if she had?

A familiar pang tightened Garrett's stomach into

knots. It hinted at what he might have done if she had agreed, before any harsh words had been spoken. But the words had been spoken. One word, uttered through Lila's beautiful, deceitful lips had returned him to painful reality.

Elizabeth.

That name on Lila's lips had been a desecration of everything Elizabeth had been. Beautiful Elizabeth . . . innocent and good, who had never had a selfish thought. Elizabeth, who had given up her life trying to save his parents and him.

Lila was nothing like Elizabeth. He had told her that flatly, without sparing the blunt truth. Lila was hard and grasping, taking all she could get, where Elizabeth had been gentle and giving. Lila was cold and calculating where Elizabeth had been innocent of any guile. Lila was willing to sacrifice anyone and anything to save her thieving lover, where Elizabeth had sacrificed herself . . .

Garrett paused, resolute. He would not let Lila sacrifice him.

Knox walked to within a few feet of Garrett. He was breathing heavily with obvious agitation. His face was pale, his shoulders hunched belligerently forward, and his fists were twitching with obvious restraint. Silently pleading for an excuse to abandon a guise that had become more difficult than he had ever imagined it could be, Garrett waited for Knox to make the first move.

"Do you like to walk, Harrison?"

Garrett returned Knox's heated stare with a frigid gaze.

"Not especially."

"You'd better listen then, and listen good, or you'll find yourself wearing out your boot leather and not the seat of your pants on the way back to town. The next time you see me talking to Modesty, you stay away from me—from us—until we're finished. Understand?"

The war raging inside Garrett reached new heights. The damned fool . . .

"Answer me!"

"Yeah, I understand."

Taking that moment to emerge into the yard, Max glanced between the two men with surprise. His obvious confusion deepened as Knox instructed tightly, "Get that wagon moving. Right now. Harrison will be right behind you . . . won't you, Harrison?"

Garrett paused. He was so tempted . . .

"Won't you, Harrison?"

Garrett gave a stiff nod in reply.

Startled at Knox's anger, Max queried in open-mouthed amazement, "What about you? Ain't you comin'?"

"When I'm ready."

Max glanced at Garrett, then back at Knox as Knox started toward the house. "Where're you goin'?"

Knox did not bother to respond.

Suddenly furious, Garrett dug his heels sharply into his horse's sides. The animal leaped forward with a startled whinny as Max gave a yelp of surprise.

"What in hell's goin' on here?"

Not bothering to respond as well, Garrett turned his mount out toward open country. He was flying over the ground when the thought came to him that he was a fool, that everything he wanted . . . in so many ways . . . was behind him.

•

"You ain't goin' nowhere, Chesney!" Halting Billy in his tracks as the force of his words rang in the small cabin hideout they had used many times before, Forbes continued more softly, "If you take one more step, you're a dead man."

Billy turned slowly. Forbes was livid. The other men were grouped around a nearby table, silently watching. Knowing he could not depend upon them to back him up if Forbes decided to draw his gun, he kept a wary eye on Forbes's hand, hanging too close to his holster for comfort as he responded levelly, "Look, I wouldn't try to go back to Denver if I thought there was a risk."

"The problem is that you *don't* think!" Forbes's response was quick and vicious. "That posse hasn't given up chasin' us yet, and I ain't takin' no chances of you leadin' them back to us here."

Billy's patience snapped. "It's been a week and they haven't even come near this place!"

"A week ain't long enough."

"It was always long enough before!"

"It ain't long enough this time!" Forbes's jaw tightened. "I got a feelin' in my bones . . ." His narrow lips twitched spasmodically. "Yeah . . . I ain't never had a feelin' like this before. Somethin's happenin' . . ."

"Nothing's happening! They outsmarted us this time, that's all." Disregarding Forbes's growing agitation, Billy continued, "Look, they switched shipments. The moneybox we were expecting went out a day earlier or a day later, it doesn't matter which, and they sent the shipment we got in its place."

"Damned pitiful haul . . ."

"They didn't do it because they knew we were watching them, or they would've had the sheriff waiting for us."

"So you say . . ."

"I say it because it makes sense. You're not thinking clearly, Forbes. You don't like coming out on the losing end, but none of us do. We'll make it up next time. We've waited a week in this damned place and a week is enough. I've got things to do."

"Oh, no you don't." Forbes's thin, unshaven face went revealingly still. "You don't have nothin' to do that's worth your life, do you, Chesney?"

Billy paused to search Forbes's expression. Damned if he didn't think Forbes had slipped over the edge! Hell, livin' in such close quarters for the past week, it would've been impossible not to know that Forbes had been having nightmares . . . bad ones . . . every night. Picket and he had overheard Forbes telling Eaton about them . . . about a recurring dream where a big black bird hovered overhead, waiting to swoop down on him while he hid in a cave. He had told Eaton that the dream was a warning, that it wouldn't be safe for any of them to leave the hideout until the bird in his dream flew away.

Billy's agitation soared. The problem was that he had been having nightmares of his own. It had been two weeks since he had seen Eva. He didn't like leaving her that long.

Then there was Lila. He had no doubt that she had been able to shake that Pinkerton on her tail, but he was not comfortable with the time that had elapsed since he had last heard from her. He needed to get to his post office box . . . now.

And he didn't intend waiting for a phantom bird to give him permission.

Billy eyed Forbes once more. The fanatical light in Forbes's eyes brightened and his hand moved closer to the holster on his hip. Even the fact that Forbes had taken to wearing his gun in the cabin was strange.

Forbes snickered low in his throat. "You're wearin' your gun. Want to test me?"

"What are you talking about?"

"I told you, you ain't foolin' me! Whatever you're thinkin' of doin', I've already done. There ain't no way you're goin' to get a step ahead of me, Chesney, so you might as well take your chances right now."

"I'm not trying to challenge you, Forbes. I just want to get out of here."

"And I said no."

Billy took a slow breath, then came to an abrupt decision. Taking off his hat, he tossed it onto a nearby peg on the wall with a silent sigh of disgust.

"All right, I'll wait another day."

"No you won't. You'll wait until I tell you it's safe."

"All right!" His jaw rigid, Billy plopped himself into a vacant chair. He reached for the pack of worn cards nearby and glanced around the table at the wary faces there. "Who wants to play a game of poker?"

Forbes's sudden burst of laughter snapped all heads in his direction as he walked to stand at Billy's side.

"You're a crafty bastard, ain't you! You figured the odds, and you seen they weren't good. Then you figured it wasn't worth tryin' to back me down, especially when you know our supplies are runnin' out and we'll have to be gettin' some more soon, and that since you didn't spend more than a few hours with me and the boys in Denver, you're the best person to go get them for us." Forbes laughed again. "You're right . . . and you're wrong, 'cause the truth is that it ain't safe to leave here yet, and nobody's gettin' out of here until I say it is. *Comprende?*"

"Yeah."

"That's good." Forbes pulled up a chair. "Deal. I ain't got nothin' better to do."

"Yeah . . . I know."

Billy dealt the cards.

* * *

Frowning broadly, Hobbs climbed the staircase of Deer Trail's only hotel. He paused at the top and glanced around him, then started down the hallway. Pausing at the door he sought, Hobbs raised a hand to knock. Thinking better of it, he scratched his stubbled cheek and stepped back. He didn't like this.

Leaning against the wall in a deceptively casual posture, Hobbs reviewed the situation again. He had waited until Harrison, Knox, and his hired man had returned to the ranch for the day and he had then followed his usual, biweekly procedure of heading directly to town to wire a short, cryptic report to McParland in Denver. He had come to look forward to his visits to town as relief from a tedium that tested even his devout professionalism. He was getting too old for extended wilderness camping. He had come to the point in this surveillance where he had begun to look forward to a bath with an avid expectation that rivaled his youthful anticipation of a night with an obliging whore. With some embarrassment, he had faced a revealing truth that if given the choice between that obliging whore and a good hot meal at that particular point in time, the woman would come out on the short end.

Hell, he *was* getting old!

But not too old for caution.

Hobbs's weathered face creased into tight lines of contemplation. Following his usual procedure, he had gone directly to the station house upon arriving in town to send McParland his report. He had been more than surprised to find a sealed envelope waiting for him there. That envelope had delivered him to this hallway with growing uncertainty.

Speculating on that thought a moment longer, Hobbs

adjusted his gunbelt, took a deep breath, and holding himself flat against the hallway wall, reached over and knocked on the hotel room door. The response was immediate.

"Who is it?"

Hobbs paused. "The drummer."

The door jerked open and Hobbs released a relieved breath as a familiar figure stepped into the hallway, then motioned him inside.

When the door was closed quietly behind them, Hobbs was the first to speak.

"What are you doing here?"

His inquiry was met with McParland's frown. "I'll ask the questions if ye don't mind. I've been waitin' here for ye for more days than I can spare, and my patience is gettin' thin."

Hot and tired, Hobbs replied in kind. "Look, McParland, I've been following procedure to the letter. You've been getting regular reports."

"Aye, I've been gettin' reports but no action! And while Harrison and ye have been sittin', watchin', and waitin', there's been another train robbery."

"Another train robbery?"

"By Forbes's gang! Just as bold as could be, with him stealin' across the top of the train and catchin' the engineer by surprise."

"How do you know it was Forbes? Did the engineer give you a description?"

"The fella's not talkin' anymore—not to anyone. He's six feet under, with a widow and five children cryin' at his grave."

Hobbs's expression sobered. "You're sure it was Forbes?"

"The fireman survived, and although the men wore bandannas over their faces, there was no mistakin' who they were. There were five men in all, with the same general descriptions as Forbes's gang."

"Still—"

"And there was the killin' of the engineer for the sheer joy of it. The fireman said he would've gone the same way had it not been for the tall fella who held the horses speakin' up to the leader."

"The new man . . ."

"Aye. But I've a feelin' he'll be goin' the way of the engineer if he keeps up that tack—not that it's much loss. I'm not here because of him at any rate."

"Why are you here, McParland? Harrison and I have everything under control."

"Have ye now? It seems the American Bankers Association which pays our fee has its doubts."

"They deal directly with Pinkerton and you. What do they know about Harrison and me?"

"Nothin', but William Pinkerton does, and his temper's gettin' short. The reputation of the agency's at stake here, and he doesn't like bein' pressed. I had all to do to convince him that I'd take care of this without his help."

A slow anger rising, Hobbs questioned softly, "Am I to understand that my professionalism is being questioned? Because if it is—"

"Don't go gettin' on yer high horse now, Hobbs. The truth is that ye've been on this case for longer than it should take to find a lead."

"We *have* a lead. A good one, and Harrison and I are handling it. The Chesney woman sent a letter to her boyfriend. I know it was to him because she went to great pains to hide it from Knox."

"Where was the letter directed?"

Hobbs was momentarily uneasy. "I don't know."

"Ye don't know!"

"The mail clerk sealed the mail sack right after she gave him the letters and he sent it out on the train an hour later. I couldn't get him to talk about where they were addressed without getting him suspicious."

"When was that?"

"Over two weeks ago."

"If she was goin' to get an answer, she would've gotten it by now."

"Not if it *was* Forbes's gang that held up that train and Forbes was in the planning stages of the robbery. If the stories we picked up are true, he's a hard taskmaster who keeps a tight rein on his men immediately before and after a robbery. They're probably hiding out for a while."

"You're guessin'."

Hobbs paused. "Maybe I am and maybe I'm not." He paused again. "There's something else, too. Something's going on at that ranch. I haven't been able to get Harrison alone to talk, but I've gotten accustomed enough to the daily routine there to see that something's amiss."

"Like what?"

"Like something."

"You'll have to do better than that, me bucko!"

"I can't get any more specific than that right now!" Hobbs was suddenly angry. "Look here, McParland. When I took this job with Harrison, you told me you were teaming me up with one of the best operatives you had. So that means *two* of your best are on this case. Am I right?"

"That was my thought."

"Then *keep* that thought, and remember, Harrison and I are handling things. You can go back and tell William Pinkerton that we'll be winding up this case within a month."

"Ye're sure of that, are ye?"

Hobbs took a tight breath. "I'll stake my job on it."

"As well ye may." McParland nodded, his fair, boyish face creasing into an unexpected smile. "I admit to feelin' good at yer confidence. Bill Pinkerton's been on my back, and Forbes has been a difficult man to catch."

"Forbes may not know it, but he's nearing the end of the line. I've got a feeling about this Chesney woman. She's the key, all right. Harrison's gotten quite close to her. He's sure of it, and so am I."

"All right, ye've convinced me. What's left is for me to convince the Pinkertons. A month, ye say?"

Hobbs nodded.

"I'll keep ye to yer word."

"You may do it with confidence."

"Aye. I will." Appearing to suddenly relax, McParland smiled more broadly. In well-worn pants and shirt, with a vest sufficing in lieu of his usual jacket, and with a gun slung low on his narrow hips, he looked no more or less than the average man on Deer Trail's main street, except for the smile flashing his legendary Irish charm as he said, "Well, business is done for a little while and it's time to socialize. I've the feelin' ye've not had much time for it of late."

"You're right." Hobbs hesitated, the abrupt switch of McParland's mood making him wary. "I don't have much time for it now, either. I have to get back to the ranch to take over the watch on the Chesney woman when Harrison rides out in the morning."

McParland's brows rose speculatively. "Ye've a few hours yet, have ye not?"

"I have."

"Time enough for a drink or two. I've a half-hour or so to spare before the next train back to Denver.

I've purchased a bottle of some good Irish brew, and two glasses are waitin' to be filled."

McParland's capacity for liquor was also legendary, although it was clear that drink had never interfered with his work. Somehow Hobbs knew this night would not be the exception.

"I was about to get a hot meal and a bath . . ."

"A hot meal and a bath!" McParland gave a short laugh and slapped Hobbs's back with amusement. "A bath takin' precedence over a man's drink. Aha! That's a sign of age, all right. The next thing ye know ye'll be puttin' a bath on equal footin' with a night with a woman. Then ye must beware." Laughing again, McParland nodded. "A drink or two and ye may be excused. Come now. It's agency policy to send our men off with a smile."

Hobbs hesitated. "I thought company policy forbade drinking on the job."

"Well, ye aren't workin' now, are ye, my fine fellow? And neither am I. Come on. Let's get to it."

Hobbs walked casually toward the staircase to the lobby a half hour later. He knew McParland would wait until he cleared the hallway and would then leave as well. The thought crossed his mind that he had become a better actor than he had realized if he had been able to fool McParland with the act he had put on.

Hobbs started down the staircase as the click of a door sounded in the hallway behind him. He was suddenly amazed at his own audacity. Wind this damned case up within a month? Had he really said that? He must've been crazy. But he wasn't any crazier than Garrett Harrison was getting if he was to judge from what he had seen through the spyglass earlier that day.

Stepping out onto the street, Hobbs followed his nose toward the beckoning lights of Flossie's Restaurant.

Maybe he'd better have a talk with Harrison. Maybe this case was getting to Harrison as much as it was getting to him.

Hobbs gave a short laugh. If it was, knowing Harrison as he now did, the case *would* be wrapped up within a month . . . one way or another.

Doc paused in the upstairs hallway of Deer Trail's only hotel. He was puzzled, but his puzzlement had little to do with the condition of the bedridden patient he had just left in the room behind him.

Doc's gaze narrowed as he drew the door tightly shut. He knew that man . . . the one who had just come out of the doorway down the hall. He had spent time with him on several occasions at the Red Slipper. His name was Jake and he had said he was trying to locate lost shipments for a company in Denver.

Doc paused on that thought. Jake had been coming into town with enough regularity over the past few weeks to make his comings and goings known. Everyone knew that each time Jake left town, he headed due west.

Hmmm . . .

Doc's concentration deepened. He hadn't given the matter much thought until now, but as far as he knew, there was only one place in that direction where Jake could make a base while traveling back and forth with such regularity. He hadn't given that matter much thought either, until he had seen Jake come out of that particular room down the hall . . .

Doc's concentration tightened into a frown. He had gotten a glimpse of the man who had rented that room earlier in the week. The fella had seemed immediately familiar. It had taken a while to place him, but he had then remembered someone pointing him out the last time he was in Denver. The man had been difficult to forget with that blatantly Irish face and smile. His name was McParland. He was notorious for the work he had done in bringing down the Molly Maguire organization back East years earlier, and he was now head of the Pinkerton Detective Agency in the Southwest. Respecting the fella's position, Doc had not told anyone in gossip-hungry Deer Trail who he was, but he was beginning to wonder if—

As if in confirmation of his thoughts, McParland emerged abruptly from the room and started down the hallway. Intrigued, Doc followed closely behind.

Appearing unconcerned at Doc's presence behind him, McParland stepped out onto the street and, without a break in stride, headed toward the train station. A distance down the street, Doc saw Jake pull open the restaurant door and step inside.

Right on schedule . . .

Everybody in town knew Jake's routine by now—first a trip to the station house to send a telegram, then a hot meal, a bath, and a drink or two at the Red Slipper. He would leave town shortly afterward.

A glance in the opposite direction showed McParland in the station house doorway. The next train to Denver was due to arrive in ten minutes.

Hmmm . . .

Doc headed toward the bright lights of the Red Slipper. He checked his watch. If Jake kept to his routine, he'd be arriving for a drink in about an hour and a half. He'd have to bide his time and drink slowly tonight. He wanted a chance to talk to Jake . . . just out of curiosity.

* * *

"Ach! You see . . ."

Helga turned toward Max with obvious anxiety. Their day's work behind them, the men had returned to the ranch a few hours earlier, and Helga's concern had deepened. Modesty had spent most of her time in her room after talking with Luther in the garden earlier that afternoon. She had emerged in time to help prepare dinner, a concession she had made of late despite her obvious abhorrence for the kitchen.

Helga's old heart ached at the uncomfortable tension that had grown between Luther and Modesty within the past week. Something was wrong . . . very wrong. If she did not miss her guess, Luther was as mystified by the change in Modesty as she.

Helga had studied Modesty silently as she sat at the dinner table. Pale . . . *ja* . . . with dark shadows under her eyes that reflected restless sleep. And she was thinner . . . too much thinner. A shadow weighed more. Was she sick? Helga shook her head, confused.

Grateful that Max's devotion to her cooking had brought him back to the kitchen after supper so she might share her concern, Helga continued, "Is bad. Modesty does not eat."

"Come now, Helga." Max's raspy voice was heavy with reassurance. "I seen her plate when she sat down. It was pretty near filled."

"Ja." Helga nodded vehemently. "Was filled when she took it back to der kitchen, too."

"No."

"Ja."

"Oh, well, that still ain't no cause for alarm. Young people take things harder than us older folk, that's all. Maybe she's still frettin' about that little go-around the boss had with Garrett this afternoon."

Helga was immediately alert. "Was trouble?"

"Naw . . . not really. The boss has been a little . . . ah . . . *tense* lately."

"Is so . . ."

"He was talkin' to Miss Modesty, and Garrett kind of got in the way, that's all."

"So . . ." Helga became pensive. "Was dat man again . . ."

"Come now, Helga. You ain't bein' fair. Garrett ain't guilty of nothin' but not havin' the sense to give them two a little privacy when he should." To Helga's confused look, he responded, "You know . . . the boss was talkin' to Miss Modesty and Garrett kept interruptin'."

"Dat man no goot!"

"You're makin' a mountain out of a molehill, Helga. Garrett ain't bad. He ain't too sociable, but he's a hard worker. If it wasn't for him, there'd be no way the boss and me would be ready for them bulls next week. The way things stand, we'll be ready to drive them right out to service them cows when they arrive. That means the boss's plans will be runnin' right on schedule, and there ain't nothin' that'll make him happier than that."

"Nein. One thing make him happier . . ."

"Yeah, well . . ." Max averted his gaze. "Ain't nobody but Miss Modesty who can give him that."

"Ach, is true." Helga was suddenly sad. She didn't like the way things were going. Her old eyes had seen too much not to notice Luther's gaze straying constantly to Modesty and Modesty trying to avoid it. She had thought things were going so well, too. Once her foolish resentment against Modesty had been eliminated and she had seen the true person Modesty was, she had enjoyed the growing warmth between her dear nephew and the dear girl. She had even begun to envision the children Luther and Modesty would bring into her life.

That vision had rapidly begun to fade in the past week, leaving her desolate.

Looking up at Max, Helga sighed. She paused to consider his face as unexpected tears filled her eyes. Ach . . . Max . . . so homely. Not like her Herman. Her Herman was a handsome man. He had a round face with light, rosy skin. No wrinkles like Max. No whiskers sticking out of deep grooves in his cheeks like weeds in clover.

Helga shook her head. He was too skinny, too . . . not like her Herman who was plump and happy, with blue eyes as bright as the sky, shining even brighter when he saw her.

Helga sniffed. Max's eyes were brown . . . not blue. The gold tooth was not pretty. He did not speak the language of the old country, a sound she missed with all her heart. She wished . . .

"Aw, don't cry, Helga. Everythin's goin' to be all right. You'll see." Surprising her, Max slid his arm around her shoulder. It was surprisingly comforting as he continued with a sudden crack in his voice, "I don't like to see you unhappy. You know, you're just about the strongest woman I ever did know, and I admire that."

"Am not so strong . . ." Helga allowed herself to lean into Max's support. "Am lonely old woman."

Max's arm tightened as his voice became a conspiratorial whisper. "I'll let you in on a little secret if you'll promise not to tell anybody else."

Helga nodded. It had been a long time since someone had confided in her.

"I . . . I've been lonely, too. It ain't easy growin' older and knowin' there ain't nobody special in your life." Max paused, his face reddening as he continued haltingly, "What I'm tryin' to say is that I'm willin' to be your friend, if you're in need of one."

Helga remained silent, considering.

Max's expression uncertain, he offered, "There ain't nobody else your age around here to talk to, you know, and sometimes it feels kinda good to talk to somebody who's seen as many years pass by as you have. It's kinda comfortin'."

Helga continued her silence, and Max's dark eyes softened. "I'd feel honored if you'd turn to me for comfort in that way. Helga . . ."

"Ja."

"You're a damned good-lookin' woman, you know."

A sudden shout of laughter burst from Helga's lips. "Am *not* good-looking!"

"Yes, you are!"

"Nein. Was *never* good-looking."

"You are, I say!"

"Am fat!"

"I like big women."

"Am old!"

"So am I."

Helga shook her head and indicated her sagging jowls. "Too many chins . . ."

"Them chins look real good on you."

All trace of her former tears gone, Helga smiled broadly, feeling the warmth of Max's offer in her heart. *"Ja,* we be friends." Picking up the knife on the table nearby, Helga sliced off a generous piece of leftover cake and slipped it onto a plate. She held it out to Max. "You eat."

Max's eyes took on a glow. "You sure know how to seal a friendship." He moved closer. "And I—"

The sound of Modesty's step in the doorway turned both their heads toward her as she paused briefly there.

"Oh." Modesty appeared flustered. "I thought Luther was in here."

"Nein. Is outside." Helga smiled. "You want cake?"

"No . . . thank you. I'm not hungry."

Modesty was gone in a moment, and Helga's former light mood faded. She looked up again at Max. "Ach, you see! Does not eat . . ."

Optimistic to the end, Max nodded. "The boss'll make everythin' right."

Her doubts remaining, Helga watched as Max picked up a fork and started to eat with obvious enjoyment. She turned back to the doorway through which Modesty had disappeared as quickly as she had come, her concern deepening. The smacking of Max's lips grew louder as the thought registered in the back of her mind that she would never be truly certain whether it was her cooking or her companionship Max preferred. But of one thing she was sure. It was good to have a friend.

Lila raised a shaking hand to her hair and smoothed it nervously as she walked through the dining room toward the outer door. The sun had set a short time earlier, dinner had been eaten, and Luther had retired from the house with Garrett walking slowly at his heels.

Bastard . . .

Tears choked Lila's throat. He had done it purposely, she was certain . . . that snide glance, the deliberate way he had turned his back on her.

Slowing to a stop, Lila took a firm hold on her emotions. She was slipping into Modesty Parkins again, and she didn't like herself. With a supreme effort she summoned the return of Lila Chesney . . . the woman who faced her anxieties and disappointments head on, with a smile on her face, however forced. But the effort was wasted. She could not smile now for fear of deceiving Luther any further. He needed to know it was over, even if she could not yet say the words.

True, she could not say those words, but there were other words that needed to be spoken between Luther and her. She needed to go to town. It had occurred to her that while she had been suffering all the torment of the damned this past week, a letter from Billy could have been waiting in Deer Trail for her . . . a letter that could set her free. She would impose upon Luther's goodness, beg him if necessary, to take her to town to find out.

Stepping out onto the porch, Lila hesitated. She had stepped into the shadows once before with disastrous results. She did not intend to make that same mistake again.

Walking carefully around the side of the house, Lila looked toward the barn. The whirr of a nighthawk's wings sounded close by, as did its soft, comforting call, but Lila paid it little mind as she stared at the tall figure moving there. Luther . . . there was no mistaking him this time.

Releasing a relieved breath, Lila started rapidly toward him, aware that he did not see her approaching. She was about to call out when a rough hand clamped over her mouth, muffling her frightened scream as she was abruptly snatched from her feet.

Dragged back into the shadows of the great tree to her rear, Lila felt the hard trunk of the tree against her back and Garrett's voice in her ear as he uncovered her lips and demanded, "What's so urgent that you're chasin' after the boss at this time of night, Lila?"

"That's none of your business!"

"Oh, isn't it? I think I've already proved to you that your business is my business."

"The only thing you've proved to me is that you're everything I thought you to be, a deceitful thief wh-who uses people—nothing more!"

"If I didn't know better, I'd think you were describin' yourself, Lila darlin'."

"Maybe, but at least I'm not a lonesome cowboy looking for a woman to do him another *true service.*" Lila paused, her voice bitter. "You got what you wanted. Why don't you leave me alone?"

"Because . . ."

Garrett's hand had slipped to her hair. His angry touch grew more gentle, and Lila's throat tightened.

He was remembering. She knew, because she was remembering, too—the tantalizing pleasure of his fingertips moving in the heavy tresses . . . the bittersweet pain as his grip tightened to hold her fast under his kiss . . . as his mouth sank deeper into hers, coaxing, seeking . . .

A shiver moved down Lila's spine. Filled with self-loathing and desperate to have him release her, she whispered harshly, "You're wasting your time."

"Am I?" Garrett's voice dropped a notch lower. "Maybe I am, but I don't think so. You haven't forgotten the night we were together. I can see it in your eyes."

"Just like I can see it in yours?"

Garrett's shadowed face tightened. "We've got unfinished business between us."

"What business?"

"You know what business as well as I do."

"No, I don't."

"You're finished playin' games with me, is that it, darlin'?" Garrett's voice hardened. "You'd rather play with Knox while you're laughin' behind his back."

"That's not true. I don't want to hurt Luther."

"Then why are you doin' it? Why are you stayin' here? What are you waitin' for? *Who* are you waitin' for. Tell me, Lila! Damn it, tell me!"

"No."

"Yes!"

"You wouldn't believe me if I told you."

"I might . . . if you told me the truth."

"I can't."

"Tell me . . ." Garrett cupped her face with his hands, suddenly kissing her with a bruising passion that shook her to the core. Trembling, as well, Garrett drew back, repeating in a ragged whisper, "Tell me. I want to know. I have to know who could make Lila Chesney do something she doesn't want to do. I want to know his name . . . and I want to meet him, because when I do—"

Lila reacted sharply to the threat in Garrett's voice. "Who said it's a man?"

Jerking her flush against him, Garrett crushed her close, hissing as his mouth descended to cover hers, "It's a man all right . . . damn you . . ."

Garrett's kiss deepened, drowning out thought and fear. Weak with the power of wanting him, knowing that as her hunger for him grew, his soared to demanding need, Lila fought her surging response with all her might. Clasping her closer still, Garrett shuddered as he whispered between frantic kisses, "This is all an act, isn't it, darlin'. You knew I was out here waitin' for you, didn't you? You had to come."

"I didn't!"

Garrett's hands were stroking her back, her buttocks, curving to capture her breast in eager, loving caresses as he continued breathlessly, "You knew I could hardly keep my eyes off you at the table tonight. You knew

I've been achin' for you every moment since I left your room that night."

"No . . ."

"You knew I've been relivin' holdin' you in my arms and lovin' you until I'm sick with the pain of wanting you. You knew. That's why you encouraged Luther this afternoon when you knew I was watchin'. You were gettin' even for what I said."

For what he said . . .

Elizabeth . . .

Lila's passion drained. Anger grew in its stead.

"I didn't know you were watching, but if I had, it wouldn't have made any difference. You're not important enough to me to make that difference. I'll be leaving here soon anyway. Very soon."

"You're not goin' anywhere without me."

"I'm not going anywhere *with* you! Let me go!"

"I want to know who you're expectin' to take you away from here, Lila."

Lila gave a harsh laugh. "I know the name of your lover, so you want to know mine, is that it?" Lila could not make herself say Elizabeth's name. She laughed again, feeling an aching satisfaction in Garrett's rising fury. "Never!"

"Witch! Tell me."

"Let me go, Garrett."

"Tell me who the man is, Lila. I know it isn't Knox."

"I said, let me go!"

"Tell me!"

Abruptly realizing his demands were to no avail, Garrett swept Lila up into his arms in a quick, facile movement. He was carrying her farther into the shadows despite her struggles when the sound of Luther's footsteps alerted them to his approach.

Realizing the need to halt the rush of Garrett's heedless passion, Lila called out, "Luther!" Luther's step halted. "I'm over here."

Garrett stiffened, his expression fierce as she continued in as normal a voice as she could manage, "I . . . I'd like to talk to you for a minute."

Dropping her to her feet, Garrett growled a low curse as Luther started toward them. He took a step backward. "You won't get away from me. Remember that!"

Garrett retreated into the shadows and disappeared from sight. Reacting instinctively, Lila started toward Luther. She saw the hopeful gleam in his eye as she stepped into view and she ached with the new pain she was about to deal him.

Pausing, sensing her distress, Luther slowly raised his arms to her and Lila's resolution turned to need. Unable to refuse the gentle haven she knew awaited her, Lila slipped into his embrace. She closed her eyes as Luther's protective warmth closed around her.

"You're trembling, Modesty. Darling, please, don't be upset. Whatever it is, I'll make it right."

Sliding her arms around Luther's waist, Lila held him tight. The scent of him, the strength of him, the concern in his voice—all bespoke comfort unlike any she had ever known before. Uncertain . . . uncaring if Garrett could hear her, Lila whispered words that came from the heart.

"Luther . . ." Lila's voice cracked, and she tried once more. "Luther, I wish. . . . Will you always be my friend?"

Silence stretched between them, and Lila felt a sob rise in her throat. She controlled it, forced it back, as Luther's hand rose to stroke her cheek. His light eyes somehow clear to her despite the shadows, Lila read the sincerity there as he responded slowly, emotion heavy in his voice. "If friendship is what you want from me, yes. I'll be your friend."

Savoring those words, knowing that from Luther's lips they held the solemnity of a vow, Lila whispered in response, "Yes, that's what I want."

The strength of Luther's embrace did not waver and Lila indulged its comfort for long moments before drawing back. Despising Garrett at that moment almost as much as she despised herself, Lila stepped to Luther's side and slid her arm around his waist. She leaned her head against his shoulder as they walked silently back to the house.

Witch!

Concealed in the darkness, Garrett watched Lila and Knox disappear into the house. Jealousy burned. He raked his hair with an anxious hand as he attempted to sort out his feelings. It had been no good telling himself that Lila was nothing like Elizabeth. He had never felt about Elizabeth the way he felt about Lila. He had never despised Elizabeth for her deceit while suffering a perverse need to protect her from herself. He had never wanted Elizabeth the way he wanted Lila . . . with a driving need, with a passion that threatened rational thought.

That admission causing him more pain than he could bear, Garrett consoled himself that his passion for Lila was no reflection on his love for Elizabeth . . . beautiful Elizabeth who would always be his wife in his heart. The reflection was totally on himself . . . on the man he had become.

Knowing . . . sensing with a certainty deep inside him that the whole affair was nearing an end . . . that Lila's lover would soon make his move, Garrett searched his heart. How much of his desire for Lila was tied up with his hatred of the man she protected . . . and what would he do when they met face-to-face?

It would be soon.

Thirteen

Billy's mount danced nervously underneath him as a stray mongrel barked and snapped at his hooves. Cursing, he drew back sharply on the reins, then jerked at his pack animal's lead. Again in control, he glanced at the Denver street around him. Oblivious of the clear air, the view of high-peaked mountains clad in shadowy purple visible in the distance, he felt only the heat of the midday sun beating relentlessly on his shoulders and the gnawing agitation inside him that grew stronger with each passing hour.

Civilized . . . Denver was no longer the rough mining town it once had been. It now sported a citified veneer that could easily deceive, but Billy had seen the other face of Denver. He knew the night side of a town where "disorderly houses" lined the street in open invitation. He was familiar with the saloons where rough men in careless dress who earned their money hard let it go just as easily, where the haze of tobacco smoke over the gaming tables never waned, and where the shuffling of feet and the rattle of roulette marbles combined with the musical clinking of ivory chips for a heady din that often clouded the mind to rational thought.

That part of Denver, however, was far from Billy's

thoughts as the particular building he sought came into view. His jaw tightened with frustrated anger.

Damn that Forbes! The man was getting crazier every day. Forbes was still certain that an unusual danger dogged them, but Eaton had finally convinced him that the time had come to divide the money from the robbery and split up for a while. Forbes's agitation had grown as the shares had been doled out, smaller than the proceeds from any job they had ever undertaken, and his own agitation had not been much less. It was not enough.

Billy's handsome face tightened as he nudged his horse to a faster pace. Things had changed since he had met Eva . . . sometimes too much to suit him. In the past he had used his share of the money from the robberies in whatever way appealed to him at the moment. He recalled the bright-red traveling dress and matching plumed hat he had bought for Lila with part of the proceeds from their last job. She had protested his extravagance and had quizzed him as to how he had gotten the money, but in the end she had accepted his gift. He had come to realize that, knowing the pleasure it had given him, she had accepted the gift more for him than she had for herself.

Billy's face sobered. Lila was like that. She had put his welfare ahead of her own ever since he could remember. In more sober moments he wondered if he was worth her sacrifices, but those moments were few. Instead, he had satisfied himself that Lila had looked beautiful in the outfit he had bought her, and he had been proud. He had always been proud of Lila. It hurt him to know that as much as she loved him, she was not always proud of him.

Lila's fair face faded from Billy's mind to be replaced by Eva's darker-haired image. As dissimilar as the two images were, Billy knew the women were alike in ways he had not consciously recognized at first. Silent Eva, quiet and unsmiling where Lila was quick-witted and animated . . . dark-haired Eva, whose scarred beauty grew clearer upon closer scrutiny, unlike Lila whose beauty instantly caught the eye and held it captive. Different, yet alike in their unexpected inner strength, both had worked to protect the defenseless person most precious to them at great personal sacrifice, and neither had allowed anyone to defeat her. He admired that strength in his sister. He loved it, however tentatively, in Eva.

Thought of the deprivation and humiliation Eva had suffered filled him with fury. He was determined she would never be forced to endure such treatment again.

Billy released a tense breath. Separated from the mining camp below, Eva would be safe in the mountain cabin where he had left her for a while longer. Her supplies would be running low and he would replenish them, but that was not enough. Eva deserved more. She deserved safety that would encompass her daughter's and her future as well as the present, and a life without anxiety.

Billy hesitated at that thought. He wanted a sense of permanence to be a part of Eva's future, but he did not necessarily want to be a permanent part of that future—not with Eva or *any* woman.

Billy raised his chin, his determination firming. His future lay in association with Bart Forbes, or with someone like him. For whatever else he was, Forbes was a winner. Forbes had never been wounded in a robbery. He had never been captured. He had never come away empty-handed, and with all the wanted posters bearing his name and description distributed throughout the West, he had never been positively identified. With Forbes, Billy was a winner for the first time in his life. He would not give that up at any price.

Thoughts of Lila stirring another agitation, Billy kicked his horse into a faster pace. Drawing up in front of the elaborately painted false front of Wickham's General Store moments later, Billy dismounted and dropped his horse's reins over the rail. Taking a moment to secure his pack animal's lead as well, he lifted his hat from his head, ran a casual hand through his damp, tightly curled hair, and adjusted his bandanna around his neck, using the time to scrutinize his surroundings.

Finding nothing unusual about the stream of pedestrians filing past or the seedy-looking miners engrossed in ardent conversation nearby, he entered the general store. His shopping list in the hands of a bearded clerk, he emerged minutes later. Taking a moment for another quick assessment of the area, he slipped into the brick-fronted one-story building next door and walked up to the desk.

"Howdy! Nice day." Billy flashed a disarming smile at the white-haired clerk. "The name's W. Chesney, Post Office Box Number 23. Is that a letter I see waiting for me in there?"

The old fellow turned to look, too slowly to suit Billy. He maintained his smile with difficulty as the time the fellow took to retrieve the envelope stretched into an eternity.

"Yep, there's a letter all right. Looks like it's from a lady." The words whistled through the gaping spaces between the clerk's teeth as he winked. "I can always tell."

Billy snatched the letter from the clerk's hand. His relief was intense when he recognized Lila's script.

Nodding to the clerk, Billy walked outside. He waited until he reached the walk before ripping the envelope open. A sheepish grin spread across his lips as he read:

Billy,

It looks like you aren't as smart as you thought you were. A Pinkerton found me in Salina, and we both know there is only one reason he could be asking questions about me.

I'm staying at Luther Knox's ranch, the Bar WK due west of Deer Trail. Everyone here knows me as Modesty Parkins, a woman from back East. Don't use your real name if you come here. There's been a complication that I can't explain.

I have to talk to you. If you can't come here, let me know where to meet you. Soon.

Lila

Billy's sheepish grin broadened. The note was short and not too sweet. Lila was mad all right, but she never stayed mad at him for long.

His smile fading, Billy scanned the letter once more. Deer Trail . . . a whistle-stop town. How in hell had she managed to get herself a place to hide there? He gave a short laugh. Modesty Parkins? A picture of his flamboyantly beautiful sister rose before Billy's mind. Nobody would ever believe Lila had a name like that.

Billy folded the letter. Making a snap decision, he walked back into the post office. A short time later, he handed the clerk an envelope and change for postage, then left the building.

Loading up his packhorse, Billy started back down the street without a thought to the inviting sounds coming from the saloons that lined the far end of the street. He was a man with a mission. That mission had dark eyes and hair and a giving heart reserved for him alone.

Three weeks without seeing Eva was long enough. Lila would understand the delay when he explained things to her. And he *would* explain, too . . . eventually.

Billy's wide grin flashed once more as he left the sounds of Denver behind him. *Modesty Parkins . . . ?* Leave it to Lila to fix things so that she was as snug as a bug in a rug until he could get back to her. He'd never have to worry about Lila. She wouldn't let anybody get the best of her. Not Lila.

The sun was up, spreading a golden aura across green fields still wet with dew in the distance, but the new bulls were restless. Walking the corral fence and bellowing, they strained at the restriction imposed upon them as three horseman approached with caution.

Swinging the corral gate open, Luther admitted Max and Garrett into the corral just as two bulls began testing each other, pushing heads. They backed apart, preparing to charge as Luther's shout rang out on the still morning air.

"Separate those bulls!" He moved cautiously between the two challenging animals and the third bull closest to him. He shouted again, "Hurry up before they get into it!"

Watching from the yard as Max and Garrett snapped into motion, Lila felt her heart hammer in her breast. She hadn't realized she was trembling until Helga spoke softly from behind her.

"Is no danger. Do not worry."

Lila attempted a smile, but she knew better. The scene in front of her was a mirror image of one that had been played out before her when she was a child. She had never forgotten it, or the sight of the gaping wound those horns had inflicted. The gored man had not lived.

"Max . . . watch it!"

Holding tight to the reins as his horse wheeled and leaped sideways out of the way of the younger bull in full retreat, Max held his mount steady a moment later. His low laughter rang on the morning air.

"Looks like that bull ain't no match for old Harry here!" He patted his horse's neck. "There wasn't no way he was goin' to let that bull get the best of him."

Lila released a ragged breath. Another close call.

Her hands clenched into tight fists, Lila watched as the bulls were driven out into the open and separated once more. The huge, unsettled animals had been delivered by train to Deer Trail a day earlier. The strain on the men's faces when they had finally herded the huge animals into the ranch yard had made it immediately apparent that it had not been an easy drive from town. No one had to tell her the reason. Bulls were always restless in breeding season and these Herefords were no exception.

Lila assessed the testy animals. She had never seen bulls like this before with their red-mahogany coloring, white faces, and long, curving horns. Luther was convinced that they would improve his range cattle with meat that was rumored to be tastier and with their ability to put on weight faster than Longhorns. He had taken a big chance investing in them and she hoped he was right because they were a nasty lot.

"Come on, get them moving." Luther's low command started Max cautiously forward. Fighting to keep her eyes from Garrett, riding a few feet behind, Lila was intensely conscious of the realization that he had not hesitated to ride between the two bulls when Max was threatened. There was no doubting Garrett's skill or his courage. She wondered what had turned him to a life of crime when he had obviously spent much time at honest labor.

Billy's image appeared before her mind, and she frowned. Billy and she had ridden with their father at roundup as children. She knew Billy had not forgotten what he had learned any more than she had. He was an excellent rider with honest skills, just like Garrett, yet they both . . .

Shrugging that thought from her mind, Lila watched as the three men herded the nervous bulls out into the open. It would be another long drive out to the pasture where they would be scattered among the breeding stock gathered for them, and she—

With a sudden rush, the two bulls earlier engaged were again fighting. The younger bull staggered under the bigger bull's charge, falling back on the rough ground as the third bull bellowed deeply and rushed to join the foray. Gasping, Lila watched as Max and Garrett circled them, waiting for an opening as Luther managed to keep the third bull at bay. The fight continued, the bulls straining and pushing, the younger bull being forced back farther and farther until he broke unexpectedly and started to run.

Directly in his path, Max strove to escape the animal's blind rush. The bull swung his head upward, catching him on the leg with a furious swipe. Gasping, Lila dashed toward Max as the old cowboy leaned low over the saddle, grasping his leg.

In an action that was fast and furious, Garrett was suddenly between Max and the bull, shouting and waving until the confused animal headed out into clear ground. Lila was still running toward Max when she was suddenly swept from her feet and jerked up into the air. On the saddle beside Garrett a moment later, she turned to meet light eyes that froze her with their fury as he rasped, "Don't you have any sense! That bull could've killed you!"

Lila's heartbeat was thunder in her ears as she managed a breathless, "B-but Max is hurt!"

"Max is all right, damn it! He—"

"Modesty, are you all right?"

Turning at the sound of Luther's voice, Lila felt her face flame. "I'm fine. I . . . I didn't think. All I saw was Max."

Luther's expression was stiff. "Take her back to the house, Harrison."

Turning, Luther rode toward Max as Garrett spurred his horse into motion. Lowering Lila to the ground, Garrett held his nervous horse motionless as Max and Luther made a slow approach.

Drawing up beside them, Luther ordered in an unnaturally clipped tone, "Get back to the bulls, Harrison." Ignoring Garrett's departure, he watched as Max dismounted with obvious pain. He dismounted beside the old cowboy and took his arm. "We're going to have to get Doc Bennett to look at that."

"Oh, no you ain't!" Max's face was pale, but his response was adamant. "I'm all right. It ain't nothin' . . . just a scratch."

Crouching beside Max, Lila separated the torn section of Max's trousers and grimaced at the nasty gouge just above his boot. Max was in more pain than he admitted to, but as far as she could see, the wound wasn't serious.

"Don't you go botherin' yourself, Miss Modesty." Obviously embarrassed at Lila's attention, Max took a pained step backward. "It'll be all right. I'll just pour some red-eye over it and the pain'll be gone."

"I doubt that the pain will be gone that fast, but

you're right about that red-eye." Lila smiled. "Come on inside for a minute. I'll take care of it for you."

"Aw, Miss Modesty, I—"

"Do what she says, Max."

Looking up at Luther, Lila saw the strain and concern that creased his face. Max appeared about to protest before he relented unexpectedly. "All right, but don't you go tryin' to move them bulls without me. You know you ain't goin' to get far with them critters in the mood they're in."

"Don't worry." Luther looked back at Garrett as he strove to keep the big animals separated. "We'll wait."

Restraining herself from lending Max a helping hand as he limped into the house, Lila waited until he had cleared the doorway before following. Suddenly conscious of Helga's silence, she turned to see the older woman's plump form was rigid.

She touched Helga's arm tentatively. "Aunt Helga . . ."

Aunt Helga snapped from her frozen state with a start. Her full face twitched the moment before she swallowed with obvious difficulty, then turned toward the house.

Silent, unaware of Garrett's heated glare, Lila followed.

"What are you looking at, Harrison?"

Beside him, Knox drew Garrett's gaze from Lila's back with open animosity. Too agitated to heed the danger in that challenge, Garrett responded hotly, "At a damned fool woman, that's what!"

Luther's expression hardened. "You'd better watch what you say about Modesty, or you might find yourself regretting it. If it wasn't for the way you got between Modesty and that bull a few minutes ago, I might be saying something different, but as things stand, all I'm going to say is that I don't give a damn what you think about Modesty, just as long as you keep it to yourself and do your job. Is that understood?"

Garrett returned Luther's stare, unblinking. "Yeah, it's understood."

Holding his gaze a moment longer, Luther turned back to the bulls snorting restlessly nearby. "Move that big fella away from the others and make sure he stays there. I'll take care of these two until Max comes out."

Not bothering to respond, Garrett turned to the largest of the bulls. Resisting, the big animal finally began moving under his unyielding persuasion. It was not until the bull was a safe distance from the others that Garrett realized he was shaking.

Damned fool woman! Garrett's rage abruptly returned. What in hell had Lila thought she was doing running toward the bulls like that? A responsive chill swept down Garrett's spine, and he briefly closed his eyes against the picture of those horns tearing Lila's white skin. He wanted to rage and rail at her for putting herself at risk so thoughtlessly. He wanted to shake her to within an inch of her life for having frightened him the way she had. He wanted to make her promise him that she'd never . . . *never* . . . do anything like that again. He wanted—

Gritting his teeth as the huge animal a few feet away tossed his horned head restlessly, Garrett cursed angrily and nudged his horse close enough to swipe at him with his rope. The animal retreated and Garrett took a steadying breath.

Damn it all, he knew what he wanted . . .

The long days since Garrett had held Lila in his arms

in the darkness under the tree, during which Lila had refused him even a covert glance, returned with unexpected agitation. Suddenly certain that he could not tolerate the situation between them much longer, Garrett made a decision. He would wait one more week before forcing the action any way he could.

Garrett straightened his back and glared at the snorting animal a few feet away. *Any* way he could . . .

Concealed a distance away, Hobbs watched the scene enacted below through his spyglass. Ignoring the insistent insect buzzing near his ear, he studied Harrison's stiff expression. His grip tightened on the glass as a sense of urgency tugged at his mind. He fidgeted nervously. His situation of the past few weeks had allowed him to develop a second sense about his partner that was sometimes discomfiting.

Adjusting the glass, Hobbs scrutinized the tall man's rigid posture and the tight set of his jaw. There was no mistaking it. Garrett Harrison was teetering on the edge.

Lowering his glass, Hobbs took a moment to rub a weary hand over his face. He gave a wry laugh. Harrison was teetering on the edge, and *he* wasn't far behind him. He'd had enough of this difficult surveillance, and if he wasn't so damned determined to make up for his mistake in losing Lila Chesney the first time, he knew he would be tempted to do something desperate.

Like forcing the action.

Slowly raising his spyglass, Hobbs studied Harrison's expression again. That big fella's nerves were as tight as a drum. There was something about the way he followed Lila Chesney with his gaze. He had the feeling that if something didn't happen soon . . .

The set of Hobb's lips slowly tightened.

Retreating backward with a careful crawl, Hobbs slipped down behind the rise and walked to the tree where his horse was secured and waiting. Hesitating a moment longer, he then slipped his glass into the saddlebag, mounted up, and turned deliberately toward town.

Hobbs's sweaty face was grim. He was taking a chance, and he knew it. This could be the day Lila Chesney decided to leave the ranch as soon as Knox was out of sight. He could lose her again . . . but he didn't think that would happen. He had seen her face when the old man had been gored. She had surprised him by darting into the field to see if the old fellow was all right, and his heart had pounded with fear for her safety until Harrison had swept her up onto his horse and delivered her from harm. Harrison had been just as furious, no doubt at the realization that one swipe of that nervous bull's horns could have eliminated their only lead to Bart Forbes.

No, Lila Chesney wouldn't be going anywhere today, and he would take the time that certainty had granted him to slip into town and do some necessary snooping. A letter for Lila Chesney should be arriving soon . . . very soon. Better yet, a stranger fitting a familiar description might be arriving in town at this very moment. If he was, the waiting would soon be over.

Hobbs nudged his horse to a faster pace. It would happen, or he would *make* it happen . . . soon . . .

Billy's heart began a slow pounding as his horse climbed steadily through the heavily forested terrain. The hillside had become warmly familiar to him during the past six months, despite his frequent absences. He remembered his concern when he had first installed Eva in the cabin at the top of the rise, knowing that the gulch below was barely civilized, but it had appeared as good a place as any at the time. Rumors that lead carbonate laced with high-grade silver had been found in the small mining camp below had reached him in Leadville. He had been caught up in the excitement of it, and with free time on his hands, he had decided to try his luck. He had brought Eva and the baby with him, and, unwilling to subject her to the harshness of the camp below, he had bought the cabin on the rise above him from a fellow desperate for quick cash. Eva had been happy there, and although he had had little success prospecting, he had been content. His mind, however, had not been at rest during his absences. His intention had been to buy a place somewhere better suited to a woman with a small child after this last holdup, but things had not worked out as he had planned.

Billy's lips twitched. He was to meet Forbes and the boys at the hideout in two weeks. He had no doubt Forbes would have another job set up by then, one that would net him enough with his share to do whatever he wanted. It was a matter of pride to Forbes to make up for his mistake in planning in the last robbery.

Billy's mouth turned up in a hard smile. If he knew Forbes, their next haul would be a big one.

Surveying the surrounding mountainside with characteristic caution, Billy frowned as the acrid smell of charred wood grew steadily stronger. There had been a fire . . . recently.

Billy dug his heels into his horse's sides as caution gradually yielded to apprehension. He saw no sign of forest fire on the hillside, which meant the fire had been contained. He knew there was only one place where a fire that had left so strong an odor could have raged.

The treeline thinned at the top of the rise, and Billy's heart began a ragged pounding as the shadowed outline of the cabin failed to appear. Instead, sunlight shone on the emptiness of the clearing where the cabin had stood. Kicking his mount to a faster pace, unmindful of the animal's distress, Billy emerged into the clearing a moment later. His breath caught in his throat as he viewed the burned debris that littered the ground.

Panic . . . fear . . . a sense of horrified outrage flushed Billy's mind as he leaped from his horse and took slow, uneven steps closer to stare at the few blackened uprights still remaining. The devastation was complete. No one who had been in that cabin at the time of the fire could have survived.

Suddenly shaking, his throat too thick to emit a sound, Billy allowed that reality take firm hold on his senses.

No one . . .

Returning to his horse with quick, jerking steps, Billy mounted quickly and headed back down the mountainside toward the camp below. He was traveling at breakneck speed, his packhorse stumbling behind, when he realized that he was in pursuit of denial . . . of the sudden, unbearable emptiness that had accompanied his realization that Eva might be gone from his life forever.

The kitchen was silent except for the sounds of Max's heavy breathing and Modesty's light step as she returned to his side with a basin of water. The color slowly returning to Max's face became a hot flush as she kneeled beside him.

"You don't have to do that, Miss Modesty!" He attempted to draw her to her feet. "It ain't nothin' more than a scratch, I told you."

Max flushed more deeply as Modesty resisted with a delicate smile. "I'm just going to wash the cut a little. There's no telling how much dirt was on that bull's horns. It won't take long."

Standing stiffly a few feet away from the chair on which Max sat, Helga strained to hold herself upright as Modesty rolled up Max's pants leg and cleansed his wound. A thickness rose in her throat as the blood was wiped away to reveal the nasty gash, and a strange lightheadedness assaulted her. She gritted her teeth as Modesty then took the bottle from the table and poured the amber liquid over the clean wound.

A heavy heat moved up under Helga's eyelids as Max gasped. She took a spontaneous step forward, hardly recognizing her voice as she asked shakily, "You are all right, Max?"

Max's bloodshot eyes rose instantly to hers. She saw the concern there as he responded, "I'm all right. Are *you* all right?"

Modesty's head snapped toward her, and Helga nodded in quick reassurance that she did not feel. "*Ja,* am fine."

Silence resumed, broken only by the sound of ripping cloth as Modesty tore a worn, freshly laundered linen into strips and bound his leg. Max stood up, and Helga felt a new giddiness assault her as he turned unsteadily toward the door. His voice seemed to come from a distance as he paused at the doorway, directing his words to Modesty.

"I got to be goin' back out 'cause the boss is waitin' for me, but I thank you for your effort, Miss Modesty. I ain't sure this old leg is worth the trouble you went to, but I appreciate all you done."

Tipping his hat with a brief glance toward Helga, Max walked back out into the yard. He mounted with obvious difficulty, then rode back to join the others. Within minutes the three men had the bulls moving, and Helga released a shuddering sigh.

"Aunt Helga . . ." Realizing Modesty was beside her, Helga turned abruptly. Her sagging chins swayed at the abruptness of the movement as Modesty asked with obvious concern, "Aren't you feeling well?"

"Am fine." Helga's throat choked, and to her humiliation, her eyes filled. She struggled against her emotion, and managed a choking whisper. "Am tired. Will lie down for a while." She tilted her head toward the stove, indicating the pots bubbling there. "You will watch?"

"Of course."

Not stopping to reassure Modesty, Helga walked directly to her room. A hard sob escaped her lips as she closed the door behind her. The sound shocked her, and she forced her sagging chin up with determination.

But it was difficult . . . so very difficult. It was harder still to be reminded again, in such a frightening way, that life was fragile, a person's time short, and that in the flash of a moment all could be swept away. But most trying of all was the sudden realization that she had allowed her affections for the scruffy old cowboy to become deeply involved.

A tear moved down Helga's full cheek and she brushed it angrily away. *Nein!* Dear Herman was her husband. A part of her life had died with him. This Max . . . Helga gave a low snort as the image of the often slovenly cowboy appeared before her mind's eye. This Max was only a friend.

Another tear pursued the same path of the first, and

Helga nodded, relenting. But she had needed a friend . . . and she had come so close to losing him.

Taking a few steps to the bed, Helga lay down and closed her eyes.

She was old.

She was fat.

She was tired.

But Max did not mind. He was her friend.

She did not want to lose him.

She had not realized how much she cared.

His expression as hard and unrelenting as stone, Billy rode through the narrow, heavily rutted mining camp street at a pace that raised eyebrows and sent bearded prospectors scrambling. A wagon pulled out unexpectedly from a storefront in front of him, causing him to rein up sharply. He muttered an appropriate epithet, tempted to abandon his mount and trailing packhorse where he stood, rather than await the lumbering wagon's progress out of his path.

Reining up in front of the cabin at the end of the street, he dropped his mount's reins over the nearest hitching post and knocked on the door. His heart pounded with agitation at the pace of the dragging footsteps beyond before the door opened to Ellie Greer's lined face.

The old woman's colorless skin blanched whiter.

"Oh, it's you." She clutched the door tightly without inviting him in. "I don't know nothin'."

"Where's Eva? What happened to her?"

"I don't know, I said."

The old widow attempted to close the door in his face, but Billy was too quick for her. Forcing himself inside, he closed the door behind him and demanded once more, "Where is she?"

"How many times do I have to tell you I don't know!"

The woman took a step backward, obviously frightened, and Billy's agitation soared. Grasping her shoulders, ignoring their obvious frailty, he held her firm under his stare as he growled, "You know, all right. Tell me, damn it, or I'll make you tell me, one way or another!"

Shuddering under his grasp, the old woman nodded. She swallowed and managed weakly, "Let me go. I'll tell you if you let me go." Billy's hands snapped free and she took a step backward. "I didn't have nothin' to do with it. I didn't know nothin' about it until Pete Waller came scramblin' down the hill yellin' that he found Charlie Mosbey dead in your cabin up top."

"Dead!"

"That's right. Charlie was missin'. Pete thought he might've stumbled off somewhere to sleep off a drunk at first, but when he didn't come back, he started lookin' for him."

"What made him look for Mosbey at the cabin?"

Ellie Greer's gaze dropped from Billy's. "Charlie . . . he was real nasty when he was drunk. He saw Eva with the baby when she came here to get some milk. He kept tellin' everybody that there was no way that baby was hers . . . that she stoled it. He said he was goin' to get the baby back and teach that squaw a lesson while he was at it."

Fury and a desperation unlike any Billy had ever known pounded in his ears as he demanded, "What happened to Eva and the baby?"

"I don't know, I tell you! Pete went hollerin' up and down the street, heatin' everybody up, tellin' everybody that Eva was an Injun and that there wasn't no Injun alive, man or woman, who should get away with killin' a white man. He had a real crazy crowd followin' him when he went back up the hill for Charlie's body, and the shoutin' only got louder after they put Charlie six feet under and started drinkin' some more. It wasn't no more than an hour later that them same fellas went back up and set the cabin on fire. Then they mounted up, drunk as most of them was, and started out after her."

Billy's chest was heaving, his hands balled into tight fists as he rasped, "Did they find her?"

"They didn't say nothin' when they came back, but it's my thinkin' that nobody was goin' to find Eva and that baby . . . not if she didn't want them to . . . not with that Injun blood in her. They came trailin' back real quiet, nursin' their achin' heads and mumblin' about them damned squaws, but they didn't say much else."

Billy paused to allow his heart to catch up with his tongue, finally managing, "How long ago did all of this happen?"

"A day or so after you left. Must be . . . about three weeks."

Three weeks . . .

Billy closed his eyes. Three weeks while he was wasting time babying Forbes's nightmares.

Billy snapped his eyes open. "Pete Waller . . . is he still around?"

Taking another step backward, Ellie shook her grey head. "You ain't goin' after him, are you? It ain't worth it. He's nothin' but a sneaky coward. He'd shoot you in the back as soon as look at you."

"IS HE STILL AROUND?"

Ellie Greer blinked. "Yes."

"Where?"

"His claim's on the north side of the creek."

Billy was halfway through the doorway when the old woman called out harshly, "Wait!"

Billy turned back, twitching with suppressed agitation. His eyes narrowed as old lady Greer raised her chin and spoke with unexpected sharpness.

"I got somethin' to say to you, and you'd better listen, and listen good. Watch yourself with that Pete Waller. It ain't that I care what happens to *you*. I got the feelin' that you ain't worth much more than Waller, but there was somebody who didn't feel the same. Eva was a good woman, and her Injun blood didn't change that. You won't be findin' her if you're lyin' facedown by the creek a few minutes from now."

Old lady Greer raised her chin a notch higher. "Take a good look at me. What do you see? I ain't pretty no more, am I? I'm just a tired old lady who grew old before her time and who don't have nothin' more than a couple of goats to keep her company until she dies. And when I do die, there ain't goin' to be nobody who cares." The old woman's eyes narrowed into pinpoints of light that penetrated deep inside Billy as she rasped, "That's what you'll be doin' to Eva if you get yourself killed. And if that's what you want . . ." Ellie Greer paused to clear her throat as her eyes filled unexpectedly. She continued with obvious determination. "If that's what you want, you ain't no better than I thought you was. Now get out of here, and don't come back! I seen enough of your type and I seen enough of you."

Turning her back, the old woman walked to the stove. She did not look up as Billy pulled the door closed behind him.

* * *

Bending low over his shovel, Pete Waller dumped another load into the rocker box beside him. Waiting as water washed through the riffles there, he picked out a piece of rock, then tossed it away with disgust, spitting on the bank for emphasis. He had had a damned hard day. He was hot and sweated up. He smelled bad, and he knew that before the day was done, he'd smell worse. If he didn't know better . . . if others weren't doing better than he, he'd think this whole territory was already played out. It was just his luck that—

The sound of heavy footsteps on the gravel bank behind him turned Pete Waller toward the sound. His eyes bulging, he raced for his gun lying nearby as a hand clamped down on his shoulder and raised him from his feet. Tossed high into the air, he came down hard on his back as an enraged Billy Chesney grabbed his gun and tossed it into the creek. Scrambling to his feet, Waller stumbled backward as Chesney advanced threateningly toward him.

Spittle drooled from Waller's thick lips as Chesney drew closer. Damn Charlie to hell for what he had done to him! He had known from the first it was a mistake to mess with this big fella's woman. That little-boy smile he flashed around hadn't fooled him none. He had seen the coldness in his eyes and the swagger to his walk that showed he wasn't no gold-seekin' wanderer like the rest of them. And he had seen death in a man's eyes before, just like he saw it in Chesney's now.

Chesney came to within a few feet of him, and fear exploded from Pete's lips in a frightened plea.

"Hold on, Chesney! I didn't have nothin' to do with your woman!"

"Liar!"

"I didn't! I went up lookin' for Charlie but he was already dead. He was stiff as a board."

"Where is she?"

"I don't know!" Pete slid a few steps backward. "We . . . we couldn't find no trace of her."

"You were gone a long time chasing after her. Don't lie to me, Waller." Chesney's eyes pinned him, sending little shivers of fear down his spine as Chesney towered over him. "'Cause if you do, you won't live to regret it."

"I told you the truth!"

"What did you do with the burro?"

"What burro? There wasn't no burro at the cabin."

"You couldn't find the trail of a woman carrying a baby and draggin' a burro behind her?"

"We couldn't find nothin'. There wasn't even no supplies in the cabin." Waller gave a short laugh. "There wasn't nothin' left worth stealin'."

"Tell me the truth, Waller . . ."

"I'm tellin' you the truth!" Glancing around him at the heavy foliage lining the creek, Waller knew there was no help forthcoming. Panicking, he spoke in a desperate, whining plea. "I told Charlie to leave your woman alone. I told him you'd be back and there'd be hell to pay, but he kept talkin' about that baby not bein' hers, and about givin' it back to some white folks who could take better care of it than a thievin' Injun could. And he kept talkin' about what he'd heard about Injun women bein' real wild when you pinned them under you. He said he was goin' to sample—"

His words choked off by the tight fist that twisted his shirt under his throat, almost lifting him from his feet, Waller gulped. He pleaded with new intensity, "I told him not to go up there! I thought he listened to me, but when he didn't come back . . ."

"Where is she?"

"I think she headed northeast. Northeast! That's all I know."

"Why?"

"We found the remains of what looked like a place she camped."

"Why didn't you tell me that before?"

"Hell, we wasn't even sure it was her camp! We wasn't sure of nothin', we was so drunk most of the time. After a while we just gave up and came back."

Chesney's chest was heaving, and Pete could feel his intensity as Chesney grated, "If I find out you lied to me . . ."

"I didn't! Ask any of the others. They'll tell you the same thing."

Chesney hesitated. A hard smile hovered around his lips as he asked unexpectedly, "What're you going to do if you ever see Eva again, Waller? What are you going to say?"

"I . . . I ain't goin' to do or say nothin'! Ch-Charlie didn't listen to me and he got what he had comin'. As far as I'm concerned, it's all over."

"What about the others in your little party?"

"They won't do nothin'. They forgot about it all already. Hell, they didn't like Charlie none nohow."

Suddenly releasing him, Chesney stepped back. His threatening green eyes narrowed into slits. "If I find out you hurt her, I'll be back."

"I didn't do nothin' to her!"

Chesney turned abruptly, and Waller released a tense breath. He gulped once more as Chesney's low voice grated over his shoulder, "If you touched her, I'll be back . . ."

Waller was riveted to the spot with the sound of that deadly promise as Chesney disappeared from sight.

Suddenly scrambling into movement, Pete dashed to his lean-to and started throwing supplies onto his blanket. He had taken a chance returning to this camp. He had known from the beginning that Chesney might come back. He had gotten away with that pack of lies he had told him this time, but he knew damned well if that big fella found out what *really* happened . . .

Wrapping up the blanket, Waller ran to his packhorse and strapped it on. Returning to the creekbank for his tools and lantern, he glanced around him. He had everything he needed. Anybody was welcome to the rest. He'd be long gone if Chesney came back looking for him again.

Waller shivered and mounted up. He rode off dragging his packhorse behind him, never looking back.

Doc Bennett walked up the early-morning street, the expression on his unshaven face dour. The sun was shining but the air was unnaturally heavy for so early in the season. He had been feeling real good before the previous evening when running footsteps on the walk outside his window had raised his head. He had started toward the door as a heavy pounding began and had opened it to Timmy Barnes's excited face.

"My mom's ready, Doc!" The wide-eyed ten-year-old had been breathless, his chest heaving. "My pa told me to come and get you real quick!"

Grabbing his bag, Doc had followed Timmy back down the street to the little house near the end, his mind filled with trepidation. Mary Barnes had not had an easy pregnancy, and he had not expected one. She had had several miscarriages, which accounted for the lapse between Timmy and the child she was about to deliver, and he had not been too certain how things would go. Almost six hours later, however, Mary had delivered not one, but *two* healthy babies, a boy and a girl.

Doc's expression tightened. His practiced eye had judged that spanking-new Marianne and Bennett Barnes had weighed in at nearly seven pounds each, which had eliminated worry over their welfare. The difficulty, however, lay with Mary. He had just stopped off to check on her again, and her condition had not changed. She was weak . . . terribly weak. The delivery had been difficult and she had lost a lot of blood. He did not presently fear for her life, but he knew that without help she could fare badly.

Doc shook his head. She would need that help for an extended period of time . . . a month, at least. There was only one woman who could spare that much time for Mary.

Deer Trail's best and only restaurant came into view, and Doc pushed his way through the doorway.

"How's Mary, Doc?" Horace Neely's gravelly voice piped up immediately from a table at the rear.

Doc frowned at the rotund storekeeper. "Don't nothin' that happens in this town escape you?"

"Nothin' much, except how Mary's doin'. I heard it wasn't easy."

"I'd say it wasn't. Havin' two instead of one doubles the trouble, you know."

Horace motioned Doc toward him. "Sit down, Doc. Breakfast is my treat today. I've got the feelin' you earned it."

"I'm thinkin' Mary put a hell of a lot more work into it all than I did, but I'll accept your offer. I'm warnin' you though, I ain't good company this mornin'."

"That so?" Horace's smile flattened into a straight

line. "The truth be known, neither am I. I'm pretty annoyed."

Doc raised his wiry brows. "I should think you'd be happy. You just got yourself two new customers for your store."

"Yeah, and I got one customer I'd like to get rid of." Horace hesitated, then darted a cautious look around them before continuing softly. "You know that fella who's been driftin' in and out of town of late . . . that Jake Hobbs?"

Doc was immediately alert. "Yeah, I know who you mean. What about him?"

Horace shrugged. "He's too damned nosy to suit me. The mail from Denver came in yesterday on the train, and there he was, right at my counter when it was delivered to the store. He said he was lookin' for somethin' for himself, but he asked all kinds of roundabout questions that all pointed toward Miss Modesty out at Luther's ranch. His eyes just about bugged out of his head when he saw the letter that came for her."

Doc was suddenly still. "That so?"

"That's so, but I was too fast for him. I picked up the letter and slipped it out of his sight, and I could tell he was pretty mad about it, even if he did keep up a steady line of talk that made no sense at all. I'm thinkin' of tellin' Luther about him the next time he comes into town."

"Sounds like a good idea." Doc paused, adding casually, "Where's that letter right now?"

"Right here in my pocket." Slapping his jacket confidently, Horace smiled. "I couldn't trust that fella not to sneak up to them boxes and slip it out when I wasn't lookin', so I wasn't about to leave it there." Horace slapped his pocket again. "And this is where that letter's goin' to stay until that little lady comes to town to pick it up."

"Where's the letter from?"

"From Denver . . . from a lady Miss Modesty met on the train on the way here by the name of W. Chesney."

"Is that right?"

Horace nodded. "Miss Modesty told me about her."

"I bet Modesty's real anxious to hear from her . . . her not havin' any friends out here and all." Doc paused. "You know, I'm ridin' out there today . . ."

"Why's that?"

"I'm goin' to see if Helga will come back to take care of Mary. Her and Mary are good friends, and Mary'll be comfortable with her."

"What about Luther? Don't he need Helga?"

Doc's temper slipped. "This is an emergency! Hell, it's damned near life and death for Mary if she don't get some help that's guaranteed to keep her off her feet! Modesty's a capable woman. She can take over at the ranch."

Horace shook his head. "Luther ain't goin' to like that. He don't want nobody talkin' about Miss Modesty and him."

"Well, that's too damned bad! My patient's life is at stake, and if people want to talk, they can talk!" Doc's face screwed up into a squinting threat that he pointed directly at the storekeeper. "But they'll have to answer to me if they do!"

"How come you're ridin' all the way out there? Why don't Harry Barnes go? It's his wife."

"It's his wife, all right. And she's too proud to let him go askin' for help for her. She told him she'll take care of things herself while he's away."

"What did he say to that? Ain't he goin' to—"

"Stop askin' stupid questions, Horace. You're gettin' on my nerves."

Surprising him, Horace laughed. "I guess you're right."

Somewhat mollified, Doc studied Horace's florid face. "I can take that letter to Modesty for you while I'm at it, if you like."

Horace halted mid chew, swallowed, then nodded his head. "Good idea! That'll put an end to that Jake fella's snoopin'."

Apparently pleased, Horace shouted toward the rear of the restaurant where pans clanged and pots rattled. "Hey, ain't nobody comin' out here to take Doc's order? He ain't got all day, you know!"

Finishing the last of his breakfast a short time later, Doc stood up, shook Horace's beefy hand, and slipped Modesty's letter into his pocket. He emerged onto the street and touched the pocket where Modesty's letter rested. Somehow, he had a feeling that bringing the letter to Modesty would as likely save a life as bringing Helga back for Mary would.

Doc turned toward the livery stable. In his mind he was already heading due west.

A sudden shadow blocked the light of the sun that had been beating on Lila's uncovered head the morning long. She looked up from the washtub where it seemed she had spent the major part of her life since arriving at the Bar WK. She frowned up at the sky. As if in answer to her speculation, the sun peeked out encouragingly from behind a cloud. Lila sighed with relief as she looked at the long line of laundry she had already hung. Aunt Helga had finally emerged from her room and resumed her place in the kitchen. The older woman's normally high color had returned, but there had been something about the look of her that had kept Lila in the kitchen longer than she normally would have remained. She had finally convinced herself that she was worrying unnecessarily when Aunt Helga had taken out her baking tins and began mixing *der kuchen.* She had not asked the older woman why she was making one of the cakes she normally saved for special occasions. She thought she knew.

The memory of Aunt Helga's sudden blanch of color when she had seen Max's wound earlier in the morning returned. There had been terror in the woman's eyes when Lila had turned briefly and caught her gaze. She had seen a tragic memory shadowed there. She knew those shadows had held the older woman immobile throughout Max's ordeal, and she knew Aunt Helga could not easily forgive herself that lapse.

Sighing, Lila squeezed out the last of the linens and walked wearily to the line. She pinned it there with a moment's regret that the task that had occupied her mind had been completed.

The water dumped and the tub restored to its nail on the barn wall, Lila paused to look at the rolling land around her. It was silent and peaceful, bathed in a sun that would soon hit the summit. What now? How could she occupy her mind enough to keep at bay thoughts of the strong arms that had swept her from her feet that morning and the pale eyes that had looked into hers with such fury.

Lila's heart resumed a heavy beating as her lips flattened into an angry line. Garrett had been right, of course. She had behaved stupidly. She knew better than to get close to those bulls, but she hadn't been thinking clearly. It seemed she hadn't been able to think clearly since the first time those angry pale eyes had met hers

. . . not to speak of the tumult that had accosted her emotions after the night Garrett had climbed through her window and—

Her heel catching unexpectedly on an exposed root, Lila stumbled. Staggering awkwardly forward a few steps, she managed to catch her balance, then cursed aloud. She turned toward the kitchen window, grateful that she was far enough away not to be overhead, and then cursed again.

It was *his* fault . . . all of it! Lila's anger soared. *He* had done this to her! He had started an ache deep inside her that would not quit . . . an ache she was forced to fight every moment of the day in order to keep it from turning to longing. In that night of loving he had revealed to her a part of himself that she had somehow sensed behind that cold facade. He had burned the husky sound of his voice and the memory of his tender passion into her brain, and he had awakened her to a need she had never known before.

Then he had left her . . . leaving that need behind him.

Lila raised her hand to her forehead and pushed an errant wisp of hair back. She raised her face to the sun, hoping to burn that need from her mind, hoping to eliminate without a trace the memory of Garrett's incredible gentleness, of the anguish in his voice that so clearly mimicked her own when he had said he wanted her. But she knew she could not. It was fixed firmly inside her, a gaping, weeping wound that would not heal.

The sun beat warmly into her skin, and Lila sighed. Catching herself in that sign of weakness, she suddenly snapped open her eyes. Was she insane? Garrett Harrison was a nasty, arrogant bastard who had not hesitated to tell her he wanted her, but who did not think her worthy of speaking the name of the woman he truly loved.

The ever-present knife of pain inside Lila sliced more keenly, forcing her chin higher. She was not the sweet, innocent Elizabeth, and knowing what she did now, she was glad she was not. Unlike Elizabeth, she knew Garrett Harrison for the man he truly was. And, damn it, she would make herself forget him!

The sound of a wagon approaching in the distance snapped Lila abruptly from her raging thoughts. Looking up, she felt a slow warmth permeate her agitated spirit as Doc Bennett's familiar figure came into view. She began walking rapidly toward the front yard. She met the wagon breathlessly when it pulled up in front, and her greeting was straight from the heart.

"What a surprise! What are you doing out here, Doc? You're not reading minds now, are you?"

"Well, well! It looks like somebody here is happy to see me! Whose mind would I be readin', Modesty darlin'? Would it be yours? Are you tryin' to tell me you were thinkin' about this old man?"

"I was."

Doc stepped down from the wagon. He looked as seedy as usual with his ragged, unevenly cut hair and unshaven face. His bulbous nose fairly glowed, but the color appeared to be more from the sun than from attention to the bottle, and Lila was glad. It occurred to her that although Doc was as homely as sin, he had one of the nicest faces she had ever seen.

Lila paused in her scrutiny. There was something about Doc's eyes that did not allow the jovial sound of his voice to ring true. That thought was reflected in her guarded tone as she added, "We had an accident here this morning. Max—"

"Damn! What next?" Doc reached back for his bag. "What happened? Where is he?"

Lila walked beside him as he started toward the house. "He went out with Luther and Garrett, scattering bulls, but not before one of them got him."

"Where?"

"In the leg."

"How bad was it?"

Lila shrugged. "I can't exactly say, but—"

"You forget, I've seen you in action, young lady. I'll take your assessment of a wound any day."

"It looked to me that it was more painful than dangerous. I washed it off and poured some whiskey over it."

"Good . . ."

"And I wrapped it up as best I could."

Doc nodded. "I suppose it couldn't be too bad if he was able to mount up and ride out again."

"He barely managed it."

Doc nodded again. He reached into his bag and withdrew a few familiar packets. "You know what these are. Tell Max to take them every couple of hours. If it looks like the wound is festerin', you tell him to get right into town to see me."

Halting at the front door, Lila turned toward Doc with surprise. "Does that mean you won't be staying until the men come home?"

Doc smiled. "I ain't exactly here on a social call, Modesty dear." Looking up as Helga appeared in the doorway, Doc smiled, addressing her directly. "I came to bring you some news, Helga."

Surprising her, Helga stiffened. "*Ja,* what it is?"

"Mary Barnes had her baby last night."

Helga did not smile. "*Ja?* Is all right?"

"Well . . ."

Helga took an anxious step forward and Doc waved his hand. "Don't get excited. Mary had twins . . . a boy an a girl."

The news did not get the reaction from Helga that Lila expected. Instead, the older woman waited expectantly as Doc continued.

"Mary had a hard time. She lost a lot of blood." Helga's expression tightened and Doc hastened to add, "She'll be all right, but she's goin' to need a lot of help for a while. Harry's schedule's goin' to take him out of town for a few days startin' tomorrow. There ain't nobody he can get to take over for him on this run and Mary'll be alone except for Timmy."

"I come."

"Wait a minute, Helga." Doc looked at Lila tentatively. "Don't you think you'd better talk to Luther first?"

"Nein. Modesty take care of dis place. I come."

"Modesty . . ." Doc looked at Lila tentatively. "I was hopin' Helga would talk it over with you, too, before she decided."

"I. . . it's all right, Doc."

"I get der clothes."

Doc gave a short laugh. "Well, I was kind of hopin' I'd get somethin' to eat here first. I've had a long ride."

"I get der food."

Helga headed abruptly for the kitchen and Lila attempted to follow, only to be restrained by Doc's hand on her arm.

"Another thing I was hopin' for was to get a chance to talk to you in private, Modesty darlin'." Something about Doc's expression tightened a knot in Lila's stomach. "I think this is the best chance we're goin' to get. Want to take a walk with me while Helga's gettin' the food ready?"

Apprehension prickled up Lila's spine. "All right."

Doc took her arm and drew her away from the house. Lila's apprehension grew. They had walked a considerable distance when Doc turned toward her and withdrew an envelope from his pocket. "This came on the train today. I thought you might be waitin' for it, so Horace let me bring it to you."

Lila accepted the envelope, struggling to control the trembling of her hand. She glanced at the return address.

"Go ahead and open it."

"I . . . I can wait to read it later."

"No, open it now, if you don't mind, Modesty darlin'. As a favor to me."

Uncertain of the reason for Doc's gentle insistence, Lila ripped open the envelope. Despite herself, her heart took a little leap at Billy's familiar scrawl. She could almost hear his light, teasing tone as she read:

Dear Lila,

I know you're mad at me, and I'm sorry for that. I'm sorry that there was a Pinkerton on your trail because of me, too, but I'm not worried about him. I know you took care of it.

We do have to talk, but I have some things to do that'll take about a week. Meet me in Denver a week from this Friday, on the 12th. I'll wait for you at the Falmouth Hotel.

Don't disappoint me, Lila honey. You know you'll always be my favorite girl.

Billy

Despite herself, tears rose to Lila's eyes with an emotion that was plain to read as she looked up at Doc.

"That ain't no letter from no lady friend in Denver, is it, Modesty darlin'?"

Unable to speak a blatant lie, Lila did not respond.

"You don't have to answer." Doc touched a finger to her brow. "You aren't wearin' them glasses anymore, are you? You never did need them, did you, darlin'?" He smiled. "No, you don't have to answer that, either, 'cause I think I knew the truth from the minute I first laid eyes on you—drunk as I was. Hell, there's too much fire inside you for you to be as shy and retirin' as you pretended to be. I ain't so old that I couldn't feel its heat."

"Doc, I didn't mean to fool you or anybody else. It just happened that way because . . . because . . ."

Lila's voice trailed away and Doc finished, "Because of the fella who wrote that letter."

Lila nodded.

"So I guess I was right in comin' here to warn you, after all."

Lila's breath caught in her throat. "Warn me?"

"There's been a fella that's been comin' in and out of town since you came to Deer Trail. He said he had some kind of business in the area and nobody gave him much thought, includin' me . . . except . . ."

Lila swallowed hard as she waited for Doc to continue. "Except he always returned to town from the same direction . . . due west . . . and you know there ain't nothin due west of Deer Trail for almost two hours' ride except this here place. I was gettin' suspicious, and then he started askin' roundabout questions about you."

Doc paused, the intensity of his scrutiny tightening. "I seen him in the hotel with another fella the other day. You ever heard of a man named McParland?"

Unable to trust her voice, Lila shook her head.

"He's the head of the Pinkerton Detective Agency in this part of the country."

Lila gasped, her eyes widening.

"I thought so." His expression almost fatherly, Doc whispered, "I knew he couldn't be after you, cause you ain't the type to have done somethin' bad enough to get a Pinkerton on your trail. I figured he had to be after that fella of yours who wrote the letter."

"Oh, Doc," A tear escaped Lila's heavily laden eyes and she brushed it away, "I . . . I wish I could tell you—"

"I know you do, darlin', but I don't want to know nothin' nohow. I just want you to know that you ain't as safe as you thought you was, and that fella of yours ain't, neither." Doc's lined face softened at her obvious distress. "Come on now, don't let Helga see you was cryin'. Old Helga and me are goin' to be leavin' here in a little while, and the rest is up to you. I'm hopin' you'll do the right thing, with Luther feelin' like he does about you and all."

"I never meant to hurt Luther."

"But things don't always work out the way we planned, do they, darlin'."

A world of meaning was in Lila's single word of response.

"No."

"There's only one thing I want to know."

"What's that?"

"Your real first name."

Lila's smile was ragged. "It's Lila."

"I knew it! You didn't look like no Modesty nohow." Doc paused. "Will you promise me somethin'?"

Lila struggled to retain her composure. "If I can."

"Will you promise me that you won't forget old Doc?"

"Oh, Doc . . ." Her heart in her voice, Lila whispered, "Never."

Holding her gaze a minute longer, Doc suddenly smiled. "That's good enough for me. Now put a smile on your face and remember—Helga, the old bag that she is, don't miss nothin'."

"Oh, Doc . . ."

They were strolling back to the house when Lila slipped her arm through Doc's. She held tight to his scrawny strength and fought the swirl of fears assaulting her.

Dark, heavy clouds thickened overhead, blocking out the brilliant sunlight that had baked Garrett's shoulders an hour earlier. Catching the brim of his hat as a sudden wind whipped viciously, he looked at the two men working a short distance away. Knox's body was stiff with frustration. He had not anticipated the endless trouble they had encountered in driving the belligerent bulls to the upper pasture. Fight after fight had broken out between the largest bull and the young challenger along the way, necessitating stop after stop that had stretched the morning hours into an eternity. The animals had finally been installed in separate pastures, but relief had proved to be premature as the largest bull made another roaring charge that demolished a row of fencing erected only a week earlier.

Garrett's dark brows knitted tighter as he studied the downed fencing. Once repaired, it would be only temporary at best. Another determined charge would net the same results as before. There was only one solution.

Knox turned, catching Garrett's speculative look. He grunted with disgust.

"This fencing isn't going to work. We're going to

have to put up a double row in order to discourage that big fella." Knox surveyed the agitated animal through squinting eyes as the wind whipped harder. "I sure hope he's worth the trouble."

"Oh, I'd say he is." Max was quick to inject a quip, despite the obvious pain he had suffered most of the day. "He's a randy piece, all right. I get the feelin' that once he sets his mind to business instead of fightin', there won't be no holdin' him back."

"You think so, huh?" Knox managed a weak smile. "But it looks like he's not goin' to get about his job until he's made us work like hell first."

Knox turned to Garrett. "Max and I will start repairing what's here while you ride back to the barn and get a few more bales of wire. I won't feel safe leaving until we have an extra row of wire along this portion of fencing."

Garrett glanced again at the rapidly darkening sky, then back at Knox, and Knox's temper snapped. "Don't tell me you're afraid of getting wet! If you are, it's too bad because we're going to get this fencing done, and the sooner you start back, the better. While you're at it, you can tell Helga we'll be late for supper." Knox paused. "You can tell Modesty . . ." He paused again. "Never mind. I'll tell her myself when I get back."

Garrett turned without response and mounted his horse. It occurred to him that under different circumstances he might have liked Luther Knox. But as things stood, he didn't. It was plain to see that Knox didn't like him much, either. He supposed that was natural . . . instinct . . . when, whether Knox consciously realized it or not, both men wanted the same woman.

Kicking his mount into motion, Garrett gave a scoffing snort. They were going to get wet, all right, but he had suffered worse. And he knew that this day's brief, physical discomfort would be nothing next to what Knox had in store for him when Lila made her move.

Knox . . . the damned fool . . . swallowing every lie Lila told him—bending to her every whim . . . wanting her . . .

A slow fury rose inside Garrett. Lila would never belong to Luther Knox.

Refusing to pursue that thought any further, Garrett spurred his horse into a gallop.

Lila's mind whirled in ever-deepening panic as she paced the spotless kitchen floor. She turned toward the pots still simmering on the stove, almost amused at her own concern that the supper Helga had started prior to Doc's arrival should not burn. She gave a weak laugh. Her world was falling down around her and she was worrying about the stew Helga had left behind.

Lila's throat choked dangerously tight. A Pinkerton in Deer Trail . . . and she thought she had been so clever. How long had he been watching her? Was there a spyglass trained on the house from a hillside in the distance right now? How could she escape him?

Lila's pacing increased. The Pinkerton, whoever he was, had not followed her to this ranch, she was certain of that. She had been alone when she had originally gotten off the train in Deer Trail. However he had found her, he had done it after she had arrived.

A sudden thought striking her mind, Lila gasped. Garrett . . . Had the Pinkerton recognized him as well? No, Doc had said the Pinkerton was asking questions about *her.* There had been no mention of Garrett. Garrett was safe, temporarily. If she left, the Pinkerton, wherever he was, would doubtlessly follow. She had a week before she met Billy in Denver . . . a week to throw him off her trail.

Halting her pacing, Lila drew herself stiffly erect. She would write a letter of explanation to Luther and she would leave as soon as the men rode out the next morning. That was the only way. She could not take the chance of speaking to him in person. She hoped he would be able to forgive her for her deceit, but she doubted he would. As for Garrett, neither could she allow him to find out about her plans. His temperament was too mercurial and he was too dangerous . . . to the safety of her and Billy. She needed him out of her life. He would forget her and go his own way once she was out of sight. He would go back to his loving Elizabeth.

But if Garrett should choose to follow her . . .

Lila's heart skipped a beat.

He would not.

Because of Elizabeth.

Tears flooded Lila's eyes. Despising herself for those tears, Lila brushed them away just as a sudden, deafening crack of thunder sounded overhead. With a few running steps, she was at the kitchen door, staring up at the leaden sky. The rumbling continued as oversize drops of rain slapped loudly against the hard-packed ground in warning of a deluge to come.

Lila glanced at the clothesline billowing in the wind. If she hurried, she had just enough time to pull the clothes in . . . just enough time to tie up that loose end, at least.

Picking up the laundry basket outside the door, Lila raced out into the yard. She worked furiously, ignoring long amber strands of hair whipping free of their confinement as the linens cracked and flapped in the heightening wind. Another deafening roll of thunder sounded as the large, chilling drops of rain fell heavier, staining the white clothes with moist spots of grey as Lila pulled them from the line.

Her hands growing clumsy in her haste, Lila was struggling to keep a long sheet from the ground when a second sense turned her abruptly to the unexpected sight of Garrett standing behind her. She gasped, her eyes darting to the spot where his mount stood alone a few feet away.

"Wh-what are you doing here?" Lila glanced again at Garrett's horse. "Where's Luther?"

Garrett's cool, grey-eyed gaze studied her intently. "What's the matter, Lila?"

"Nothing!" Realizing her response was too quick, Lila turned back to the line, her hands trembling as she struggled with the remaining pins. Garrett's large, calloused hands closed over hers, sending heated tremors snaking through her as he pulled the remaining clothes from the line and dropped them into the basket.

Ignoring the growing fury of the storm, Garrett halted her as she attempted to pick up the basket. "I asked you what's wrong."

"Nothing, I said! I have to bring the laundry inside."

Garrett glanced at the house. "Where's Helga?"

"She . . . she's inside."

"Why isn't she helping you?"

"She's resting. She doesn't feel well."

"You're lyin'."

"No!"

"She's gone, isn't she?" Garrett grasped her shoulders. "Tell me the truth, Lila."

"No . . . yes . . . All right, she's gone! Doc Bennett came for her. She was needed in town." Thunder cracked again. It began raining in earnest as Lila pulled herself free. "Let me go."

Lila reached again for the basket, but Garrett snatched it up instead. "I'll take it inside for you."

"No!"

Garrett's gaze was suddenly intense. "Why not, Lila?"

"Because I don't want you to. When are Luther and Max coming back?"

Thunder boomed and lightning cracked in a sudden barrage of sound as the heavens opened up in a frigid deluge. Rain pounded down in a chilling assault, bouncing against the ground as wild gusts whipped the drops into driving torrents. Soaked to the skin in the space of a few moments, her hair and clothing plastered against her body as water ran in rivulets down her face, Lila remained stubbornly still. Her lips quivered from the chill as she demanded over the increasing din. "Where's Luther?"

"He and Max are stayin' with the bulls until I get back."

A trembling unrelated to the raging elements began inside Lila as the driving wind whipped the last of her bound hair free of restraint to flay her with the sodden strands. Desperation giving her sudden voice, she shouted, "Why don't you leave? They're waiting for you."

The basket abandoned, Garrett took a step closer. She could see the muscular outline of his heaving chest under his saturated shirt as rain ran in a small stream from the brim of his hat onto the shrinking space between them. His voice was barely audible over the maelstrom around them.

"What are you afraid of, Lila?"

"Nothing!" She looked down at the sodden clothes in the basket beside them, tears mingling with the rain washing her cheeks. "I just want . . . want you to leave."

"No you don't, Lila darlin'." Garrett took another step, eliminating the final distance between them as he reached out for her and drew her close. "You don't want that anymore than I do. Oh, Lila, I—"

"No! Leave me alone!" Wrenching herself free, Lila ran from Garrett blindly, her feet flying across the puddled yard in a frantic bid for escape from the emotion growing inside her. The icy deluge hammering the ground did not drown out the sounds of Garrett's heavy footsteps splashing in pursuit, growing ever closer.

Breathless from her mindless flight, Lila was suddenly swept from her feet and up into Garrett's arms. Within moments his strong legs had carried them across the ground, delivering them to the protection of the barn.

The growing intensity of the storm raged beyond the barn walls as Garrett held her against his heaving chest. His ragged breath bathing her lips, his arms warm bands of steel that held her helplessly close, Garrett finally rasped, "You don't really want me to leave you, do you, darlin'?"

Garrett's question was a whispered plea that touched Lila to the soul. Her lips parting, she strained for words that did not come as Garrett carried her slowly to a mound of hay by the rear wall and lay her gently there. Lying beside her, he stroked her hair back from her face, then kissed the rain drops from her lashes, her cheeks, the curve of her jaw before settling on her mouth with a gasping sound.

Uncertain if the gasp had come from Garrett's lips or her own, Lila felt a familiar magic assume control. Lost in its wonder, she discovered anew that there was no sensation more beautiful than being in Garrett's arms, no emotion truer than the joy that suffused her when he whispered barely coherent words of love into her ear, nothing that could match this moment of realization that whatever else happened beyond the silent walls surrounding them, at this moment in time, they were meant to be together.

A glow, warmer, more brilliant than the sun, spread slowly through Lila's mind. It mirrored Garrett's image. It was reflected in his eyes and in her heart. It nurtured to full, throbbing life an emotion so intense that she cried out in overwhelming bliss as Garrett's hands freed her of her clothes to caress her with breathtaking torment. Garrett's lips against her skin raised her higher into the glowing realm. She was aching with the sheer rapture of his touch when he suddenly pulled back.

"Garrett . . ."

"I'm not goin' anywhere, darlin'."

Taking a moment to free himself of his clothes, Garrett kneeled beside her. He halted briefly to speak in an unexpectedly hesitant whisper. "I wish I could tell you . . . I wish I could say—"

Garrett's words trailed to a halt, but Lila knew what he had left unsaid. There were so many things that should keep them apart. Elizabeth . . . Luther . . . Billy . . . But they all became pale shadows that dissipated in the brilliant light of the blinding emotion that raged between them.

Indulging that emotion and indulging herself as she had not dared before, Lila drew herself to her knees beside Garrett to meet his uncertainty halfway. Her gaze trailed his face, memorizing each softened line. With the bitterness gone, it was a wonderful face . . . a handsome face . . . a loving face . . .

Lila kissed Garrett's lips lightly. Drops of water from Garrett's sodden hair trailed down his cheek and she caught one with her lips. She savored it, then followed the gleaming trail of another with her tongue as it ran down his jaw and throat onto his chest. The heat of Garrett's skin, the taste of him, raised the hunger inside her. She traced the narrow paths lower still until Garrett's breath exploded in a gasp and his arms snaked around her, crushing her close.

The hunger grew greater, the aching need stronger, as Garrett's mouth devoured hers. She strained against him, her mind filled with the glory of his flesh against hers. The fragrant hay again pillowing her, Lila welcomed Garrett as he slipped atop her. He filled her and she accepted him willingly. He plunged deeply and she met him fully. Wrapping her arms around his neck, she exalted in each deepening thrust as kaleidoscoping colors inside her mind grew brighter, as her need grew more fierce, as the exhilaration of their joining rapidly pushed her beyond control. The burst of rapture was sudden, blinding, as Garrett arched against her. Trembling with the unmatched ecstasy of the moment, Lila joined Garrett in his throbbing release, clutching him, wanting him more desperately than he would ever know.

A stillness broken only by the sounds of Garrett's heavy breathing and the unrelenting drumming of rain on the roof echoed in the silence that followed. Oblivious to the storm that raged unabated outside, Lila felt the swell of a bittersweet torment as reality gradually returned a knot of anguish that could not be denied. Garrett's weight still lay intimately upon her but their time together was quickly slipping away. She ached at the impending loss, mourning, wishing with all her heart—

"Lila . . ." Garrett raised himself above her. Her heart twisted with pain to see familiar shadows returning to his eyes as he whispered, "Come away with me, darlin'. Now . . . tonight."

Drawing his head down so their lips might meet, Lila kissed Garrett lovingly, lingeringly. Regret rang hard and deep within her as she drew back at last, her voice a pained whisper.

"I can't."

"You can."

"No . . ."

"Forget him, damn it! Whoever he is, he's not worth sacrificin' what we can have together."

"Garrett, please, don't spoil—"

"You're not makin' sense, Lila. How can I spoil what we've had by tellin' you I don't want to give it up?"

"You don't understand. I *can't* forget him."

"You can."

"I can't!"

"You will." The burning intensity of Garrett's gaze caused a sudden shudder to shake Lila's frame as he repeated softly, "I promise you, you will."

Lila shuddered again and Garrett frowned. He stroked a damp tendril back from her face, then rolled to his side, freeing her. "You're cold. Come on, get up. We'll go back to the house so you can change."

Her hands trembling as she fastened the last button on her sodden garments, Lila looked up to see Garrett fully dressed as well. The rain had abated to a steady drizzle as Lila turned toward the doorway, only to have Garrett grasp her arm and draw her back. She saw the torment in his light eyes as he whispered, "No, don't go yet."

"We have to, Garrett. The rain is stopping. Luther will be coming back."

"I said not yet, damn it!" Clasping her close, Garrett wrapped his arms around her in a fierce, breathtaking embrace. His lips moved warmly against her temple when he spoke again in an anguished whisper. "I can't get enough of you, darlin'."

Garrett's words echoed deep inside her as his mouth claimed hers once more, as the heat of rising passion momentarily eliminated the creeping chill. Drawing back as she shuddered once more, Garrett gave a soft sigh of acceptance before slipping his arm around her waist and drawing hcr against his side. Leaning against him, wishing they were free to spend their lives just so, Lila followed Garrett's lead as he urged her out into the steady drizzle toward the house.

Intensely aware of the restraint Garrett had practiced in allowing her the privacy of her room, Lila quickly changed into dry clothing. Her hair freshly bound, she drew her door open to the sound of hoofbeats in the yard. She emerged into the parlor to see Luther and Max enter the house.

His expression stiff, his clothes making broadening puddles on the wood floor, Luther looked at Lila, then at Garrett as he appeared in the kitchen doorway. He assessed Garrett's wet clothing, then slowly removed his dripping hat.

"You're a damned lucky man, Harrison. If Max and I had come back here and found you cozy and dry, that would've been the end of it."

Lila glanced at Garrett. The warmth draining from her heart, she saw the old Garrett had returned. His gaze, as cold as ice, sent a chill down her spine as he replied to Luther in a hard voice that revealed no hint of the passion they had so recently shared. "I got caught in the rain, too. I figured only a fool would stay out in that deluge, so I waited here for you to come back."

Luther's jaw tightened. "You didn't give the bulls a thought."

"I figured the storm would cool them off, and we could string that wire tomorrow."

Max limped to a chair. Going directly to his side, Lila realized Luther's voice was as close to a growl as she had ever heard it as he responded, "We'll do that, all right. All *three* of us." She raised her head as Luther asked, "Where's Aunt Helga?"

Garrett walked past her without a glance as Lila responded automatically to Luther's question. The thought struck her as Garrett opened the door and left the house without another word that his abrupt departure was perhaps the most appropriate way to have said goodbye.

Fourteen

Will Eaton ignored the whinnied protest of the horse tethered nearby as he turned sharply to face his long-time associate. Forbes and he had walked out of their cabin hideout a few minutes earlier and had begun saddling up. Forbes had chosen to keep the plan he was contemplating a secret until that moment. The reason had been immediately and infuriatingly apparent, eliciting Eaton's spontaneous response.

"You're gettin' crazier every day, you know that, Forbes!"

Eaton ignored Forbes's warning glare. He was getting damned sick of the man's nightmares and irrational behavior. If they hadn't been together so long, he would've taken off with the rest of the men when the money had been doled out. The truth be known, he wouldn't blame any one of them if they didn't come back for the scheduled meeting a week from now.

He continued hotly. "What in hell's wrong with you? Are you tryin' to get us all killed?"

"There wouldn't be no point in that, now would there." Forbes gave an eerie laugh, and Eaton's anger flared higher.

"You wouldn't think so, to hear what you've been

plannin'. You have to be crazy thinkin' to hit the same train carryin' the same bank's money again. It's too soon!"

"That's why they won't expect it."

"You're crazy!"

"I'm gettin' tired of hearin' you say that, Willie *boy* . . . and I'm givin' you fair warnin'. Say it once more, and you're goin' to be sorry."

"Don't threaten me, Bart, old *boy.*" Eaton's expression turned mean. "You don't scare me like you do the others."

"Maybe I should."

"Maybe that should go both ways."

Silent for long moments as tension crackled between them, Forbes gave a sudden harsh laugh. "Yeah, maybe it should." He paused. "You ain't comfortable with the way I've been handlin' things lately, are you?"

"No, I ain't." Eaton did not relent. "All that talk about your dreams and that threat hangin' over us. You forget about it quick enough when you start plannin' another job, don't you? I'm startin' to think it was just a way of keepin' control of that money you didn't want to part with."

"You're wrong there. There's somethin' happenin' out there. I can feel it."

"Yeah . . . and I suppose it has to do with Chesney."

Wariness entered Forbes's expression. "What are you talkin' about?"

"I'm talkin' about the way you've been on Chesney's back lately."

"Since when have you been standin' up for Chesney?"

"I ain't, but you're makin' the rest of the boys nervous . . . like they're wonderin' when you're goin' to start on them. It ain't safe makin' them feel that way."

Forbes's small eyes narrowed. "You don't get it, do you?"

"I sure as hell don't."

Forbes paused for a long moment, cautiously considering his next words. "We've been ridin' together a long time, Eaton. What do you see when you look at Chesney?"

"I don't see nothin' special, that's for sure."

"I'll tell you what I see when I look at him. I see myself about fifteen years ago, and I ain't sure I like it."

"You *are* crazy!"

"No, I ain't!" Forbes's body tensed, and Eaton recognized a need for caution as Forbes continued. "You ain't lookin', so you ain't seein'. I noticed it the first time I seen him. There's somethin' about him. It's in the way he looks and listens to everythin' that's goin' on around him, like he's analyzin' it. He puts me in mind of myself when I first hooked up with Quantrill."

"So? What's that supposed to mean?"

"It means I can almost read Chesney's mind. He's thinkin' that he's finally where he's meant to be . . . that he's finally somebody, just like I was finally somebody when I found my place with Quantrill."

"What's wrong with that? I'd think you'd be glad."

"Yeah?" Forbes maintained a heavy stare. "I told you, I ain't so sure. Chesney's smart. I'm wonderin' if he's too smart."

"What're you talkin' about?"

Forbes's response was slow and heavy with menace. "You still don't understand, do you? The truth is that I have a feelin' I know what might've happened if Quantrill hadn't been wounded when he was and put out of commission. I get the feelin' that I wouldn't have been satisfied takin' his orders too much longer when

I had already learned as much as I could from him. I get the feelin' that if some bluebelly, hadn't stopped him, *I* might've."

The intense light in Forbes's small eyes sent an unexpected shiver down Eaton's spine. He gasped with disbelief. "Hell, you're always talkin' about that time with Quantrill bein' the best of your life!"

"It was."

Eaton shook his head, confused.

"It ain't that hard to figure out. I figured there wasn't no more use in followin' when I could be leadin'."

"Y-you don't mean that . . ."

The intense light in Forbes's gaze sharpened as Eaton's voice trailed away. "Maybe I do, maybe I don't."

"Christ!"

Forbes laughed. "Ain't no use gettin' religion now."

Eaton blinked. Regaining his voice, he pressed, "If you're thinkin' that way, why don't you get rid of Chesney? Tell him you don't need him no more. We can get along without him."

"That won't work."

"Why not?"

"'Cause I say it won't. Besides, I kind of took a likin' to him."

"A likin' to him!"

"Yeah. He's keepin' me on my toes. I'm goin' to give that young fella as much rope as he'll take and see what happens."

"You're cra—" Eaton halted abruptly. His expression turned hard as he continued. "Just as long as you don't decide to take the same kind of *likin'* to me . . ."

"No chance of that. We're old friends." Forbes's expression lightened unexpectedly. "Besides, you ain't no threat to me. You ain't smart enough."

"Maybe I'm smarter than you think."

Forbes laughed again. "Come on. We're wastin' time. We got work to do."

Still smarting from Forbes's dismissal as he guided his mount down the trail behind Forbes a short time later, Eaton worked their conversation over in his mind. It occurred to him that Chesney, with his big smile and boyish appeal, wasn't as smart as Forbes thought he was if he couldn't see what was coming.

Eaton's lip ticked as his hand tightened on the reins. But Chesney would come back. Forbes was right on that score. Ridin' with the gang had gotten into Chesney's blood, all right.

A sudden thought popped into Eaton's mind. If Chesney *was* as smart as Forbes thought he was, he was really in trouble. He'd be watchin' his back and tryin' to anticipate Forbes. He'd try to be ready for whatever Forbes was goin' to do . . . and that would be his first mistake. Forbes was still the fastest gun he had ever seen . . . faster than Chesney or any one of them in the gang. If Chesney thought he—

Eaton halted the rapid progression of his thoughts. What was he worryin' about, anyway?

Forbes was Chesney's problem, not his.

Eaton kicked his horse to a faster pace.

And he was damned glad of it . . .

Her hands trembling so badly that she was barely able to close the catch, Lila picked up her carpetbag and took a long, slow look around the small bedroom she had used for the past few weeks of her life. The modest furnishings had grown warmly familiar, almost homey. She suffered a strange sense of despair realizing that she would never see them again, and she—

A glimpse of herself in the washstand mirror drew Lila's thoughts to a sudden halt. Wearing the same brown traveling clothes and bonnet that she had worn upon her arrival at the ranch, she had lost even the small trace of her own personality that had gradually begun to emerge during her residence there. She was again the simple brown wren, Modesty Parkins.

Lila grimaced at the sight. Despite the length of time she had assumed that personality, it was still miles away from her own in every way. She itched to shed her disguise while realizing, with a depth of pain that was almost overwhelming, that she was not truly ready to shed the new friends her disguise had brought her at this isolated ranch in the middle of nowhere.

Pulling the ranch-house door closed behind her, the envelope she had left behind on the dining-room table heavy on her heart, Lila viewed the roll of the land and the modest house behind her through a growing mist of tears. She listened to the sweet silence she had once abhorred with a lingering sadness. She recalled the friends who would soon despise her. She ached with an ache that would not cease for the love of a cold-eyed man . . . a love that could not be.

And she wondered if at that very moment, a furtive figure was watching her say her last silent goodbyes.

That furtive figure in mind, Lila forced a smile as she walked determinedly toward the wagon she had readied earlier, and threw her bag into the rear. Holding the horse steady with a sharp command, Lila climbed up onto the seat, slapped the reins against the horse's back, and raised her chin as the wagon jerked abruptly forward.

Swallowing against the tightening thickness in her

throat, Lila held herself erect as the wagon rolled down the road at a steady pace. She would be in Deer Trail within two hours. The Denver train would arrive shortly afterward and she would be gone. She had two hours to say her goodbyes. Two hours to *lament* her goodbyes . . . two hours to put her goodbyes forever behind her.

Lying on his stomach at his vantage point not far away, his eye to his spyglass as Lila's wagon drove down the trail at a steady pace, Jake Hobbs gave a restrained shout of jubilation. It was finally happening!

Jumping to his feet, taking only a moment to brush the dust from his clothes and to wipe away the perspiration that had already accumulated on his brow despite the morning hour, Jake scooped up the few belongings still scattered around his makeshift camp and shoved them into his saddlebag. Mounted a moment later, he kicked his horse into motion.

Following at a safe distance as Lila Chesney's wagon wound its way toward Deer Trail, Jake allowed a satisfied smile to settle into the deeply etched lines on his face. He hadn't made any mistakes this time. Lila Chesney had emerged from the house in her mousey traveling garb, but he had taken nothing for granted. He had trained his spyglass on that face . . . that beautiful face . . . and he had been certain this time that it was Lila Chesney and no other.

Jake nodded. He had taken a big chance going into town and following the mail delivery to the general store the previous day. Luck had been with him for a change with the arrival of the letter for Lila Chesney on that morning's train, but he had been more than irritated when that overstuffed storekeeper had guarded it like it was pure gold. He had silently cursed when

Neely had slipped the letter into his pocket, thinking he might have aroused the fellow's suspicion. He had been vastly relieved to discover that Doc Bennett's pending trip to the ranch was the reason.

Hobbs paused at that thought. He was still uncertain if Neely had gotten suspicious, but the visit had been a calculated risk worth taking. It was now just a matter of keeping his distance and following Lila straight to her boyfriend . . . and then following him straight to the rest of the gang.

Jake's thoughts slipped to Harrison, laboring on fencing for another long day . . . another long, wasted day, and his smile stretched a trace wider. It served Harrison right . . . sleeping in a nice comfortable bed all the while he had been stretched out on the hard ground for more weeks than he cared to remember. Harrison would be surprised to find Lila Chesney gone when he returned, but Harrison would also have the consolation of knowing that he was right behind her. Harrison would have no trouble picking up their trail. He'd see to that.

Lila Chesney's wagon slipped momentarily out of sight on a curve of the road, and Jake spurred his horse into a canter. Reining back when the wagon was again within view, he rubbed his palm against his stubbled cheek, consoling himself that in no more than another week or so, he'd be done with the disguise he had been forced to maintain, and with the same damned clothes he had been wearing for a longer time than he cared to remember. Hell, when he finally took them off for good, he might even celebrate by burning them . . . and maybe doing a victory dance around the fire! And then he'd—

Suddenly frowning, Jake drew his wandering thoughts to a halt. There'd be time to think about celebrating when Forbes and his gang were finally behind bars—but he was sure of one thing. Not the least satisfying part of that celebration would be the admission he intended to get from McParland, and maybe even the Pinkertons themselves, that they had made a mistake when they had doubted Harrison and him for a single minute.

Lila Chesney's wagon continued to bounce steadily along ahead of him, and Jake nodded to himself in silent resolution. Yes, sir, he had an apology coming . . .

The wagon jumped and bounced along the rutted road as Lila maintained a steady hand on the reins. The sun's steady climb into the morning sky had brought with it a heat that baked her damp skin and a reluctant breeze that did little to cool it. But Lila was oblivious to the weather's subtle torment, preoccupied as she was with thoughts that gave her little rest.

Regrets, anxiety, despair, and a growing agitation had continued to assault her mind until she was certain of only one thing. She needed to get away, for Billy's sake, for Luther's sake, and for her own . . .

Garrett's face flashed before Lila's mind, his pale eyes accusing, but Elizabeth's image was tormentingly close behind.

You're nothin' like Elizabeth. Elizabeth is good and innocent and pure . . .

Truth had been harsh and unforgiving as Lila had forced herself to face it squarely in the darkness of the night past. The first truth had been her certainty that Garrett wanted her with all his heart . . . *now* but not *forever.* Elizabeth was his "forever" kind of woman. The second truth had been that although Garrett did not see her that way, Lila *was* a "forever" kind of woman. She could never be satisfied with less.

Forcing those lingering thoughts from her mind as Deer Trail loomed ahead, Lila fought an inclination to glance behind her. She had not seen anyone, but she knew she was being followed.

Entering town, Lila turned off directly into the livery stable in the first step of a plan she had formulated during the previous sleepless night. A warning bell rang in her mind at the bearded proprietor's interest when she notified him Luther would pick up the wagon in the morning. She flashed him a disarming smile, adding a soft comment about going shopping in Denver for a few days before picking up her carpetbag and turning toward the door.

Her smile discarded the moment she reached the street, Lila walked quickly, her gaze focused and determined. Great puffs of black smoke swirled in the distance as she approached the station house. A screeching train whistle reverberated against the hills as she purchased her ticket. She was standing ticket in hand as the train rattled into the station. She was poised and ready when the train ground to a halt in front of her.

Boarding the train the moment it stopped, Lila walked to the rear of the semicrowded car. Sitting, she purposely placed her carpetbag on the seat beside her, then turned toward the window to scan the platform with a deceptively casual gaze. The stationmaster, with his drooping mustache and sour expression, stood in the doorway of the station house—nothing unusual, she was sure. A boy with a spotted dog trailing at his heels ran across the platform and moved out of sight. Two casually dressed ranchers boarded. A laughing young couple dressed for a holiday followed. They assumed seats as Lila rubbed a trembling hand across her brow. She had not realized she was perspiring. She was about to reach for a handkerchief when she saw *him.*

He was walking with two other men, apparently engrossed in earnest conversation, but Lila knew instinctively that it was the Pinkerton.

Running over the description Doc had given her of the Pinkerton in her mind, Lila appraised the fellow more closely. He was a short man, thin and wiry, dressed casually, almost slovenly. He sported a bushy mustache, and had greying hair that was roughly cut. Underneath his hat, his hairline was receding.

His hat . . . with a faded snakeskin band . . .

Lila's heartbeat escalated to a roaring thunder in her ears as she averted her gaze. She was looking into her carpetbag when the man entered the car, still conversing. She glanced up in an offhand manner, the heavy hammering of her heart seeming to come to a sudden stop as she glimpsed the fellow's face more clearly.

Lila withheld a gasp.

The drummer!

Withdrawing a handkerchief from her bag, Lila turned back to the window. Shock heavily tinged with an unconscious relief tingled along her spine as she dabbed at her brow with a delicate hand. This Pinkerton was the same man who had followed her from Salina. He had no interest in Garrett. Garrett was safe—free to leave the ranch whenever he chose . . . free to follow whatever life he chose.

A supreme sadness surged within Lila. She hoped he would choose well.

But in the meantime . . .

Lila looked out the window as the whistle blasted and the train jerked into motion. She stared at the scenery gradually rolling past, her mind racing. She had eluded this Pinkerton once before. Now that she had identified him, it would be that much easier to do it a second time.

She was sure . . .

Hobbs laughed aloud and gave Sam Potter's shoulder a hearty wack. Settling back in his seat, he listened to the conversation progressing around him in the rail car, intensely grateful to have met these fellows as he had approached the station. Drinking acquaintances from the Red Slipper Saloon, they had provided him the perfect cover upon boarding the train. Lila Chesney had not given him a conscious glance.

Pulling down his hat lower on his brow, Jake reacted with another guffaw to an off-color joke and an elbow poked sharply into his ribs. He glanced out the corner of his eye as the conductor reached Lila Chesney and punched her ticket. The fellow's voice carried with surprising clarity over the din of clacking wheels and coarse laughter.

"Goin' to Magnolia . . . is that right, ma'am?" He leered down into Lila Chesney's upturned face. "That's the last stop before Denver. I'll be sure to let you know when we reach it."

Jake heard Lila's whispered word of thanks, and was grateful that he had had the foresight to buy a ticket for Denver. It would've been just like that nosy bird to call attention to the fact that Lila and he were getting off at the same stop.

Jake gave a low snort, only to have his ribs jabbed sharply as another round of laughter burst from the men around him. A coarse voice questioned in his ear, "Did you hear that one, Jake?"

Jake forced a lopsided grin. "Sure enough did! I don't know how you fellas can remember all them jokes."

Liquor heavy on his breath, Sam assured, "This ain't nothin'! We ain't even got started yet."

Jake nodded, maintaining his grin with sheer strength of will. Heaven help him and his poor, sore ribs, he believed every word.

"MAGNOLIA! NEXT STOP, MAGNOLIA!"

The conductor's call rang over the rattle of the crowded rail car. Appearing beside her, the persistent fellow leaned down to speak directly to Lila, so close that she could feel his hot breath against her cheek and could see the little spots of decay on his yellowed teeth.

"Magnolia's the next stop, ma'am. Magnolia's one of my favorite homes away from home." He winked and smiled more broadly. "If you're intendin' to spend some time there, I'd be happy to show you around."

Drawing back, Lila withheld the retort that might have sprung to her lips if she had been sporting her true personality. Instead, she feigned a flustered manner and batted her bespectacled eyes.

"That's very generous of you to offer me your valuable time, sir, but I . . . I'm afraid my intended might object. He's so jealous . . ." She shook her head with shy disapproval. "He resorts to his gun too quickly to make me truly comfortable in accepting your offer."

His eyes popping open wide, the conductor jerked upright, then raised his cap politely. "Excuse me, ma'am. No offense intended."

"No offense taken, sir."

Satisfied at the conductor's rapid retreat, Lila turned to concentrate on the station slowly pulling into view. Her expression composed, Lila waited as the train drew to a shuddering stop. Maintaining her seat until the last person had disembarked and the first warning call had been sounded for departure, she stood abruptly to exit the car. She stepped down onto the station platform just as the train prepared to roll again, then walked quickly, without a backward glance, toward the main street.

Laughing inside at the haste with which her "shadow" would have to extricate himself from his drunken cronies in order to follow, Lila took great satisfaction at the sound of an awkward leap to the platform and a harsh grunt behind her as she continued walking.

Emerging onto Magnolia's main street, Lila surveyed the area with dismay. Except for the absence of familiar faces, it was Deer Trail all over again. She groaned inwardly. One store, one hotel, one saloon, one barber shop, one livery stable, one restaurant . . .

Lila's stomach rumbled as she glanced up at the position of the afternoon sun. She had missed her noon meal. Starting toward the restaurant, she prepared to eliminate that oversight.

Lila was back on the street a short time later, her stomach satisfied and important questions about the town answered by a talkative and cooperative waitress. It surprised her that the Pinkerton was nowhere in sight, but she knew he was watching. So certain was she that she smiled brightly for his benefit before starting briskly toward the Willows Hotel.

Her bag carefully stored in her small but adequate room, Lila stepped back onto the street and started purposefully toward the general store. The sun was making its slow descent toward the horizon when Lila carried her purchases to the counter with a Modesty-like smile for the benefit of the youthful clerk. The sum paid and her purchases carefully wrapped, she headed back to the hotel.

Pulling down the blind on the setting sun, Lila unwrapped her packages. The contents of the first package restored a temporary brightness to her eye. The pale-blue cotton dress with wide lace trim on the square neckline and sleeves was a simple enough garment, but it was a dress of incredible beauty when compared with the dowdy clothes she had been wearing for the past month. The first sight of it had raised her spirits. Her smile widening, she unwrapped the small, flat straw hat decorated with lace butterflies wrapped in tissue paper beside it.

All trace of a smile disappeared as Lila unwrapped the second package.

Glancing at the window where the dying rays of the sun shone brilliantly in a final hurrah, Lila prepared herself for the ordeal to come.

On the street below, Jake looked up at the second-floor window of the Willows Hotel. He had seen Lila Chesney draw the blind a short time earlier and he had been watching her shadow move back and forth behind the drawn blind in the time since. This was almost too easy. It was obvious that Lila Chesney was settling in for a short stay, awaiting her boyfriend. It was also obvious that she intended to look her best when he came. He had watched from a covert distance as she had shopped in the general store, sorting through the small selection of women's ready-made clothing and holding dresses up against her indecisively. He had been forced from his position of observance before she made her final purchases by a fellow who became suspicious of his interest in the general store, but the number of packages she had emerged with had been silent testimony to her enthusiasm.

Jake gave the street an assessing glance. He had

learned the hard way that he could not take any chances with the wily Lila Chesney, and that the safest place to be was as close as he could get to her without being seen. He made an abrupt decision.

Carefully installed in the room across the hall from Lila Chesney's room 12, Jake left his door open a crack and placed his chair beside it so he might watch her doorway in comfort. He saw the flickering light of the lamp already shining beneath the door and the reassuring shadow moving within.

Preparing himself for a long night, Jake glanced out the window at the rapidly darkening sky. Lila's departure from the Bar WK was an established fact by now. He could only guess what the reaction to her leaving had been . . .

The sun had dropped behind the mountain in a final blaze of glory. The brief pall of twilight had settled within the silent ranch house as Luther, incredulous, reread the neat, carefully scripted letter bearing his name.

Dear Luther,

By the time you get this letter I'll be far away from Deer Trail. I regret that I can't tell you where I'm going. I hope you will understand, although I know no amount of explanation can truly excuse what I've done.

Simply, I'm not the woman you thought me to be. My name isn't Modesty Parkins. I met the true Modesty on the train en route to Denver. The uncertainties of starting a new life in the West became too much for her, and she lost her courage. In exchange for her fare home, I convinced her to change identities with me so I might escape a dangerous situation. I used your hospitality, knowing that I would soon be leaving, just as I must now. The only trouble is, I did not think far enough ahead to realize what that deceit would entail.

I'm sorry, Luther. You'll never know how truly sorry I am. You're too good a man to have been treated as I've treated you. You believed you loved me, but the truth is that I'm not Modesty Parkins of the sweet, gentle letters and the shy, retiring soul. I never could be she.

My only consolation is that you'll one day see that I've done you a service by removing myself from your life.

Tell Aunt Helga and Max I'm sorry. I'll miss all of you.

Please forgive me, Luther, because I know I'll never be able to truly forgive myself for what I've done to you.

Sincerely,
Lila

"What does it say?"

The harsh question raised Luther's head to the stony set of Garrett Harrison's features. His mind was frozen with disbelief. They had arrived back at the ranch house a few minutes earlier after a long day raising fences. There had been no smoke coming from the chimney upon their approach, and the silent air of abandonment about the house had caused him to kick his horse into a gallop almost the moment it came into sight. He had not realized Harrison had reacted in the same way until they had slid to a stop outside, side by side. He was still uncertain which of them had made it through the doorway first.

The house had echoed with the sound of his voice as he had called Modesty's name, but Harrison had not wasted time calling out. Harrison had come back from Modesty's room to announce that her clothes were gone just as he had started reading Modesty's letter for the first time.

"I asked you what the letter says, damn it!"

Harrison's voice reverberated on the silence as Luther snapped toward the sound. He did not respond, drawing back just in time to stop Harrison from snatching the letter from his hand.

"What do you care what the letter says?" Luther's angry shock emerged in a threatening growl. "It's addressed to me, not you!"

"Oh, is that right?" Harrison sneered, as he did so well, and Luther's hands tightened into fists. He took an aggressive step forward that was halted by Harrison's next unexpected question.

"Did she sign the letter 'Lila'? Because that's her real name . . . Lila Chesney."

Startled, Luther did not respond, and Harrison's jaw hardened. "Everything that woman ever told you was a lie! She used you just like she used me and everybody else, but that isn't important right now. Where she *went* is important. I have to know wh—"

"You have to know?" A slow rage began boiling inside Luther. "If Mod—If Lila wanted you to know, she would've left this letter for you instead of me, but she didn't!"

"You damned fool! Let me see that letter."

"No."

Harrison's eyes grew heavy with threat. "Don't force me to take it from you, Knox."

The growing heat of their exchange somehow comforting, Luther responded with equal intimidation, "You can always try . . ."

"Wait a minute, damn it!" Max limped between them. He turned to assess their warring expressions with obvious puzzlement. "Things are movin' too fast! What in hell's goin' on here? It looks to me like neither of you are sure, and both of you are ready to fight over not knowin'."

"I know, all right. Knox is the one who's in the dark."

"Yeah, you know. That's why you want to see the letter."

Harrison's jaw jerked spasmodically at Luther's sharp retort. He responded harshly. "I know Lila isn't the person you thought she was . . . that the real Modesty Parkins went back East and Lila took her place. That's what she told you in that letter, isn't it?"

The truth in those words a blow he was not expecting, Luther was momentarily speechless.

"I also know that Doc must've delivered a letter from her boyfriend yesterday and that she's on her way to meet him right now. I want to know where that is."

"How do I know anything you say is true?" Regaining his voice as anger flushed anew, Luther edged forward aggressively, "I never did trust you."

"Yeah," Harrison's sneer deepened. "You trusted Lila, and look what it got you."

"Bastard!" Hardly recognizing the sound of his own voice, Luther attempted to push Max aside. "Get out of my way, Max!"

"I ain't goin' nowhere!" Firmly retaining his stance between them, Max continued. "If you're intendin' to get to each other, you're goin' to have to run over me, and I'm tellin' you now, that ain't goin' to be too easy!"

"Get out of the way, I said!" Luther was trembling with rage.

"Wait a minute, Knox." Responding in Max's stead, Harrison directed a hard glance into Knox's eyes. "Max is right. Fightin' isn't goin' to get us anywhere." He paused, and Luther felt the scrutiny of those cold grey eyes reach down deep inside him. "If you're ready to listen, I'll explain everythin'."

Suddenly uncertain if he really wanted to know the truth . . . uncertain if he wanted to have the realization that Modesty was gone from him forever confirmed by a ruthless man who was not what he appeared to be, Luther did not respond.

The silence lengthened, and Max spoke abruptly. "If the boss don't want to know what this is all about, I sure enough do." And when Luther made no comment, "Out with it, then! What in hell's goin' on?"

The deadening ache inside Luther expanded as Harrison started to speak. It deepened into pain as Harrison's explanation washed over him, trailing on. The words continued, meaning little except that Modesty was gone, meaning little except that he would never see her again, meaning little except that Modesty had never . . . not for a moment . . . loved him.

Brilliant shafts of moonlight shone on the road ahead of Garrett, lighting his way with the brightness of day as he maintained a steady pace toward town. Bathed in the silver glow, the landscape moved in silent, shifting shadows which he unconsciously measured, then dismissed as he reviewed in his mind the hour most recently past.

Lila was gone, damn her! He knew now that Doc must have delivered a letter from her lover when he had come for Helga the previous day. Nothing else made any sense.

Restraining a sudden need to shout and rail, to curse aloud, Garrett spurred his horse to a more rapid pace. He recalled Lila's nervousness when he had appeared at the ranch before the storm broke. The letter from her lover had already been received and her plans made. She had tried desperately to make him leave, and he wondered now how much of that desperation had been a desire to escape *him.*

The damp, earthy scent of the barn returned to mind as did the echo of rain drumming on the roof, the crackle of lightning and the boom of thunder overhead, and Garrett felt a familiar emotion assault him. He had been so certain that Lila's dark eyes had met his with honesty as he had held her in his arms. He recalled the touch of her lips against his cheek and the delicate pressure of her mouth against his skin. He remembered her quiver of rapture when their naked flesh had touched for the first time and the unexpected strength of her arms clutching him close. Her lips had parted in welcome and it had been beautiful between them, a mutual, loving exchange that had been meant to be from the first moment their eyes had met. None of it had been feigned . . . not for him.

The thickness in Garrett's throat grew dangerously tight, and he breathed deeply in an attempt at control. He had read the letter Lila had left for Knox. She had begged Knox's forgiveness, but she had left him no word. He realized now that he shouldn't have expected anything else. In leaving, Lila had said it all.

But the *final* word had not yet been spoken.

Garrett took another steadying breath. Hobbs was watching Lila now, wherever she was. She wouldn't get away this time.

Garrett's expression grew grim as a fierce anger, barely contained, soared to life inside him. Lila Chesney . . . saloon woman, cheap tart, supreme actress who would do anything to protect the worthless criminal who was her lover. He despised her for her deceit, and he despised himself for believing her.

With a low rumble of disgust, Garrett swept off his hat and ran his hand through his hair in a gesture of supreme agitation. Then, replacing the hat firmly, he squared his shoulders and forced a solemn admission. He had wanted Lila yesterday with a desire that had bordered on desperation. He would've done almost anything to have her.

But that was not the worst of it.

Taunting Garrett unmercifully, stabbing him with a pitiless knife of pain as he continued steadily onward, was a truth he need make himself face before it was too late. That truth was simple. Despite all that had been done and all he would yet do, he wanted her still.

A peculiar agitation crawled up Hobbs's spine. He fidgeted in his surveillance of Lila Chesney's room and turned to look at the morning sunlight shining against the drawn blind behind him. Still seated on the same chair he had assumed the night before in order to watch Lila Chesney's closed door, he was stiff, uncomfortable, and weary to the bone. The light under her door the previous night had been extinguished after the first hour, allowing him to relax a bit with the knowledge that Lila had retired, but he had not followed suit. He had not been willing to take the chance.

Still . . .

Rubbing his hand over his unshaven face, Jake squinted at the closed door opposite him. Something wasn't right. It was already past midmorning and she hadn't yet emerged from her room. Jake's stomach sounded a loud reminder of its emptiness and his frown tightened. It didn't make sense that Lila Chesney would still be sleeping. She had been an early riser at the ranch for too long to break the habit so abruptly and too much was due to happen soon for her to remain leisurely abed. No, something wasn't right.

Slowly standing, Jake kicked back his chair and surveyed the hallway carefully. Finding it empty, he walked the few steps across the hallway. His ear to the door, he listened intently . . . and heard nothing. Deciding to take a chance, he knocked on the door.

Behind his own door in a flash, he waited for a response. There was none.

A new anxiety rising, Jake scanned the hallway once more and stepping out quickly, knocked again. Back in his room, he waited in vain for a response. Cursing under his breath as realization began taking hold, he strode boldly into the hallway and rattled Lila's doorknob. There was no sound of movement behind the closed door and Jake briefly closed his eyes.

Not again. . . !

An uncharacteristic anger flaring, Jake applied the weight of his shoulder against the door once, twice . . . On the third attempt the door sprang open and Jake stepped inside a small room that was a duplicate of his own across the hall. A bed, dresser, a washstand, a night table with a lamp . . .

. . . and a roughly cut silhouette dancing from a cord in front of the window . . .

Two steps to the lamp revealed that most of the oil had been dumped into the washbowl and he groaned inwardly. The explanation was infuriatingly simple. The paper silhouette, moving in the subtle breeze in front of the lamp, had provided the shadows of movement he had seen under the doorway the previous evening. With most of the fuel removed, the lamp had burned out after an hour or so, creating the illusion that Lila had retired for the night.

Damn it all, she had done it again!

Turning back to the bed, Jake looked at the familiar brown traveling dress and bonnet carefully spread out on the bed, adding insult to injury. The message was clear and humiliating.

Snapping into movement, Jake left the room and started down the staircase toward the first floor. Out on the street in a minute, he raced toward the train station.

Incredulous, Garrett stared at Hobb's flushed face. "What do you mean, you lost her?"

"I mean just what I said, damn it! She slipped away from me just like she did the first time. I'm ashamed to say, I underestimated her. That Lila Chesney's the craftiest woman I've ever encountered."

Barely in control of his emotions, Garrett stared down at the smaller man. Hot, angry words rose to his lips, only to slip away at the man's obvious discomfiture. Suddenly realizing he was trembling, Garrett stepped back in an attempt to assess the situation more rationally.

It had been a hard ride from the Bar WK during the night, but he had made it to Deer Trail with plenty of time to spare for the morning train. The train had delivered him to Magnolia, the destination of Modesty Parkins, as the entire populace of Deer Trail seemed aware. He had stepped down on the platform in time to see Hobbs inside the station house, frantically quizzing the stationmaster, but the quizzing had been to no avail. The stationmaster had not seen Modesty Parkins, or anyone who looked like her, get on the train.

Back outside on the platform as the morning sun rose in the sky, Garrett felt frustration soar.

"She had to go somewhere! We can check the livery stable later, but I think it's safe to say Lila is smart enough not to have taken off across open country alone. The fastest and safest means of transportation is the train."

A sudden thought striking him, Garrett inquired abruptly, "Let's go over this whole thing again from the minute Lila arrived in Magnolia. What did she do, step by step?"

Hobbs frowned. "She was a tricky little piece, all right. She probably had me spotted from the beginning. When I think how she waited until the last minute to get off the train . . . I damn near broke my neck jumping off after her!"

Garrett was not amused. "Where did she go from the station?"

"She went to the restaurant to eat. From there she went to the hotel to get a room. A few minutes later she came out and went to the general store to do some shopping."

"Shoppin'? That didn't strike you as strange?"

"Not a bit. You should've seen her, trying those dresses against her. She was looking to get rid of that godawful brown dress. She did, too." Hobbs's lips twitched. "She left it behind on the bed at the hotel."

"What did she buy?"

"How the hell do I know?"

"I thought you said you were watchin'?"

"Not close enough to see what she bought. But she came out with a load of packages and she—" Hobbs's small eyes suddenly popped wide. "You don't suppose she—?"

Not bothering to respond, Garrett turned back toward the stationhouse at a run.

The outline of the mountains stood clear and majestic against the blue sky of Denver as Lila looked out the window of her room at the Falmouth Hotel. The night she had spent there had been filled with the sounds of civilization for which she had once longed. The rattle of wagons had continued under her window long into the night, along with the hoorahs of cowboys riding into town, sounds of raucous music floating on the night breeze, and the drone of conversation sprinkled with bursts of laughter that seemed to come from every quarter. She had even convinced herself that she could hear the clicking of the roulette wheel and the clatter of chips, but she knew that to be impossible.

But somehow, through it all, she had experienced none of the expected sensation of coming home.

Drawing her head abruptly back inside, Lila turned to look into the washstand mirror beside her. The bright-blue cotton dress she wore was a perfect match with the color of the sky outside her window. It added a sparkle to her face and a lift to her unsmiling eyes. The white lace of the bodice lay appealingly against the rise of her breasts and the matching sash around her waist accented its narrowness in a way that turned heads at every quarter.

Raising a hand to her upswept hair, Lila tucked in an errant curl. She surveyed the soft waves piled atop her head critically, noting that the glimmer of the shiny strands, freed from the severe coiffure she had been forced to maintain for so long, accented the patrician curve of her brows and the incredible length of sable lashes that surrounded her dark eyes. Atop the silky mass, the small straw hat adorned with lace butterflies was perched cockily.

Lila surveyed her sober reflection.

Lila Chesney had truly returned.

Still staring at her reflection, Lila heard a voice in the back of her mind sound a soft contradiction and her eyes fluttered briefly closed.

The voice was right. The old Lila Chesney had not returned because she no longer existed. Something had changed her.

A familiar sadness sprang to life inside Lila. She knew what that something was. She had seen love in Garrett Harrison's gaze . . . she knew she had . . . however briefly. She had returned that love . . . however briefly. She had felt the icy facade around Garrett's heart melt while she had lain in his arms and she had seen the bitterness leave his eyes. The true Garrett, the innermost Garrett, carefully concealed, had been exposed to her then, and the tenderness had flowed freely. His gentle passion haunted her, as did the rasp of hunger in his voice when he had said her name, and memory of the need . . . the mutual, soul-shaking need they had met and consummated in the most beautiful of ways.

The revelation of the other side of Garrett, the vulnerable, loving side, had been fleeting. Causing her endless pain was the realization that in leaving him, she would never see that side of him again.

A knot of pain deeper than any she had ever experienced squeezed tight inside Lila. Elizabeth had known that side of Garrett. It had not been necessary for Garrett to say the words for Lila to know that Elizabeth would enjoy that side of him forever. She had read it in his eyes.

Turning, Lila looked at the carpetbag lying on the bed beside her. The first smile of the day tugged at her lips as she leaned down and opened it to look at the boy's trousers and shirt lying on top.

So, the Pinkertons weren't as smart as they were rumored to be!

Lila removed the pants and shirt and placed them on the bed. The red suspenders followed, along with the boots and bandanna. Her sad smile broadened at the sight of the broad-brimmed hat crushed on the bottom. The Pinkerton had not a chance in the world of finding her now.

Lila's smile faded as she conceded that luck had been with her every step of the way from the moment she had arrived in Magnolia. The waitress in the restaurant, appearing starved for conversation, had talked nonstop for the duration of her meal. She had rattled off a detailed history of the town and its inhabitants, without blinking an eye at more intimate affairs, and with a nudge of encouragement, had related their connection to the arrival of the railroad. Included in her monologue had been the scheduled departure times of the Denver train, which Lila had smilingly tucked away for future use.

After dropping off her bag at the hotel, she had gone to the general store where she had observed herself being observed through the store window. A careful word to the proprietor had sent a fellow outside to move her shadow farther down the street, enabling her to make her purchases without being seen.

Back at the hotel, she had watched herself being watched from the street. Making sure to make enough passes by the window to assure the Pinkerton of her room, she had drawn the blind closed, had prepared a rough silhouette from the cardboard dress box, and had changed into the boy's clothing she had bought. She had then watched from behind the drawn blind, waiting for the Pinkerton to abandon the street.

The moment she had awaited had not been long in coming. Springing into action the moment the Pinkerton started walking toward the hotel lobby, Lila had then affixed the silhouette where it might move on the gentle breeze to create flickering shadows underneath the doorway, snatched up her carpetbag, jammed the oversize hat onto her head to cover her upswept hair, and had waited, hidden near the rear staircase at the end of the hall, for the Pinkerton to show his face.

The plan had worked like clockwork. The Pinkerton had arrived in the hallway a few minutes later and had slipped into the room across the hall from hers. Her heart pounding with the realization that she was about to escape him, Lila had slipped down the rear staircase and out into the darkened street. A half hour later, her disguise unchallenged, she had boarded the train for Denver.

But her precautions had not ended there.

Slipping into the crowd after arriving in Denver, Lila had then gone directly to a small hotel nearby and checked in. Her heart still pounding, she had changed into the clothes she now wore, had left the hotel by the back entrance, and had never looked back.

Certain she had taken enough precautions to elude the most determined of pursuers, Lila had then gone directly to the Falmouth Hotel and registered. Comfortably ensconced in a room that afforded her a clear view of the street, she now waited for Billy to arrive.

But waiting was more difficult than she had imagined.

Billy's image popped before Lila's mind, and Lila shook her head, taking silent exception to its constant smile. She had once believed her smile to be constant, too. She had carefully cultivated that constant smile, but the short weeks she had spent at a ranch in the middle of nowhere had revealed the lie that had lain behind it.

The truth was simple. The life she had formerly made for herself had merely filled empty time. She knew now that fulfillment did not lie in bright lights, pretty clothes, and laughter that lasted long into the night. Neither did it lie in a quiet ranch in the middle of nowhere where neither sun nor patience faltered. It lay in the arms of the man whose love lit a flame inside her that would not die.

Lila's throat choked tightly as she struggled against tears. She was suddenly furiously angry with Billy for having brought her to this sad realization when she had previously believed herself content. She yearned to shout at him, to curse and howl her anger. She longed to attack that smile and strike it from his face.

No . . . Lila shook her head, regretting her momentary anger. She didn't want that, for somehow she knew that without that smile, Billy would be as bereft as she.

Removing her hat, Lila placed it on the bed and sat wearily. Yes, waiting was the hardest part . . . as was remembering . . .

Fifteen

He was desperate to find her.

Holding his horse to a careful pace, Billy rode down Auraria's main street. The sun was setting, tinting the blue-gray of the sky with gracefully swirled streaks of pink and gold, but he was oblivious of the brilliant celestial display as he assessed the pedestrians crowding the narrow boardwalks on either side of him. Another mining town filled with strangers . . . another muddy street . . . more bearded faces and inquisitive gazes that would change from surprise to wariness when he inquired about the whereabouts of a slender, half-breed woman with a golden-haired child.

Eva's sober face returned before his eyes. The picture of the child he had begun to think of as his own accompanied it, and Billy's anxiety soared. It was almost more than he could bear. He had been searching for them for two weeks without finding a trace. It was almost as if Eva and her baby had disappeared from the face of the earth.

That thought haunted him.

Rubbing a weary hand across his eyes, Billy was suddenly conscious of the fact that he had not shaved recently. Neither had he bathed or slept, or even taken the time to eat as panic had begun making deep inroads into his mind.

Where could Eva and Christina be? Central City, Black Hawk, Russell Gulch, Golden, and now Auraria . . . He had followed Clear Creek, stopping at every town and mining camp along the way, but he had found no sign of them. He had searched his mind, trying to remember everything Eva had ever told him about her past, but there had been no clue there. Even if there were, he could not make himself believe that she would return to an area where she was well known when she believed herself pursued for killing a man.

Billy's thoughts returned again to Pete Waller as they had so many times in the past two weeks, and a murderous rage possessed him. If the man had lied . . . if Waller's band of drunken vigilantes had done anything to Eva . . .

Billy reined his mount to a slower pace as he approached the saloon at the end of the street. He was exhausted and hungry. It was time to stop and clear his mind of the agony of his thoughts so he might be able to think more lucidly.

His horse tied up in front, Billy walked through the doorway of the Silver Nugget Saloon and strode directly to the bar. He did not notice the assessing gaze of the brunette near the doorway as the bartender slid a drink in front of him. Nor did he hear her coming up behind him as he emptied his glass in a gulp.

"Hello, partner." The sultry brunette slid her hand onto his shoulder and smiled up at him sympathetically. "It looks like you really needed that drink."

Billy did not attempt a smile.

The brunette moved closer. She stroked his bristled cheek with her fingertips as she lowered her dark-eyed gaze to his lips. "Is there anythin' else you might be needin'? You look to be real cute under them scratchy whiskers. A little trail dirt don't put me off none, you know."

Billy paused with his refilled glass midway to his lips. The first drink had burned his throat all the way down and the stirring warmth had already begun heating his insides. He remained silent as the saloon girl assessed him boldly, as her gaze moved over his face, the stretch of his shoulders and chest, then traveled to his narrow waist and hips to touch a more intimate portion of his anatomy.

"You look to be a real man, honey. You seem kind of edgy, but I can take the edge off if you'll let me."

Billy's superior height gave him a bird's-eye view of the white flesh that swelled above the bodice of the woman's bright-green dress, but he gave it only a passing glance. Instead, he concentrated on the face beneath the paint of her profession. It was a young face. For all the harshness of her voice and the experience easily read in her eyes, she didn't look to be more than eighteen or nineteen years old. He shook his head.

The young woman's lips abruptly flattened into a straight line. "See somethin' you don't like?"

Taking a moment to toss down his second drink, Billy tapped the bar for another, then motioned the barkeep to pour one for the saloon girl as well. The courtesy pleased her, restoring her smile as he asked, "What's your name?"

"Dolores. What's yours?"

"How old are you, Dolores?"

Dolores took a short, backward step. "Oh, hell, don't tell me that beneath all them good looks, you're one of them do-gooders wantin' to reform me!"

Billy shook his head. "No chance there. I can't even reform myself."

Dolores's smile returned. "That's a relief."

"You were saying something about wanting to do something for me . . ." Billy paused as the warm body scent of the young woman reached his nostrils. It was lush and invitingly familiar. He emptied his glass again, continuing slowly. "If you're looking to please, I've got something you could do. I'm looking for somebody . . ."

"You're lookin' for somebody. I should've knowed." Dolores tossed down her drink with revealing expertise. "It's a woman, ain't it?"

"That's right."

Dolores gave a short laugh.

"A woman with a baby . . ."

Dolores's laughter faded. "What do you want with a woman and a kid?"

"I need to find them." Surprising himself, Billy was momentarily unable to continue. Regaining control a moment later, he spoke hoarsely. "She's a half-breed, about your age, with a scar on her cheek."

"A scar . . ." Dolores's young face hardened. "Did *you* mark her?"

"No. I'd never hurt her. I just need to find her."

"The baby . . . is it yours?"

Billy hesitated, realizing for the first time he wished it otherwise as he replied, "No, it isn't."

"The woman's yours, though."

"Yeah."

"How come she left you?"

"She didn't. She got scared because something happened, and she took off before I came back. I've been trying to find her ever since."

"Yeah?" The young woman hesitated. "So why're you tellin' me all this?"

"I need some help, and I figure you'd be a good person to give it to me."

"Yeah? Maybe so, but I ain't seen no woman with a baby comin' into town alone . . . especially a half-breed."

"Look . . ." Billy straightened up, pausing as his head reeled. He cursed, realizing he should've known better than to drink when he hadn't eaten for so long. He made a sudden decision. "You got a room upstairs?"

Dolores's eyes brightened with renewed interest. "I sure do."

"I want it for the night."

Dolores beamed. "That'll be my pleasure, handsome."

"I'll double whatever you get for the night, and then some if you'll take a little time off to do me a favor."

Dolores appeared confused. "What are you talkin' about?"

"Look . . ." His earnest expression filled with anxiety, Billy continued. "I came in here tired and hungry, and now I'm a little drunk. I need to sleep, but I'm running out of time. I need somebody to ask around for me . . . to get the answers to some questions . . . somebody who won't have any trouble getting the kind of information I need . . . somebody I think I can trust to make a real effort."

The young saloon girl was momentarily silent. "What makes you think you can trust me?"

Swaying, Billy considered the question. "That's a good question. My only answer is that everybody probably knows you around here and won't have any problem talking to you. I figure you're about the same age as Eva, and it looks like you didn't have any easier life than she did. So I figure you can understand what I mean when I say my woman needs me right now." Billy paused, then gave a short laugh. "Almost as much as I need her."

Dolores's painted face sobered. "You're tellin' me you want my room for yourself . . . alone . . . is that it?"

"You got it right."

"That all you want?"

"Yeah."

Dolores's brow drew into a thoughtful frown for a few moments before she responded abruptly, "All right. It's a deal."

Billy paused, not a trace of a smile left in him as he fought to keep himself upright. "Where's your room?"

"Where's the money?"

"First things first . . ."

Dolores turned toward the staircase at the rear of the crowded saloon and Billy followed close behind.

Seated on the side of Dolores's bed as she stood over him, her womanly lushness pressed closer than necessary, Billy counted out several bills. He looked up and pressed them into Dolores's hand. He grasped her hand as she attempted to withdraw it.

"Don't wake me up unless you find out something." He paused and continued a trace more softly, "I'm trusting you, Dolores. If I find out you took my money and didn't do what you promised . . ."

Snatching back her hand, Dolores counted the bills. She flashed a smile. "Don't go botherin' your head about that. This is more than I make in a week and I ain't about to risk your wantin' it back. I'll just tell Buck at the bar that I'm takin' the night off, then I'll ask up and down the street about your woman. If anybody knows anythin' about her, I'll find out."

Warning heavy in his increasingly slurred voice, Billy pressed once more. "I'm tired and I'm a little bit drunk, but I'm still the fastest hand with a gun you'll ever see, so if you got any ideas . . ."

"You just lay back and close your eyes, honey." Dolores patted his hand. "I'll take it from here. A half-breed with a kid, huh?"

"A blond baby . . ."

Dolores's mouth dropped with surprise. "Hell! Anythin' else you forgot to tell me?"

"Her name's Eva Nielsen and she's probably traveling with a small pack animal and trying to avoid being seen."

"Well, if she's in town, I'll find her."

"I'm counting on you."

The door clicked closed behind Dolores. The sound echoed in the room as Billy laid back against the bed and closed his eyes. He was drifting off to sleep when he realized that desperation made strange bedfellows . . . that a woman he would have had no thought for except to bed a few months previous, now held no appeal except for what she could find out for him about the woman he loved . . .

Yes, the woman he loved . . . Eva.

It was true. He loved her.

Awakening with a start as the bed creaked noisily, Billy snapped to a seated position just as Dolores lay down beside him. He glanced toward the window to see the first light of dawn edging through the drawn blind. He turned back as she spoke.

"Relax. I'm tired and I ain't got no place else to sleep."

Billy fought to clear his mind. "What did you find out?"

"Nothin' . . . nothin' much, that is."

Anticipation prickled along Billy's spine. "I asked you what you found out."

Dolores heaved a tired sigh. "That woman wasn't never in this town, at least as far as I could find out. Nobody I talked to saw her, either. I spent most of the night goin' up and down the street, visitin' every saloon along the way. My feet are killin' me. I ain't used to spendin' so much time standin' up."

Dolores's small smile flashed. It faded quickly when she saw Billy was not amused. "Then I decided to talk to everybody in the Iron Kettle. It's the most popular eatin' place around. Charlie the cook . . . he didn't never see her, but he said he remembered hearin' somethin' about a half-breed woman and a blond baby."

Dolores paused. "The baby was a girl, right . . . with big blue eyes? Charlie said the fella he talked to said he heard somebody talkin' about her, sayin' he never seen nothin' like them big blue eyes on that baby girl, especially with her mama bein' a squaw . . ."

Billy stiffened and Dolores frowned. "Don't go gettin' upset. I'm just tellin' you what Charlie said. He said he heard that squaw killed a fella somewhere along Clear Creek, and that a bunch of fellas went out after her. He said he didn't know what happened to her, but he wasn't takin' any bets that anybody'd ever see her again."

Billy's heart started a heavy pounding. "Who told Charlie all this?"

"I don't know. I don't know that Charlie remembers who, either."

"What else did he say?"

"He didn't say nothin' else." Dolores hesitated and

looked up at him with a measuring stare. Billy felt the growing heat of that stare as she whispered, "Your woman's gone, and it don't look like you're goin' to find her." She continued more softly. "I'm sorry, I truly am, but people die every day out here, young and old, and others disappear without a trace. It . . . it ain't as if it's the end of the world unless you make it be that way. I learned that the hard way, and I learned there's a little comfortin' that goes a long way when somebody's feelin' low."

Her small, dark eyes growing moist, Dolores raised her hand to slip the strap of her dress off her shoulder. A rounded white breast exposed, she smiled tentatively. "I'm tired, but I ain't that tired that I'm not willin' to give you the comfort you're needin'. You're a nice fella, and you're hurtin'. I know what it's like to hurt like you're hurtin' now. Come on, let me do somethin' for you."

Unable to draw his gaze from Dolores's face, Billy felt a hot flush transfuse him. His world had just crashed around him, and this young whore hoped to fix it all with the warmth of her body. With her hard facade stripped away, however, Dolores's youth came shining through . . . as did the sincerity of her gesture.

Not conscious of his intent, Billy lowered his head to brush Dolores's lips with his. Her arms closed around his neck, but he unwound them with gentle determination.

"No. Thanks, Dolores."

Slipping his legs over the bed, Billy slipped into his boots, then stood up to look down at Dolores's open invitation once more. He had no difficulty refusing it.

Billy reached into his pocket and withdrew a few more bills. He lay them on the night table in silent gratitude.

"What did you say that cook's name was?"

Dolores drew up the bodice of her dress. "Charlie, at the Iron Kettle, down the end of the street."

The door clicked closed behind him, and Billy paused in the hallway with a darkening thought. He ran his hand through his tightly curled hair, then slipped his hat down squarely onto his brow and walked toward the staircase.

Time was running short, but he would find Eva. He loved her. He only hoped he hadn't realized too late how deeply he loved her.

"Is true? I did not believe . . ."

Her small eyes wide, Helga stood stock-still, staring at Max's sad face. A small whimper from the babe in her arms turned to a low wail, prompting her to resume the steady rocking she had only recently abandoned. Glancing down at the cradle opposite her, she saw little Marianne Barnes busily sucking her thumb and she released a relieved sigh. Little Bennett had not yet found that thumb and his misery was growing. Another look at Max where he stood uneasily near the doorway of the small, tidy Barnes cabin, and Helga made a snap decision.

Taking baby Bennett's small hand in hers, she rubbed his thumb against his lips. He immediately seized hold and began sucking contentedly. Helga's smile was brief.

"Dis is goot."

The small male child was in his cradle, his mother asleep in the next room, and his older brother busy outside when Helga turned back to Max. In truth, her heart was aching. Everyone in town knew that Modesty had left the Bar WK and had not returned, but few knew the reason for her leaving. She had suffered in ignorance of all that had happened at the ranch, hearing only rumors. It was time to find out the truth.

Helga took a short step toward Max, loathing to ask the question for fear of the response she might receive. Encouraged, Max took a step forward as well, and Helga felt the ache inside her deepen. He was the same old Max. His cheeks were not clean-shaven, his clothes were not fresh, and his boots were not clean . . . but his face was honest and his eyes were warm when he looked at her.

Ja, she had missed him . . .

Tears filled Helga's eyes. Even the happiness that the two new babies had brought to the Barnes household had not raised her spirits from the deadening shock of Modesty's abrupt departure from town and the realization of all her dear Luther must be suffering.

Helga took a deep breath. "Is true? Modesty was not der real Modesty?"

"It's true, all right."

A single tear fell onto Helga's lined cheek.

"Now don't you go gettin' yourself all upset, Helga." His former hesitation forgotten in the face of her tears, Max came to stand at her side. He slid an awkward arm around her plump, rounded shoulders. "I admit to feelin' bad, too. I really liked Miss Modesty. She kind of touched my heart, and I was lookin' forward to the day when she and the boss would make it permanent between them, but . . . but . . ." He shook his head, and Helga felt his arm tighten. "Some things just ain't what they seem, I guess. The boss didn't tell me the whole story and I didn't ask, 'cause it ain't none of my business." He paused. "It don't look like the boss can make himself talk about it, anyways. Maybe you was right about her from the first."

"Nein." Helga shook her head vigorously. "Was not

right. Modesty . . ." She halted. "What is der real name?"

"The boss said her real name is Lila."

"Lila was goot person. I see something wrong when she come . . . *ja* . . . but I see later in der eyes dat she was goot person." Helga shook her head, unconscious of the new tear that fell. "What did Luther say?"

"He ain't said much of nothin' since Miss Mod—I mean Miss *Lila* left."

Helga's eyes again filled to brimming. "Ach, so much sadness . . ."

"Aw, Helga . . ." Drawing her closer, Max patted Helga's shoulder comfortingly. "Don't cry. The boss sent me into town to get some things. He said to make sure you was all right, and to tell you not to worry about the gossip . . ."

"Is gossip? People talk?" Helga's spine went ramrod stiff. "No one gossip to me!"

Max smiled. His gold tooth glinted familiarly. "Nobody would dare, and I'm right proud to be able to say that." Appearing suddenly conscious of their intimate posture, Max took a wary step back. "Anyways, I have to be goin'. The boss is workin' alone out there, you know, with Garrett and Miss Mod—I mean Miss *Lila* gone."

Helga felt a familiar animosity rise. "Dat big fella. He was bad one . . ."

A sudden wariness sprang into Max's eyes as he responded cautiously, "He was a hard man, but he wasn't such a bad fella, even if the boss and him didn't part friends, exactly. I expect the boss'll tell you more when you see him."

"Is goot he is gone."

Max shrugged. "We sure could've used his help for a little while longer." He looked up from under his shaggy brows to add hesitantly, "The Bar WK has gotten to be a real lonesome place."

Helga's eyes misted once more. She looked at the nearby cradle and shook her head. "Am needed here, yet. Cannot come back to cook."

"Oh, it ain't the cookin' I mis—I mean *the boss* misses. I'm thinkin' he misses you."

A slow warmth started inside Helga, dulling the ache. "*Ja,* I miss, too."

Turning toward the table behind her without speaking, Helga withdrew a piece of brown paper from a drawer and wrapped the remaining portion of a cake she had baked the previous night in it. Retrieving a basket from the wall, she placed the package inside and held it out to Max with a smile.

"Here. For you and Luther. Something sweet to make Luther smile."

Accepting the basket, Max held it carefully. "I thank you kindly, Helga. We'll sure appreciate it, but if you're hopin' to make the boss smile, I'm thinkin' you're goin' to have to wrap Miss Modesty in a package, and send her back to the ranch, too."

Leaving with a tip of his hat and a lingering glance, Max pulled the door closed behind him. Still staring at the closed door for long moments afterward as a myriad of feelings assaulted her, Helga heard Max's final comment echo in her mind.

If you're hopin' to make the boss smile, I'm thinkin' you're goin to have to wrap Miss Modesty in a package, and send her back to the ranch, too.

Ja, he was right. Only Modesty could make Luther smile now.

Helga nodded sadly . . . then froze.

Ja, only Modesty . . .

* * *

The sounds of Denver's noontime traffic grew louder as Billy, with growing impatience, guided his mount along the congested street. Delivery wagons, passenger vehicles, individual horsemen, and pedestrians darting in and out between, along with casual shoppers seeming more intent upon enjoying the warm sunshine than in following a prescribed path, were part and parcel of the bustling scene for which he had little patience.

His agitation mounting, Billy fastened his gaze on the familiar brick-front building at the end of the street. Familiar also was the thickness that sprang into his throat and his sense of panic at the realization that this was his last hope. If there was no word from Eva at his post office box . . .

Unable to face that last thought, Billy halted it abruptly. His weeks of searching had come to a dead end with his conversation with the cook in Auraria. Everything the thin, seedy-looking fellow had known had been based on idle talk overheard in the restaurant. He had told himself there was no need to accept Charlie's pessimistic outlook. He would not allow himself to believe anything else but that Eva and her child were safe somewhere, waiting for him to find them.

Through it all, however, memory of Pete Waller's fear haunted him. He did not want to believe Waller's fear had been born of guilt . . .

His patience exhausted, Billy nudged his horse to a faster pace, ignoring the angry remarks of pedestrians forced to scramble out of his way. He dismounted outside the post office, suddenly realizing he was shaking. Taking a moment to compose himself, he started toward the entrance as his mind jeered at his foolishness in telling Eva about his post office box . . . when he wasn't even certain she could write.

Inside, Billy approached the counter. His step slowed as his gaze focused on his post office box, situated directly behind the elderly clerk. It was empty.

The clerk turned toward him. Billy could not make himself move as the fellow squinted at him curiously.

"Can I help you, young fella?"

"Box number 23 . . . there's nothing in it. Has all the mail been sorted for the day?"

The old fellow smiled suddenly, exposing his gap-toothed smile. "Well, now, it's B. Chesney, ain't it? I hardly recognized you. You look like you've been travelin' for a while."

Billy nodded. "Yeah, I've been traveling. What about the mail?"

"Everythin's in them boxes. There won't be no more mail until later this afternoon." The old fellow studied his face, then added with unexpected sympathy, "You're lookin' for a letter from your lady, I suppose. I remember her handwritin'. It was real nice. I can always tell by the handwritin' what kind of person writ a letter. She'll be writin' to you soon, all right. Come back later."

Turning without reply, Billy was back at his horse's side in a few fast steps. His hand on the saddle horn, he paused before mounting. Sick with disappointment, with worry, and with the growing fear that he would never see Eva again, he raised himself slowly into the saddle. Seated, he turned back in the direction from which he had come. He had three appointments to keep. The first was at the Falmouth Hotel . . . the second with Forbes and the boys . . . and the third—

An icy calm touching his mind, Billy wondered if Waller was already counting his limited tomorrows.

* * *

Lila walked quickly along the crowded Denver street. The buzz of the busy thoroughfares had become exceedingly familiar during the week she had spent at the Falmouth Hotel, but the pulsing heartbeat of the growing frontier city left her strangely cold. Glancing inside as she passed one of the many saloons on the street, Lila listened to the clatter of the roulette wheel and the jingling of chips. She glanced at the brightly-clad women briskly employed in various jobs there and attempted to imagine herself working among them again. The thought held little appeal.

Telling herself that her old enthusiasm would return once she could allow herself to return to the Lila Chesney of old, to the woman whose painted smile never faltered and whose eye-catching gowns caused many a male heart to skip a beat, Lila continued down the street. Her gaze was less casual than it appeared as she scanned her immediate vicinity. Caution was automatic, but Lila knew it was needless. She would not see the lined face of the drummer in the crowd. Nor would she see Garrett's tall, broad frame outlined against the sun. She had shaken the former from her trail with surprising ease, and the latter . . . Lila raised her chin in a valiant gesture that belied her inner despair. The latter had other trails to follow that were closer to his heart.

A glance at her reflection in the store window stimulated a frown as Lila clutched her purse more tightly. It was lighter than it had been a week ago. Part of the reason for its light weight was the new afternoon gown she now wore, a necessary purchase due to her unexpectedly prolonged stay. The garment was more conservative than she would normally have worn, despite the appealing rose color that lent a blush to her cheeks and emphasized the naturally dark lashes that lined her sober eyes. The need to distance herself from her true identity had forced a compromise in her attire of which she did not totally approve. She did approve of her hat, however, with the saucy tilt to its straw brim and the delicate artificial roses clustered along the crown. She had needed that hat to bolster a morale that had begun declining more with each passing day.

Oh, Billy, Billy . . .

Lila was close to despair. Billy was days late in meeting her. Her brother's hostile attitude toward commitment in any form had fostered a tardiness that had often raised her ire, but she worried nonetheless.

Lila's lips tightened angrily. Well, Billy wasn't going to get away with it this time. Damn him, he had uprooted her! He had forced her into a situation that had changed her life forever while he went merrily along his way.

Did he care? No!

Lila's fists tightened as she stepped into the lobby of the Falmouth Hotel and turned toward the staircase. She would let Billy know in no uncertain terms that she was angry when he finally arrived. She would tell him that he had gone too far this time and that he—

"Lila . . . ?"

Her heart jumping at the sound of the familiar voice behind her, Lila turned abruptly. Familiar green eyes met hers and at the flash of Billy's broad smile, Lila dashed across the lobby into her brother's arms. Laughing, crying, Lila hugged Billy with all her might. Spontaneous words of welcome tumbled from her lips, returned by him in kind as her anxious arms refused to relinquish him.

Finally drawing back, Lila felt a momentary tug of concern at the flash of sadness in Billy's eyes as he brushed joyful tears from her cheeks. His smile faltered as he whispered, "I'm sorry, Lila. I—"

"No, not here. Let's go upstairs." Slipping her arm around Billy's waist, the comforting feel of him briefly dimming the persistent ache that bore the name of another light-eyed man, Lila looked up at her brother with a tremulous smile. Billy slid his arm around her in return as they turned toward the staircase.

Blood ties were never stronger. Familial love was never deeper.

All anger was forgotten.

No, damn it, no!

Restraining a sudden lurch forward, Garrett watched through the lobby window of the Falmouth Hotel as Lila and the tall stranger walked up the staircase, arms wrapped lovingly around each other. The sounds of the street behind him had faded from his ears as he had witnessed their joyous reunion. He had ached at the strength of Lila's embrace as she had run into her lover's arms, at the sight of her tear-streaked, jubilant face raised over the fellow's broad shoulder. Her beautiful face had been filled with love . . .

Straining for control, Garrett did not feel Hobbs's elbow poke into his side, or Hobbs's low, victorious chuckle.

A furious jealousy consumed him.

A long, frantic search had finally yielded Lila's location a few days earlier, but he had soon discovered that the easy part was over. Watching Lila from a distance, remembering their last day together as she waited for another man had been almost more than he had been able to bear. Always beautiful, Lila had grown even more beautiful in his eyes as he had maintained an enforced distance from her. Always desirable, she had become more desirable still as she had shed the last remaining shreds of a personality that was not hers. He had found it increasingly difficult to make himself remember that Lila did not belong to him . . . that except for the few moments when they had lain in each others' arms, she had *never* belonged to him.

His gaze riveted to the backs of Lila and her lover as they neared the top of the staircase, Garrett recalled the time *his* arms had held her close . . . when the rain drumming on the roof and the sounds of the storm crashing and booming around them had orchestrated the wonder of Lila's sweet flesh flush against his, the warmth of her breath fanning his lips, the scent of her rain-soaked hair filling his nostrils, the taste of her mouth, sweeter than any taste he had ever known, and the warmth of her body enclosing him, holding him captive inside her, making them one.

With growing anguish, Garrett realized that he had withdrawn physically from Lila that day, but in his heart they were still joined. He had forced himself to walk away from her when Luther had appeared unexpectedly in the doorway of the house, to make his gaze turn cold even while his emotions had still burned hotly inside him. It had not occurred to him in his wildest imaginings after he had made his emotionless exit from the house that Lila would exit his life just as emotionlessly the next morning, leaving only emptiness behind her.

He had hated Lila when he had discovered she was gone.

But the hatred had been a lie.

It had not been until the moment a few minutes ago when another man had stepped out of the shadows to claim her that he had realized how great a lie it had been.

He wanted Lila more than he had ever wanted another woman.

He *needed* her more than he had ever needed another woman.

He would not . . . he could not . . . let her go.

Garrett's thoughts flickered unexpectedly. The shadows of jealous rage shifted in his mind. A vow signed in blood regained clarity. The echo of that vow, engraved into his soul by years of commitment, sounded clearly once more. It held him immobile as the scent of charred wood and burning flesh, the helpless screams that had reverberated in his dreams, returned with jarring impact.

The past confronted the present . . .

Lila and her lover reached the top of the stairs.

No! Lila belonged to him! She could not have loved him as she had loved him, she could not have welcomed him inside her, she could not have responded as fully and as passionately to him if she had loved another man!

Lila and her lover disappeared abruptly from view and Garrett's blood rage returned. It exploded in a burst of fury. His restraint snapped.

Hobbs grasped Garrett's arm, halting his sudden lunge forward.

"Where do you think you're going!"

"Let go!"

"I asked you where you're going!"

Garrett was momentarily beyond response as Hobbs studied his partner's flushed face. The monotony of the surveillance they had maintained since they had found

Lila Chesney at the Falmouth Hotel several days ago had given Hobbs the opportunity to observe Harrison more closely. A deep concern had formed in Hobbs's mind during that time . . . a concern that was now abruptly confirmed.

Harrison had slipped over the edge.

His light eyes cold with menace, Harrison repeated, "Let go of my arm . . ."

"What's wrong with you, Harrison?"

"That's none of your business."

"That's where you're wrong!"

Pulling Garrett into the alleyway beside the hotel with surprising strength, Hobbs stared up at his partner assessingly. The set of Garrett's jaw rang a warning bell in Hobbs's mind as Garrett grated, "If we lose Lila Chesney again because of you . . ."

"You're not fooling me, Harrison!" Hobbs's gaze met Garrett's in direct challenge. "Those two aren't going anywhere, and you know it. You saw the way they greeted each other. They're going to be locked up behind closed doors for a while, enjoyin' every minute of it, and if I don't miss my guess they're—"

"Shut up!"

"What?"

"I said, shut up!"

Hobbs staggered backward from Garrett's unexpected thrust, regaining his balance as Garrett stepped back out onto the walk. Starting after him on a run, Hobbs emerged onto the street in time to see his partner enter the Falmouth lobby. He caught Garrett by the arm at the top of the staircase, only to be taken aback as Garrett turned toward him with a vicious, warning snarl.

"I'll tell you one more time . . ."

The situation was suddenly clear. Hobbs was incredulous. "You're personally involved with the Chesney woman, aren't you? I didn't want to believe it! Hell, I didn't think you could be that much of a fool!"

Garrett's gaze moved to Lila Chesney's door and Hobbs felt a rush of panic. "You can't go in there, Harrison! You'll ruin months of work. We'll never get another chance to get Forbes. We . . ."

Perspiration rose on Hobbs's brow as his voice trailed away. Harrison wasn't listening. Months of investigation, Harrison's and his reputation, his own personal guarantee to McParland hung in the balance. He had to do something!

"Harrison!"

Hobbs's prolonged hiss echoed in the hallway as Garrett jerked free of his grip. Frozen with disbelief, Hobbs watched as his partner strode up to Lila Chesney's door. He held his breath as Garrett paused for a fraction of a moment before ramming the door open with a mighty thrust of his shoulder . . .

Lila jumped to her feet as the door of the room burst open to reveal Garrett's threatening stance. An astonished gasp escaped her lips at the same moment that she noted the subtle movement of Billy's hand toward his gun.

"Billy . . . No!"

Jumping between the two men, Lila regained her voice as the door slammed shut behind Garrett. The aura of heavy, pulsating danger radiating from Garrett appeared to shrink the room as he stood, broad shoulders hunched forward, his hand dangling cautiously close to his holstered hip.

Breathless, Lila gasped, "What are you doing here, Garrett? How did you find me?"

"Get out of the way!"

"No!"

Turning back to Billy, Lila grasped his arm as he attempted to push her aside. "No . . . please, Billy. You don't have to worry about him. He's not the law."

Billy's narrowed gaze met Garrett's. The menace that had replaced the loving, brotherly emotion visible there a few minutes ago stole Lila's breath. Its heated intensity matched the magnitude of Garrett's imposing intimidating presence and her heartbeat quickened. This was the Billy she did not know . . . the part of him she had chosen to believe did not exist. But it was real . . . too real . . . as he spoke to Garrett in direct challenge.

"Who the hell are you? What are you doing here?"

Lila's voice faltered as she answered in his stead. "He . . . he's someone I met while I was hiding from the Pinkerton."

"Get out of the way, Lila. Now!"

Lila responded to Garrett's command with instinctive fury. "No, I won't get out of the way! You don't have the right to give me orders and I don't intend taking any. This is *my* room! I don't know how you found me, but you weren't invited here."

"He was, though, wasn't he . . ." Garrett's voice was a lethal growl. "I told you to get away from him . . ."

Incredulous at the frightening bent of the confrontation, Lila exclaimed, "This is crazy! You're angry at me for leaving the ranch without telling you, is that it, Garrett? Are you here for an explanation? If you are, that's between you and me. It has nothing to do with Billy."

"You don't have to protect me, Lila." His expression unchanged as he watched Garrett intently, Billy continued. "I'm not a little boy anymore. I can take care of myself."

"That's right!" Lila turned on Billy with sudden rage. "You're not a little boy, and nor is Garrett, but neither of you has accepted the responsibilities of manhood. Neither of you *earns* a living. You steal it! You do what you want to do without thinking about its effect on others because you don't care! But when the situation is reversed . . ." Lila's voice cracked unexpectedly as she glanced between the two men she loved, "The two of you are facing each other as enemies while you're more alike than I ever wanted to believe . . . in ways that I'm ashamed to acknowledge. Damn you both!"

Regaining control a moment later, Lila retained a rigid stance between the two men. "Shoot . . . go ahead! End each other's misery! And end mine, too, so I don't have to see my brother and the man I—"

"Your brother!" Garrett's shocked exclamation brought Lila's tirade to an abrupt halt. He glanced at Billy, then back at her. "Why didn't you tell me he was your brother?"

Lila raised her chin. "It wasn't any of your business."

Garrett took a hard step forward. "Wasn't it?"

But the ice in Garrett's glacial glare was melting. Lila felt its overflow building under her own lids. She shot a quick look at Billy, noting that he observed the rapidly changing tenor of emotions between Garrett and herself with caution.

Garrett reached out for her and Billy hissed sharply, "Don't touch her!"

"I'm not going to hurt her." When his statement had no effect on Billy, Garrett hesitated briefly, then took a step back. "All right. Look, I'll take my gun by the handle and throw it on the bed if that'll convince you. This is a misunderstandin'." He looked again at Lila. "A goddamned hell of a misunderstandin' . . ."

Taking Billy's silence for acquiescence, Garrett drew his gun slowly from his holster and threw it on the bed.

And Lila held her breath . . .

Jake Hobbs held his breath.

Standing in the hallway outside Lila Chesney's room, he heard no gunshots, no raised voices, just the low drone of conversation . . . then silence.

Vacillating between anxiety and relief, Jake silently cursed Garrett Harrison, McParland, and all the Pinkertons combined, knowing only one, undeviating certainty at that moment. He would do everything and *anything* he needed to do to get his man. It was a matter of personal integrity that brooked no exceptions. With or without his partner, he'd get his man . . .

Defenseless by his own choice, Garrett faced the steely green eyes of the man across from him. He had just made a damned foolish move, and he knew it. A phrase rolled unconsciously across the back of his mind.

A man who died for love . . .

Both astounded and blackly amused by his own stupidity, Garrett watched the fellow cautiously. The man was Lila's brother, but he was also a thief and a murderer. Whatever had made him think he would hesitate to shed blood again?

Billy Chesney spoke softly, drawing his gun. "Get out of the way, Lila."

Lila's face whitened. She backed up protectively against Garrett, challenging her brother stiffly. "Put your gun down, Billy. If you want to shoot him, you'll have to shoot me, too. Is that what you want?"

Billy did not move.

"Put your gun down, Billy." Lila paused, her icy calm faltering. "Please . . ."

Billy's threatening stare flickered briefly. Still focused on Garrett, he demanded softly, "What is this fella to you, Lila?"

"Nothing. His name's Garrett Harrison He's . . . a friend . . ."

"I'm a hell of a lot more than a friend, and you know it!"

"You are?" Lila raised her chin defensively. "I don't remember any conversations between us that indicated anything else." She laughed harshly. "As a matter of fact, I remember you mentioning a woman named Elizabeth . . ."

Elizabeth . . . Garrett was suddenly incensed as a familiar pang stirred to life inside him. "Elizabeth has nothin' to do with this!"

"She doesn't?" Lila took a steadying breath. "I suppose that says it all . . ."

Interrupting their exchange, Billy growled, "What's this all about, Lila? Who is this fella?"

Garrett stared at Billy Chesney. A plethora of images assaulted his mind. Bart Forbes . . . McParland . . . Elizabeth. The scent of charred wood returned . . .

Garrett's jaw hardened. Lila had inadvertently saved him from his own stupidity. It was not too late to rescue his cause.

"You don't have to worry about me, Chesney. I followed Lila here, not you. From the looks of things, you're the one who Pinkerton was after, so I'd say you and I are both in the same boat."

"What's he talking about, Lila?"

Lila's lips tightened. "The law's after him. I saw the wanted poster."

"What's he wanted for?"

"Bank robbery."

His gaze intently assessing, Billy Chesney turned toward Garrett once more. "Is that right?"

"Yeah, that's right."

"How do I know you won't bring the law down on me?"

That question too close to the truth for comfort, Garrett shrugged. "Ask your sister. It wasn't me who was hidin' from a Pinkerton at that ranch."

"Is he telling the truth, Lila?"

Garrett held his breath until Lila nodded. "Yes, he is."

Billy Chesney considered his sister's response. "Do you want me to get rid of him, Lila?"

"No!"

"What do you want me to do? Do you want to talk to him?"

"No."

Garrett's voice dropped an intimate notch lower. "Yes you do, Lila."

Chesney considered his sister's uncertain expression for a long moment, then slid his gun slowly back into his holster. "It looks to me like you've got something to settle with this fella. Do you want me to leave?"

Lila grasped her brother's arm. "We haven't had a chance to talk, Billy."

Billy's smile flashed. The brief transformation was acute, and Garrett was momentarily stunned at the resemblance between brother and sister that had gone unnoticed before. Also apparent was the warmth between them as Billy slid his arm around Lila's shoulders.

"Don't worry. I'm not going far . . . just to get

cleaned up so I can think a little more clearly. Is that all right?"

Lila clung to him. "Promise?"

"Yeah." Chesney's smile faded as he motioned toward Garrett with his head. "But if you'll take my advice, you'll get rid of him. He's not the kind for you, Lila."

Garrett responded with instinctive heat. "Lila doesn't need your advice, Chesney!"

All trace of his former warmth gone, Billy turned sharply toward Garrett. "Maybe she doesn't, but I'm giving it to her anyway. She's too good for the likes of a wanted man. You know it and I know it. But Lila makes her own decisions. I'm going to leave the two of you alone because my sister says you're all right, but if you try anything . . ."

Controlling the urge to wipe the warning from Billy Chesney's youthful face, Garrett growled in return, "You don't scare me, so don't waste your breath. Lila's safe with me because I'll keep her safe . . . not for any other reason. Take as long as you want. We'll be here when you get back."

Chesney absorbed the warning in Garrett's response with a cold smile. "Fine. We understand each other." Billy brushed Lila's cheek with his lips. "I'll be back."

Nodding, Lila followed her brother's slow departure with a gaze that spoke more loudly than words, and jealousy again twinged inside Garrett. It occurred to him as the door closed behind Billy that his jealousy had added a new complication to the affair . . . a dangerous complication . . . of which Hobbs was unaware as he wisely kept his distance from the scene.

The click of the lock echoed hollowly on the silence of the room as Billy pulled the door closed behind him . . . as Lila turned to Garrett . . .

* * *

"Why did you leave without telling me, Lila? I deserved more than that from you."

"Did you?" Lila controlled an urge to laugh, knowing it would emerge with a hysterical sound. She could not afford to let Garrett know how the sight of him had affected her, how her heart had leaped with joy in the moment before fear had assumed its place. She was still afraid, but her fear no longer stemmed from the unexpected confrontation between Billy and Garrett. The confrontation between Garrett and herself was more intimidating, because she had little protection against it.

Anger her only viable defense, Lila forced immunity to the caress of Garrett's gaze, choosing instead to recall Elizabeth's innocent, youthful image. The effect was instantaneous, reflected in her sharpened tone.

"This is a waste of time, Garrett. You shouldn't have followed me here."

Garrett took a step closer. "Did you really think I wouldn't?"

Lila willed her eyes to remain cold despite the slow quivering that started inside her. "I didn't think you'd be able to find me. I took great care . . ."

"To escape me or the Pinkerton?"

Lila was instantly alert. "What do you know about the Pinkerton?"

Garrett's eyes reflected her wariness. "I know you wouldn't have gone to the trouble of a disguise and changin' hotels to escape me."

"You think not?"

"Damn it, Lila, stop lyin' to me!"

Garrett gripped her roughly by the shoulders. Her

skin burned at his touch, evoking memories she did not dare recall as she rasped, "Let me go!"

"Are you afraid again, Lila?" Garrett's voice slipped to a low caress as he drew her closer. "Just as you were afraid that last day, before the storm broke? I've thought about that afternoon every minute of the day since you left. I ached with wantin' you until I could think of nothin' else. I don't know what drove you away, but I know it wasn't what happened between us. It couldn't have been that."

"You're wrong, Garrett." The quivering inside Lila began assuming control as Garrett's rough grip turned gentle, as his hands caressed the flesh he had unwittingly bruised moments earlier.

"No I'm not, darlin'."

Suddenly tight against the lean length of him, struggling against the mesmerizing warmth slowly pervading her, Lila closed her eyes. Garrett's lips brushed her cheek, the corner of her mouth, tempting, coaxing a response she would not allow even as his lips met and covered hers.

Rigid under his kiss, Lila heard Garrett's frustrated rasp as he drew back. "Talk to me, Lila. Tell me what you're afraid of and I'll make it right."

"How can you make it right?" Firmly extricating herself from Garrett's embrace, Lila took a deep breath. "Well . . . you were right in one way. I didn't leave the ranch solely because of you. The Pinkerton was in Deer Trail. Doc told me. He saw him with a man named McParland . . ."

Garrett's subtle reaction did not escape Lila. "I see you know the name. Doc did, too. He described the Pinkerton agent who was with McParland, and it was easy enough to pick him out on the train when I left Deer Trail. I had no difficulty slipping away from him once I had the advantage. At least I thought I didn't . . ." A new fear suddenly dawning, Lila felt a rush of panic. "But if you found me . . ."

"Don't worry about the Pinkerton. I found you because I know how determined and clever you are. I have the feeling that the Pinkerton wouldn't give you that much credit. That would've been his first mistake."

"But—"

"Don't worry about the Pinkerton." Garrett's handsome features became sober and intent. "If need be, I'll take care of him."

A slow horror grew within Lila. "Is that what you think I want—to have you kill a man to protect me . . . or Billy?" Lila shook her head in disbelief. "Do you really think I could build a life with a man who has blood on his hands . . . that I could—"

Lila halted abruptly, a knife of pain inside her slashing deeply. "But you're not offering me a lifetime, are you, Garrett . . ." The gaping wound gushed her life's blood as Lila raised her chin. "You're saving your lifetime for Elizabeth."

"I told you. Leave Elizabeth out of this!"

"How can I? She's standing between us now!"

"Lila . . ." Garrett's voice was suddenly hoarse with anguish as he clutched her shoulders once more. "Will you believe me if I tell you that when you're in my arms, no other woman enters my mind?"

The rumble of crumbling defenses sounded softly in Lila's mind. Garrett's handsome face was close to hers . . . so close that she could see the hint of desperation in his eyes as he awaited her response . . . so close that she could feel his powerful body trembling with the passion he restrained. She wanted to feel that passion encompass her. She wanted to be absorbed into his quivering strength. She wanted the ecstasy of knowing that she was as much a part of him as the arms that would enclose her, as the lips that would caress hers . . . *as the heart he had saved for someone else . . .*

A slow futility pervaded Lila's mind. It was useless to yearn. Garrett had loved her with supreme tenderness and beauty the day of the storm. She had loved him back, withholding nothing, but the emotion between them, so brilliant and consuming, had quickly paled when reality had returned. Garrett had then returned to his "forever" woman in his mind. She knew instinctively that she could never be to Garrett what Elizabeth was to him. She did not want to suffer the agony of trying.

Seeking a steady tone, Lila managed in a whisper that was gentle despite the resolution behind it, "No, Garrett, that's not enough. It could never be enough."

Appearing stricken by her response, Garrett was long moments before responding. When he finally spoke, his voice was a low monotone of barely controlled emotion.

"Elizabeth, she . . . you could never understand about her. She's . . . special. She's in my heart forever. She's a part of me."

A violent rage suffused Lila. She didn't want to hear Garrett speak about his love for Elizabeth! Each word he spoke twisted the knife of pain deeper. She was not the innocent his dear Elizabeth was. Unlike Elizabeth, circumstances had forced her from the innocence and purity Garrett seemed to value so highly. Refusing to feel shame, Lila raised her chin higher.

"Elizabeth was a virgin when you took her for the first time. . . . That's right, isn't it, Garrett?"

The grey velvet of Garrett's eyes began to harden.

"Yes, she was . . ."

"And I wasn't."

"No."

"She had never loved a man before you . . ."

"That's right."

"And I had . . . you're uncertain of how many . . ."

Garrett's eyes shot sparks of angry fire. "That's right."

"Elizabeth would never betray you . . . would never look at another man. She would wait for you forever."

"That's right . . ."

"She's sweet and honest and pure. She would give her life for you."

Garrett went completely still. Lila did not need to hear him say the words. The answer was in his suddenly rigid stance and in the fury that had replaced the love formerly shining in his eyes.

"I'm right, aren't I? You want me . . . but you want to keep Elizabeth, too . . . always above me, truer, more honest, more loving, more sincere . . ."

"Shut up!"

"No, I won't shut up!"

"You don't know what you're talkin' about!"

"Oh, yes, Garrett, I do! I learned the hard way what it means to be second best to a 'good' woman. I learned it years ago when I was young and inexperienced and looking for someone who could save my brother and me from the frightening world we had escaped into. I learned then that conditional love was really no love at all. I learned that it took everything and gave nothing in return. I learned that the loving beauty of the moment, no matter how intense, was far overshadowed by the aftermath of tears that followed . . . and I became determined never to shed those tears again."

Garrett shook his head in vehement denial. "It wouldn't be that way with us."

"Yes, it would, because I could never be satisfied to

be second best, Garrett. The thought would eat me up inside until I made you as miserable as I was."

"Lila, darlin' . . ." Garrett stroked her cheek, the tenderness of his touch as much a torment as his words as he whispered, "The greater misery would be to be apart . . ."

"Maybe." Retaining control with sheer strength of will, Lila whispered in a pained hiss, "But I'd grow to hate myself, and when I did, I'd hate you, too. I don't want to hate you, Garrett."

"Lila, darlin' . . ."

"Don't say anything else, please. Just answer one question for me . . . truthfully." Garrett did not respond as Lila pressed softly, "Can you honestly tell me that if I walked into your arms right now, you could put Elizabeth out of your mind forever?"

"Lila . . ."

"Could you say that, Garrett?"

Garrett took a shuddering breath. "No."

The pain that single word delivered more than she could bear, Lila took a rigid step backward. "Leave my room, Garrett."

"Lila, please . . ."

"Leave now!"

Her anguish so intense that she feared she would expire, Lila viewed the torment etched deeply on Garrett's handsome face.

Oh, God, he *did* love her . . .

But he did not love her enough . . .

Garrett turned slowly toward the door. Her heart shattering further with each step he took, Lila withheld her brimming tears, knowing he would not turn back as he opened the door, stepped into the hall, and drew the door closed behind him.

The image of Garrett remained before Lila's eyes for

long moments. His anguish was carved into her heart with cruel, slashing strokes.

She was bleeding again.

So badly that she feared she would not survive.

Silent and immobile, Garrett stood rigidly in the hallway outside Lila's room. He had had no response to her words or to the pain he had witnessed grow greater with each syllable she had uttered. Elizabeth's name on Lila's lips had left him defenseless.

Garrett closed his eyes briefly. Lila asked too much. He could not forget the sacrifice Elizabeth had made for him. He could not strike from his mind the debt he owed to Elizabeth and his parents, a debt he had vowed to pay. He could not explain to Lila that the brother she loved so dearly would suffer in payment of that debt. She would not understand because she would not choose to understand that the brother she had protected all her life deserved whatever price he would pay.

Garrett drew himself slowly erect as reality hardened into pained acceptance. Lila had been right all along. Elizabeth, and all that her memory entailed, would be forever between them.

Sixteen

The shadows of afternoon had shifted, sending a pale, semilight into her small hotel room, but Lila was oblivious to the passage of time. Her tears exhausted, she lay silently abed as the tormenting scene played over and again in her mind. Garrett had no defense against the truths she had forced from him, just as she had no defense against the pain his honesty had inflicted. It was over and done. Garrett was gone from her life forever.

But the agony lingered on.

A deep sob rose again in Lila's throat, erupting in a wracking spasm that stole her breath. Garrett, whose anguish was as deep as her own, whose love for Elizabeth was unyielding despite the hunger for her she had read in his eyes. She had shared that hunger. She shared it still.

Her tears returning full measure, Lila did not hear the door open behind her or the sound of Billy's step until he was beside her, raising her from the bed to dry her tears. Held in his comforting arms, she poured out her heartache without restraint, knowing that her brother, far better than anyone else, understood.

Silent, her sobbing stilled, Lila rested quietly in

Billy's protective embrace. She stirred as he drew back from her, startled at the unexpected distress that accompanied the sympathy she read in his eyes.

"I'm sorry, Lila."

Lila remained silent, sensing more than his words conveyed.

"This is all my fault."

"No, I—"

"Yes, it is." Billy's youthful, clean-shaven face was filled with remorse. "You were right in everything you said to me earlier. I claimed to be a man, but I went about proving it in all the wrong ways."

"I . . . I didn't mean what I said, Billy."

"Yes you did." Billy stroked a damp wisp of hair back from her cheek, his smile flashing briefly. "You've said the same things before, but I never heard you. I never truly understood until now."

The misery Lila read in her brother's eyes matched her own, momentarily overwhelming her own grief as Billy's face grew unexpectedly stiff. She saw an unexpected quiver of his lips the moment before he whispered hoarsely, "It's strange the way things worked out. You found a man to love, and he made you second best. I found a woman to love, and *I* made her second best . . . to my own selfishness. Harrison and I are both the same kind of fools. The only difference is that I realize now what I've lost . . . when it's too late."

Billy's lips twitched again. "I've lost her, Lila."

Compassion undimmed by her own distress sobered Lila's tear-streaked face. Billy was suffering. She took his hand.

"Tell me what this is all about. I want to know."

His fleeting smile beautiful for all its sadness, Billy gripped Lila's hand tightly in return. A world of emotion in his hoarse tone, Billy said softly, "Her name is Eva . . ."

"Leave me alone, Hobbs!"

"Like hell I will!" Glancing uncertainly around the long mahogany bar that stretched toward the entrance of the Trail's End Saloon, Hobbs frowned. Night had fallen and the action within was in full swing. The clatter of chips and the ring of the roulette wheel competed with the growing din of conversation at nearby tables, shouted hoots of laughter from tipsy customers along the bar, and a racy ditty sung by a saloon girl at the piano in the far corner of the room. Having fended off female advances for the first half hour, Garrett and he had settled into a tense conversation during which he had finally obtained a sketchy account of the proceedings in Lila Chesney's room earlier that afternoon.

He hadn't liked what he had learned.

Satisfied that their sharp exchange had not been overheard, Hobbs moved closer to Garrett as the bigger man leaned over his refilled glass.

"You're damned lucky you didn't blow the whole investigation, busting into that room like you did! Months of work would've gone down the drain, and I don't mind telling you that I wouldn't have taken it lightly!"

Garrett slanted Hobbs a black look. "I didn't blow it, though, did I?"

"That was sheer luck! There wasn't a bit of professionalism involved."

"I don't give a damn about professionalism!"

Garrett's increasing aggressiveness drew the attention of nearby patrons, and Hobbs frowned. "This isn't exactly the place to discuss it."

"I didn't bring it up. You did." Garrett's expression

darkened. "If you're so concerned about Lila's brother gettin' away, you should be watchin' his room right now."

"He isn't going anywhere tonight. He bedded his horse down at the livery stable before he got cleaned up and paid for a night in advance. He stopped off at the post office before he went back to rent a room a few doors down from his sister. I nosed around at the post office afterward, and the fella there said Chesney was real anxious about a letter he was expectin' . . . from a woman . . . and that Chesney said he'd be back after breakfast to see if it came in on the morning train."

"Maybe that was all an act to throw you off."

"No, I don't think so. And even if it was, it's easy enough to see the hotel entrance from here. I haven't taken my eye off it for a minute."

"A Pinkerton to the core . . ."

Hobbs reacted with growing heat to Garrett's deprecating sneer. "That's right, Harrison, and proud of it! At least I haven't let a woman turn me around in circles until I'm not sure which way I'm going!"

Garrett's lips tightened. "You don't know what you're talkin' about, Hobbs. I know the way I'm headed." He gave a hard laugh. "Maybe that's the problem."

"And maybe it isn't! Correct me if I'm wrong, Harrison. You swore an oath when you took this job, didn't you?"

Garrett did not bother to respond.

"Somehow I've got the feeling that oath doesn't mean as much to you as your own personal motivation does, so I'll tell you this now." His lined face flushing, Hobbs stared into Garrett's light eyes. "That oath means something to me, and so does my reputation, which you're putting in danger with your unprofessional conduct."

Garrett's expression turned grim. "I told you once, and I'll tell you again, there isn't anythin' in the world . . . not *anythin'* . . . that's going to get in the way of my gettin' Forbes."

"So you say." Hobbs took a deep breath. "I want you to stay away from Lila Chesney . . ."

"You what?"

"I want you to stay away from her . . . keep your distance . . . maintain a covert surveillance until her brother makes a move toward Forbes."

A slow rage twitched on Garrett's sober face. "I don't take orders from you or anybody else."

"Your personal involvement with Lila Chesney is too dangerous!"

"I can handle it!"

"I don't think so!"

"I don't care what you think . . ."

Hobbs drew his wiry frame slowly erect. "I'm warning you now, Harrison. I'll do anything I have to do in order to get Forbes and his gang."

The emphasis of his words explicit, Garrett responded slowly, "So will I."

"I told you before, I don't think so."

"And I told *you* before, I can handle it!"

"Look, Harrison . . ."

"I'm tired of talkin'." Tossing down the last of his drink, Garrett slapped some money on the bar and turned abruptly. "You can watch that hotel until dawn if you want . . . or you can rent a room down the hall from Lila and her brother and get a good night's sleep . . . like I'm goin' to do. In any case, I'll see you in the mornin'." Garrett paused. "Just make sure *Lila* doesn't see you, or that'll be the end of it all for sure."

Hobbs's lip twitched. "Don't worry. I won't underestimate her again."

A hard smirk his only reply, Garrett turned toward the door. Moments later he was striding across the brightly lit street toward the entrance to the Falmouth hotel.

As Hobbs seethed . . .

Twisting and turning in bed, Garrett glanced at the night sky outside the unshaded window of his room. It glowed with reflected lights from the city beneath as echoes of revelry from the Trail's End and similar establishments up and down the street punctuated the silence of the night with ceaseless regularity. Garrett knew, however, that he could not lay blame for his sleeplessness on anything but the turmoil within him.

The closeness of the poorly ventilated room suddenly more than he could bear, Garrett stood up abruptly and walked to the window. A night breeze touched his bare chest, cooling him, but Garrett knew the relief was temporary.

A persistent agitation returned as Lila's tearful image again assaulted his mind. He had not wanted to make Lila cry. His intentions had been different by far. Garrett frowned, recalling the jealous rage that had possessed him when he had first seen Billy Chesney. But rage had turned to shock, and shock to shame when he had realized the full extent of his wrongful judgment of Lila.

He had been a fool.

Taking the few short steps to the washstand in the corner of the room, Garrett poured water into the bowl and splashed his face and hair liberally in an attempt to clear his mind. The water dripped down onto his chest, making snaking paths between the short, dark hairs sprinkled there as he picked up the cloth hanging nearby and dried himself absentmindedly.

Running a hand through his damp hair, Garrett glanced at the frowning image staring back at him in the washstand mirror. He then turned toward the nearby chair, snatched up his shirt and pants, and slipped them on without conscious thought. His boots followed. He was striding toward the doorway of his room before he realized a decision had been made.

A soft pounding on the door stirred Lila from her troubled sleep. Resisting wakefulness, she did not immediately respond. It had been too difficult to fall asleep after Billy had left her, his sorrow adding to her own.

Again the pounding . . .

Suddenly awake, Lila felt her heart jump. Billy . . . the Pinkerton . . .

On her feet in a moment, Lila raced to the door. She jerked it open with a gasp, motionless at first sight of the towering figure silhouetted against the light of the hall.

The glow from behind held Garrett's features in dark relief. Unable to assess his mood, Lila willed the heavy pounding of her heart to cease as she asked, "What do you want, Garrett?"

"I want to talk to you, Lila."

"We've said everything that needed to be said. I don't want to talk anymore."

Lila attempted to close the door, only to have Garrett's arm shoot out to hold it fast. "No, we didn't say everythin' that needed to be said. *I* didn't, anyway. Lila . . ." Garrett's voice dropped to a tortured whisper that shook

Lila to the soul as he continued. "I . . . I owe you an explanation."

"You don't owe me anything."

"I do. Please, Lila . . . let me come in."

The request was mere formality. With the simple thrust of his arm, Garrett already held the door open despite Lila's determined effort to shut it. She knew that should he choose to force entry, she would be unable to stop him. Those circumstances aside, Lila also knew that Garrett was waiting for her permission. Somehow, she could not refuse him.

Stepping back, Lila allowed Garrett into the room, then moved to the night table to raise the flame on the lamp. Flickering shadows danced against the wall as she turned toward him, suddenly aware of the thin layer of cotton batiste that separated her nakedness from his gaze. Reaching for her wrapper, she slipped her arms into it and belted it tightly. She thrust back her unbound hair, the memory of Garrett's mumbled wonder as he had run his fingers through the flowing tresses returning to raise a slow heat to her face.

"What do you want to tell me, Garrett?"

Able to see Garrett clearly in the improved light of the room, Lila saw the responsive tic of his cheek. She saw the shadows of an anguish too deep for tears shifting in his eyes as he replied, "I want to talk about Elizabeth."

"No!" Her heart suddenly racing, Lila took an involuntary step backward. "You bastard! I don't want to hear about her!"

"I want you to understand . . ."

"I understand! I've understood all along. You love Elizabeth with your heart and soul . . . but you *want* me. It's not going to be that way. Not tonight . . . not tomorrow . . . not ever again!"

"Lila, please believe me." With a few quick steps, Garrett grasped her arms, prohibiting further retreat. His gaze silver slivers of light, pinned her, holding her immobile. "I didn't come here for that. I want peace between us."

"I'll be at peace when you leave. Let me go!"

"If you won't listen for yourself . . . listen for me."

Garrett's strong hands were trembling. Lila could feel the vibrations of that trembling shake her, tottering her defenses.

"Please . . ."

Despising herself for her weakness, Lila briefly closed her eyes. "All right. Tell me whatever you want to tell me . . . then go."

Allowing herself to be drawn to the side of the bed, Lila sat stiffly as Garrett drew her down beside him. His restraining grip slipped to her hands, which he held tightly, willing her gaze to meet his.

"I . . . I think it's important for you to understand who Elizabeth is."

Lila remained rigidly still. "All right. Who is she?"

"My wife."

The shock of those two words stole Lila's breath. Bastard! Thief! Adulterer! And he had made her no better than he!

But those words did not leave her lips. Instead came a whispered question. "Where is she?"

"In Kansas."

"Why aren't you with her now?"

Garrett's hands tightened painfully. "Because she's dead."

Dead.

Lila was momentarily unable to speak.

"When did she die?"

"Years ago. I've lost count."

"But you've never stopped loving her."

"No. I never will. You see . . ." Garrett shuddered. Silver ice melted, filling his eyes to brimming. "I was wounded during the war. I wasn't expected to live, so I was sent home to my parents' house, where Elizabeth was staying. The town was attacked by Quantrill's raiders. They were determined to kill every Union soldier they saw, but they didn't stop there. It was wanton murder . . . bloody destruction. Women and children . . ." Garrett faltered, then continued purposefully. "When the raiders came within sight, Elizabeth and my parents carried me down into the cellar where I would be safe. My father went out to talk to them. They killed him. My mother rushed to his side as the raid continued. Elizabeth ran out to help her. I watched through the cellar window as she reached them. She was terrified, and I couldn't help her. The barn burst into flames and Elizabeth looked up at it. I knew what she was thinking. The wagon and the horses were our only means of escape. She wanted to get them out of the barn. I tried to call her. I tried to tell her to come back when she started toward the barn."

Garrett paused, his expression tortured as Lila remained mesmerized by the horror of the tale.

"But she couldn't hear me. She slipped into the barn and disappeared from sight. My mother stood up. She was shaking. She called Elizabeth, and when there was no response, she ran toward the barn and followed Elizabeth inside." Garrett paused again. "A few minutes later there was a loud crack and the barn exploded fully into flames. And they were gone."

Lila started to speak, but her voice failed her. She tried again. "You . . . you never saw them again?"

"I saw where their remains were buried—not far

from what was left of the house after the raiders sacked it."

"They didn't find you."

"No."

Lila was trembling, too, when Garrett continued. "My parents . . . they died cruelly, but they died together, the way they hoped it would be. Elizabeth died alone. She was too young to die. If it hadn't been for me . . . if she hadn't tried to get to the wagon to save me . . ."

"You don't know that. Maybe she . . ."

Garrett's gaze did not falter. "The last thing Elizabeth said to me was that she wouldn't let them get me, that she'd find a way to get me away from there . . ."

Not aware that tears trailed down her cheeks, Lila whispered, "I'm sorry, Garrett. I'm so sorry."

"I'm sorry, too. But bein' sorry wasn't enough then, and it isn't enough now."

Lila was suddenly confused. "What are you saying? That you had to get even? Is that why you've done terrible things . . . robbed banks . . ."

Garrett glanced up, startling Lila with the sudden heat of his gaze. "Am I any worse than your brother?"

Lila's pain increased. "No . . . you aren't." She took a deep breath. "You aren't any better, either. Oh, Garrett, it doesn't have to be this way . . . not anymore! Don't you see? You can put all this horror behind you."

Garrett shook his head. "No I can't."

"You can."

"Not yet."

"When? When a bullet catches up with you . . . or when a posse sits you on a horse and ties a rope around your neck? Garrett, think what you're doing!"

"I've thought . . . I've thought it over many times." Garrett raised his hand to stroke the tears from her cheeks. "I've thought about it until I can't stand thinkin' about it anymore."

Garrett's gaze intensified as his hands trembled against her cheek. Lila responded instinctively to that touch, and a sudden fear assaulted her. She was weakening. The plea in Garrett's voice was melting her resolve as he whispered, "It was different with Elizabeth and me. I had known her all my life. She and I . . ." His voice faltered. "I've never wanted any woman the way I want you, Lila. I can't look at you without wanting to touch you." His hand slid to her hair to stroke it lightly. "I can't touch you without wanting to kiss you." He briefly touched his mouth to hers. His voice dropped to a throbbing whisper. "And I can't kiss you without wanting to make you a part of me."

His arms sliding around her to clutch her desperately close, Garrett rasped, "Let me love you, Lila. It'll be right and good between us."

Lila strained to retain the last fading shred of her resolve. "No, Garrett. I . . . I don't want to spend the rest of my life looking over my shoulder and wondering when the law will catch up with you. I've had a sample of that life. It's too hard. It takes too much." Lila shook her head, the pain of her next words excruciating. "I . . . I don't want to love you, and I don't want you to love me."

But Garrett was working a familiar magic as he brushed her hair, her temple, her cheek with a kiss, then whispered against her lips, "It's too late for that, Lila. And it's too late for regrets. There's only one thing left for us . . ."

"Garrett . . ."

Lila's last trailing protest was smothered by the warmth of Garrett's mouth against hers as she surrendered to the aching need within her.

Garrett's embrace tightened, and Lila gasped with the wonder of it as his mouth pressed more deeply into hers. She reveled in the hard, muscled weight of him as he pressed her back against the bed, consuming her with his kiss. She sighed as Garrett's hand moved beneath her nightdress to stroke her intimately. She rose to his touch and her heart soared as he freed her of her inhibiting garments. Her breasts cried for his caress and Garrett complied, covering them with worshipful kisses. Suckling, adoring, loving, he set her soul afire as she clutched his head against her. She was not conscious of the soft groans that escaped her lips, driving him to greater depths of tender frenzy. She was drowning in his loving . . .

Garrett drew back suddenly, and Lila opened her eyes. An intense sense of abandonment drew a soft protest from her in the moment before he cupped her face with his trembling hands to speak in an impassioned whisper.

"Don't worry, I won't leave you. I'll never leave you again, darlin'. You're mine and I'm goin' to mark my claim on you tonight so there'll be no doubtin' it anymore."

Drawing himself to his feet beside the bed, Garrett held Lila's gaze with his as he stripped away his clothes. His powerful body bared, he stood unexpectedly still as her searching gaze wandered the tight lines of passion in his face, as it slipped down the muscular column of his neck to trace the broad expanse of his shoulders. He maintained his silence as she took in his firmly muscled chest, the narrow tapering of his waist, his flat male hips. She heard his quick intake of breath, saw his breathing grow more ragged as her gaze lingered on the hard, firm rise of his passion.

The aching need within her expanded, flushing a new

heat through her veins as Lila slowly raised her eyes to his. Garrett held his arms out to her and she rose from the bed as if drawn by invisible bonds. She took a step toward him, stopping short when he whispered, "No . . . wait. Let me look at you . . . just for a moment."

The lamp's pale light lent a glowing translucence to Lila's fair skin as she remained obediently still, allowing Garrett the same moment of chaste worship that he had allowed her. Her breath caught in her throat as he smoothed the long, curling length of her hair with his gaze, as he explored the delicacy of her womanly perfection with growing hunger, as he stroked every inch of her flesh with a gaze so intimate, so palpable, that it left her trembling. The catch in his voice touched her soul as he whispered, "You're beautiful, Lila . . . the most beautiful woman I've ever seen. I've never wanted anyone the way I want you . . ."

Garrett took a step forward, narrowing the separation between them as he took a lock of hair from her shoulder and raised it to his lips.

"Your hair smells like flowers . . . it tastes like the sun. I've dreamed of touchin' it . . . touchin' you." Closing the final distance between them, Garrett traced the planes of Lila's cheek with his mouth, lingering, adoring. He brushed her lips with his, drawing away even as her mouth clung hungrily. He trailed his caress down her neck, worshiping the curve of her shoulder, the rise of her breasts. He found the burgeoning crests once more, and Lila arched her back as he bathed them with the moist heat of his kisses. Slipping to one knee, Garrett crouched beside her, pursuing the curve of her hip to the flat, white skin of her stomach. His calloused palms moved erotically against her back, smoothing and stroking, drawing her into his caresses as his mouth slipped lower still.

A new level of anxious anticipation rose within Lila as Garrett nudged the tight, moist curls between her thighs. She murmured an incoherent word that drew Garrett's gaze up to hers. The glow of passion in its silver depths mesmerized her as he whispered, "I need this, darlin', as much as I need you. I need to love you, to know every part of you, to know you belong to me . . . completely."

His gaze still holding hers, Garrett cupped Lila's buttocks in his palms. He drew her forward as he lowered his mouth to brush the gleaming ringlets between her thighs with his lips. Her eyes fluttered closed as his mouth slipped lower still, as he found the tender slit below. Her breath caught in her throat as his tongue slid into the moistness there to search it with loving tenderness. Her knees weakened as he found the bud of her passion and drew from it with loving abandon.

Her heart pounding, Lila closed her eyes, helpless against the waves of riotous sensation assaulting her as Garrett laved the tender delta with his kiss. Her thighs separated as his kisses deepened. She opened to him fully, gasping and whimpering as she climbed higher into a realm of ecstasy she had not known before. She was flying high above the brilliant sphere, in a world of heightened color and emotion as a gentle throbbing that had begun within her deepened rapidly, assuming control. Her knees weakened as it threatened to overwhelm her, and Lila stiffened in momentary apprehension.

"Lila, look at me."

Obeying his soft command, Lila looked at Garrett. She saw an urgency that reflected her own as he whispered, "Don't hold back. Give to me. Give all you have to give and I'll give *you* all I have to give in return. I promise you that, darlin'."

Lowering his mouth to her once more, Garrett urged, "Now, darlin' . . . give to me now."

Lila's sharp gasp echoed in the room as Garrett's kiss surged more deeply than before. A hot flood of emotion swelled as the gasp lingered, increasing to a cry that did not cease, as the rapture of the moment overflowed into deep, involuntary spasms, as her body shuddered again and again its sweet, ecstatic tribute to the joy of Garrett's loving.

Sinking weakly to her knees, her culmination complete, Lila opened her eyes again at the softness of the bed beneath her and Garrett's weight warm against her. Garrett's handsome face was marked with loving solemnity as he stroked her cheek gently, then whispered, "This is the way it was meant to be between us, darlin'."

Still unable to speak for the emotion choking her throat, Lila slid her arms around Garrett's neck as he raised himself to thrust home within her at last. Reveling in the swell of him, in the rasp of his breath in her ear as he began the ageless rhythm of love, Lila met him thrust for thrust. Her exhilaration mounted as his tempo increased, as the renewed urgency within soared higher . . . higher . . .

Ecstasy surrounded them like a fiercely glowing light, as they trembled on the brink. The light burst into flame and Lila clutched Garrett close, joining him, exalting in the rapture of the moment as his powerful body shuddered its ultimate, silent tribute to the wonder they had shared.

Stillness reigned in the aftermath of their lovemaking. A tear slipped down Lila's cheek as Garrett raised his head at last, as he slid his arms under and around her and drew her into a tight embrace to rasp in hoarse confirmation, "Yes, this is the way it was meant to be . . ."

The night deepened. The lamp sputtered. The flame died. The darkness enclosed them, sealing them in . . . in each other's arms . . . their joy complete.

Until . . .

The sound of flapping wings—the courier of darkness—the scent of burning wood . . .

The nightmare returned.

Flames, hot and greedy, intruded into Garrett's dreamless sleep. They awoke in him a familiar fear there was no escaping as the sound of pounding hooves vibrated through his shaking frame. The horsemen's ghoulish shouts grew louder as he looked toward the barn to see flames stretching hungry fingers toward the sky. Mired in helpless terror, Garrett watched as his father and mother were trampled under the merciless hooves, as an agonized scream raised his gaze to a female figure emerging from the doorway of the burning barn.

The woman was aflame, her light hair blazing as she turned pale, frenzied eyes toward him. A familiar powerlessness held him fast as she started toward him, arms outstretched in a silent plea. The agony of his impotence grew greater, slashing mercilessly at his innards, even as the unexpected emergence of another female figure from the burning barn drew a shocked gasp from his lips.

The second woman started toward him, also ablaze, her dark eyes meeting his in silent, agonized appeal. He struggled harder against the mire holding him fast, succeeding in pulling first one foot free, then the other.

Startled at his freedom, he lurched forward in mindless quandary as he glanced between the two women.

Pale eyes struck with pain implored him.

Dark eyes filled with anguish beseeched him.

An explosion rocked the ground as the burning barn burst into oblivion. The rain of fire ignited him. The flames seared him. He was being consumed even as he strained to reach . . . to reach—

Garrett snapped open his eyes, suddenly awake. Perspiring and shaken, he was momentarily disoriented as his gaze raked the unfamiliar room around him, coming to rest on Lila where she slept beside him. He reached toward her with trembling uncertainty, the terror of his dream still vividly real. Her skin was cool and smooth to his touch. She turned toward him in sleep, her face serenely and exquisitely at peace.

Garrett took a steadying breath and wiped his arm across his brow. His breathing gradually returning to normal, he drew Lila cautiously into the curve of his body. The sweet warmth of her a matchless solace, he drew her closer. Lila moved, fitting herself comfortably against him, and Garrett closed his eyes. He breathed deeply, allowing himself these moments of intimate joy, knowing that when all was said and done . . . the nightmare remained.

Uncharacteristically, Billy came slowly awake. His mind clouded from his restless sleep, he glanced around him at the small hotel room lit by the first morning rays of sun. His thoughts falling into place, he raised a hand to his brow.

It had been a damned long night. He did not care to count the mornings he had awakened in recent weeks, panic gnawing at his mind at the realization that

Eva had slipped another day farther away from him. It occurred to him that he had reached the end of the trail here in Denver. He ached with the thought that he might never hold Eva in his arms again. He longed with a longing that would not die for the sight of her sober face, to feel the loving warmth of her in his arms, to hear the soft purr of her voice when she said his name.

Eva and Lila . . . the two women he loved. One was lost to him, while the other . . .

Billy's torment deepened. He had never seen Lila cry as she had the previous night. He hadn't liked feeling helpless against her tears, and he hadn't liked knowing that only her concern for him had been able to lift her from her despair.

Damn that bastard, Harrison. Was he too blind to see that Lila was worth a hundred Elizabeths . . . *whoever* she was? Didn't he realize that when Lila gave her love it was forever, and that her love would never falter? Because of Harrison, Lila was suffering a torment she didn't deserve. Because of Harrison, Lila—

His raging thoughts coming to an abrupt halt, Billy shook his head in silent refutation. It wasn't Harrison's fault. It was his own. He had taken advantage of Lila's love, knowing she would never withhold it. He had gone his way without thoughts of how the life he chose would affect hers. He had forced her into a situation where she had not been free to leave because of him, and Harrison had assumed the advantage.

His jaw firming even as a wave of regret washed over him, Billy determined that Harrison would never assume the advantage over Lila again.

Throwing back the coverlet, Billy stood up and looked out the nearby window. Early-morning traffic had already started on the street, foretelling another busy day. Billy reached for his clothes. He would have a busy day, too. He would do today what he would have done earlier if he had been the man he had thought himself to be. He would go to his sister and do for her as she had always done for him. When he was satisfied at her comfort, he would go to the post office despite the certainty deep inside him that it would be to no avail. When both those tasks were accomplished, he would leave town to go to his meeting with Forbes and the boys.

Billy frowned as he straightened his shirt, ran a cursory hand over his hair, and picked up his hat. He was days late for that meeting with Forbes. It would not bode well for Forbes's mood when he appeared, but that thought did not bother him as much as it formerly might, for he had another matter to attend that overshadowed it.

His rendezvous with Waller would follow. Whatever Forbes's plans, it would not wait.

Billy turned toward the door, his boyish face set, the liquid green of his eyes cold. He yanked it open, stepped into the hall, and turned toward Lila's door.

Morning sunlight slitted through the window shade but Garrett did not choose to awaken Lila as she lay sleeping at his side. He had stirred countless times after his disturbing dream the night before, uncertain if the womanly softness of Lila pressed against him was indeed a dream . . . uncertain what he would do if he discovered it was.

Lowering his face to Lila's hair, spread out like a brilliant fan on the pillow beside him, Garrett breathed deeply of the scent of the heavy strands, allowing the fragrance to work its magic on his mind. Free of perfume, and innately sensual because it was Lila's alone, it recalled to him passionate moments when the heat of their joining had raised that scent higher. He recalled the wonder of Lila's fragile softness lying beneath him, the arching of her back and the parting of her lips when he had entered her and filled her with his need. She had gasped his name, the extravagant length of her lashes fluttering against her cheeks as ecstasy had slowly gained control. He had not wanted those moments to end.

Careful not to disturb Lila, Garrett slipped his finger into a curling tendril at her hairline. He smiled as the silky wisp adjusted itself, curling around his finger to bind it tightly. Lila had slipped into his heart in the same way. She had wrapped herself around it with her unyielding spirit and she had bound his heart more tightly with each passing day until he had become hopelessly entangled in her silken web.

Unrest returned as Garrett recalled the time when his desire for her had only increased his agitation, when he had attempted to convince himself that he despised her, when he had wanted to believe she was all the things she wasn't and had avidly anticipated the satisfaction of bringing an end to the deceit she practiced.

That thought stinging, Garrett drew back. It was not Lila who now practiced the deceit between them. It was he.

The shame of that deception rose anew. Lila had listened to him with compassion when he had talked to her. She had trusted him completely while he had maintained his deceit by carefully neglecting to correct basic misconceptions. He had conquered her final resistance with half truths, and she had loved him. She had given herself to him totally, while he—

Garrett closed his eyes as the agony of his nightmare

abruptly returned. He had loved Elizabeth with youthful exuberance and passion. A portion of his heart was forever hers and the pain of the sacrifice she had made for him was carved deeply there. The years of emptiness and lack of love in his life that had followed had changed him, hardened him, had erected a wall around his heart that no one had been able to scale. Until Lila.

Garrett despaired as the past and the present vied for preference in his heart . . . knowing the debt remained . . . knowing it must be paid.

Would Lila forgive him when she discovered the truth? *Could* she forgive him?

Lila stirred, and Garrett's love rose in a great, overwhelming swell. He could not lose her. He *would* not lose her. Drawing her close, he covered her parted lips with his, kissing her deeply, seeking to prolong the present so he might—

A sharp knock on the door drew Garrett back abruptly. He looked down at Lila as she struggled to full wakefulness. Her gaze met his, and a smile touched her lips. He ached at that smile. He wished he—

Another knock, and Garrett threw back the coverlet. He drew on his pants as Lila rose from the bed, her smooth, naked flesh pale in the semilight of the room in the moment before she slipped into her wrapper and tied it around her. She walked to the door just as another knock sounded . . . then Billy's voice.

"Lila, are you all right?"

Garrett stood behind Lila as she unlocked the door and drew it open. He did not smile when Billy looked at his sister, then at him, his face darkening.

A new respect glimmered to life inside Garrett as Billy held his sister's gaze and inquired with unexpected gentleness, "Are you sure this is what you want, Lila?"

Garrett slid his arm around Lila, willing her response. He watched her expression closely. He saw her valiant effort at a smile.

"I . . . I don't know if this is what I really want, Billy. All I know is that right now, it can't be any other way."

Billy's gaze lingered on his sister's face. It turned cold when he looked at Garrett with silent animosity and stated flatly, "He's not good enough for you, Lila. I've known a dozen just like him with wanted posters waiting in every town. He's trouble. You deserve more than what he'll give you." Billy paused, his gaze returning to Lila. "But I want you to be happy. If *he's* what'll do it for you . . ." He paused again. "I just want you to be sure."

Lila's dark eyes brimmed. "I know you do, Billy."

Billy frowned at the rumpled bed behind them. "I suppose this isn't the best time to talk. I've got some things to do, anyway. I'll come back later."

Turning to Garrett the moment the door was again closed, Lila whispered, "I'm sorry, Garrett. I had to be honest with him."

"I know."

"I . . . I didn't mean to hurt you."

"I know." Garrett drew her into his arms.

"Garrett . . ."

They spoke no more.

Silently cursing from his observation point on the staircase landing, Hobbs pulled his hat low onto his forehead and started up toward the second floor, passing Billy Chesney as he started down.

Grateful that Lila Chesney's door had snapped shut, Hobbs continued past, waiting only until her brother had cleared the staircase before turning abruptly to follow him back down. He glanced again at Lila's door in passing, anger stiffening his expression into resolution.

Harrison had been standing behind Lila in the doorway. The damned fool! It had been obvious the previous night that the woman had Harrison tied up in knots, but he had not realized the extent to which Harrison would go to free them.

He was still uncertain.

It was apparent, however, that Harrison had still managed to maintain his cover. He had learned that much from the few words of conversation he had overheard at the doorway. But he also knew Harrison was operating without a plan, playing it from one moment to the next. That was dangerous . . . too dangerous. For all the gilding on his reputation, Harrison had proved that he was now too undependable to be trusted fully to do his job.

Stepping down into the lobby, Hobbs waited the few minutes for Chesney to step onto the street before continuing forward. It was time to put into effect an alternate plan that he had been considering during the night. The plan was risky and timing was essential, but he had little choice. Harrison, damn him, had forced his hand!

His eye on Chesney's back as the fellow continued down the walk, Hobbs stepped out onto the street.

Billy continued down the walk at a rapid pace. His mind was racing, and his patience was tested to the limit by the confusion of mercantile stores and restaurants in the midst of early-morning trade while those establishments appealing to night traffic accepted deliveries to replenish stocks depleted by hard-drinking patrons the night before.

Moving around a pile of crates temporarily abandoned on the walk in front of him and mumbling an appropriate warning to a barking dog nearby, Billy looked toward the brick-fronted building at the end of the street. His stomach churned. His encounter with Lila a few minutes before had upset him. He had not expected to see Harrison standing behind his sister in her room, or its obvious implication.

He didn't like it.

Searching his mind, Billy sought to interpret the instinctive animosity between Harrison and himself. Somehow, there was more to it than his objection to Harrison's involvement with Lila. There was something about the way Harrison looked at him that raised the hackles on his spine. He didn't trust him.

Whatever his feelings about Harrison, one glance had revealed that Lila was helpless against her feelings for the man. He sympathized with his sister's plight. He had had no defense against his feelings for Eva. The force of those loving emotions, however, had slowly turned to enmity against those who had driven Eva away from him. That enmity now compelled him just as relentlessly as love.

His gaze still trained on the post office at the end of the block, Billy cursed under his breath. The morning train would arrive within the hour . . . an hour that would stretch into eternity until the mail sacks were emptied and the contents sorted. He glanced toward the restaurant across the street.

The smell of fresh coffee and frying bacon assaulted Billy as he walked through the restaurant doorway.

Seated, his breakfast in front of him minutes later, he determinedly picked up his fork. Appetite had deserted him, but he had learned the hard way, at a very young age, that life went on.

His expression sober as Pete Waller's face returned to mind, Billy took grim consolation in knowing that for a certain few, life was destined to go on for only a little while longer.

Resolute, Billy raised his fork to his mouth.

His breakfast finished, Billy approached the post office, his heart drumming. The morning train had arrived on time. He could put the moment off no longer.

Halting inside the doorway, Billy paused as his eyes adjusted to the dim interior light. The clerk's back was to him as he sorted the last of the letters in his hand, blocking view of box number 23. Billy held his breath as the clerk moved, allowing him clear sight of the box's contents.

Empty.

His throat constricting painfully, Billy was unable to move as the clerk turned toward him with his familiar, gap-toothed smile.

"Sorry. No mail for you."

Billy did not respond.

"A lady was here lookin' for you earlier this mornin', though." He took a step forward and peered over the counter toward the rear corner of the room. "Yeah, she's still here . . . There she is."

Billy turned slowly in the direction the clerk indicated. Stunned incredulity held him momentarily motionless as a slender figure moved out of the shadows there.

"Billy . . ."

Elation exploded within Billy. Closing the distance between them in a few quick steps, he swept Eva off her feet and into his arms, a joy so intense coursing through him that he could not speak as he crushed her close. His mouth finding hers at last, he indulged the familiar warmth of Eva, the sweet taste of her mouth that was hers alone as he drew her closer still.

Trembling, realizing that Eva was just as shaken, as he drew back, Billy assessed her anxiously. She was thinner, painfully so. Exhaustion was plainly written in the shadows of her face, but she was well and whole, and more beautiful to him at that moment than any woman he had ever known.

His throat so thick that he could barely speak, Billy managed, "I thought I had lost you."

Tear-filled eyes overflowing, Eva whispered in a quaking voice, "I was so afraid. It's been so long. I . . . I wasn't sure you still wanted me."

"You weren't sure I still wanted you?" Billy clutched Eva painfully close, but his anger at her uncertainty was self-directed as he rasped, "I want you, all right."

A whimper from the bench behind turned them toward the child lying there, still confined in a canvas sling. Releasing Eva, Billy reached for the babe with a choked laugh. His shaky smile broadened at Christina's gurgling response as he scooped her high into the air. The realization of all he had almost lost suddenly acute, he turned back to Eva and slid his other arm around her to include her in a silent embrace.

Billy's head snapped up as the clerk interrupted with a chuckle. "Seems like you found the lady you was lookin' for." The old man winked, then nodded respectfully to Eva. "I'm mighty glad. There ain't enough happy endin's for an old fella like me these days."

The old man's words rang in Billy's mind as he

emerged into the brilliant sunlight of the street. Curling his arm protectively around Eva as she held the child, he drew her toward the Falmouth Hotel.

Observing from a distance, Jake Hobbs squinted against the sun's bright glare as the unlikely couple made their way down the street.

So, Chesney had gotten himself a half-breed woman and a child . . .

Intuition acquired over years of detective work tugged uncomfortably at Hobbs's mind. He didn't like the unexpected turn of events. The scene of joyous familial reunion he had witnessed through the post-office window would not conform with the free and easy lifestyle of Forbes's gang. He sensed a major disaster in the offing for the investigation to which he had devoted months of his life . . . the investigation on which his reputation depended.

The couple crossed the street as Jake's mind sorted the obvious facts. The woman had been separated from Chesney for a while . . . probably by some misadventure if he was to judge from appearances. She had looked exhausted and unnaturally thin. She certainly would need some rest before any traveling could resume. That would guarantee him a few hours . . .

His expression intense, Hobbs watched until Chesney and his woman disappeared through the hotel entrance. Turning abruptly, he started in the opposite direction.

Lila paused with a brush against the upward sweep of her hair as Garrett turned to glance at the brilliant morning sunlight streaming through the window. Loving memories sent a hot flush to her cheeks as she studied

Garrett's outline in relief against the golden glow of the world outside the silent room. The strength of his profile and the firm line of his jaw . . . the heavy, dark hair lying against his neck . . . an incredible stretch of shoulder . . . the power of muscular arms that had held her so possessively . . . narrow waist and hips . . . long, strong legs . . . He was a beautiful man.

Her eyes briefly closing in remembered ecstasy, Lila recalled Garrett's whispered words of love as he had worshiped her body with his. Her response has been almost debilitating in its depth, excluding all else from her mind but the sound of that voice, the touch of Garrett's hands, and the heat of his flesh against hers. But the rapture of their physical union had been eclipsed by another, gradual realization as Lila had lain in Garrett's arms. In sharing the horror of his past, he had allowed her a glimpse of his inner self, giving of himself in a way that she knew instinctively he had never given before.

Lila swallowed against a sudden thickness in her throat. Yes, she loved him . . . Where once she could not, she now admitted that to herself and she—

Appearing disturbed by something outside the window, Garrett moved, suddenly frowning. In that instant, the old Garrett returned, his light eyes hardening as he adjusted his gunbelt to settle it comfortably low on his hips. The old Garrett was still a stranger she could not understand. She wondered if she ever would.

As if sensing her thoughts, Garrett turned toward her. At her side in a few steps, he drew her against the muscular wall of his chest and dipped his head to trail his lips against her neck. When she did not immediately respond, he pulled back, concerned.

"Somethin' wrong, darlin'?"

Sober, Lila touched the gunbelt at his waist. "You

weren't wearing a gun when you knocked at my door last night. I suddenly realized that I liked it better that way."

Garrett's brief smile was forced. "It's not safe for a man in these parts without a gun, darlin'."

"Most especially a man with a price on his head."

Garrett's gaze became wary. "That's right."

Despite the wariness, Lila saw love in the warm, velvet eyes that had moments earlier been grey ice. She saw a spark of passion, carefully controlled, as she slid her arms around his neck. She fitted herself against him, deliberately fanning that spark as she whispered, "Do you love me, Garrett?"

Garrett did not respond. He had expressed his feelings for her in so many ways during the past night, each lovingly explicit, but he had not said the words. That lapse hung between them, growing ever larger as she pressed, "Do you, Garrett?"

"Lila . . ."

"Why can't you say the words?"

A slow torment grew in Garrett's eyes. "Words are only sounds, Lila . . ."

"No, they aren't. They mean much more. *I'm* not afraid to say them. I love you, Garrett."

Garrett's intense gaze flickered, and a slow apprehension crawled up Lila's spine. A silent war raged behind his eyes as he whispered, "How can you doubt how I feel about you, darlin'? How can I convince you?"

"You can say the words . . ."

Garrett's hand slid up to cup the back of her neck. His fingers massaged the delicate nape as he whispered, "You're in my blood, darlin'. I wanted you the first moment I saw you, when I wasn't sure if the next minute would be my last. That wantin's grown stronger every day until there isn't a moment that thoughts of you don't haunt me, when I don't want you and need you . . ."

"Wanting isn't loving."

A silent torment grew to life in Garrett's eyes. "Lila, darlin' . . ."

"You can't say the words, can you, Garrett?"

"Lila, please try to understand."

"Understand what? That you're sacrificing your future for the past? What happened to Elizabeth and your parents was terrible, but it's over and done. Nothing can change it and nothing can bring them back, especially not making the same mistakes and changing yourself into the same kind of person as the men you hated." She shook her head. "It just doesn't make any sense . . ."

"It does."

"No! The only sense it makes is that you're trying to die, just like they died—violently . . . without reason. I don't want to be any part of that kind of horror."

"You said—"

"I said I love you, Garrett, and I do." Realizing the situation was rapidly moving out of control and into a direction from which there could be no return, Lila continued with increasing emotion, "I . . . I love the man who came to me last night, Garrett, the gentle man who loved me with his heart and soul, even if he didn't say the words. I don't know this other man—the one who lives by his gun. I don't want to know him! I want to forget he ever existed!"

"It's too late for that."

"No, it isn't." An urgent plea entered Lila's voice. "This is a big country. We can leave Denver and go someplace where you aren't known. I saw you working on Luther's ranch. You know cattle and—"

"This argument is a waste of time!" His arms suddenly snaking around her, Garrett crushed her against him. His voice was shaky as he whispered against her hair, "I wish I could explain . . ."

Her heart aching at the torment in Garrett's voice as it trailed into silence, Lila whispered, "You *can* explain it to me, Garrett. I want to understand."

Garrett shook his head, his grip tightening. "You couldn't . . . I can't . . ."

Breaking free with a sudden thrust, Lila took a few steps backward, incredulous. "You can't? Or do you mean, you won't? What's going on inside your mind, Garrett? What's so terrible that you can't share it with me? What's compelling you to—"

"That's my business!" Garrett's expression grew suddenly stiff. "I don't want to talk about it anymore!"

Aghast at Garrett's sudden hostility, Lila whispered, "I love you, Garrett. I can't watch you destroy yourself because of an old grief."

"I already told you—"

"I know what you told me, but if you really love me . . . if you really *want* me—"

"All right, damn it! I love you!" Grasping her arms to hold her rigidly in place, Garrett demanded, "Is that what you wanted to hear? I love you!"

Lila did not respond. The words were right, but everything else was wrong. Instead of love, she read desperation in Garrett's gaze. The words were not enough to overcome the confused anxiety that forced her shaken whisper. "You love me . . . but not enough."

"Enough for what? What else do you want from me?"

Lila paused for a shuddering breath. "I want you to love me enough to put the past behind you. It has to be that way or else I can't—"

"Don't say it, Lila . . ." Garrett's voice grew suddenly gruff. "Don't give me an ultimatum. Don't force me to choose between you."

"*Between* you . . . between Elizabeth and me?" Lila shook her head, her incredulity growing. "Elizabeth is dead! Nothing can bring her back. Your devotion to the past is destroying your present and your future. Can't you see that?"

"Lila . . ." Garrett swallowed tightly. "I've spent too many years—"

"Wasted years . . ."

"No."

"Yes!"

"Listen to me, Lila!"

"I'm done listening! And I'm done wanting and loving a man who feels guilty for loving me . . . a man who's determined to bring me to grief for loving him!"

"Lila . . ."

"No! I don't want to hear it! There's only one thing I want to know. Can you put the past to rest?"

"Not yet!"

"Not yet? You mean not now . . . not ever."

"Lila . . ."

Lila took a short step back. "Please leave, Garrett."

"No, damn it, I won't!"

"Please leave!"

"No."

Lila's eyes were suddenly blazing. "You will if I have to throw you out myself!"

"Lila, you're not thinking clearly. Remember last night . . . this morning . . . It can be like that again. It can be like that for—"

"Get out, I said! Get out!"

Shaking violently, Lila jerked the door open and stood there rigidly, her hand on the knob. "I don't want you. I don't need you. Don't come back."

"You don't mean that."

Locking Garrett's gaze with hers, Lila held it fast as she whispered in a quaking voice, "I never meant anything more . . ."

Garrett's eyes sudden shards of ice that sliced at her heart, he turned abruptly and walked out the door.

Lila stood in the frigid aftermath of their turbulent parting. She closed the door behind him, realizing with sudden, heartbreaking certainty that loving Garrett as she did, wanting him with all her heart, she could not have had it any other way.

Breathless sounds of loving had faded from the room, leaving an exalting silence as Billy and Eva lay in each other's arms. Glancing toward the floor nearby where Christina lay on cushions fashioned into a mattress that had immediately lulled the exhausted child into sleep, Eva turned back to Billy once more. She kissed him lightly, the sweet wonder of his mouth against hers flushing her with a new heat. Resisting the deepening of that kiss as she looked up into her lover's fair, emotion-filled face, she reached up tentatively to trace the line of his brow with her calloused fingertips, then slid her hand into his hair. The thick, reddish-brown curls enveloped it as she slid herself up higher against him. Her dark-nippled breasts brushed his chest as she spread tender kisses against his hair, touching his temple, the curve of his ear, the line of his jaw. She heard his low groan, only to be startled as he gripped her arms to restrain her loving assault. Holding her fast for a silent moment, he touched the freshly healed scar on her arm, his expression resolute.

"No, Eva. I won't let you put me off any longer. I want to know how you got this wound."

Fear seizing her heart, Eva whispered, "Th-there is no use in walking the same path of tears over and again."

"I said I want to know."

"What's done is done."

"Tell me."

Eva averted her eyes. "What sense is there to it?"

"Eva, look at me." Billy forced her face up to his. She saw his lips contort with emotion the moment before he whispered, "I love you, Eva. I didn't realize how much until I almost lost you. I swore to myself that if I found you again, I'd spend the rest of my life proving those words to you. But I can't put all this behind me unless I know what happened. I have to know . . ."

Fear tempered the joy of Billy's declaration of love as Eva hesitated in response. Eva felt the ecstasy of his touch as he stroked her scarred cheek with his fingertips, then her lips. His tenderness more than she could withstand, she whispered, "The wound is nothing. It has healed and the pain is gone. What's important is that we're together again."

"Tell me."

Hesitating a moment longer, Eva took Billy's hands in hers. She placed them against her breast and held them captive there as she whispered, "This heart you feel pounding . . . it beats for you, Billy. It comes to life only when I am in your arms. If you love me as you say you do, you'll—"

"Eva . . ."

". . . you'll forgive all trespasses made against me, for my sake. Will you promise me?"

"Tell me, Eva. I must know."

"Billy . . ."

"Please . . ."

Realizing no choice was left to her, Eva glanced briefly away. Shadows of a remembered terror returned to her eyes as she looked back at him and began slowly, "Charlie Mosbey was a bad man. He saw Christina and me on the street when I went to Mrs. Greer's for milk after you left. He said Christina couldn't be mine . . . that I stole her. He came to the cabin in the middle of the night to take her away from me." She paused. "I killed him."

Billy's hand tightened on hers as a tremor shook Eva, urging her on. She continued in a voice surprisingly void of emotion. "I packed the supplies onto my burro and ran away, but Charlie Mosbey's friends followed me. I couldn't travel fast because of Christina. They caught up with me in the darkness of the second night." Eva took a breath. She released it with another shudder. "I was so afraid . . . I heard scrambling in the darkness around me, and then I heard drunken shouts. I put out the lantern and picked up Christina just as the shooting started. One of the bullets . . ." She touched the scar on her arm. "I grabbed the gun and started running. Christina was so exhausted she didn't even cry, but I was afraid that the next bullet might . . ." Pausing to regain her composure, not realizing tears were cascading down her cheeks, Eva continued in a whisper. "They were shooting wildly. I heard my burro braying with pain, but I didn't stop. They were so drunk . . . I heard someone cry out. They stopped shooting then because they realized they were shooting each other."

Eva looked up into Billy's distraught expression. "I kept running until I couldn't run anymore. Then I found a place . . . an abandoned cabin. I barricaded myself inside and waited with the gun ready, but they never came. I sneaked back when I thought it was safe. My burro was lying dead where he had fallen, but the supplies hadn't been touched. I carried the supplies back to the cabin and stayed there until my arm healed. I started out for Denver then, but I was afraid . . . afraid that when I found you, *if* I found you, you wouldn't want me anymore."

Eva's anguish becoming his own, Billy swallowed tightly. "I didn't realize how much I wanted you until I thought you were gone. I blame myself for all of this. None of it would've happened if I hadn't left you alone and unprotected."

"No, it wasn't your fault!" Eva despaired at his obvious distress. "It was Charlie Mosbey . . ."

Billy's expression grew pained as he caught her hand in his. "I knew the situation I was leaving you in, Eva, and I knew the danger, but I left anyway. I told myself that you'd be all right, that other things were more important. I told myself that my feelings for you were only temporary and they'd soon fade. I *wanted* them to fade, because I resented the way you made me feel. I didn't want to love you, darling. It wasn't part of my plan . . ."

Billy gave a short, choked laugh, then drew her closer. His lips moved against hers as he whispered, "But I was wrong . . . more wrong than I've ever been. I didn't stop thinking about you for a minute while I was gone. I wanted to get back to you sooner . . . but I couldn't. When I finally returned and found you had disappeared . . ."

Billy paused, emotion momentarily overwhelming him. "I searched for you, and with every day that passed I realized more clearly how big a fool I really was. I told myself that if I ever found you again, I'd never let you go. But I couldn't find you and I knew I had failed you again."

"No, you didn't! I—"

"Yes, I did. If you hadn't found me . . ." Billy's voice trailed away only to grow stronger as he whispered in fervent promise, "I'll never fail you again, darling." His gaze uncertain, implored her. "Do you believe me, Eva?"

"I believe you." Eva pressed her mouth lightly against his. "I love you, Billy."

The soft green of Billy's eyes filled. He gave a short, choked laugh. "Love is so damned hard. There's only one part that's easy."

Billy drew Eva tight against him and a singing joy began in Eva's heart as their lips met, as they gave full vent once more to the tumultuous, *easy* part of love.

Seventeen

Garrett walked rapidly down the hotel staircase. His strong, even features were hard as stone, the powerful line of his shoulders aggressively rigid in reflection of his turbulent parting from Lila moments earlier. Reaching the bottom, Garrett jerked his hat brim down further on his forehead, shading the furious glint in his light-eyed gaze as it searched the lobby tensely. Lila's parting words and the obvious pain they had caused her were with him still. Both had cut him to the bone, twin wounds that gushed his life's blood even as another concern nagged viciously at his mind.

Damn that Hobbs! Something was wrong. He had seen Hobbs watching the hotel from a position across the street that was entirely too conspicuous from Lila's window. Hobbs was too much the professional not to have realized Lila would see and recognize him if she looked out. It had occurred to him after his first moment's shock that his silent partner had seen his outline in the window and was attempting to get his attention.

Garrett's lips tightened into a grim line. Well, if that had been his intention, Hobbs had gotten what he wanted, all right. His resulting agitation had been reflected in the turn his conversation with Lila had taken immediately afterward. His regrets were many, but they did not change the result or the sense of impending disaster growing greater within him with each passing minute.

Pausing in the lobby doorway, Garrett surveyed the street. Hobbs was nowhere to be seen. He stepped out onto the walk, his irritation rising.

"So, there you are, Harrison."

Garrett turned abruptly, his frown tightening at Hobbs's unexpected appearance beside him. "That's right, it's me. You wanted me out here, didn't you? There couldn't be any other reason for that prank you pulled a little earlier. It was almost as stupid as meetin' me here where anybody comin' down the staircase can see us."

Allowing Garrett to pull him a few steps down into the alleyway between the two buildings, Hobbs turned toward him with a hard smile. "You don't really think I'm stupid, Harrison, and that's what's agitating you. You're right. I wanted you out of that room . . . quick . . . and I knew there was only one way I was going to do it."

"Why? What's so important that you'd take that kind of a risk?"

Hobbs's lined face tightened. "You're the one who was taking the chance, and you know it. You're not responsible for your actions with that woman."

"I damned well am!"

"You were with her last night."

"That's none of your business!"

"I'd say it is. Everything you do connected with this case is my business . . . but that's all beside the point now. I've taken the matter out of your hands."

"Is that right?" An edge of panic made sharp inroads into Garrett's mind as he grabbed Hobbs's shirtfront in a grip that all but raised the smaller man from his feet. "What did you do, Hobbs?"

"Let me go, Harrison."

"Tell me . . . *now.*"

"I said, let me go."

Garrett snapped his hands free and Hobbs fell a short step backward. He faced Garrett squarely. "I talked to the sheriff."

"You did what?"

"I had no alternative. I haven't studied human nature all these years without learning something along the way. Another day and you'd have told the woman everything."

"I wouldn't!"

"Deny it all you want, I wasn't going to take the chance. The sheriff'll be here within the hour. He's gathering a posse on the next street right now."

"A posse!" Garrett glanced out toward the street. "What in hell did you tell him?"

"I told him I had found a member of Forbes's gang and that he was holed up in a room in the hotel with a woman."

"With a woman!" Fury surged white hot inside Garrett. "You brought Lila into this?"

"Lila Chesney had nothing to do with it. Chesney is in his room right now with a woman and a child."

"A woman and child!"

"The baby is blond and the woman's a half-breed. The baby looks to be his. But that isn't all I told the sheriff. I told him he could get two for one if he was careful because there was another wanted man right down the hall."

"Another . . ."

"I showed him your wanted poster. As far as that sheriff's concerned, you're wanted dead or alive."

"You bastard!"

Hobbs's expression did not change. "I wasn't taking any chances on you wangling your way out of this. I'd say you have about fifteen minutes to convince Lila Chesney that you saw a posse forming on the next street and you're not sure who it's for, you or her brother. I made sure that there were several horses hitched to the rail in back of the building, enough for all of you to make a run for it."

"This story you want me to tell Lila doesn't make any sense, and you know it!"

"Just tell her you came back because you want her to go with you. I'm going back out on the street where I can be seen 'accidentally' from Lila Chesney's window, just like before. She'll believe you when she sees me, and if she believes you, her brother will, too. Chesney will run for the safest place he can think of. That'll be Forbes's hideout. We know it's around here somewhere. He won't have any choice but to take you with him. Then we'll get them." Hobbs's eyes hardened. "We'll get them all."

Incredulous, Garrett studied his partner's face. The man was ice inside . . .

"I won't involve Lila in this."

Hobbs's expression did not change. "You're wasting time."

Turning abruptly, Hobbs stepped back out onto the street. A sudden flush of panic besetting him, Garrett snapped into motion. Back in the lobby moments later, he scaled the stairs to the second floor of the hotel two at a time. He was breathless and relieved of all choice when he pounded on Lila's door.

Her heart jumping to a racing beat at a sudden

pounding at her door, Lila looked up. Wiping the last trace of tears from her cheeks, she paused cautiously.

"Who is it?"

"Open up, Lila!"

Responding instinctively to the threat of panic in Garrett's tone, Lila pulled the door open. Her breath escaped in a gasp at first sight of his agitation as he stepped inside and pushed the door shut behind him.

"What happ—"

Garrett grasped her arms. "There's a posse forming on the next street. It's headed here—for your brother and me."

Startled and confused, Lila rasped, "What are you talking about? Nobody knows either of you are here."

"They know we're here, all right. I heard somebody talkin' on the street. You're bein' watched right now by the same fella I noticed lookin' up at your window earlier. If you don't believe me, look for yourself!"

Garrett's obvious agitation forcing her to comply, Lila moved closer to the window. She followed his direction as he motioned. "Over there, standing partially hidden behind that upright . . ."

"Where? I—" Lila gasped as the man's familiar face moved briefly into view. "Oh, God, it's the Pinkerton . . ."

A wild shuddering besetting her, Lila rasped, "You came back to warn Billy?"

"I don't give a damn about Billy." Garrett's light eyes grew cold at the mention of her brother's name. "I came back because I don't want you in the middle of this when that posse comes." He grasped her arm. "We have to get out of here—now!"

"I can't. I have to warn Billy!"

"You don't have time."

"No!"

Jerking her arm free, Lila pulled open the door and

ran down the hallway. Pounding at Billy's door moments later, she rasped, "Let me in, Billy! Hurry! The sheriff—"

The door snapped open to Billy's white face. Behind him, Lila saw a small, dark woman reach for a child lying nearby. Her mind registered the name Eva, as Billy's narrowed gaze snapped from her to Garrett and back.

"What's the matter, Lila?"

"A posse's forming on the next street. Garrett says they're on their way here. It's that Pinkerton who followed me from Deer Trail! He's watching my window from the street outside. I thought I had lost him, but—"

Interrupting, Billy turned unexpectedly to Garrett, reaching for his gunbelt as he questioned tightly, "You came back to warn *me?* Why?"

Incredulous, Lila pleaded desperately, "What difference does it make? They'll be here any minute!"

"I don't trust him . . ."

"I don't trust you, either, Chesney, and you can be damned sure I didn't come back to warn you!" Garrett's open animosity snapped Lila's head toward him as he grated tightly, "I didn't want Lila gettin' caught up in the middle of a shootout. Stay here if you want, but Lila's comin' with me."

"She's not going anywhere with you!"

"We don't have time for this!" Lila's incredulity soared at the instinctive dislike between the two men. "We have to leave now! Billy, please . . ."

Billy's tense gaze snapped back to her face the moment before he asked abruptly, "Do you trust him, Lila?"

Her throat suddenly tight, Lila glanced up at Garrett. Did she trust him when he said he had come back to save her? Did she believe he loved her? She swallowed tightly.

"Yes."

Her single word of response snapped Billy into motion. Securing his gunbelt on his hips, he reached into his pocket and withdrew his money pouch. Turning to the silent woman behind him, he placed the pouch in her hand and squeezed her fingers tight around it. A sob rose in Lila's throat at the love briefly displayed in her brother's eyes as he whispered into the woman's frightened face, "Take this, Eva. Get Christina out of here now. Walk out the front entrance as if nothing's wrong and then go to another hotel and wait. Don't worry. I'll come for you as soon as I can."

Lila swallowed tightly as Eva's thin face twitched. The young woman's eyes dark with anxiety, she nodded in silent assent the moment before Billy pressed his mouth briefly to hers, his hand lingering as he urged her out the door.

Billy turned back to Lila when they moved out of sight, his lips in a sober line. "It's too dangerous for you to stay here, Lila. I'll take you with me."

"Oh no you won't!" Moving unexpectedly to block the doorway, Garrett growled, "Lila's not goin' anywhere without me!"

"Get out of my way, Harrison!"

Billy's hand slipped to his gun. Her heart leaping, Lila grasped it tightly. "Billy, please . . ."

A silent moment passed before Billy's hand dropped to his side. "All right, let's go."

Down the rear staircase within minutes, Lila gasped as Garrett swept her into the air and deposited her on a horse at the hitching rail. Mounted beside her in a moment, he rasped, "Stay close to me. If you can't keep up, let me know."

"Don't worry about Lila." Billy wheeled his horse around, continuing sharply. "She can handle herself—and what she can't handle, *I* will. Let's go!"

Following Billy as he started for the rear of the alley, Lila turned briefly toward Garrett as he took up a position behind her. The ice in his gaze started a new trembling inside her.

Emerging onto a side street, Lila kept close to Billy's rear as he moved quickly down a maze of alleyways before arriving at the outskirts of town. Glancing tensely behind to find no one visible in pursuit, Billy leaned low over his saddle and kicked his horse into a full gallop. Following suit, Lila heard the sound of Garrett's horse following protectively at her rear. It was her sole consolation as the sudden reality dawned that they were fugitives.

The sun had begun a slow descent toward the horizon when the overgrown trail began to widen. Riding in the lead, Billy maintained a steady pace despite his mount's obvious exhaustion. Like him, Garrett had little thought for their horses' condition as he glanced around him, studying the terrain, committing it as carefully to memory as he had the twisting route that had delivered them to the isolated retreat coming into sight in the distance.

Garrett appraised the cabin silently. Crudely built, with a lean-to for horses visible in the rear, it blended with the surrounding terrain so well that it was almost invisible to the eye at a distance—the perfect hideout for a gang on the run.

His heartbeat quickening, Garrett assessed Lila silently as she rode in front of him. He noted the courageous tilt of her head, but the slump of her shoulders was revealing and his anxiety deepened. His admiration for her had grown as she had kept up the frantic pace without difficulty throughout the long afternoon, but she was exhausted.

As if sensing his perusal, Lila turned abruptly toward him. Her beautiful face sober, her dark eyes pensive, she held his gaze briefly before facing front once more, but the damage had been done. He had seen the vulnerability there, the uncertainty and the fear as the cabin loomed closer.

Garrett swallowed tightly as a sudden realization dawned. Hobbs had been correct. Given another day, perhaps even a few more hours, he would have gone back to Lila's room, taken her into his arms despite her objections, confessed the full scope of his deception, and allowed her to make a choice.

But that option was now gone.

He had underestimated Hobbs. He had not taken into full account his partner's dedication to his work or the harsh reality, clear to him only within the tense few hours just past, that to Hobbs, Lila was merely another spoke in the wheel rolling toward the capture of a dangerous felon and his gang. She had no identity, purpose, or worth to him other than for that purpose, and was easily sacrificed toward that end.

The astute judge of character that he was, Hobbs had calculated Garrett's growing passion and the risks presented and had reacted spontaneously and shrewdly. With one bold stroke, Hobbs had forced his hand, knowing that to confess his deception under the pressure of a potentially disastrous situation could have proved cataclysmic for all.

But disaster still threatened. It lay in wait within the cabin and Garrett chafed at the danger to which Lila would be exposed.

The lean-to in the rear of the cabin suddenly within clear view, Garrett saw several horses tethered there.

He had no doubt to whom those horses belonged.

The remembered scent of burning wood returned vividly to Garrett's nostrils as familiar cries rebounded in his mind. Hatred swelled hot and sharp within him and Garrett's hands balled into tight fists on the reins.

The time had finally come.

Tension crackled on the silence of the small cabin as Billy stood just inside the doorway. He glanced at Garrett Harrison's grim expression, at Lila's white face, then turned back to Forbes's silent fury.

"I told you, I didn't have any choice! A Pinkerton spotted me and a posse was closing in. I had to get away fast."

Livid, Forbes took an aggressive step forward. "What I want to know is why you brought them two along with you! You know the rules! Nobody comes here but us. Nobody!"

"You don't have to worry about Lila . . ."

"I worry, all right!" Forbes's flush darkened. "I don't trust women. I never have. They turn on you like a snake if you give them half a chance. They ain't good for nothin' more than a quick—"

Billy interrupted coldly. "Lila's my sister. She wouldn't do anything that could hurt me."

Forbes swept Lila in open assessment. His expression was snide as he addressed her directly. "Is that right? You wouldn't do nothin' to hurt your brother?" He gave a sharp laugh. "But you don't give a damn about me or the boys here, do you?"

"I told you, she's all right!"

"Yeah, I heard you." Forbes turned toward Harrison

abruptly, and Billy felt his skin crawl. He had seen that look in Forbes's eyes before. Harrison had been staring at Forbes from the moment they had entered the cabin minutes earlier and Forbes didn't like it. He knew that if Harrison didn't do something soon to clear the air between them, they'd be carrying him out the door feet first. Billy's stomach tightened. He didn't want Lila to be a part of something like that. He needed to—

"What about you, Harrison?" Forbes's gaze narrowed into menacing slits. "Are you all right, too?"

"Sure he's all right! I wouldn't have brought him here if—"

"The big man can talk for himself, Chesney!" His gaze trained on Garrett's face, Forbes pressed, "You *can* talk, can't you?"

Billy's hands moved subtly toward the gun at his hip as he glanced around the small, silent room. Eaton was sitting by the fireplace, his beefy shoulders hunched forward as he watched the scene with an unrevealing expression. Picket and Ricks were sprawled on nearby chairs, their casual postures belying the intensity of their stares. They all knew Forbes well enough to sense what was coming.

Billy looked back at Garrett Harrison as the big man responded quietly. "Yeah, I can talk. What do you want to hear?"

"You're a real cute fella, ain't you!" Forbes's cheek ticked warningly. "But I don't like cute fellas who come to my hideout uninvited no more than I like smart fellas who bring them here. What have you got to say for yourself, Harrison? It'd better be somethin' good or you might not be doin' much talkin' anymore."

His mind moving in rapid jumps, Billy saw the fear that widened Lila's eyes and he silently cursed. Calculating the safest place to thrust her if the shooting started, he was rigidly poised for action as Harrison replied, "I don't do much talkin'. Action is more to my likin'. It's been that way since the war, and it isn't about to change now."

"The war?" Forbes's hand remained carefully poised. "What color did you wear?"

Harrison's response was quick and defensive. "Grey, and I'm proud of it!"

Lila turned sharply toward Harrison, but the big man's gaze was intent on Forbes as Forbes pressed, "Gray, huh? Ain't that a shame? You lost the war, didn't you?"

Harrison's expression darkened. "As far as I'm concerned, the war isn't over."

Forbes's sharp crack of laughter echoed on the cabin's silence. "That why you got a wanted poster out on you . . . because you're still fightin' the war?"

"I got a war of my own goin' now. And it isn't about to be over until I'm ready to let it be over."

The crawling feeling on the back of Billy's neck tightened. He saw Lila's growing incredulity at Harrison's response. She was getting a view of the bastard that she had never seen before, and he knew it was cutting her deep. He hadn't wanted her to find out the kind of man Harrison was in such a painful way.

Billy looked at Bart Forbes. Neither did he want her to discover the true viciousness of which Forbes was capable. He had made a mistake bringing her here. He had to get her out as soon as possible . . . and away from Harrison. He knew instinctively, neither would be easy.

Obviously enjoying his tormenting, Forbes pressed Harrison harder. "That right? You got your own war goin'? You about to fight a battle in that war right here, when you're outnumbered? That ain't so smart."

"I've faced worse odds before."

"What outfit were you with durin' the war?"

Harrison stiffened. "That's none of your business."

"Oh, ain't it? Or maybe you don't like tellin' nobody because you're not too proud of—"

"I'm proud enough!" The big man's hands tightened. "I was with General Pemberton at Vicksburg. The Yankees didn't beat us there. They starved the city out. They didn't leave any choice but surrender."

"Surrender . . ." Forbes gave a scoffing laugh. "Pemberton surrendered to Grant, didn't he . . . just handed over his sword like the coward—"

"This's gone far enough, Forbes." Suddenly on his feet, Eaton walked forward, his face florid with anger. "I ain't about to listen to no more, even if I know you're only puttin' this fella on, and I ain't about to let you goad a fellow Confederate into a fight just for the hell of it."

Silent for long moments as the tension thickened, Forbes shrugged. "I was just checkin' the big fella out. He's a little hotheaded for my tastes . . ."

Gruff laughter from the men behind him jerked Forbes's head toward them sharply. "What's so funny?"

Eaton ignored the question, addressing Harrison directly. "Forbes has got a strange sense of humor, bein's every one of us here wore grey as well as he did." Turning toward the bottle on the table, Eaton filled a few glasses. He picked up the nearest one and raised it solemnly. "To them who didn't win and who ain't about to surrender."

Forbes, the last to pick up his glass, stared intently at Harrison as the big man downed his drink in a gulp. Waiting expectantly, Billy heaved a silent sigh of relief as Forbes downed his drink as well. Empty glass in his hand, Forbes turned unexpectedly to Lila.

"As for you . . ."

Harrison's arm snaked out to curl around Lila's shoulder. "She belongs to me."

Billy paused to consider his sister's uncharacteristic silence. Her unusual pallor and the shock visible in her eyes worried him. Billy became more concerned still as she disengaged herself from Harrison's arm and moved to stand at his side.

Forbes's laughter echoed in the silent cabin. "Looks like the lady don't agree! Hell, that's like a woman, ain't it?" Turning back to the table, Forbes poured himself another drink, but Billy wasn't fooled. It wasn't over yet.

Watching as Harrison seated himself on a nearby bunk, Billy was struck with a sudden premonition . . . the abrupt feeling that he might never see Eva's face again.

Lies! They were all lies!

Seated silently beside Billy as the halting conversation around the table grew gradually more relaxed, Lila attempted to control the shuddering that had begun inside her the moment Garrett had started to speak. His gaze unmoving from Forbes's malevolent expression, Garrett had not blinked as one lie after another rolled off his lips. The impact of that shock was with her still.

Lila attempted to sort the startling statements in her mind, suddenly uncertain. Which was the true Garrett? Was he the vicious ex-Confederate she had glimpsed only a few minutes earlier, or the ex-Union soldier who had suffered a tragic loss at the hands of the very Confederates he now defended? Was the story about Elizabeth and his parents all a fabrication he had dreamed up especially for her? Was Elizabeth alive and waiting for him somewhere? Was Garrett intending to return to her?

A new trembling beginning inside her, Lila looked again at Garrett where he sat silently across from her. His face was the same . . . strong, even features, dark brows shadowing eyes that had returned to piercing grey ice. The overwhelming size of him, always intimidating, was also the same, but the man inside . . .

Lila raised a hand to her pounding head as an unexpected giddiness assailed her. Billy's arm snapped around her. The light green of his eyes darkened with concern.

"Are you all right, Lila?" She felt his arm tighten at her nod. She heard the true regret in his voice as he whispered, "I'm sorry about all this, honey. You don't know how sorry I am."

A prickling sensation at the back of her neck caused Lila to turn abruptly to meet Garrett's gaze . . . the hard, cold gaze of a stranger . . .

"You surprise me, you know that, Forbes." Eaton's amused voice cut into Lila's thoughts, drawing her attention as he continued. "You take every chance you get to tell them war stories you're so fond of. How come you ain't tellin' Harrison about your glory days?"

Forbes poured himself another drink, remaining silent as Eaton gave a short laugh. "Forbes is a hero, did you know that? Him and me was in the same outfit, both of us wearin' that grey uniform you're so proud of, but it was Forbes who outdone himself. Quantrill was so impressed that he made Forbes one of his lieutenants. You should've seen him when we was with Quantrill in Kansas. He didn't let a single bluebelly get away . . . not a one!"

Quantrill . . . Kansas . . .

A slow realization, hot and paralyzing, began creeping across Lila's mind as Eaton continued. "We was with Quantrill in Lawrence. Quantrill had been workin' himself up to that one for weeks. He hated that town since the days of the Border War and he swore he was goin' to make every man pay for the way he was treated there." Eaton laughed again. "We gathered outside the town before daybreak, about four hundred and fifty of us. We closed off all the roads so nobody could escape, and at dawn we stormed into town. Hell, it was like shootin' fish in a barrel! We hit the Eldridge Hotel first, and after it was surrendered, we set it on fire and scattered over the town. That measly pocket of raw recruits they had stationed there was no match for us, and when they was gone, we made sure we finished off all the other men in town, uniformed or not. By ten o'clock there wasn't a buildin' or a man left standin' anywheres around!"

Lila did not feel Billy's arm tighten around her as ripples of shock swept over her. She saw nothing but Garrett's impassive facade as Eaton continued. "Quantrill . . . that was a man . . ."

Suddenly on her feet, Lila started toward the door.

"Where are you goin'?" Forbes's voice was harshly nasal.

Holding herself steady with supreme strength of will, Lila responded with equal abruptness. "Outside."

"You don't need to go out."

Lila raised her chin, desperation forcing a coolness to her tone she did not feel. "Yes, I do."

Forbes stood and took a belligerent step forward. Billy stood as well as Eaton interrupted the uneasy scene in a voice tinged with disgust. "What's the matter with you, Forbes? The lady needs some privacy."

"Yeah?" Lila could feel the bite of Forbes's gaze. "Is that right?" He turned to bark, "Sit down, Chesney!"

before addressing her again with a familiar sneer. "Take all the time you want, lady, but don't get no ideas about goin' nowhere. Remember, your brother and me'll be waitin' for you to come back . . . and I ain't a patient man."

Intensely aware of the warning in Forbes's words, Lila turned toward the door. Within moments she had slipped into the pale light of dusk. Standing outside, her hand on the door latch, she breathed deeply in an attempt to still her quaking.

Oh, God, now she knew . . .

"Where do you think you're goin', Harrison?"

Suddenly realizing he had risen automatically to his feet, Garrett turned back toward the sound of Forbes's rasping inquiry. "Eaton ain't finished them war stories yet."

"It isn't war stories I've got on my mind right now." Barely controlled, Garrett continued tightly. "And I'm not about to let anybody stop me from talkin' to my woman."

"Your woman?" Forbes's hoot of laughter echoed in the silent cabin as he turned toward Billy. "What's the story here, Chesney? Is your sister his woman or is Harrison just indulgin' in some wishful thinkin'?"

Garrett shot Chesney a sharp glance. He was surprised by the steel in Chesney's boyish features as he responded, "That's my sister and Harrison's business."

Forbes's expression went slowly cold. "Are you tellin' me to mind my own business, Chesney? Because if you are—"

"Damn it, Forbes, I've had enough of this!" Snapping to his feet, Eaton slapped his hand down on the table, the sharp crack of sound startling everyone in the room as he continued hotly. "You're bound and determined to make a fight of this tonight, ain't you? Well, I ain't about to find myself in the middle of a shootout just because you got some kind of bee in your bonnet about Chesney!"

"I ain't got no bee in my—"

"You and I know better, Forbes, and I ain't goin' to argue with you! Harrison wants to go out to talk things over with the woman. You don't have no worries there. She ain't goin' nowhere without her brother."

"Says you."

"Yeah, that's right." Eaton glanced toward Garrett. "Go ahead out if you want. Just remember, if we hear you makin' any move toward them horses in the back—"

Not bothering to respond, knowing he was going out into the yard after Lila at any cost, Garrett turned toward the door. Closing it behind him, he stared out into the descending darkness. A slender shadow moved in the purple twilight, and Garrett strode directly toward it.

"Don't come near me . . ." Her voice emerging in a tortured rasp, Lila halted Garrett within a few feet from her. She stretched her arms out in front of her as if to ward him off as he took another step forward. "Stay back, I said!"

"Lila . . ."

"Don't say anything. I don't want to hear any more lies."

"Lila, darlin' . . ." The pain in Lila's voice registered deep inside Garrett despite his anxiety. "It's too dangerous for us to argue here."

Lila's voice dropped to a harsh whisper. *"You're* the danger here . . . a danger no one recognizes. I know who you are . . ." The heated flood of emotion that flushed hotly to Lila's face was visible even in the meager light as she rasped, "You told Forbes that story about being a Confederate at Vicksburg. I couldn't understand why you were lying to him. Then I realized that maybe you weren't lying to *him* . . . that maybe you had lied to *me* when you told me about Elizabeth."

"I didn't lie to you . . . not about that."

"I was at a complete loss until Eaton started talking about Lawrence. Then everything started falling into place." Lila took a choking breath. "You knew about Billy being a part of Forbes's gang all along. You found me somehow at the Bar WK and waited for me to lead you to Billy. You knew I would sooner or later if you stayed close enough to me . . . if you made me trust you . . ."

Lila took another shaken breath, her voice emerging in a hiss. "You're a Pinkerton . . ."

Garrett stiffened, but there was no denial. The slow dread of confirmation sweeping over her, Lila continued in an incredulous hush. "All the while I was running from that other fellow, the drummer . . . all the while I believed myself safe in your arms, you were using me . . ."

"No, Lila, that isn't true! Darlin', listen to me!" Grasping her arms, Garrett held her fast despite her desire to break free. She heard the anguish in his deep plea as he whispered, "We don't have much time. You're in danger here, and your brother is, too."

"Don't tell me about danger!" Lila was shuddering, the realization that she was responding to the thread of torment in Garrett's voice despite her revulsion sent shock waves through her confused mind. Furious, she spat, "You're the one who's really in danger! One word from me and Forbes will—"

"Is that what you want?" Pulling her against the hard

wall of his body, Garrett wrapped his arms around her, binding her to him with his strength as he whispered hoarsely against her hair, "I never expected . . . I never intended this to happen, darlin'. You were just another lead when Hobbs first brought up your name. Then when we found you . . ."

Lila stared up at Garrett, cursing the shadows shielding him. "You were working with that other man all along . . . laughing at me. You used me . . . used my anxiety about my brother against me."

"I didn't know he was your brother. I thought—"

"You didn't know he was my brother!" Another harsh realization dawned, cutting Lila deeply. "No, of course not! You thought he was my lover, didn't you! Lila Chesney, saloon woman of easy virtue, an easy mark . . . and I fell right into your trap!"

"It wasn't like that! Lila, listen to me."

"No, I'm tired of listening, and I'm tired of being used!" Incensed, Lila was again struggling. "Let me go, damn it!"

"You have to listen to me, Lila!"

"No!"

"Damn it, be still!"

"Let me go or I'll—"

"Or you'll what?" Garrett held her fast. His voice was harsh with threat, his breath hot against her lips. "You don't have any damned choice other than to keep quiet about this. You saw the kind of man Forbes is. Don't think Eaton or the others are any different! If they find out your brother brought a Pinkerton here, they'll kill us all without batting an eye."

Lila's struggles came to an abrupt halt. "They wouldn't hurt Billy!"

"You don't really believe that . . ."

Momentarily silent, Lila rasped, "You thought of

everything, didn't you . . . even a way to make me betray my own brother."

"No, I didn't! I never wanted . . . I never thought . . ."

A sound behind them jerked Lila and Garrett's gazes toward the cabin doorway where Eaton's rounded figure was silhouetted against the light from within. They remained silent as he called, "Are you out there, Harrison?"

Garrett stiffened, his arms tightening spontaneously around her as he responded gruffly, "Yeah, I'm out here."

"Forbes is gettin' tired of waitin' . . ."

"That's too bad because he's goin' to have to wait a few damned minutes longer!"

Eaton gave a brief, mirthless laugh. "I wouldn't make him wait too long . . ."

Pausing until Eaton had walked back inside, Garrett jerked Lila into the shaft of light from the doorway. His gaze clear to her for the first time, he whispered earnestly, "Look at me, Lila, and listen to me, because your life depends on it. I haven't been completely truthful with you in the past, but I'm telling you the truth now when I say everything's gone too far for you to try to turn it around now. The only thing you can accomplish is to get yourself hurt. I don't want that to happen. Darlin', please . . ."

"Bastard!" Lila shuddered, hating the part of herself that wanted desperately to believe him.

Garrett continued hoarsely. "You're right. I lied to you. I manipulated your concern for your brother to my advantage. I sacrificed your trust to find Forbes. I did all those things, but I didn't lie—I'm not lying now—when I say I love you."

Suddenly enraged, Lila jerked herself free of Garrett's

grasp. Her single word of response was passionately intense.

"Liar!"

Back at the cabin door in a flash, Lila paused to wipe her face free of tears. She raised her chin, willing away all sign of weakness as she opened the door. Suddenly conscious of Garrett's presence close behind her, she walked into the room and silently assumed her seat.

The cabin door snapped closed, shutting out the slim shaft of light that had rent the encroaching darkness outside. Silent shadows within the foliage stirred. Shifting, they gradually took on human form as Jake Hobbs raised himself from his concealed position and peered at the silhouettes moving against the carelessly draped windows.

Hobbs's eyes narrowed. He hadn't heard it all, but the fury in Lila Chesney's shaking voice and Harrison's low, passionate response could not be missed. Harrison obviously had been upset, but he knew Harrison's anxiety was not for himself.

Making a sudden decision, Hobbs slipped out of the shadows and moved closer to the cabin. He listened to the low rumble of conversation within, slowly raising himself so he could peer through the slitted window covering. Harrison was seated on a bunk, his expression unrevealing as Chesney and his sister sat nearby in silence. The heavy fellow who had come to the door was playing cards at the table with three other men, one of whom could only be Bart Forbes. A harsh snap of conversation between the men confirmed that fact and Hobbs felt a hot rush of satisfaction.

They were all there . . . ready and waiting . . .

Hobbs slipped back into the shadows. In a moment he was gone.

The rhythmic, croaking sounds of night rang outside the small cabin, reverberating in a silence within that was broken only by uneven snores and the almost imperceptible movement of the tall man in his bedroll on the floor.

Turning slowly to his back, Garrett surveyed the sleeping forms around him. He looked at the lower bunk nearby, his gaze stopping cold as Bart Forbes shifted in sleep. Every muscle in his body tightening, Garrett viewed the man's easy repose. The dreamless sleep of the conscienceless . . .

Struck with sudden rage, Garrett struggled to control his trembling. Burned into his mind was the moment of confrontation when he had walked through the cabin door and met Forbes face-to-face for the first time. He had recognized Forbes immediately. Years spent in that devoted quest had flashed before his eyes in a kaleidoscope of fragmented, painful images that had left him momentarily impotent against the overwhelming swell. He had been silently stunned that a man so depraved, so evil as to epitomize the word, could be so unimpressive in size and stature.

But then he had seen Forbes's eyes. It had all been written there, in the shift of his slitted, erratic gaze and in the inherent cruelty traced in the downward slant of the lines that marked his face. Transfixed, he had read every dissolute thought, every act of wanton brutality, and his outrage had soared. So subservient did he become to the turbulence of his emotions for those few, paralyzing moments that he had been powerless against them.

And then he had heard Lila's name.

It had hit him then . . . the full danger in her exposure to Forbes. Cursing himself, reading Forbes's instantaneous animosity toward him, he had fallen back on instinct, carefully manipulating Forbes by telling him what he knew the fellow would want to hear. But he had underestimated Forbes's vicious bent. He had no doubt that Forbes would have attempted to sate the blood lust that had glowed in his eyes had it not been for Eaton's unexpected interference.

Garrett closed his eyes briefly against realization of what might have happened then . . . at the risk he had inadvertently exposed Lila to with his momentary lapse. His only consolation had been in seeing Chesney's concerned glance at Lila and the subtle movement toward the gun on his hip that signified he would have used that gun to protect his sister at any price.

Garrett searched the shadowed cabin with his gaze in further assessment. Picket—thin, dark, and cautiously silent—had folded his gangling frame into the bunk bed above Forbes early in the evening, but the ploy had not fooled Garrett. The fellow had been observing everything that happened from his perch, without blinking an eye.

Ricks, his perpetual grimace exposing tobacco-yellowed teeth as he scratched his matted beard with maddening consistency, had spoken only in gruff whispers to Eaton and Picket. Ricks had scrutinized Forbes in a watchful silence that had caused Forbes to flare up on several occasions before the fellow had finally slapped down the cards and followed Picket's example to retire for the night.

Eaton . . . A taste as bitter as bile rose in Garrett's throat as he recalled Eaton's boastful praise.

Quantrill . . . that was a man . . .

Garrett's heart began a furious pounding. Eaton had not mentioned that Quantrill had gotten his due when he had been shot while raiding in Kentucky . . . or that it had taken him a month to die.

Garrett's small smile was cold. He would remind Eaton of his praise of Quantrill soon . . . very soon.

His gaze flicking to the man lying in his bedroll a few feet away, Garrett perused Billy Chesney's sleeping figure. He frowned, uncertain. Chesney was the odd man out here. Younger than the others by some fifteen years, he also appeared to have a shorter history in their game if he were to judge by the disparaging comments made by some of the other members of the gang. He sensed that Chesney had been accepted begrudgingly by them and that they were uncomfortable with the volatile, silent rivalry that radiated from Forbes's intense scrutiny of the younger man. The situation spelled a danger he could not fully understand and had not anticipated.

Looking to the far corner of the room where Lila lay, as he had so many times since the cabin had gone dark, Garrett felt a wave of almost debilitating anxiety overwhelm him. Loyalty and love for her brother had brought her to this particular peril, but he was not totally free of blame. He had compounded the problem now facing them by losing her trust when he needed it most. He needed to restore that trust before it was too late.

Making a sudden decision, Garrett threw back his blanket and drew himself up to his knees. Beside Lila in a few strained moments, he paused, looking down into her sleeping face. An aching hunger for her surged to pain as he reached out to touch her unbound hair, a gleaming halo in the pale light streaming through the ragged window coverings. He remembered its fragrance, its silky texture, its warmth . . .

Lila's clear face twitched. An expression of abject sorrow slipped over her small, perfect features, stimulating a corresponding sorrow within him as her lips parted with a soft sound of despair. The single tear that slipped from the corner of her eye to trail into the curling tendrils at her temple more than he could bear, Garrett leaned over her to brush the damp silver path with his lips. One taste not enough, Garrett touched his mouth to hers, his breath catching in his throat as Lila's lips moved under his. The taste of her was sweet, intoxicating, calling for more as he slipped his arms around her, drawing her close. He—

"Get away from her, Harrison . . ."

A voice to his rear snapped Garrett toward the sound as Lila awakened abruptly. Meeting Billy Chesney's furious gaze, Garrett heard Lila's soft exclamation.

"Garrett . . . Billy . . . What happened?"

Garrett grasped Lila's fluttering hand, holding it steady as she drew herself to a seated position. "I wanted to talk to you."

"Yeah . . ." Billy Chesney sneered. "You wanted to talk . . ."

Garrett's anger flared. "It's none of your damned business what I wanted to do, Chesney!"

"It's my business, all right!" Inching closer, his voice a rasping hiss, Chesney glared into Garrett's face. "My sister doesn't want any part of you."

"Your sister can talk for herself!"

"Not when she's sleeping she can't, and I'm not going to let you go crawling all over her when she can't defend herself!"

"Lila doesn't have to defend herself against me."

"That isn't the way it looked to me."

"I don't give a damn how it looked! If you really cared about your sister you'd—"

"How much *Billy* cares about me was never in doubt." The ice in Lila's gaze returned. "Leave me alone, Garrett."

"You heard her, Harrison . . ."

Lila turned stiffly to her brother. "I can take care of this, Billy. I've made it clear enough how I feel."

"That's right, and the bastard hasn't moved an inch. So I think it's time to get some things straight, once and for all." Billy's green eyes sparked fire as he addressed Garrett with growing heat. "I don't like you, Harrison. There's no way I would've let you come here if it hadn't been for my sister. I don't know what happened between the two of you, but it looks like she's come to her senses somehow, and I'll be damned if I'll let you force yourself on her again."

"You hypocritical bastard . . ." His anger rising, Garrett returned the heat of Chesney's ire. "You've done nothin' but take from your sister. It's your fault she's in the middle of this now, and she—"

"Right . . . you're right . . ." Billy interrupted Garrett with a low growl. "I let her down, but I'm not about to do it again by letting her get bowled over by somebody else who's going to let her down. You're not good enough for her, Harrison."

Lurching forward, Garrett grasped Billy's shirt in a twisting grip that caught the younger man off guard. "I told you this is none of your damned affair and I'm not going to—"

A sudden kick from behind sending him sprawling, Garrett raised himself to hear Forbes interject harshly, "You ain't doin' nothin', Harrison!"

His gun snapping into sight as Garrett started toward him, Forbes laughed low in his throat, a chilling sound that crawled up Garrett's spine as Forbes continued. "It's time for some plain talk, so here it is. I don't give a damn about the woman. The whole damned lot of you can have her for all I care, but if there's any trouble in this cabin, it's goin' to be *me* who makes it . . . understand? I didn't want Harrison or the woman here, but now that they are, I'm not takin' any damned chances. Nobody's leavin' this cabin until I'm ready to make my move."

Billy's light eyes narrowed. "I don't know what you got in mind, Forbes, but I'm taking my sister out of here as soon as I think it's safe for us to get back on the road."

Forbes laughed again . . . a laugh filled with menace. "Sounds like you're goin' to give me the excuse I've been waitin' for, Chesney. But just remember, my gun don't make no distinction between a man or a woman . . . and you know I mean what I say."

Garrett cursed under his breath as Billy snapped, "What've you got in mind, Forbes?"

Forbes's small eyes turned hard. "You've queered this place for us for good . . . you know that. I wouldn't put it past this big bastard to find a way to collect the reward on us by leadin' the law back here as soon as he gets a chance."

"You're crazy! Harrison's wanted by the law, too. There's no way he—"

"Don't tell me there's no way! There's always a way if you want to do somethin' bad enough. But it won't make no difference after we pull our next job. We'll have enough money to move on west, where nobody'll find us."

Billy stiffened. "How long are we supposed to wait to pull this job?"

"Don't get anxious, Chesney." Forbes laughed again. "Only three days."

"Three days . . ." Silent, Garrett saw Chesney glance at Lila. "I guess three days'll be all right."

"You're damned right it will!" Forbes swung his gun again between the two men in silent warning. "Get back to your bedrolls and stay there. If I find either one of you sneakin' around again, it'll be the last time."

Unwilling to respond, Garrett drew himself to his feet. He returned to his bedroll, noting that Chesney did the same. His gaze flicked back to Forbes as the man walked slowly toward him.

Halting a few feet away, Forbes leaned down to pick up Garrett's gunbelt. "This stays with me until you leave."

Forbes turned back to his bunk, and Garrett cursed under his breath as he strained to see into the corner of the room. Lila was no more than a rigid outline against the meager moonlight streaming through the window, but he felt her distress.

Forbes's nasal tone cut the uneasy silence with a final warning. "Remember what I said. Don't give me the chance I'm waitin' for. I won't turn it down . . ."

Looking back at Lila, Garrett saw her sudden quiver of movement before she lay down abruptly and turned to her side. A sense of impending disaster never stronger in his mind, Garrett stared up at the ceiling in silent frustration.

There had to be a way . . .

Lila struggled to control her convulsive shuddering as she drew her blanket up over her shoulders. Pulsating tension radiated from the darkness around her as a fear deeper than any she had ever known trailed down her spine.

What had she done?

Controlling the sob that rose to her throat, Lila attempted to force the sound of Garrett's deep voice from her mind.

I didn't lie to you when I said I loved you . . .

Pain twisted sharply within her. She had been trapped by Garrett's lies and she had allowed those lies to trap Billy as well.

Another fear suddenly accosting her, Lila recalled the small man . . . the drummer. What had Garrett said his name was? Hobbs? Where was he now? Had he followed them to this place? Was there a posse surrounding the cabin at this very minute?

Lila paused in an attempt at rationality. No, Billy had taken too many precautions. No one had followed them here. Garrett would need to sneak away to alert his fellow Pinkerton, but there was little chance of that now.

Suddenly uncertain which of the many threats in this small cabin was the most dangerous, Lila felt the urge to laugh hysterically. She was at a complete loss, forced into keeping a perilous secret from her brother simply because knowing might put him in even more danger . . . forced to watch and wait helplessly because all other options had been taken from her.

Lila's frustration soared.

There had to be a way . . .

Eighteen

Lila walked swiftly back up the heavily foliated trail toward the cabin, agitation gnawing at her. The frightening incident with Forbes the previous night was still fresh in her mind. It haunted her, dulling the effect of the brilliant sunshine filtering through the leafy cover overhead and the sweet scent of the morning air. She had been allowed a few minutes privacy to visit the stream and bathe. She knew Forbes had taken great pleasure in the warning he had issued as she had walked out the door, reminding her whom she left behind. She had seen the spontaneous tightening of Billy's expression and she had wondered then, as she had many times since she had entered the cabin the day before, how Billy could have associated himself with such a despicable man.

Smoothing back a sun-bleached strand of hair that had escaped her careless topknot, Lila paused as the cabin came into view within the trees. She despaired at the thought of returning to the tension of Forbes's veiled gaze, the silent question in Garrett's light eyes, and the quandary she could not escape.

Oh, Garrett . . . Rising tears choked Lila's throat. Why did you say you loved me? Why did you eliminate my defenses one by one until I had given you my heart full measure when you only meant to betray me?

Closing her eyes, Lila submitted to the flood of memories assaulting her: Garrett's tender, hungry abandon when they first came together and the rise of an emotion that equaled in scope and then surpassed the fire of their former conflict; the sound of rain drumming on the roof and the sweet smell of hay beneath them as crashes of thunder orchestrated their ardent lovemaking; the softly flickering light of her hotel room and a passion so fierce and consuming that she still trembled in its wake; the bittersweet joy of revelation and the sound of Garrett's quaking voice as he opened his heart to her to relate . . .

The memories turned abruptly cold.

Lies . . .

Lila opened her eyes, inadvertently releasing the tears confined there. She had believed Garrett completely. She had pleaded with him to leave a life that had never existed for him, not knowing that the man returning her fervent gaze, the man who held her intimately in his arms, who claimed to love her, was deceiving her.

I didn't lie when I said I love you, Lila.

No, not true! Lila spoke silently, directly into the grey velvet eyes of the image in her mind. *Vengeance was always your true love. You lusted after it with a passion that paled the anemic emotion you felt for me. You pledged your troth to it long ago, with an unholy vow more powerful than any we could ever make to each other.*

Oh, Garrett . . . how much I could have loved you . . .

Taking a stabilizing breath, Lila brushed away her tears. She had been a fool, but that was over and done. She must now find a way to ensure that Billy would not suffer for her mistakes. She had three days before anyone would be allowed to leave the cabin . . . three days to come up with a plan.

That thought in mind, Lila started forward again only to halt abruptly at a stirring in the trees ahead of her. Her heartbeat escalating to a roaring thunder in her ears, Lila fell a step backward, slipping into the foliage beside the trail. She crouched, straining her eyes . . .

Another brush of movement . . . A man moved briefly into view. Gasping, Lila saw another man . . . and another! The glint of steel caught a ray of morning sunlight, and Lila's heart turned to lead in her chest. There were so many of them! Their guns were drawn as they moved closer to the cabin. No one inside would stand a chance if they—

Springing to her feet, Lila began running toward the cabin. She called out . . . !

Snatched from her feet from behind before the sound could emerge, Lila was dragged helplessly backward. A hand clamped tightly across her mouth muffled her cries as a male voice hissed into her ear, "Be quiet! You can't save any of them now. All you can do is start a bloodbath. Is that what you want?"

Struggling wildly, fighting the unrelenting grip of her captor, Lila managed a glance behind her. The shock of recognition left her momentarily weak. It was he . . . the drummer . . . the man wearing the hat with the faded snakeskin band!

Lila's senses returned abruptly, raising a great swell of hatred as she fought harder, her arms swinging wildly, her feet kicking as she was held above the ground with a strength that belied the man's modest size. She was still struggling vainly when the man rasped, "Don't be a damned fool! Do you want everybody in that cabin to get killed!"

Her captor's sobering words halted Lila's protest, availing him the opportunity he sought as he pressed relentlessly into her ear, "Why do you think we're waiting out here? We could've gone in ten minutes ago, but we didn't want it that way."

Lila sought to respond past the hand clamped over her mouth. She saw the Pinkerton's gaze narrow as he began to speak. "I'll take my hand away if you give me your word not to cry out. Will you do that?"

Lila nodded.

The Pinkerton studied her intently. "You know what'll happen if you're lying to me now. Your brother's in there . . . and Harrison. Bad things have a way of happening when bullets start flying."

Lila nodded vigorously. She breathed deeply as the Pinkerton's hand fell from her mouth.

Lila Chesney turned to face Hobbs squarely. Her dark eyes wide saucers of reflected fear, her creamy skin blanched of color, a stark contrast with the brilliance of her upswept hair, the delicate perfection of her features unmoving and her womanly body intent, she appeared a frightened doe, frozen, expectant.

Hobbs's understanding for Harrison's plight was suddenly never clearer.

"Your name is Hobbs . . ."

Hobbs was momentarily incensed. "So, Harrison did tell you about me!"

Answering his question with one of her own, Lila Chesney pressed uncertainly, "What are you going to do?"

"What do you think we're going to do? The Agency's been after Bart Forbes for a long time. You were the only lead we had. I thought for a while it wasn't going to pay off, but it did. We've got him now, and we aren't going to let him get away."

"I don't care about Forbes or the others. I don't care about anybody but Billy. He isn't like the rest. He—"

"He's part of the gang, isn't he?"

"Yes, but—"

"But what?" The graceful curve of Lila Chesney's jaw twitched as Hobbs pressed. "Your brother's not going to get any special treatment from us . . . not unless you earn it for him."

"What do you mean?"

"You know what I mean. If you cooperate with us, we'll do our best for him. At the very least, he'll stand a chance of getting out alive."

Lila's dark eyes searched his face for the truth of his response. The incredible length of her long, sweeping lashes fluttered against her cheeks as she summoned strength from deep within her, and Hobbs was momentarily entranced. Damn . . . it was no wonder Harrison had fallen under this woman's spell! As hard a case as he himself was, he wasn't so sure he would've acted any differently if she had—

Lila's gaze was again intent. "How do I know I can trust you to keep your word?"

Hobbs gave a low snort. "What choice do you have?"

An angry flush colored cheeks previously void of color as Lila hesitated, then spoke abruptly. "All right. What do you want me to do?"

"I have one question." Hobbs's scrutiny intensified. "Is your brother the only person in there you're interested in helping?"

Lila did not respond, forcing Hobbs to continue. "I don't mind telling you that your brother isn't my concern. He's in there because he chose to be in there, but

I'll be damned before I'll throw a good Pinkerton to the wolves without making a try to save him."

Lila Chesney's lips tightened. "What do you mean?"

"What do you think'll happen if Forbes finds out we've got the place surrounded? Hell, he'll figure it all out in an instant. He'll turn on Harrison, and if Harrison isn't fast enough with his gun—"

"Forbes took Garrett's gun last night."

Hobbs's jaw tightened. "Well, that's the end of it for him."

Lila swayed unexpectedly. Hobbs grasped her arm to steady her, only to have her shake him off. "I'm all right."

Annoyed, Hobbs pressed, "Well, what are you going to do about it?"

"What *can* I do?"

Hobbs was silent for long moments before speaking. "I'm in charge out here. The sheriff and his men are waiting for my signal before they make a move, because they know I've got a man in there, but I don't mind telling you that their trigger fingers are twitching. If you're going to help, you're going to have to work fast."

Fear flickered across Lila's beautiful face, changing abruptly to determination. "Tell me what you want me to do."

His anxiety carefully concealed, Hobbs began slowly. "Here's the plan . . ."

Garrett glanced toward the spot where his gunbelt lay across Forbes's bunk, his stomach churning. The incident with Lila the previous night had turned into a fiasco that had given Forbes the opportunity he had been seeking to take his gun. There had been no way he could have objected without starting a war he could not win. He had yielded with little grace, and Forbes had enjoyed every moment of it.

Glancing toward the table where Forbes was sitting with his men, he watched the dispute ensuing with little satisfaction. Eaton, Picket, and Ricks were united in their objection to striking the same train again so soon, with Billy Chesney wisely abstaining. Chesney was no fool. He knew Forbes was angry, and he also knew the danger in that man's anger.

Garrett's scrutiny intensified. Eaton was talking while Picket and Ricks nodded in agreement, but the outcome of the discussion was a foregone conclusion. He had less than three days to figure out a way to contact Hobbs.

His agitation growing, Garrett looked toward the window again. Lila was out there somewhere. She was taking too long to come back. He didn't like it. If she had done something foolish, he—

As if in response to his thoughts, the door opened abruptly. Lila stood hesitantly in the opening, the sunlight from the yard beyond glowing against her hair, a glittering halo framing her sober face as she glanced toward the table where the men were gathered. He saw her take a short, relieved breath when Forbes glanced at her briefly and turned back to his men. She looked at Garrett then, her gaze lingering with a tight control that caught his own breath in his throat. He took a spontaneous step toward her, the sudden warning in her eyes halting him abruptly as a slow realization began forming in his mind.

His heart beginning a heavy pounding, Garrett looked out into the yard beyond Lila, then back at her stiff face. Confirmation was written in Lila's sudden flush.

Hobbs . . .

Panic touched Lila's gaze briefly before she raised her chin and walked casually toward the table where Billy Chesney stood observing the heated discussion. She stopped beside her brother and touched his arm, looking up at him as he turned toward her. She whispered a few words, only to have Forbes turn abruptly toward them.

"What are you whisperin' about?"

"She said—"

"She can talk for herself, Chesney!" Forbes focused on Lila's unsmiling face. "I asked you what you said."

"I told Billy his horse was lying down out back and that he didn't look good."

"What do you know about horses?"

"Lila knows as much about horses as any man. She—"

"Maybe *I* should go out and check on that horse myself." Forbes's gaze tightened, pinning Lila. "What would you think of that?"

Lila shrugged. "Suit yourself, but if somebody doesn't check on him soon, you're going to be short one horse when you leave here."

"No, we ain't. We'll just use Harrison's . . . or yours. Neither of you will be needin' your horses for a while."

Billy took an aggressive step forward. "What do you mean by that?"

"Just what I said! You don't think I'm goin' to turn these two loose when we go to hit that train." Forbes's short bark of laughter was harsh. "Hell, I thought you was smart, Chesney! They're goin' to stay right here, tied up in nice little packages until we come back."

Billy's boyish face grew livid. "You're not going to tie my sister up."

"I ain't, huh?" Forbes rose slowly to his feet, his

hand moving a cautious distance from his hip. "Who's goin' to stop me?"

"I've had enough of this!" Springing suddenly to his feet, Eaton stepped between the two men, forcing Lila a staggering few steps backward against Forbes's bunk. She sat weakly as Eaton continued hotly. "You're gettin' crazier every day, Forbes, what with those dreams that keep warnin' you to be careful, and now this wild scheme that's goin' to get us all killed. I don't give a damn about Chesney or them other two he brought along with him. You're gettin' to be a bigger threat to us than they could ever be! I told you before, and now I'm tellin' you for the last time . . . I'm not about to go ridin' into the hands of the law just because you want to prove somethin' to yourself!"

"Is that right, Eaton?" Forbes's tone took on a sinister note. "What do you intend doin' about it."

On their feet in a moment, Picket and Ricks moved backward cautiously, watching as Eaton and Forbes faced each other with ominous intent. Billy's warning glance brought Lila immediately to her feet as well. She retreated rapidly to stand at Garrett's side.

Startled, Garrett accepted the gunbelt Lila slipped from behind her skirt as she whispered, "Hobbs is outside with the sheriff. He's coming in in a few minutes. I didn't get a chance to warn Billy. Please—"

"What's goin' on over there? What are you two whisperin' about?"

Livid, Forbes started toward them, only to have Billy grip his arm roughly. "Leave her alone."

"Take your hand off me!"

"I'm warning you, Forbes. Leave my sister alone."

"You got a short memory, don't you, Chesney? You ain't no match for me with a gun. And if you're expectin' help from that big fella over there, you're wrong because his gun is lying' on my—"

Forbes's words turned to a growl of rage as he glanced toward his bunk to see Garrett's gunbelt gone. His hand flashed to his hip as Billy shouted, "No!"

Reacting instinctively, Garrett thrust Lila to the floor, covering her body with his as gunshots echoed within the cabin. He scrambled to withdraw his gun from his holster as Forbes fell to the floor, as the cabin door burst open and the firing began in earnest.

Gunshots . . . loud, in rapid succession, shook the room, accompanied by sharp cries of pain and the thuds of bodies hitting the floor.

Silence.

Straining his gaze through the acrid mist of gunsmoke, Garrett raised his gun to see Picket clutching a wound in his shoulder. He snapped an anxious gaze toward the motionless forms on the floor.

Eaton, his bulk crumpled into an inert heap . . . Ricks, moaning softly . . . Forbes, his lifeless eyes staring upward . . .

Chesney . . .

Stunned, Lila raised herself from the floor. Garrett's expression was anxious, his grey eyes dark with concern as he drew her to a seated position beside him. She felt his hands tremble as he touched her face, her hair, her shoulders and arms, searching. She heard his rasp of relief at finding her whole, but the emotion of the moment escaped her as her gaze jerked to the still forms lying on the floor a short distance away.

A slow, keening wail beginning inside her, Lila was on her feet in a moment. Swaying, she brushed off Garrett's supporting grip as she took a few staggering steps forward, then fell to her knees beside Billy. She touched his chest, her heart leaping as she felt it moving in shallow breaths. Looking up at Garrett, she rasped, "He's alive! Quick . . . help him!"

Billy's eyelids flickered at the sound of her voice. Unconscious of the sob that escaped her lips, of the tears cascading down her pale cheeks, Lila looked again at the rapidly expanding stain on his chest. She turned to the men behind her, her voice a broken plea.

"Please . . . he needs a doctor."

The scramble of footsteps behind her produced a grey-haired man who dropped to Billy's side. She watched as Billy's chest was bared to reveal a ragged hole there, and she gasped aloud.

"Billy . . . oh, God . . ."

Billy's eyelids flickered again. They rose slowly, but the brilliant green beneath was glazed as his gaze fastened uncertainly on hers. Leaning forward, Lila stroked Billy's cheek, her voice a shaken whisper.

"Don't worry, Billy, you'll be all right."

His gaze wavering, Billy grasped her hand. "Promise me . . ."

His breath spent, Billy was not immediately able to continue, and Lila leaned closer. His face was grey, his lips pale. Sudden realization shaking her, she clasped his hand tighter, straining to hold the life that was rapidly waning.

"What do you want me to promise, Billy? Tell me. Talk to me, Billy, please!"

Retaining her gaze with obvious difficulty, Billy whispered, "Eva . . . tell her . . ." His breathing was ragged, but he forced himself to go on. "Tell her . . . sorry . . . love her. Help her . . ."

"Why are you saying these things, Billy?" Panic tightened Lila's throat, raising the timbre of her voice as she clutched his hand tighter. "You're going to be all right."

"No . . ."

"Yes, you are! You—"

"Promise . . ."

"Billy . . ."

"Promise . . ."

"I promise. Billy . . ."

Billy's eyelids fluttered closed. Lila heard a rattle low in his chest . . . heard a single, fiercely gasping breath.

Stillness.

"No!"

Filled with a rage greater than any she had ever known, Lila gripped Billy's shoulders and shook him roughly. "Open your eyes, Billy. Open your eyes!"

There was no response.

Reality striking a mortal blow, Lila was suddenly unable to breathe. Billy would never open his eyes again! He would never flash his boyish smile or fold her into a laughing embrace. He would never again say her name.

Billy was gone . . .

Gasping, Lila did not react to the strong arms that gripped her shoulders, drawing her to her feet. She felt nothing as she was drawn against a broad chest, as strong arms closed around her. She did not protest as a hand gripped her chin, raising her gaze to grey eyes as soft as velvet . . . grey eyes that—

Her eyes suddenly snapping wide, Lila shoved roughly at Garrett's chest, freeing herself.

"*You* did this!"

"No, Lila, I—"

"You planned it all from the beginning!" Lila's words escaped with a sob. "You lied to me! You made me trust you, then you used my trust! You made me *kill* Billy . . ."

"No! You didn't kill Billy, and neither did I. Billy made his choice. He—"

"He didn't choose to die!"

"He didn't—"

"Liar!"

"Listen to me, Lila."

"Liar!"

"Lila, please . . ."

"Liar!"

"I love you, Lila."

"Liar, liar, *liar!*"

Her rage overwhelming, Lila took a swaying step backward. The glint of metal on the floor nearby caught her eye, and she scrambled toward the gun lying there. Snatching it up into her hand, she turned in a rapid movement. The world stood still in the flashing moment Garrett's shocked gaze met hers . . . as she raised the gun . . . as she leveled it and pulled the trigger!

The blast of gunfire . . . a cry of pain.

Shock.

Incredulity!

Darkness.

The rattle of a wagon . . . a canine whine . . . an occasional burst of laughter . . . the echo of casual conversation . . .

Lila awakened slowly from a dreamless sleep as sounds from the street made slow inroads into her unconsciousness. Disoriented, she blinked at the brilliant shaft of sunlight shining across her bed, at the dust motes dancing in its glow. She touched the coverlet stretched lightly over her, glanced around her at the unfamiliar room, her gaze coming to an abrupt halt at first sight of the short, thin fellow standing a few feet away.

The man approached her bed, and Lila's breath caught in her throat. He was clean-shaven now, his clothing meticulously clean, his hair freshly cut, but she recognized him instantly. The drummer . . . the man wearing the hat with the faded snakeskin band. Hobbs.

"I see you're feeling better. You've been unconscious for several days."

Several days . . . Lila closed her eyes.

"The doc says you'll be all right. It was just the shock."

Lila's breathing grew rapid. The echo of gunshots . . . the red wash of blood . . . No, she didn't want to think. She didn't want to remember—

"There's somebody here who wants to talk to you."

"Lila . . ."

Lila gasped as Garrett stepped between them.

The snap of the door closing behind Hobbs registered in Lila's mind as Garrett moved closer. He was tall and strong, the black of his hair gleaming, his dark brows furrowed, his gaze intense. She watched in silence, her breathing growing more agitated as he came to sit beside her bed. But his skin was pale, his expression strained as he drew closer.

"No, I'm not a ghost. You didn't even pull the trigger. You fainted. The gun discharged when it fell from your hand. No one was hurt."

A slow trembling started inside Lila. "No, you're wrong. Someone was hurt. Billy . . ."

"Lila, you have to understand . . ."

"What do you want me to understand?" Trembling, Lila rasped, "That you're a Pinkerton . . . that my brother was a criminal . . . that he deserved to die?"

"No, he didn't. Lila, listen to me . . ."

"Why? So you can explain that you did what you had to do? I don't believe that. I'll never believe that!"

"Lila, please . . ." Garrett's handsome face twisted into a mask of pain. "Billy—"

"Don't speak his name!"

"Lila, please . . ."

"Go away."

"Please, darlin' . . ."

"Go away!"

"Lila, I want to tell you—"

"I can never forgive you . . . never."

"Lila, let me explain—"

"LEAVE ME ALONE!"

The door opened. A grey-haired man she had seen once before entered as Lila pleaded wildly, "Make him go! I don't want him here . . . not now . . . not ever!"

The doctor took her hand. "Don't excite yourself, Lila. It isn't good for you."

"Make him go!"

At the doctor's sharp nod, Garrett turned toward the door. Black devastation overwhelmed her as the door clicked closed behind him.

Her breathing ragged, Lila turned away. She had lost Billy, and she had lost the man she loved. This Garrett . . . this malevolent stranger who had just left . . . was the man who had killed them both.

Sobbing, Lila buried them with her tears.

Nineteen

The grey stillness of dawn had yielded to another day, with brilliant sunshine and blue sky stretching unmarred above the Bar WK as far as the eye could see. A crisp breeze stirred the air, the forerunner of the change of seasons as Luther walked silently across the ranch yard. His cleanly cut features sober, his mind intent, he gave little notice to the advance of fall tingeing the hillside foliage with color or the high-pitched whinny of the new colt prancing in the corral.

The scent of baking bread wafted from the kitchen window, cutting into his thoughts, and Luther raised his head. Aunt Helga had returned to the ranch a few weeks earlier, declaring that Mary Barnes and her twins no longer needed her. She had boldly inquired if he wanted her to stay. The silent commiseration in her eyes almost more than he had been able to bear, he had nodded and taken in her bags. He had regretted his ungracious acceptance of her generous offer in the time since, but he knew Aunt Helga understood.

The simple comforts of life to which he had grown accustomed during Aunt Helga's former residence had returned with her—hot meals, clean clothes, the life a woman brought to a house. Max had found it difficult to hide his pleasure at Aunt Helga's return, and Luther had been startled by the bond that had developed between his good-natured hired hand and his blunt but well-meaning aunt without his realization. He had been ashamed of the envy that had beset him, an envy that still nagged at times, despite his greatest efforts to dispel it.

Modesty . . . The name produced the same deadening sense of loss each time it appeared in his mind. Modesty was gone, but she had not left empty-handed. She had taken with her the satisfaction he had previously obtained from simple accomplishments, and the joy he had formerly found in each new day. But most damaging of all, she had stolen his dreams, in which his vision of the future and thoughts of their life together had become hopelessly entwined.

Luther paused, bitterly amused. He could not seem to make himself understand that Modesty had never truly been Modesty. He could not seem to get it through his head that the woman he had grown to love with all his heart had never really existed at all.

Lila had explained that to him in her farewell note when she had left without saying goodbye.

Garrett Harrison had explained the rest.

No one, however, had explained why he could not forget her.

Taking a moment to push the corral gate closed, Luther looked back at his limping bay, then turned toward the house. He had returned from the high pasture when his mount had come up lame that morning. Max had manufactured an excuse to accompany him back, and Luther had not been able to refuse him despite the need to repair the downed fencing that had greeted them that morning. His new bulls were an aggressive lot. They allowed nothing to stand between them and what they wanted . . . unlike he himself, who had been a fool.

In the time since Modesty . . . *Lila* . . . had left him, Luther had reviewed the time they had spent together over and again in his mind, wondering how different things might have been if he had taken a more forceful course. Modesty . . . *Lila* . . . had cared for him. He was not so great a fool that he had not read the signs in the warmth of her gaze, in her halting whispers, and in her growing contentment in his arms. He was also not so great a fool that he had not realized when she had begun drawing back from him.

The clear, honest blue of Luther's eyes darkened with silent anger and the generous curve of his mouth grew tight. Harrison—a Pinkerton—had supplied the reason for Lila's deception. Her love for a wanted man had been stronger than her growing feelings for him. Strangely, he knew that Harrison, the bastard that he was, had been able to accept the hard truth of Lila's love for that unknown man no more easily than he.

Stepping up to the door of the house, Luther cleaned his boots carefully before walking into the parlor. The room was silent and empty . . . like him. He walked to the side window, frowning at the barren laundry lines visible in the backyard where Modesty . . . no, *Lila* . . . had met him with a smile among the billowing linens. He looked at the garden with weeds now abounding, remembering . . .

He ached with remembering.

A sound in the distance drawing him abruptly from his thoughts, Luther turned toward the front window. His first sight of the approaching wagon in the distance hardened his frown.

The wagon drew nearer.

The occupants became identifiable.

Luther was unable to move as his heart began a rapid pounding. His chest heaving, his sober face flushing with anger, he watched the wagon draw steadily closer.

Max was in heaven. The smell of baking bread, the comfortable warmth of a kitchen filled with its scent, the heartening, reassuring presence of the oversize, buxom woman who bustled between table and stove as she added chopped vegetables to the pot steaming there . . . Max sighed contentedly.

"That food smells mighty good, Helga."

"Ja?" Helga turned abruptly toward him, her sagging jowls swaying. "You like? Is goot. *Mein* Herman like, too."

Max frowned. Helga had not mentioned *"mein* Herman" too often since she had returned to the ranch. He had believed at first it was a conscious effort in view of Luther's distress, but as the weeks had passed, he had begun to tell himself it meant more.

Max's old heart gave a little leap. He knew it meant more to *him* because never . . . *never* . . . had he been happier.

The guilt of his thoughts flushing his face with color, Max was grateful Helga was otherwise involved and did not notice his sudden discomfort. It was not as if he was indifferent to Luther's distress. Rather, it was the comfort he took from Helga's presence that had given his days new meaning . . . the realization that she was there preparing for their return while they worked, that she would be waiting with her clipped words of encouragement should they appear disheartened, and the knowledge that she, too, had begun to take simple pleasure from the hours that they spent alone, talking in the kitchen after supper.

Helga turned toward him in the course of her work and Max felt his smile reach to the tip of his toes. He surveyed her soft grey hair, always neatly bound; her large, slightly protruding eyes, still keen and brightly inquisitive; her rounded, rosy cheeks, the sign of a woman who had come to terms with the years; and her full lips, which often spoke curt, sometimes harsh words never meant to harm.

Helga was beautiful.

A swell of warmth rising within him, Max knew the time was fast approaching when he would be forced to speak his thoughts. If it was not today, it would be tomorrow when—

"Ach, what is dis? Someone comes?" Helga moved closer to the side window and stared at a wagon coming into view on the portion of road visible there. Gasping, she turned abruptly toward him, excitement flushing her full face. "Is Doc's carriage! Is Doc and *her!"*

Beside Helga in a moment, Max peered through the shiny windowpane, then swallowed tightly. "You're right. They're here!"

Max took a deep breath.

The time had come.

Helga was still gaping through the window when Max took her arm and turned her firmly toward him. His voice wobbled briefly as he began, "H-Helga, there's somethin' I got to say . . . and I got to say it right now." Nervous tremors crawled up Max's spine as he took another strengthening breath. "I . . . I know you've been hopin' and waitin' for this day to come since you mailed that letter. I've been waitin' for this day, too, but not exactly for the same reason. You see, it came to me that once that wagon gets here, things'll be out of our hands. Things might change, and I wanted you to know that what I got to say ain't influenced by anythin' other than what I really feel."

"Something is wrong?" Helga's keen eyes studied Max's obvious anxiety. Her response was typically short. "You must speak."

Max gulped. His hairy brows twitched. "All right, I will. I've been doin' a lot of thinkin' these past few weeks, Helga. I've been thinkin' that I'm not as young as I used to be. The bloom of youth has faded, but . . . uhh . . ." Max's voice momentarily failed. Regaining it, he continued in a rush. "But since I got to know you real good over these past few months you restored a youth to my heart that was gone for many years."

Max flushed. His Adam's apple bobbed vigorously as he forced himself to continue. "What I'm tryin' to say is that I can't think of nothin' I'd like better to do with the time I got left than to spend it with you . . . gettin' closer and sharin', givin' what we can to each other . . ." His eyes bulging, Max swallowed hard, "Lo-lovin' each other . . ."

Helga's eyes bulged as well.

"What is dis?"

"I'm sayin' that I ain't got much to offer you, Helga. Just a few dollars tucked away in the bank in town, a horse, my health, and a heart full of love that I want to give to you. I . . . I'm tryin' to tell you that I love you, Helga, and I want you to be my wife."

Helga's jaw dropped.

The silence between them, long and extended, ticked by with Max's mouth growing more dry with each passing second. Her face flushing bright red, Helga snapped her mouth closed at last. She attempted to speak, was unable, and tried again.

Finally successful, Helga stammered, "You want to *marry?"*

"Ja. I mean, yes. I mean . . ." Max shook his head in absolute confusion. "What I mean is that I want to marry you more than I ever wanted anythin' in the world."

Helga's mouth opened again but no sound emerged, and Max silently groaned. She tried again, her words finally emerging with honest incredulity.

"Am homely!"

"That ain't true!"

"Am old!"

"I ain't so young myself."

"Am fat!"

"Not too fat for me."

"Have *three* chins!"

"And each one of them damned fascinatin' . . ."

Helga paused. She shook her head. Appearing almost dazed, she whispered, "You are not like *mein* Herman. *Mein* Herman was handsome man. Had blue eyes, like der sky . . . not brown. Der skin was soft and pink . . . no whiskers sticking out of wrinkles on der cheeks . . . no gold tooth in der mouth . . ."

Max's heart squeezed tight in his chest. He took a step back, his eyes filling. His distress intense, he was about to turn away when Helga reached a stubby hand toward him. She rested it warmly on his chest, her eyes filling as well.

"You are not like *mein* Herman, but you make *mein* heart full." Helga moved a step closer. "Am old woman, but can see brown eyes are as goot as blue, when dey are true." She reached up to touch his cheek. "Can see der skin is tough, but der heart is not." Helga's voice failed uncharacteristically, and Max's throat choked full with emotion as she touched his lips. "Der gold tooth . . . it does not change words dat come from der heart." Her small smile tremulous, Helga whispered, "Der gold tooth is beautiful. Will marry you, Max. Will be goot wife . . . and will love you."

His heart suddenly filled to bursting, Max threw his arms around Helga. The cushion of her soft flesh against him was more wonderful than he had dreamed, and he sighed with wonder as her strong arms gripped him firmly in return. Drawing back, he tilted up her chins . . . all three of them . . . his heart singing as he pressed his mouth to hers. He drew back several blissful moments later, a chuckling coming from the bottom of his heart at the widening of Helga's eyes as his faithful old soldier rose firmly against her to salute the occasion.

Kissing her again briefly, Max drew Helga against his side. He then forced his gaze through the windowpane, aware that Helga did the same as the approaching wagon drew to a halt in the front yard. A happy but tense silence between them, they each held their breath . . .

Luther's lean body went rigid as the rattle of the approaching wagon halted outside the front door. He did not move at the sound of light footsteps advancing. An overwhelming swell of heated emotions rose in him as a knock sounded at the door. The second knock started him slowly forward, his breathing ragged. He drew the door open.

The uneasy silence lengthened as Luther searched the sober face returning his gaze. Anger and pain forced a harshness to his tone as he finally spoke.

"What are you doing here?"

The woman standing in front of him was dressed conservatively in a traveling dress of a somber hue. Her sandy-brown hair was confined in a tight bun under a bonnet that did nothing to enhance the smooth, plain lines of her face as she looked up at him through small, round glasses. She was familiar to him without being truly familiar at all, and Luther's heart lurched to a new depth of aching. He had once awaited this woman's arrival with eager anticipation, but her appearance now did nothing more than increase his bitterness.

Unwilling to make the first move, Luther stood stiffly as Modesty Parkins stared up at him. Her serious gaze blinked and her throat worked convulsively as her look of uncertainty expanded to a subtle trembling. Her thin lips twitched in the moment before she began softly.

"Hello, Luther. I . . . I'm late in arriving . . . too late for many things, I know. I don't know if I'm welcome here, but I had to come."

Modesty paused, awaiting a reply. When it did not come, she blinked again, then continued. "I couldn't live with myself any longer . . . not with the terrible thing I did to you. I made a mistake . . . a mistake I've regretted with all my heart from the first day I arrived back in New York. I cursed myself for being a timid, spineless fool and for allowing panic to overwhelm me before I traveled those last few miles to meet you face-to-face. I know I have no right to ask your forgiveness, or to expect it, but I cannot rest unless the words are said."

Modesty searched Luther's still face for a sign of encouragement. When there was none, her voice dropped to a new level of sadness. "My regrets are deeper than you will ever know. I know you've suffered because of my cowardice and that words will never erase the memory or the pain. You have every right to despise me and you may never forgive me, b-but I'm sorry, Luther . . . so very, very sorry. If I had it to do over again . . ." Modesty gave a short, unexpected laugh. The sound caught strangely in her throat, emerging as a sob as she forced herself to continue. "But we can't change the past. We can only regret it with all our hearts . . . as I do now. Luther . . ." Modesty reached out a hand that hung tentatively in the short distance between them as she rasped, ". . . if you could forgive me . . . please."

All emotion frozen inside him, Luther surveyed Modesty's small, plain face. She was Modesty as he had originally expected her to appear, with none of Lila's perfection of feature. She was frightened, uncertain—the woman of the shy, gentle letters who had endeared herself to him as she had gradually revealed a side of herself now hidden behind her grief. He knew her regrets were many and sincere, just as his were. He was familiar with that kind of pain.

If he could change the past . . .

But he could not.

He had no choice but to go on.

A smile somehow beyond him, Luther accepted her hand.

Twenty

A uniformed guard walked silently ahead of Lila, leading her through winding corridors that were long and grey. The air was stale. Sounds echoed: footsteps, the opening and closing of heavy, metal doors, occasional angry shouts.

No words were spoken as the corridors came to an end and she was admitted into a small room. The door snapped closed behind Lila and she looked around her. The room was no different than the others she had seen since arriving. The walls were grey, almost colorless. It was simply furnished with a long, scarred table and chairs. Small windows, set high on each of two walls, were barred.

A deep sadness within her, Lila waited, her heart leaping at the sound of footsteps approaching from the room beyond. A sound at the door . . . the rattle of the knob . . . the door opened . . .

Lila gasped at the thin male form silhouetted briefly in the doorway. She did not move as the guard urged the man into the room with brief instructions and closed the door behind him, leaving them alone.

Lila's breath escaped in a sudden gasp.

"Billy . . ."

Rushing toward her brother, Lila threw her arms around him. She hugged him tight as he slid his arms around her in return. Locked in a silent, bittersweet embrace, they did not speak for long moments. Lila was still incapable of speech when Billy drew back at last.

His youthful face contorted briefly with emotion as he tried to speak. His short laugh was choked. "So, I guess you're glad I'm not dead after all." He laughed again. "Damn, I'm happy to see you, Lila. I didn't know how much I could miss you."

"I missed you, too, Billy."

Her heart an aching lump lodged in her throat, Lila swallowed hard. Billy was thinner, even younger in appearance after his narrow escape from death. She raised her chin, consoling herself that he would regain his former weight and strength now that he was well again.

Lila forced a smile. "You're looking better, Billy. Stronger."

"Yeah." Billy touched her cheek with trembling fingers. "I guess prison agrees with me."

"Oh, Billy." Lila's voice was pained. "I'm so sorry. I didn't want this to happen."

"Neither did I. I couldn't quite believe it at first. I kept going over everything in my mind while I was lying in that bed in the hospital, wondering if the next day would be my last. He attempted a smile. "It took me a long time, but I finally came to terms with everything." His smile grew sad. "You always were the smart one in the family. Too bad I was too hardheaded to listen to you."

A familiar agitation stirred inside Lila, raising the heat of tears. "This is all my fault. If it wasn't for me, you wouldn't be in here now."

"No . . . no, that isn't true." Billy drew her with him to some nearby chairs. "They would've caught me sooner or later. I know that now. I suppose it's better they caught me sooner, before I wasted any more years, or before I—"

Choosing not to complete that thought, Billy seated Lila and sat opposite her. Leaning forward, he took her hands in his. "Lila, I have some things that I should've said to you earlier . . . that I would've said if I hadn't been too involved in my own selfish little world to think of anybody but myself. That's why I wrote and asked you to come as soon as I got here, because I wanted to set some things straight."

"I would've come sooner, Billy, but I wasn't even sure they had transferred you here."

"I know . . . I know."

"Oh, Billy . . ."

"Listen to me, Lila. I want to apologize to you."

"No." Lila shook her head, adamant. "No."

"Yes . . . please. Eva finally told me everything. She told me how sick you were after I was shot. She told me how you suffered."

"I . . . I thought you were dead. I thought they were lying to me when they told me you weren't, and I didn't believe them." Lila took a deep breath against the remembered horror. "There was so much blood. I was certain I had heard you take your last breath." She shuddered. "I told *him* I'd never forgive him for that . . ."

"Garrett Harrison . . ."

Lila could not make herself say the name. "I trusted him, Billy. I believed every word he told me, and I made you trust him, too. He betrayed my trust. He betrayed me, and he made me betray you."

"You didn't do anything to me. I did it to myself. Lila, look at me." Forcing her to meet his steady gaze, Billy whispered, "I've done a lot of thinking. I've gone around and around about all this, and now that I look back on it, I ask myself why I got involved with Forbes in the first place. He was a cold-blooded killer, Lila. And the truth is, if he didn't end up killing me, I probably would have become just like him."

"No!"

"Yes . . ."

Lila shook her head, incredulous. "Why . . . why did you stay with him if you believed that?"

Billy's lips tightened, his anger tinged with self-disgust. "Because I was too stupid to see things as they really were. Because I was vain enough to believe I was smarter than Forbes was . . . that I could manipulate him just like I had manipulated everyone else. Because I was living high and I was filled with the excitement of it all. Because I believed I could surpass Forbes in everything with just a little more experience. Because for a while . . . too long a while for me to admit with comfort . . . I not only wanted to be like Forbes, I wanted to *be* Forbes."

Billy refused to flinch under Lila's shocked gaze. Instead, he continued quietly. "Forbes knew it. He was waiting for me to make my move. It was a cat-and-mouse game we were playing, with me too damned much of a fool to realize that Forbes was the cat, and the result of the game was a foregone conclusion. But then I met Eva . . ." Billy's jaw twitched revealingly. "Everything started changing then. I started to realize that sooner or later I was going to have to make a choice. But that choice was taken away from me suddenly, without warning, and Eva was gone. You know what happened then, Lila. It was too late when I realized what was really important to me. There had been too much water under the bridge . . ." Billy halted abruptly, frowning. "But I didn't ask you to come here to talk about my mistakes. I wanted you to come so I could see you and thank you."

"Thank me?"

"For helping Eva . . ."

"Oh." Lila's slow smile was tremulous and sincere at the mention of the quiet, soft-spoken woman she had come to know so well. "She loves you, Billy. She's going to wait for you. She has a job now. A good one. A woman named Molly McCann needed someone to help her at her boardinghouse in Denver. It was perfect for Eva and the baby."

"Eva told me you arranged that for her and you've been watching out for her. She's happy there, and she feels safe." Billy nodded, his eyes again moist. "I've told myself I'll make it all up to Eva when I get out . . . and I will." Billy paused, his scrutiny intensifying. "But there's only one way I'll be able to forgive myself for everything I put *you* through, Lila. I have to know you're happy. Are you happy?"

The ache inside Lila deepened as she forced a smile. "I'm doing fine." She winked and curled a shoulder clothed in bright-green velvet forward as she cocked her head flirtatiously. "Don't I look happy? I'm back working at a job I do well. There's not a man within three hundred miles who can beat me with a deck of cards, but that doesn't stop them from trying. Those stubborn fellas are making me rich."

"Lila, honey . . ." Billy's gaze pinned hers. "Answer me. Are you happy?"

Lila's bright facade faded under Billy's direct assault. Her eyes filled with her whispered reply. "I suppose . . ."

"What will it take to make you really happy, Lila?"

"I don't know."

"Can Garrett Harrison make you happy?"

The deadening ache within Lila deepened. "No. Not anymore."

Billy swallowed with obvious emotion. "I . . . if you knew I didn't bear Harrison any hard feelings for what he did, could you forgive him?"

"It's too late."

"Lila . . ." A new maturity reflected in his gaze, Billy whispered, "I've said this before, but I've never meant it more than I do right now. I want you to be happy."

Releasing her hands, Billy stood up and drew Lila to her feet beside him. Sliding his arms around her, he hugged her again.

"Be happy, Lila, please . . . for me."

Releasing her unexpectedly, Billy walked back to the doorway where he had entered. Lila was still standing when he left her . . . when he slipped out of sight.

About to turn away, Lila was stopped by the muffled exchange beyond the door.

She knew that voice . . .

Frozen with incredulity, Lila was unable to move as the door opened again and a taller man stepped into the room.

Garrett . . .

Struck rigid with the sudden assault of memories, Lila recalled the sweet scent of hay and the rumble of thunder as Garrett's arms held her close. She saw shadows flickering against a hotelroom wall and relived a sweet silence broken only by gasps of loving sounds . . .

Garrett advanced toward her without speaking. He was the Garrett of old, massively proportioned, darkly intense, menacing in stature and demeanor . . . the Pinkerton who had betrayed her.

His gaze met hers and the metamorphosis began.

Eyes of grey steel melted to liquid silver filled with anguish. Strong features set in stone softened with longing. Powerful arms capable of crushing strength reached out to her in mute appeal. That appeal touched her heart. She—

Harsh reality abruptly intruded, turning Lila sharply toward the door. Her hand on the knob, she heard Garrett's whispered rasp. "Lila, please . . ."

The sound sliced viciously at her heart as Lila turned back to Garrett with sudden fury.

"Please . . . I hear you speak the word, but I don't know what you mean, Garrett. Please *what?* Please forgive you for using me? Please ignore your betrayal? Please forget that you made me suffer the pain of believing my brother died in my arms because of you? Please strike everything from my mind simply because my brother miraculously survived? Please forget that it was all a lie, each time you held me in your arms, each time you kissed me, each time you made love to me, and each time I loved you in return?"

"No . . . no, it wasn't!" Grasping her arms with open distress, Garrett whispered, "I never lied when I said I lo—"

"No! I won't listen!" Lila wrenched herself free. "You don't love me! You don't love anyone! You've forgotten how!"

"Lila, listen to me." Garrett took a short step closer. "You're right. Yes . . . I had forgotten how to love. All those years of searchin' . . . hatin' . . . took their toll. I was empty inside when I found you, but then things started to change. I hated you for that. I told myself what I felt for you was nothin' more than the same lust I had felt for other women over the years. I was sick with guilt for lovin' you. Like a damned fool, I struggled with my feelin's, cursin' myself, cursin' you, followin' the whole damned charade through until it was too late to turn back."

Shaken, Garrett continued. "Then there he was, standin' in front of me—Forbes, the man I had been seekin' for more years than I could remember. But there was no sense of elation or victory at havin' finally tracked him down. All I felt was a growin' fear that it would happen again, that when all was said and done, I would lose the woman I loved!"

Touching her cheek with trembling fingertips, Garrett rasped, "I haven't been able to get that day out of my mind. I keep seein' and hearin' everythin' that happened over and again. Forbes turnin' with his gun drawn, your gasp when I pushed you out of the way, the sound of your body hittin' the floor at the same moment the gunfire started. And I remember the fear . . . oh, God . . . the fear, that when the shootin' was over—"

Momentarily silenced by emotion, Garrett paused before continuing. "All those years of searchin' . . . When it was over at last and Forbes was lyin' on the floor dead, I didn't even care. All that mattered was that I could see in your eyes that I had lost you just as completely as if his bullet had struck your heart."

Garrett's throat convulsed with emotion. "I tried to tell myself you'd feel differently when you came out of shock and realized Billy wasn't dead. But you didn't. I told myself that when Billy recovered, everythin' would be all right. But it wasn't."

Pausing once more, his light eyes anguished, Garrett whispered, "I know you hate me, Lila. I suppose I can't blame you, but I want you to know that when I held you in my arms . . . when I made love to you, there was never anyone between us . . . never. I loved you then. I love you now."

His chest heaving from the strain of emotions held

strictly in check, Garrett whispered softly, "There's just one thing I have to know. You said you loved me, too, before it all went bad. Did you love me . . . really love me . . . even for a little while?"

So shaken that she could barely stand, Lila managed a trembling nod.

His voice filled with the agony of his words, Garrett questioned, "Lila, darlin', if you loved me . . . why couldn't you forgive me?"

Love . . . forgive . . .

The words hung on the air between them, prolonging the pain. They joined the echoes of other words that returned to reverberate in Lila's mind.

Be happy, Lila . . . please, for me.

Love . . . forgiveness . . . happiness . . .

You're sacrificing your present and your future for the past, Garrett! The past is over and done. Nothing can change it . . . especially not making the same mistakes again. It doesn't make any sense . . .

No, it didn't make any sense.

Lila's gaze traced Garrett's impassioned face. This man had hated her. He had fought loving her with all his strength. He had lost the battle, but the love had survived.

A sudden tremor shook Lila. She had hated Garrett, too. She had also fought loving him with all her strength, but somehow the love had survived.

Forgiveness . . . love . . . happiness . . .

Oh, God . . . Lila's breath escaped in a sob. Garrett had spent so many years in bitterness, excluding love from his life. She had almost done the same . . .

Her eyes welling with all the words she could not speak, Lila took a tentative step forward. She saw a spark of hope spring to life in Garrett's eyes as his gaze raked her face. She felt the spark burst into flame as his arms closed around her with a soft, gasping sound. She felt the blaze encompass them both as she turned her mouth up to his to bury the past at last with a silent pledge as deep as a vow.

Loving her, knowing he would never again let her go, Garrett returned that vow wordlessly, passionately, with all his heart.

Epilogue

The room was silent except for the early-morning chirping of birds and the whinny of a horse echoing from the sunswept roll of land beyond the open window. The bed was warm, the covers thrown back as two figures lay intimately entwined.

The perspiration of mutual passion still moist between them, Garrett raised his head to look down into Lila's still face. Skin like cream—peach cream where it had been touched by the sun . . . dark, passionate eyes, now closed, resting a thick fan of lashes against her flushed cheeks . . . small features too perfect to seem real . . . a generous mouth, a giving mouth, a loving mouth, for which his desire never ceased. His heart skipped a beat. She was beautiful, and she was his.

Lila opened her eyes. She brushed his cheek with a loving touch he had come to know well and he caught her hand with his. He turned the palm to his lips. His eyes closed briefly as he tasted it, as a familiar hunger surged anew, despite the lovemaking recently past.

God, he loved her . . . He loved the scent of her, the taste of her, the feel of her. He had not believed his feelings for her could possibly increase in scope, but they had. They had grown until each waking moment was impressed with Lila's image, until each thought rang with the sound of her name, until every hope and dream that entered his mind bore her mark upon it. She was his love, his life, his wife . . . his tomorrow. It was a wonder to him how he had managed to live without the joy of her. He knew he never could again.

Garrett's gaze grew solemn. His Pinkerton days over, he was a rancher and a husband. His nightmares had been dispelled and he was whole again—all because of Lila. Lila's love had been strong, consistent, and heart-stoppingly passionate, almost a match for his own. Yet, for a short time after their marriage, Lila's heart had not been at peace. She had written a letter then, and he recalled the day the letter bearing the Bar WK seal arrived in return. She had been puzzled at the unfamiliar feminine script and was stunned to discover that it had belonged to Modesty Parkins. She had gasped with surprise upon learning that Modesty had become Modesty Parkins Knox, and she had laughed aloud to learn that Max and Helga had also wed.

Despite his reservations as to the wisdom of it, they had visited the Bar WK after that. Modesty's serious, myopic gaze had turned briefly to Luther where he had stood at her side and she had slid her hand into his as she had told Lila with characteristic hesitation that appeared half apology, half pride, "I haven't been sorry that I took the chance to try again—not for a moment."

Luther had drawn Modesty against his side briefly in a tender gesture, and Lila's smile had beamed as Modesty had ushered her toward the house.

Garrett's jaw slowly tightened. But he had read the truth in Luther's eyes in that one unguarded moment as Lila had turned away. He had seen the love . . . the yearning that still remained.

Looking up, Luther had caught his scrutiny. A lifetime had passed in that moment. Jealousy, anger, and soul-chilling fear had raced across Garrett's mind before reason had abruptly returned and he had forced himself to remember that Lila was his wife, that she loved him, and no one else.

Striking his jealousy aside for Lila's sake, Garrett had fallen in behind the two women with Luther. But in their hearts both men had known that Lila would always stand between them.

"Garrett . . . what's wrong?"

Garrett forced a smile. He needed no one to tell him that a truth which would be painful to all and could not be changed was better left unrevealed.

Garrett's smile warmed. Slipping to the bed beside her, Garrett lowered his head to kiss the white skin of Lila's abdomen, still smooth and flat despite the babe that grew within. He knew the joy she felt in carrying his child, and he knew her happiness had been increased tenfold when Eva had returned from visiting Billy with the news that he would be released from prison in time for the babe's birth.

Once seeming damaged beyond repair, Lila's world had become one of bright tomorrows. Lila's world was his world. It had been that way since the first moment he had seen her. That would never change.

Stroking the delicate flesh of Lila's stomach once more, Garrett looked down into her eyes as he responded lightly to her question, "I'm thinkin' I'm not so sure I'll like sharin' your attention with this other fella in a few months . . ."

Lila gave a short laugh. "Oh, Garrett, you—"

Gasping as Garrett turned in a quick shift of movement that found the lush, naked length of her lying atop him, Lila laughed again. Her smile slowly faded as she supported herself above him, the crests of her breasts brushing his chest and her hair a brilliant curtain around her flawless countenance. She whispered, "In that case, I suppose we should make the best of our time together while we can . . ."

Lowering her mouth to his, Lila kissed him. Her ardor was filled with the passion of a past consigned to the shadows, of a love lost and regained, and with an eagerness for all the loving days to come.

The passion lingered. It surged to flame.

He loved her. She loved him. Garrett and Lila.

Always.